The
DA VINCI CODE

ALSO BY DAN BROWN

Angels & Demons

Deception Point

Digital Fortress

The
DA VINCI CODE

SPECIAL ILLUSTRATED EDITION

DAN BROWN

BANTAM PRESS

LONDON · TORONTO · SYDNEY · AUCKLAND · JOHANNESBURG

TRANSWORLD PUBLISHERS
61-63 Uxbridge Road, London W5 5SA
a division of The Random House Group Ltd

RANDOM HOUSE AUSTRALIA (PTY) LTD
20 Alfred Street, Milsons Point, Sydney,
New South Wales 2061, Australia

RANDOM HOUSE NEW ZEALAND LTD
18 Poland Road, Glenfield, Auckland 10, New Zealand

RANDOM HOUSE SOUTH AFRICA (PTY) LTD
Endulini, 5a Jubilee Road, Parktown 2193, South Africa

The original hardcover edition of THE DA VINCI CODE was
published in 2003 by Bantam Press,
a division of Transworld Publishers

Book design and layout by Judith Stagnitto Abbate / Abbate Design

A catalogue record for this book is available
from the British Library.
ISBN 0593 054253

Photo research by Photosearch, Inc., New York
All image and photo credits are listed on pages 459–463.

Printed in Germany

3 5 7 9 10 8 6 4

Papers used by Transworld Publishers are natural, recyclable products
made from wood grown in sustainable forests. The manufacturing processes conform to the
environmental regulations of the country of origin.

FOR BLYTHE. . .AGAIN.

MORE THAN EVER.

AUTHOR'S NOTE

WHEN I WAS FIRST APPROACHED with the idea of creating an illustrated edition of *The Da Vinci Code,* I was intrigued. One of the most common questions I'm asked by readers is where they can go to *see* all of the art, architecture, locations, and symbols described in the book. This illustrated edition seemed like the perfect answer.

For me, the process of researching the rich history and images associated with this story was a wondrous journey of discovery, and it's thrilling now to see these visuals interspersed with the text of *The Da Vinci Code.* It is my hope that these images shed new light, spark new questions, and, above all, serve as an entertaining companion to the story.

DAN BROWN
October 2004

The
DA VINCI CODE

✺ F A C T :

The Priory of Sion—a European secret society founded in 1099—is a real organization. In 1975 Paris's Bibliothèque Nationale discovered parchments known as *Les Dossiers Secrets,* identifying numerous members of the Priory of Sion, including Sir Isaac Newton, Botticelli, Victor Hugo, and Leonardo da Vinci.

The Vatican prelature known as Opus Dei is a deeply devout Catholic sect that has been the topic of recent controversy due to reports of brainwashing, coercion, and a dangerous practice known as "corporal mortification." Opus Dei has just completed construction of a $47 million National Headquarters at 243 Lexington Avenue in New York City.

All descriptions of artwork, architecture, documents, and secret rituals in this novel are accurate.

THE DEATH OF THE VIRGIN, CARAVAGGIO

LOUVRE MUSEUM, PARIS
10:46 P.M.

Renowned curator Jacques Saunière staggered through the vaulted archway of the museum's Grand Gallery. He lunged for the nearest painting he could see, a Caravaggio. Grabbing the gilded frame, the seventy-six-year-old man heaved the masterpiece toward himself until it tore from the wall and Saunière collapsed backward in a heap beneath the canvas.

As he had anticipated, a thundering iron gate fell nearby, barricading the entrance to the suite. The parquet floor shook. Far off, an alarm began to ring.

The curator lay a moment, gasping for breath, taking stock. *I am still alive.* He crawled out from under the canvas and scanned the cavernous space for someplace to hide.

A voice spoke, chillingly close. "Do not move."

On his hands and knees, the curator froze, turning his head slowly.

Only fifteen feet away, outside the sealed gate, the mountainous silhouette of his attacker stared through the iron bars. He was broad and tall, with ghost-pale skin and thinning white hair. His irises were pink with dark red pupils. The albino drew a pistol from his coat and aimed the barrel through the bars, directly at the curator. "You should not have run." His accent was not easy to place. "Now tell me where it is."

"I told you already," the curator stammered, kneeling defenseless on the floor of the gallery. "I have no idea what you are talking about!"

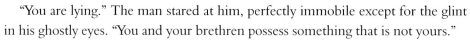

"You are lying." The man stared at him, perfectly immobile except for the glint in his ghostly eyes. "You and your brethren possess something that is not yours."

The curator felt a surge of adrenaline. *How could he possibly know this?*

"Tonight the rightful guardians will be restored. Tell me where it is hidden, and you will live." The man leveled his gun at the curator's head. "Is it a secret you will die for?"

Saunière could not breathe.

The man tilted his head, peering down the barrel of his gun.

Saunière held up his hands in defense. "Wait," he said slowly. "I will tell you what you need to know." The curator spoke his next words carefully. The lie he told was one he had rehearsed many times . . . each time praying he would never have to use it.

When the curator had finished speaking, his assailant smiled smugly. "Yes. This is exactly what the others told me."

Saunière recoiled. *The others?*

"I found them, too," the huge man taunted. "All three of them. They confirmed what you have just said."

It cannot be! The curator's true identity, along with the identities of his three *sénéchaux,* was almost as sacred as the ancient secret they protected. Saunière now realized his *sénéchaux,* following strict procedure, had told the same lie before their own deaths. It was part of the protocol.

The attacker aimed his gun again. "When you are gone, I will be the only one who knows the truth."

The truth. In an instant, the curator grasped the true horror of the situation. *If I die, the truth will be lost forever.* Instinctively, he tried to scramble for cover.

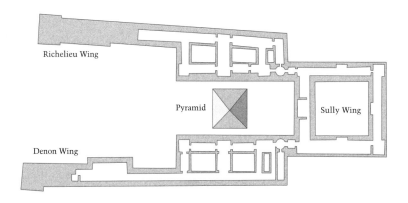

LOUVRE MUSEUM

The gun roared, and the curator felt a searing heat as the bullet lodged in his stomach. He fell forward . . . struggling against the pain. Slowly, Saunière rolled over and stared back through the bars at his attacker.

The man was now taking dead aim at Saunière's head.

Saunière closed his eyes, his thoughts a swirling tempest of fear and regret.

The click of an empty chamber echoed through the corridor.

The curator's eyes flew open.

The man glanced down at his weapon, looking almost amused. He reached for a second clip, but then seemed to reconsider, smirking calmly at Saunière's gut. "My work here is done."

The curator looked down and saw the bullet hole in his white linen shirt. It was framed by a small circle of blood a few inches below his breastbone. *My stomach*. Almost cruelly, the bullet had missed his heart. As a veteran of *la guerre d'Algérie,* the curator had witnessed this horribly drawn-out death before. For fifteen minutes, he would survive as his stomach acids seeped into his chest cavity, slowly poisoning him from within.

"Pain is good, monsieur," the man said.

Then he was gone.

Alone now, Jacques Saunière turned his gaze again to the iron gate. He was trapped, and the doors could not be reopened for at least twenty minutes. By the time anyone got to him, he would be dead. Even so, the fear that now gripped him was a fear far greater than that of his own death.

I must pass on the secret.

Staggering to his feet, he pictured his three murdered brethren. He thought of the generations who had come before them . . . of the mission with which they had all been entrusted.

An unbroken chain of knowledge.

Suddenly, now, despite all the precautions . . . despite all the fail-safes . . . Jacques Saunière was the only remaining link, the sole guardian of one of the most powerful secrets ever kept.

Shivering, he pulled himself to his feet.

I must find some way. . . .

He was trapped inside the Grand Gallery, and there existed only one person on earth to whom he could pass the torch. Saunière gazed up at the walls of his opulent prison. A collection of the world's most famous paintings seemed to smile down on him like old friends.

Wincing in pain, he summoned all of his faculties and strength. The desperate task before him, he knew, would require every remaining second of his life.

OBERT LANGDON awoke slowly.

A telephone was ringing in the darkness—a tinny, unfamiliar ring. He fumbled for the bedside lamp and turned it on. Squinting at his surroundings he saw a plush Renaissance bedroom with Louis XVI furniture, hand-frescoed walls, and a colossal mahogany four-poster bed.

Where the hell am I?

The jacquard bathrobe hanging on his bedpost bore the monogram: *HÔTEL RITZ PARIS.*

Slowly, the fog began to lift.

HÔTEL RITZ, PARIS

Langdon picked up the receiver. "Hello?"

"Monsieur Langdon?" a man's voice said. "I hope I have not awoken you?"

Dazed, Langdon looked at the bedside clock. It was 12:32 A.M. He had been asleep only an hour, but he felt like the dead.

"This is the concierge, monsieur. I apologize for this intrusion, but you have a visitor. He insists it is urgent."

Langdon still felt fuzzy. *A visitor?* His eyes focused now on a crumpled flyer on his bedside table.

THE AMERICAN UNIVERSITY OF PARIS

proudly presents

AN EVENING WITH ROBERT LANGDON

Professor of Religious Symbology, Harvard University

Langdon groaned. Tonight's lecture—a slide show about pagan symbolism hidden in the stones of Chartres Cathedral—had probably ruffled some conservative

PAGAN SYMBOLS AT CHARTRES CATHEDRAL, FRANCE

feathers in the audience. Most likely, some religious scholar had trailed him home to pick a fight.

"I'm sorry," Langdon said, "but I'm very tired and—"

"*Mais, monsieur,*" the concierge pressed, lowering his voice to an urgent whisper. "Your guest is an important man."

Langdon had little doubt. His books on religious paintings and cult symbology had made him a reluctant celebrity in the art world, and last year Langdon's visibility had increased a hundredfold after his involvement in a widely publicized incident at the Vatican. Since then, the stream of self-important historians and art buffs arriving at his door had seemed never-ending.

"If you would be so kind," Langdon said, doing his best to remain polite, "could you take the man's name and number, and tell him I'll try to call him before I leave Paris on Tuesday? Thank you." He hung up before the concierge could protest.

Sitting up now, Langdon frowned at his bedside *Guest Relations Handbook*, whose cover boasted: SLEEP LIKE A BABY IN THE CITY OF LIGHTS. SLUMBER AT THE PARIS RITZ. He turned and gazed tiredly into the full-length mirror across the room. The man staring back at him was a stranger—tousled and weary.

You need a vacation, Robert.

The past year had taken a heavy toll on him, but he didn't appreciate seeing proof in the mirror. His usually sharp blue eyes looked hazy and drawn tonight. A dark stubble was shrouding his strong jaw and dimpled chin. Around his temples, the gray highlights were advancing, making their way deeper into his thicket of coarse black hair. Although his female colleagues insisted the gray only accentuated his bookish appeal, Langdon knew better.

If Boston Magazine *could see me now.*

Last month, much to Langdon's embarrassment, *Boston Magazine* had listed him as one of that city's top ten most intriguing people—a dubious honor that made him the brunt of endless ribbing by his Harvard colleagues. Tonight, three thousand miles from home, the accolade had resurfaced to haunt him at the lecture he had given.

"Ladies and gentlemen . . ." the hostess had announced to a full house at the American University of Paris's Pavillon Dauphine, "Our guest tonight needs no introduction. He is the author of numerous books: *The Symbology of Secret Sects*, *The Art of the Illuminati*, *The Lost Language of Ideograms,* and when I say he wrote the book on *Religious Iconology,* I mean that quite literally. Many of you use his textbooks in class."

The students in the crowd nodded enthusiastically.

"I had planned to introduce him tonight by sharing his impressive curriculum

CHARTRES CATHEDRAL

vitae. However . . ." She glanced playfully at Langdon, who was seated onstage. "An audience member has just handed me a far more, shall we say . . . *intriguing* introduction."

She held up a copy of *Boston Magazine.*

Langdon cringed. *Where the hell did she get that?*

The hostess began reading choice excerpts from the inane article, and Langdon felt himself sinking lower and lower in his chair. Thirty seconds later, the crowd was grinning, and the woman showed no signs of letting up. "And Mr. Langdon's refusal to speak publicly about his unusual role in last year's Vatican conclave certainly wins him points on our intrigue-o-meter." The hostess goaded the crowd. "Would you like to hear more?"

The crowd applauded.

Somebody stop her, Langdon pleaded as she dove into the article again.

"Although Professor Langdon might not be considered hunk-handsome like some of our younger awardees, this forty-something academic has more than his share of scholarly allure. His captivating presence is punctuated by an unusually low, baritone speaking voice, which his female students describe as 'chocolate for the ears.' "

The hall erupted in laughter.

Langdon forced an awkward smile. He knew what came next—some ridiculous line about "Harrison Ford in Harris tweed"—and because this evening he had figured it was finally safe again to wear his Harris tweed and Burberry turtleneck, he decided to take action.

"Thank you, Monique," Langdon said, standing prematurely and edging her away from the podium. "*Boston Magazine* clearly has a gift for fiction." He turned to the audience with an embarrassed sigh. "And if I find which one of you provided that article, I'll have the consulate deport you."

The crowd laughed.

"Well, folks, as you all know, I'm here tonight to talk about the power of symbols . . ."

THE RINGING of Langdon's hotel phone once again broke the silence.

Groaning in disbelief, he picked up. "Yes?"

As expected, it was the concierge. "Mr. Langdon, again my apologies. I am calling to inform you that your guest is now en route to your room. I thought I should alert you."

Langdon was wide awake now. "You sent someone to my *room?*"

"I apologize, monsieur, but a man like this . . . I cannot presume the authority to stop him."

"Who exactly *is* he?"

But the concierge was gone.

Almost immediately, a heavy fist pounded on Langdon's door.

Uncertain, Langdon slid off the bed, feeling his toes sink deep into the savonnerie carpet. He donned the hotel bathrobe and moved toward the door. "Who is it?"

"Mr. Langdon? I need to speak with you." The man's English was accented—a sharp, authoritative bark. "My name is Lieutenant Jérôme Collet. Direction Centrale Police Judiciaire."

Langdon paused. *The Judicial Police?* The DCPJ was the rough equivalent of the U.S. FBI.

Leaving the security chain in place, Langdon opened the door a few inches. The face staring back at him was thin and washed out. The man was exceptionally lean, dressed in an official-looking blue uniform.

"May I come in?" the agent asked.

Langdon hesitated, feeling uncertain as the stranger's sallow eyes studied him. "What is this all about?"

"My *capitaine* requires your expertise in a private matter."

"Now?" Langdon managed. "It's after midnight."

"Am I correct that you were scheduled to meet with the curator of the Louvre this evening?"

Langdon felt a sudden surge of uneasiness. He and the revered curator Jacques Saunière had been slated to meet for drinks after Langdon's lecture tonight, but Saunière had never shown up. "Yes. How did you know that?"

"We found your name in his daily planner."

"I trust nothing is wrong?"

The agent gave a dire sigh and slid a Polaroid snapshot through the narrow opening in the door.

When Langdon saw the photo, his entire body went rigid.

"This photo was taken less than an hour ago. Inside the Louvre."

As Langdon stared at the bizarre image, his initial revulsion and shock gave way to a sudden upwelling of anger. "Who would do this!"

"We had hoped that you might help us answer that very question, considering your knowledge in symbology and your plans to meet with him."

Langdon stared at the picture, his horror now laced with fear. The image was gruesome and profoundly strange, bringing with it an unsettling sense of déjà vu. A little over a year ago, Langdon had received a photograph of a corpse and a similar request for help. Twenty-four hours later, he had almost lost his life inside Vatican City. This photo was entirely different, and yet something about the scenario felt disquietingly familiar.

The agent checked his watch. "My *capitaine* is waiting, sir."

Langdon barely heard him. His eyes were still riveted on the picture. "This symbol here, and the way his body is so oddly . . ."

"Positioned?" the agent offered.

Langdon nodded, feeling a chill as he looked up. "I can't imagine who would do this to someone."

The agent looked grim. "You don't understand, Mr. Langdon. What you see in this photograph . . ." He paused. "Monsieur Saunière did that to himself."

Chapter 2

ONE MILE AWAY, the hulking albino named Silas limped through the front gate of the luxurious brownstone residence on Rue La Bruyère. The spiked *cilice* belt that he wore around his thigh cut into his flesh, and yet his soul sang with satisfaction of service to the Lord.

Pain is good.

His red eyes scanned the lobby as he entered the residence. Empty. He climbed the stairs quietly, not wanting to awaken any of his fellow numeraries. His bedroom door was open; locks were forbidden here. He entered, closing the door behind him.

The room was spartan—hardwood floors, a pine dresser, a canvas mat in the corner that served as his bed. He was a visitor here this week, and yet for many years he had been blessed with a similar sanctuary in New York City.

The Lord has provided me shelter and purpose in my life.

Tonight, at last, Silas felt he had begun to repay his debt. Hurrying to the dresser, he found the cell phone hidden in his bottom drawer and placed a call.

"Yes?" a male voice answered.

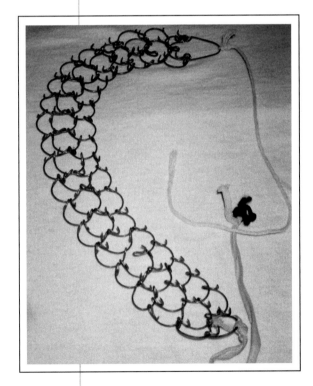

CILICE BELT

"Teacher, I have returned."

"Speak," the voice commanded, sounding pleased to hear from him.

"All four are gone. The three *sénéchaux* . . . and the *Grand Master* himself."

There was a momentary pause, as if for prayer. "Then I assume you have the information?"

"All four concurred. Independently."

"And you believed them?"

"Their agreement was too great for coincidence."

An excited breath. "Excellent. I had feared the brotherhood's reputation for secrecy might prevail."

"The prospect of death is strong motivation."

"So, my pupil, tell me what I must know."

Silas knew the information he had gleaned from his victims would come as a shock. "Teacher, all four confirmed the existence of the *clef de voûte* . . . the legendary *keystone.*"

He heard a quick intake of breath over the phone and could feel the Teacher's excitement. "The *keystone.* Exactly as we suspected."

According to lore, the brotherhood had created a map of stone—a *clef de voûte* . . . or *keystone*—an engraved tablet that revealed the final resting place of the brotherhood's greatest secret . . . information so powerful that its protection was the reason for the brotherhood's very existence.

"When we possess the keystone," the Teacher said, "we will be only one step away."

"We are closer than you think. The keystone is here in Paris."

"Paris? Incredible. It is almost too easy."

Silas relayed the earlier events of the evening . . . how all four of his victims, moments before death, had desperately tried to buy back their godless lives by telling their secret. Each had told Silas the exact same thing—that the keystone was ingeniously hidden at a precise location inside one of Paris's ancient churches—the Eglise de Saint-Sulpice.

"Inside a house of the Lord," the Teacher exclaimed. "How they mock us!"

"As they have for centuries."

The Teacher fell silent, as if letting the triumph of this moment settle over him. Finally, he spoke. "You have done a great service to God. We have waited centuries for this. You must retrieve the stone for me. Immediately. Tonight. You understand the stakes."

Silas knew the stakes were incalculable, and yet what the Teacher was now commanding seemed impossible. "But the church, it is a fortress. Especially at night. How will I enter?"

With the confident tone of a man of enormous influence, the Teacher explained what was to be done.

WHEN SILAS hung up the phone, his skin tingled with anticipation.

One hour, he told himself, grateful that the Teacher had given him time to carry out the necessary penance before entering a house of God. *I must purge my soul of today's sins.* The sins committed today had been holy in purpose. Acts of war against the enemies of God had been committed for centuries. Forgiveness was assured.

Even so, Silas knew, absolution required sacrifice.

Pulling his shades, he stripped naked and knelt in the center of his room. Looking down, he examined the spiked *cilice* belt clamped around his thigh. All true followers of *The Way* wore this device—a leather strap, studded with sharp metal barbs that cut into the flesh as a perpetual reminder of Christ's suffering. The pain caused by the device also helped counteract the desires of the flesh.

Although Silas already had worn his *cilice* today longer than the requisite two hours, he knew today was no ordinary day. Grasping the buckle, he cinched it one notch tighter, wincing as the barbs dug deeper into his flesh. Exhaling slowly, he savored the cleansing ritual of his pain.

Pain is good, Silas whispered, repeating the sacred mantra of Father Josemaría Escrivá—the Teacher of all Teachers. Although Escrivá had died in 1975, his wis-

THE DISCIPLINE

dom lived on, his words still whispered by thousands of faithful servants around the globe as they knelt on the floor and performed the sacred practice known as "corporal mortification."

Silas turned his attention now to a heavy knotted rope coiled neatly on the floor beside him. *The Discipline*. The knots were caked with dried blood. Eager for the purifying effects of his own agony, Silas said a quick prayer. Then, gripping one end of the rope, he closed his eyes and swung it hard over his shoulder, feeling the knots slap against his back. He whipped it over his shoulder again, slashing at his flesh. Again and again, he lashed.

Castigo corpus meum.

Finally, he felt the blood begin to flow.

Chapter 5

THE CRISP APRIL AIR whipped through the open window of the Citroën ZX as it skimmed south past the Opera House and crossed Place Vendôme. In the passenger seat, Robert Langdon felt the city tear past him as he tried to clear his thoughts. His quick shower and shave had left him looking reasonably presentable but had done little to ease his anxiety. The frightening image of the curator's body remained locked in his mind.

Jacques Saunière is dead.

Langdon could not help but feel a deep sense of loss at the curator's death. Despite Saunière's reputation for being reclusive, his recognition for dedication to the arts made him an easy man to revere. His books on the secret codes hidden in the paintings of Poussin and Teniers were some of Langdon's favorite classroom texts. Tonight's meeting had been one Langdon was very much looking forward to, and he was disappointed when the curator had not shown.

Again the image of the curator's body flashed in his mind. *Jacques Saunière did that to himself?* Langdon turned and looked out the window, forcing the picture from his mind.

Outside, the city was just now winding down—street vendors wheeling carts of candied *amandes,* waiters carrying bags of garbage to the curb, a pair of late-night lovers cuddling to stay warm in a breeze scented with jasmine blossom. The Citroën navigated the chaos with authority, its dissonant two-tone siren parting the traffic like a knife.

"*Le capitaine* was pleased to discover you were still in Paris tonight," the agent said, speaking for the first time since they'd left the hotel. "A fortunate coincidence."

Langdon was feeling anything but fortunate, and coincidence was a concept he did not entirely trust. As someone who had spent his life exploring the hidden interconnectivity of disparate emblems and ideologies, Langdon viewed the world as a web of profoundly intertwined histories and events. *The connections may be invisible*, he often preached to his symbology classes at Harvard, *but they are always there, buried just beneath the surface.*

"I assume," Langdon said, "that the American University of Paris told you where I was staying?"

The driver shook his head. "Interpol."

Interpol, Langdon thought. *Of course.* He had forgotten that the seemingly innocuous request of all European hotels to see a passport at check-in was more than a quaint formality—it was the law. On any given night, all across Europe, Interpol officials could pinpoint exactly who was sleeping where. Finding Langdon at the Ritz had probably taken all of five seconds.

As the Citroën accelerated southward across the city, the illuminated profile of the Eiffel Tower appeared, shooting skyward in the distance to the right. Seeing it, Langdon thought of Vittoria, recalling their playful promise a year ago that every six months they would meet again at a different romantic spot on the globe. The Eiffel Tower, Langdon suspected, would have made their list. Sadly, he last kissed Vittoria in a noisy airport in Rome more than a year ago.

"Did you mount her?" the agent asked, looking over.

Langdon glanced up, certain he had misunderstood. "I beg your pardon?"

"She is lovely, no?" The agent motioned through the windshield toward the Eiffel Tower. "Have you mounted her?"

Langdon rolled his eyes. "No, I haven't climbed the tower."

"She is the symbol of France. I think she is perfect."

THE EIFFEL TOWER

Langdon nodded absently. Symbologists often remarked that France—a country renowned for machismo, womanizing, and diminutive insecure leaders like Napoleon and Pepin the Short—could not have chosen a more apt national emblem than a thousand-foot phallus.

When they reached the intersection at Rue de Rivoli, the traffic light was red, but the Citroën didn't slow. The agent gunned the sedan across the junction and sped onto a wooded section of Rue Castiglione, which served as the northern entrance to the famed Tuileries Gardens—Paris's own version of Central Park. Most tourists mistranslated Jardins des Tuileries as relating to the thousands of tulips that bloomed here, but *Tuileries* was actually a literal reference to something far less romantic. This park had once been an enormous, polluted excavation pit from which Parisian contractors mined clay to manufacture the city's famous red roofing tiles— or *tuiles*.

As they entered the deserted park, the agent reached under the dash and turned off the blaring siren. Langdon exhaled, savoring the sudden quiet. Outside the car, the pale wash of halogen headlights skimmed over the crushed gravel parkway, the

ARC DU CARROUSEL

rugged whir of the tires intoning a hypnotic rhythm. Langdon had always considered the Tuileries to be sacred ground. These were the gardens in which Claude Monet had experimented with form and color, and literally inspired the birth of the Impressionist movement. Tonight, however, this place held a strange aura of foreboding.

The Citroën swerved left now, angling west down the park's central boulevard. Curling around a circular pond, the driver cut across a desolate avenue out into a wide quadrangle beyond. Langdon could now see the end of the Tuileries Gardens, marked by a giant stone archway.

Arc du Carrousel.

Despite the orgiastic rituals once held at the Arc du Carrousel, art aficionados revered this place for another reason entirely. From the esplanade at the end of the Tuileries, four of the finest art museums in the world could be seen . . . one at each point of the compass.

Out the right-hand window, south across the Seine and Quai Voltaire, Langdon could see the dramatically lit facade of the old train station—now the esteemed Musée d'Orsay. Glancing left, he could make out the top of the ultramodern Pom-

MUSÉE D'ORSAY

pidou Center, which housed the Museum of Modern Art. Behind him to the west, Langdon knew the ancient obelisk of Ramses rose above the trees, marking the Musée du Jeu de Paume.

But it was straight ahead, to the east, through the archway, that Langdon could now see the monolithic Renaissance palace that had become the most famous art museum in the world.

Musée du Louvre.

Langdon felt a familiar tinge of wonder as his eyes made a futile attempt to absorb the entire mass of the edifice. Across a staggeringly expansive plaza, the imposing facade of the Louvre rose like a citadel against the Paris sky. Shaped like an enormous horseshoe, the Louvre was the longest building in Europe, stretching farther than three Eiffel Towers laid end to end. Not even the million square feet of open plaza between the museum wings could challenge the majesty of the facade's breadth. Langdon had once walked the Louvre's entire perimeter, an astonishing three-mile journey.

Despite the estimated five weeks it would take a visitor to properly appreciate the 65,300 pieces of art in this building, most tourists chose an abbreviated experience Langdon referred to as "Louvre Lite"—a full sprint through the museum to see the

VENUS DE MILO

WINGED VICTORY

PYRAMID ENTRANCE TO THE LOUVRE

three most famous objects: the *Mona Lisa, Venus de Milo,* and *Winged Victory.* Art Buchwald had once boasted he'd seen all three masterpieces in five minutes and fifty-six seconds.

The driver pulled out a handheld walkie-talkie and spoke in rapid-fire French. *"Monsieur Langdon est arrivé. Deux minutes."*

An indecipherable confirmation came crackling back.

The agent stowed the device, turning now to Langdon. "You will meet the *capitaine* at the main entrance."

The driver ignored the signs prohibiting auto traffic on the plaza, revved the engine, and gunned the Citroën up over the curb. The Louvre's main entrance was visible now, rising boldly in the distance, encircled by seven triangular pools from which spouted illuminated fountains.

La Pyramide.

The new entrance to the Paris Louvre had become almost as famous as the museum itself. The controversial, neomodern glass pyramid designed by Chinese-born American architect I. M. Pei still evoked scorn from traditionalists who felt it destroyed the dignity of the Renaissance courtyard. Goethe had described architecture as frozen music, and Pei's critics described this pyramid as fingernails on a chalkboard. Progressive admirers, though, hailed Pei's seventy-one-foot-tall transparent pyramid as a dazzling synergy of ancient structure and modern method—a symbolic link between the old and new—helping usher the Louvre into the next millennium.

"Do you like our pyramid?" the agent asked.

Langdon frowned. The French, it seemed, loved to ask Americans this. It was a loaded question, of course. Admitting you liked the pyramid made you a tasteless American, and expressing dislike was an insult to the French.

"Mitterrand was a bold man," Langdon replied, splitting the difference. The late French president who had commissioned the pyramid was said to have suffered from a "Pharaoh complex." Single-handedly responsible for filling Paris with Egyptian obelisks, art, and artifacts, François Mitterrand had an affinity for Egyptian culture that was so all-consuming that the French still referred to him as the Sphinx.

"What is the captain's name?" Langdon asked, changing topics.

"Bezu Fache," the driver said, approaching the pyramid's main entrance. "We call him *le Taureau.*"

Langdon glanced over at him, wondering if every Frenchman had a mysterious animal epithet. "You call your captain *the Bull*?"

The man arched his eyebrows. "Your French is better than you admit, Monsieur Langdon."

My French stinks, Langdon thought, *but my zodiac iconography is pretty good.* Taurus was always the bull. Astrology was a symbolic constant all over the world.

The agent pulled the car to a stop and pointed between two fountains to a large door in the side of the pyramid. "There is the entrance. Good luck, monsieur."

"You're not coming?"

"My orders are to leave you here. I have other business to attend to."

Langdon heaved a sigh and climbed out. *It's your circus.*

The agent revved his engine and sped off.

As Langdon stood alone and watched the departing taillights, he realized he could easily reconsider, exit the courtyard, grab a taxi, and head home to bed. Something told him it was probably a lousy idea.

As he moved toward the mist of the fountains, Langdon had the uneasy sense he was crossing an imaginary threshold into another world. The dreamlike quality of the evening was settling around him again. Twenty minutes ago he had been asleep in his hotel room. Now he was standing in front of a transparent pyramid built by the Sphinx, waiting for a policeman they called the Bull.

I'm trapped in a Salvador Dalí painting, he thought.

Langdon strode to the main entrance—an enormous revolving door. The foyer beyond was dimly lit and deserted.

Do I knock?

Langdon wondered if any of Harvard's revered Egyptologists had ever knocked on the front door of a pyramid and expected an answer. He raised his hand to bang on the glass, but out of the darkness below, a figure appeared, striding up the curving staircase. The man was stocky and dark, almost Neanderthal, dressed in a dark double-breasted suit that strained to cover his wide shoulders. He advanced with unmistakable authority on squat, powerful legs. He was speaking on his cell phone but finished the call as he arrived. He motioned for Langdon to enter.

"I am Bezu Fache," he announced as Langdon pushed through the revolving door. "Captain of the Central Directorate Judicial Police." His tone was fitting—a guttural rumble . . . like a gathering storm.

Langdon held out his hand to shake. "Robert Langdon."

Fache's enormous palm wrapped around Langdon's with crushing force.

"I saw the photo," Langdon said. "Your agent said Jacques Saunière *himself* did—"

"Mr. Langdon," Fache's ebony eyes locked on. "What you see in the photo is only the beginning of what Saunière did."

CAPTAIN BEZU FACHE carried himself like an angry ox, with his wide shoulders thrown back and his chin tucked hard into his chest. His dark hair was slicked back with oil, accentuating an arrow-like widow's peak that divided his jutting brow and preceded him like the prow of a battleship. As he advanced, his dark eyes seemed to scorch the earth before him, radiating a fiery clarity that forecast his reputation for unblinking severity in all matters.

Langdon followed the captain down the famous marble staircase into the sunken atrium beneath the glass pyramid. As they descended, they passed between two armed Judicial Police guards with machine guns. The message was clear: Nobody goes in or out tonight without the blessing of Captain Fache.

Descending below ground level, Langdon fought a rising trepidation. Fache's presence was anything but welcoming, and the Louvre itself had an almost sepulchral aura at this hour. The staircase, like the aisle of a dark movie theater, was illuminated by subtle tread-lighting embedded in each step. Langdon could hear his own footsteps reverberating off the glass overhead. As he glanced up, he could see the faint illuminated wisps of mist from the fountains fading away outside the transparent roof.

"Do you approve?" Fache asked, nodding upward with his broad chin.

Langdon sighed, too tired to play games. "Yes, your pyramid is magnificent."

Fache grunted. "A scar on the face of Paris."

Strike one. Langdon sensed his host was a hard man to please. He wondered if Fache had any idea that this pyramid, at President Mitterrand's explicit demand, had been constructed of exactly 666 panes of glass—a bizarre request that had always been a hot topic among conspiracy buffs who claimed 666 was the number of Satan.

Langdon decided not to bring it up.

As they dropped farther into the subterranean foyer, the yawning space slowly emerged from the shadows. Built fifty-seven feet beneath ground level, the Louvre's newly constructed 70,000-square-foot lobby spread out like an endless grotto. Constructed in warm ocher marble to be compatible with the honey-colored stone of the Louvre facade above, the subterranean hall was usually vibrant with sunlight and tourists. Tonight, however, the lobby was barren and dark, giving the entire space a cold and crypt-like atmosphere.

"And the museum's regular security staff?" Langdon asked.

"En quarantaine," Fache replied, sounding as if Langdon were questioning the integrity of Fache's team. "Obviously, someone gained entry tonight who should not have. All Louvre night wardens are in the Sully Wing being questioned. My own agents have taken over museum security for the evening."

Langdon nodded, moving quickly to keep pace with Fache.

"How well did you know Jacques Saunière?" the captain asked.

"Actually, not at all. We'd never met."

Fache looked surprised. "Your first meeting was to be tonight?"

"Yes. We'd planned to meet at the American University reception following my lecture, but he never showed up."

Fache scribbled some notes in a little book. As they walked, Langdon caught a glimpse of the Louvre's lesser-known pyramid—*La Pyramide Inversée*—a huge inverted skylight that hung from the ceiling like a stalactite in an adjoining section of the entresol. Fache guided Langdon up a short set of stairs to the mouth of an arched tunnel, over which a sign read: DENON. The Denon Wing was the most famous of the Louvre's three main sections.

"Who requested tonight's meeting?" Fache asked suddenly. "You or he?"

The question seemed odd. "Mr. Saunière did," Langdon replied as they entered the tunnel. "His secretary contacted me a few weeks ago via e-mail. She said the curator had heard I would be lecturing in Paris this month and wanted to discuss something with me while I was here."

"Discuss what?"

"I don't know. Art, I imagine. We share similar interests."

Fache looked skeptical. "You have *no* idea what your meeting was about?"

Langdon did not. He'd been curious at the time but had not felt comfortable de-

LA PYRAMIDE INVERSÉE

manding specifics. The venerated Jacques Saunière had a renowned penchant for privacy and granted very few meetings; Langdon was grateful simply for the opportunity to meet him.

"Mr. Langdon, can you at least *guess* what our murder victim might have wanted to discuss with you on the night he was killed? It might be helpful."

The pointedness of the question made Langdon uncomfortable. "I really can't imagine. I didn't ask. I felt honored to have been contacted at all. I'm an admirer of Mr. Saunière's work. I use his texts often in my classes."

Fache made note of that fact in his book.

The two men were now halfway up the Denon Wing's entry tunnel, and Langdon could see the twin ascending escalators at the far end, both motionless.

"So you shared interests with him?" Fache asked.

"Yes. In fact, I've spent much of the last year writing the draft for a book that deals with Mr. Saunière's primary area of expertise. I was looking forward to picking his brain."

Fache glanced up. "Pardon?"

The idiom apparently didn't translate. "I was looking forward to learning his thoughts on the topic."

"I see. And what is the topic?"

Langdon hesitated, uncertain exactly how to put it. "Essentially, the manuscript is about the iconography of goddess worship—the concept of female sanctity and the art and symbols associated with it."

Fache ran a meaty hand across his hair. "And Saunière was knowledgeable about this?"

"Nobody more so."

"I see."

Langdon sensed Fache did not see at all. Jacques Saunière was considered the premiere goddess iconographer on earth. Not only did Saunière have a personal passion for relics relating to fertility, goddess cults, Wicca, and the sacred feminine, but during his twenty-year tenure as curator, Saunière had helped the Louvre amass the largest collection of goddess art on earth—labrys axes from the priestesses' oldest Greek shrine in Delphi, gold caducei wands, hundreds of Tjet ankhs resembling small standing angels, sistrum rattles used in ancient Egypt to dispel evil spirits, and an astonishing array of statues depicting Horus being nursed by the goddess Isis.

"Perhaps Jacques Saunière knew of your manuscript?" Fache offered. "And he called the meeting to offer his help on your book."

Langdon shook his head. "Actually, nobody yet knows about my manuscript. It's still in draft form, and I haven't shown it to anyone except my editor."

ISIS HOLDING A SISTRUM RATTLE

EGYPTIAN ANKH

Fache fell silent.

Langdon did not add the *reason* he hadn't yet shown the manuscript to anyone else. The three-hundred-page draft—tentatively titled *Symbols of the Lost Sacred Feminine*—proposed some very unconventional interpretations of established religious iconography which would certainly be controversial.

Now, as Langdon approached the stationary escalators, he paused, realizing Fache was no longer beside him. Turning, Langdon saw Fache standing several yards back at a service elevator.

"We'll take the elevator," Fache said as the lift doors opened. "As I'm sure you're aware, the gallery is quite a distance on foot."

Although Langdon knew the elevator would expedite the long, two-story climb to the Denon Wing, he remained motionless.

"Is something wrong?" Fache was holding the door, looking impatient.

Langdon exhaled, turning a longing glance back up the open-air escalator. *Nothing's wrong at all,* he lied to himself, trudging back toward the elevator. As a boy, Langdon had fallen down an abandoned well shaft and almost died treading water in the narrow space for hours before being rescued. Since then, he'd suffered a haunting phobia of enclosed spaces—elevators, subways, squash courts. *The elevator is a perfectly safe machine,* Langdon continually told himself, never believing it. *It's a tiny metal box hanging in an enclosed shaft!* Holding his breath, he stepped into the lift, feeling the familiar tingle of adrenaline as the doors slid shut.

Two floors. Ten seconds.

"You and Mr. Saunière," Fache said as the lift began to move, "you never spoke at all? Never corresponded? Never sent each other anything in the mail?"

Another odd question. Langdon shook his head. "No. Never."

Fache cocked his head, as if making a mental note of that fact. Saying nothing, he stared dead ahead at the chrome doors.

As they ascended, Langdon tried to focus on anything other than the four walls around him. In the reflection of the shiny elevator door, he saw the captain's tie clip—a silver crucifix with thirteen embedded pieces of black onyx. Langdon found it vaguely surprising. The symbol was known as a *crux gemmata*—a cross bearing thirteen gems—a Christian ideogram for Christ and His twelve apostles. Somehow Langdon had not expected the captain of the French police to broadcast his religion so openly. Then again, this was France; Christianity was not a religion here so much as a birthright.

"It's a *crux gemmata,*" Fache said suddenly.

Startled, Langdon glanced up to find Fache's eyes on him in the reflection.

The elevator jolted to a stop, and the doors opened.

Langdon stepped quickly out into the hallway, eager for the wide-open space afforded by the famous high ceilings of the Louvre galleries. The world into which he stepped, however, was nothing like he expected.

Surprised, Langdon stopped short.

Fache glanced over. "I gather, Mr. Langdon, you have never seen the Louvre after hours?"

ELABORATELY JEWELED *CRUX GEMMATA*

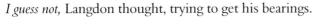

I guess not, Langdon thought, trying to get his bearings.

Usually impeccably illuminated, the Louvre galleries were startlingly dark tonight. Instead of the customary flat-white light flowing down from above, a muted red glow seemed to emanate upward from the baseboards—intermittent patches of red light spilling out onto the tile floors.

As Langdon gazed down the murky corridor, he realized he should have anticipated this scene. Virtually all major galleries employed red service lighting at night—strategically placed, low-level, noninvasive lights that enabled staff members to navigate hallways and yet kept the paintings in relative darkness to slow the fading effects of overexposure to light. Tonight, the museum possessed an almost oppressive quality. Long shadows encroached everywhere, and the usually soaring vaulted ceilings appeared as a low, black void.

"This way," Fache said, turning sharply right and setting out through a series of interconnected galleries.

Langdon followed, his vision slowly adjusting to the dark. All around, large-format oils began to materialize like photos developing before him in an enormous darkroom . . . their eyes following as he moved through the rooms. He could taste the familiar tang of museum air—an arid, deionized essence that carried a faint hint of carbon—the product of industrial, coal-filter dehumidifiers that ran around the clock to counteract the corrosive carbon dioxide exhaled by visitors.

Mounted high on the walls, the visible security cameras sent a clear message to visitors: *We see you. Do not touch anything.*

"Any of them real?" Langdon asked, motioning to the cameras.

Fache shook his head. "Of course not."

Langdon was not surprised. Video surveillance in museums this size was cost-prohibitive and ineffective. With acres of galleries to watch over, the Louvre would require several hundred technicians simply to monitor the feeds. Most large museums now used "containment security." *Forget keeping thieves out. Keep them in.* Containment was activated after hours, and if an intruder removed a piece of artwork, compartmentalized exits would seal around that gallery, and the thief would find himself behind bars even before the police arrived.

The sound of voices echoed down the marble corridor up ahead. The noise seemed to be coming from a large recessed alcove that lay ahead on the right. A bright light spilled out into the hallway.

"Office of the curator," the captain said.

As he and Fache drew nearer the alcove, Langdon peered down a short hallway, into Saunière's luxurious study—warm wood, Old Master paintings, and an enormous antique desk on which stood a two-foot-tall model of a knight in full armor. A handful of police agents bustled about the room, talking on phones and taking notes. One of them was seated at Saunière's desk, typing into a laptop. Apparently, the curator's private office had become DCPJ's makeshift command post for the evening.

"Messieurs," Fache called out, and the men turned. *"Ne nous dérangez pas sous aucun prétexte. Entendu?"*

Everyone inside the office nodded their understanding.

Langdon had hung enough NE PAS DÉRANGER signs on hotel room doors to catch the gist of the captain's orders. Fache and Langdon were not to be disturbed under any circumstances.

Leaving the small congregation of agents behind, Fache led Langdon farther down the darkened hallway. Thirty yards ahead loomed the gateway to the Louvre's most popular section—*la Grande Galerie*—a seemingly endless corridor that housed the Louvre's most valuable Italian masterpieces. Langdon had already discerned that *this* was where Saunière's body lay; the Grand Gallery's famous parquet floor had been unmistakable in the Polaroid.

As they approached, Langdon saw the entrance was blocked by an enormous steel grate that looked like something used by medieval castles to keep out marauding armies.

"Containment security," Fache said, as they neared the grate.

Even in the darkness, the barricade looked like it could have restrained a tank. Arriving outside, Langdon peered through the bars into the dimly lit caverns of the Grand Gallery.

"After you, Mr. Langdon," Fache said.

Langdon turned. *After me, where?*

Fache motioned toward the floor at the base of the grate.

Langdon looked down. In the darkness, he hadn't noticed. The barricade was raised about two feet, providing an awkward clearance underneath.

"This area is still off limits to Louvre security," Fache said. "My team from *Police Technique et Scientifique* has just finished their investigation." He motioned to the opening. "Please slide under."

Langdon stared at the narrow crawl space at his feet and then up at the massive iron grate. *He's kidding, right?* The barricade looked like a guillotine waiting to crush intruders.

Fache grumbled something in French and checked his watch. Then he dropped to his knees and slithered his bulky frame underneath the grate. On the other side, he stood up and looked back through the bars at Langdon.

Langdon sighed. Placing his palms flat on the polished parquet, he lay on his stomach and pulled himself forward. As he slid underneath, the nape of his Harris tweed snagged on the bottom of the grate, and he cracked the back of his head on the iron.

Very suave, Robert, he thought, fumbling and then finally pulling himself through. As he stood up, Langdon was beginning to suspect it was going to be a very long night.

URRAY HILL PLACE—the new Opus Dei National Headquarters and conference center—is located at 243 Lexington Avenue in New York City. With a price tag of just over $47 million, the 133,000-square-foot tower is clad in red brick and Indiana limestone. Designed by May & Pinska, the building contains over one hundred bedrooms, six dining rooms, libraries, living rooms, meeting rooms, and offices. The second, eighth, and sixteenth floors contain chapels, ornamented with millwork and marble. The seventeenth floor is entirely residential. Men enter the building through the main doors on Lexington Avenue. Women enter through a side street and are "acoustically and visually separated" from the men at all times within the building.

Earlier this evening, within the sanctuary of his penthouse apartment, Bishop Manuel Aringarosa had packed a small travel bag and dressed in a traditional black cassock. Normally, he would have wrapped a purple cincture around his waist, but tonight he would be traveling among the public, and he preferred not to draw attention to his high office. Only those with a keen eye would notice his 14-karat gold bishop's ring with purple amethyst, large diamonds, and hand-tooled mitre-crozier appliqué. Throwing the travel bag over his shoulder, he said a silent prayer and left his apartment, descending to the lobby where his driver was waiting to take him to the airport.

Now, sitting aboard a commercial air-liner bound for Rome, Aringarosa gazed out the window at the dark Atlantic. The sun had already set, but Aringarosa knew his own star was on the rise. *Tonight the battle will be won,* he thought, amazed that only months ago he had felt powerless against the hands that threatened to destroy his empire.

As president-general of Opus Dei, Bishop Aringarosa had spent the last decade of his life spreading the message of "God's Work"—literally, *Opus Dei*. The congregation, founded in 1928 by the Spanish priest Josemaría Escrivá, pro-moted a return to conservative Catholic values and encouraged its members to make sweeping sacrifices in their own lives in order to do the Work of God.

Opus Dei's traditionalist philosophy initially had taken root in Spain before Franco's regime, but with the 1934 publication of Josemaría Escrivá's spiritual book *The Way*—999 points of meditation for doing God's Work in one's own life—Escrivá's message exploded across the world. Now, with over four million copies of *The Way* in circulation in forty-two languages, Opus Dei was a global force. Its resi-dence halls, teaching centers, and even universities could be found in almost every major metropolis on earth. Opus Dei was the fastest-growing and most financially secure Catholic organization in the world. Unfortunately, Aringarosa had learned, in an age of religious cynicism, cults, and televangelists, Opus Dei's escalating wealth and power was a magnet for suspicion.

"Many call Opus Dei a brainwashing cult," reporters often challenged. "Others call you an ultraconservative Christian secret society. Which are you?"

"Opus Dei is neither," the bishop would patiently reply. "We are a Catholic Church. We are a congregation of Catholics who have chosen as our priority to follow Catholic doctrine as rigorously as we can in our own daily lives."

"Does God's Work necessarily include vows of chastity, tithing, and atonement for sins through self-flagellation and the *cilice?*"

"You are describing only a small portion of the Opus Dei population," Aringarosa said. "There are many levels of involvement. Thousands of Opus Dei members are married, have families, and do God's Work in their own communities. Others choose lives of asceticism within our cloistered residence halls. These choices are personal, but everyone in Opus Dei shares the goal of bettering the world by doing the Work of God. Surely this is an admirable quest."

Reason seldom worked, though. The media always gravitated toward scandal, and Opus Dei, like most large organizations, had within its membership a few misguided souls who cast a shadow over the entire group.

Two months ago, an Opus Dei group at a midwestern university had been caught drugging new recruits with mescaline in an effort to induce a euphoric state that neophytes would perceive as a religious experience. Another university student had used his barbed *cilice* belt more often than the recommended two hours a day and had given himself a near-lethal infection. In Boston not long ago, a disillusioned young investment banker had signed over his entire life savings to Opus Dei before attempting suicide.

Misguided sheep, Aringarosa thought, his heart going out to them.

Of course the ultimate embarrassment had been the widely publicized trial of FBI spy Robert Hanssen, who, in addition to being a prominent member of Opus Dei, had turned out to be a sexual deviant, his trial uncovering evidence that he had rigged hidden video cameras in his own bedroom so his friends could watch him having sex with his wife. "Hardly the pastime of a devout Catholic," the judge had noted.

Sadly, all of these events had helped spawn the new watch group known as the Opus Dei Awareness Network (ODAN). The group's popular website—*www.odan.org*—relayed frightening stories from former Opus Dei members who

INTERIOR CHAPEL, OPUS DEI, NEW YORK

warned of the dangers of joining. The media was now referring to Opus Dei as "God's Mafia" and "the Cult of Christ."

We fear what we do not understand, Aringarosa thought, wondering if these critics had any idea how many lives Opus Dei had enriched. The group enjoyed the full endorsement and blessing of the Vatican. *Opus Dei is a personal prelature of the Pope himself.*

Recently, however, Opus Dei had found itself threatened by a force infinitely more powerful than the media . . . an unexpected foe from which Aringarosa could not possibly hide. Five months ago, the kaleidoscope of power had been shaken, and Aringarosa was still reeling from the blow.

"They know not the war they have begun," Aringarosa whispered to himself, staring out the plane's window at the darkness of the ocean below. For an instant, his eyes refocused, lingering on the reflection of his awkward face—dark and oblong, dominated by a flat, crooked nose that had been shattered by a fist in Spain when he was a young missionary. The physical flaw barely registered now. Aringarosa's was a world of the soul, not of the flesh.

As the jet passed over the coast of Portugal, the cell phone in Aringarosa's cassock began vibrating in silent ring mode. Despite airline regulations prohibiting the use of cell phones during flights, Aringarosa knew this was a call he could not miss. Only one man possessed this number, the man who had mailed Aringarosa the phone.

Excited, the bishop answered quietly. "Yes?"

"Silas has located the keystone," the caller said. "It is in Paris. Within the Church of Saint-Sulpice."

Bishop Aringarosa smiled. "Then we are close."

"We can obtain it immediately. But we need your influence."

"Of course. Tell me what to do."

When Aringarosa switched off the phone, his heart was pounding. He gazed once again into the void of night, feeling dwarfed by the events he had put into motion.

FIVE HUNDRED MILES AWAY, the albino named Silas stood over a small basin of water and dabbed the blood from his back, watching the patterns of red spinning in the water. *Purge me with hyssop and I shall be clean,* he prayed, quoting Psalms. *Wash me, and I shall be whiter than snow.*

Silas was feeling an aroused anticipation that he had not felt since his previous life. It both surprised and electrified him. For the last decade, he had been following *The Way,* cleansing himself of sins . . . rebuilding his life . . . erasing the violence in his past. Tonight, however, it had all come rushing back. The hatred he had fought so hard to bury had been summoned. He had been startled how quickly his past had resurfaced. And with it, of course, had come his skills. Rusty but serviceable.

Jesus' message is one of peace . . . of nonviolence . . . of love. This was the message Silas had been taught from the beginning, and the message he held in his heart. And yet *this* was the message the enemies of Christ now threatened to destroy. *Those who threaten God with force will be met with force. Immovable and steadfast.*

For two millennia, Christian soldiers had defended their faith against those who tried to displace it. Tonight, Silas had been called to battle.

Drying his wounds, he donned his ankle-length, hooded robe. It was plain, made of dark wool, accentuating the whiteness of his skin and hair. Tightening the rope-tie around his waist, he raised the hood over his head and allowed his red eyes to admire his reflection in the mirror. *The wheels are in motion.*

Chapter 6

AVING SQUEEZED beneath the security gate, Robert Langdon now stood just inside the entrance to the Grand Gallery. He was staring into the mouth of a long, deep canyon. On either side of the gallery, stark walls rose thirty feet, evaporating into the darkness above. The reddish glow of the service lighting sifted upward, casting an unnatural smolder across a staggering collection of Da Vincis, Titians, and Caravaggios that hung suspended from ceiling cables. Still lifes, religious scenes, and landscapes accompanied portraits of nobility and politicians.

Although the Grand Gallery housed the Louvre's most famous Italian art, many visitors felt the wing's most stunning offering was actually its famous parquet floor. Laid out in a dazzling geometric design of diagonal oak slats, the floor produced an ephemeral optical illusion—a multidimensional network that gave visitors the sense they were floating through the gallery on a surface that changed with every step.

As Langdon's gaze began to trace the inlay, his eyes stopped short on an unexpected object lying on the floor just a few yards to his left, surrounded by police tape. He spun toward Fache. "Is that . . . a *Caravaggio* on the floor?"

Fache nodded without even looking.

PARQUET FLOOR OF THE GRAND GALLERY IN THE LOUVRE

The painting, Langdon guessed, was worth upward of two million dollars, and yet it was lying on the floor like a discarded poster. "What the devil is it doing on the floor!"

Fache glowered, clearly unmoved. "This is a crime scene, Mr. Langdon. We have touched nothing. That canvas was pulled from the wall by the curator. It was how he activated the security system."

Langdon looked back at the gate, trying to picture what had happened.

"The curator was attacked in his office, fled into the Grand Gallery, and activated the security gate by pulling that painting from the wall. The gate fell immediately, sealing off all access. This is the only door in or out of this gallery."

Langdon felt confused. "So the curator actually captured his attacker inside the Grand Gallery?"

Fache shook his head. "The security gate *separated* Saunière from his attacker. The killer was locked out there in the hallway and shot Saunière through this gate." Fache pointed toward an orange tag hanging from one of the bars on the gate under which they had just passed. "The PTS team found flashback residue from a gun. He fired through the bars. Saunière died in here alone."

Langdon pictured the photograph of Saunière's body. *They said he did that to himself.* Langdon looked out at the enormous corridor before them. "So where is his body?"

Fache straightened his cruciform tie clip and began to walk. "As you probably know, the Grand Gallery is quite long."

The exact length, if Langdon recalled correctly, was around fifteen hundred feet, the length of three Washington Monuments laid end to end. Equally breathtaking was the corridor's width, which easily could have accommodated a pair of side-by-side passenger trains. The center of the hallway was dotted by the occasional statue or colossal porcelain urn, which served as a tasteful divider and kept the flow of traffic moving down one wall and up the other.

Fache was silent now, striding briskly up the right side of the corridor with his gaze dead ahead. Langdon felt almost disrespectful to be racing past so many masterpieces without pausing for so much as a glance.

Not that I could see anything in this lighting, he thought.

The muted crimson lighting unfortunately conjured memories of Langdon's last experience in noninvasive lighting in the Vatican Secret Archives. This was tonight's second unsettling parallel with his near-death in Rome. He flashed on Vittoria again. She had been absent from his dreams for months. Langdon could not believe Rome had been only a year ago; it felt like decades. *Another life.* His last correspondence from Vittoria had been in December—a postcard saying she was headed to the Java Sea to continue her research in entanglement physics . . . something about using satellites to track manta ray migrations. Langdon had never harbored delusions that a woman like Vittoria Vetra could have been happy living with him on a college campus, but their encounter in Rome had unlocked in him a longing he never imagined he could feel. His lifelong affinity for bachelorhood and the simple freedoms it allowed had been shaken somehow . . . replaced by an unexpected emptiness that seemed to have grown over the past year.

They continued walking briskly, yet Langdon still saw no corpse. "Jacques Saunière went this *far*?"

"Mr. Saunière suffered a bullet wound to his stomach. He died very slowly. Perhaps over fifteen or twenty minutes. He was obviously a man of great personal strength."

Langdon turned, appalled. "Security took *fifteen* minutes to get here?"

"Of course not. Louvre security responded immediately to the alarm and found the Grand Gallery sealed. Through the gate, they could hear someone moving around at the far end of the corridor, but they could not see who it was. They shouted, but they got no answer. Assuming it could only be a criminal, they followed protocol and called in the Judicial Police. We took up positions within fifteen minutes. When we arrived, we raised the barricade enough to slip underneath, and I sent a dozen armed agents inside. They swept the length of the gallery to corner the intruder."

"And?"

"They found no one inside. Except . . ." He pointed farther down the hall. "Him."

Langdon lifted his gaze and followed Fache's outstretched finger. At first he thought Fache was pointing to a large marble statue in the middle of the hallway. As they continued, though, Langdon began to see past the statue. Thirty yards down the hall, a single spotlight on a portable pole stand shone down on the floor, creating a stark island of white light in the dark crimson gallery. In the center of the light, like an insect under a microscope, the corpse of the curator lay naked on the parquet floor.

"You saw the photograph," Fache said, "so this should be of no surprise."

Langdon felt a deep chill as they approached the body. Before him was one of the strangest images he had ever seen.

THE PALLID CORPSE of Jacques Saunière lay on the parquet floor exactly as it appeared in the photograph. As Langdon stood over the body and squinted in the harsh light, he reminded himself to his amazement that Saunière had spent his last minutes of life arranging his own body in this strange fashion.

Saunière looked remarkably fit for a man of his years . . . and all of his musculature was in plain view. He had stripped off every shred of clothing, placed it neatly on the floor, and lain down on his back in the center of the wide corridor, perfectly aligned with the long axis of the room. His arms and legs were sprawled outward in a wide spread eagle, like those of a child making a snow angel . . . or, perhaps more appropriately, like a man being drawn and quartered by some invisible force.

Just below Saunière's breastbone, a bloody smear marked the spot where the bullet had pierced his flesh. The wound had bled surprisingly little, leaving only a small pool of blackened blood.

Saunière's left index finger was also bloody, apparently having been dipped into the wound to create the most unsettling aspect of his own macabre deathbed; using his own blood as ink, and employing his own naked abdomen as a canvas, Saunière had drawn a simple symbol on his flesh—five straight lines that intersected to form a five-pointed star.

The pentacle.

The bloody star, centered on Saunière's navel, gave his corpse a distinctly ghoulish aura. The photo Langdon had seen was chilling enough, but now, witnessing the scene in person, Langdon felt a deepening uneasiness.

He did this to himself.

"Mr. Langdon?" Fache's dark eyes settled on him again.

"It's a pentacle," Langdon offered, his voice feeling hollow in the huge space. "One of the oldest symbols on earth. Used over four thousand years before Christ."

PENTACLE

"And what does it mean?"

Langdon always hesitated when he got this question. Telling someone what a symbol "meant" was like telling them how a song should make them feel—it was different for all people. A white Ku Klux Klan headpiece conjured images of hatred and racism in the United States, and yet the same costume carried a meaning of religious faith in Spain.

"Symbols carry different meanings in different settings," Langdon said. "Primarily, the pentacle is a pagan religious symbol."

Fache nodded. "Devil worship."

"No," Langdon corrected, immediately realizing his choice of vocabulary should have been clearer.

Nowadays, the term *pagan* had become almost synonymous with devil worship—a gross misconception. The word's roots actually reached back to the Latin *paganus,* meaning country-dwellers. "Pagans" were literally unindoctrinated country-folk who clung to the old, rural religions of Nature worship. In fact, so strong was the Church's fear of those who lived in the rural *villes* that the once innocuous word for "villager"—*vilain*—came to mean a wicked soul.

"The pentacle," Langdon clarified, "is a pre-Christian symbol that relates to Nature worship. The ancients envisioned their world in two halves—masculine and feminine. Their gods and goddesses worked to keep a balance of power. Yin and yang. When male and female were balanced, there was harmony in the world. When they were unbalanced, there was chaos." Langdon motioned to Saunière's stomach. "This pentacle is representative of the *female* half of all things—a concept religious historians call the 'sacred feminine' or the 'divine goddess.' Saunière, of all people, would know this."

"Saunière drew a *goddess* symbol on his stomach?"

Langdon had to admit, it seemed odd. "In its most specific interpretation, the pentacle symbolizes Venus—the goddess of female sexual love and beauty."

Fache eyed the naked man, and grunted.

"Early religion was based on the divine order of Nature. The goddess Venus and the planet Venus were one and the same. The goddess had a place in the nighttime sky and was known by many names—Venus, the Eastern Star, Ishtar, Astarte—all of them powerful female concepts with ties to Nature and Mother Earth."

Fache looked more troubled now, as if he somehow preferred the idea of devil worship.

Langdon decided not to share the pentacle's most astonishing property—the *graphic* origin of its ties to Venus. As a young astronomy student, Langdon had been

BIRTH OF VENUS BY BOTTICELLI

OLYMPIC RINGS

stunned to learn the planet Venus traced a *perfect* pentacle across the ecliptic sky every eight years. So astonished were the ancients to observe this phenomenon, that Venus and her pentacle became symbols of perfection, beauty, and the cyclic qualities of sexual love. As a tribute to the magic of Venus, the Greeks used her eight-year cycle to organize their Olympic Games. Nowadays, few people realized that the four-year schedule of modern Olympics still followed the half-cycles of Venus. Even fewer people knew that the five-pointed star had almost become the official Olympic seal but was modified at the last moment—its five points exchanged for five intersecting rings to better reflect the games' spirit of inclusion and harmony.

"Mr. Langdon," Fache said abruptly. "Obviously, the pentacle must *also* relate to the devil. Your American horror movies make that point clearly."

Langdon frowned. *Thank you, Hollywood.* The five-pointed star was now a virtual cliché in Satanic serial killer movies, usually scrawled on the wall of some Satanist's apartment along with other alleged demonic symbology. Langdon was always frustrated when he saw the symbol in this context; the pentacle's true origins were actually quite godly.

"I assure you," Langdon said, "despite what you see in the movies, the pentacle's demonic interpretation is historically inaccurate. The original feminine meaning is correct, but the symbolism of the pentacle has been distorted over the millennia. In this case, through bloodshed."

"I'm not sure I follow."

Langdon glanced at Fache's crucifix, uncertain how to phrase his next point. "The Church, sir. Symbols are very resilient, but the pentacle was altered by the early Roman Catholic Church. As part of the Vatican's campaign to eradicate pagan religions and convert the masses to Christianity, the Church launched a smear campaign against the pagan gods and goddesses, recasting their divine symbols as evil."

"Go on."

"This is very common in times of turmoil," Langdon continued. "A newly

POSEIDON WITH TRIDENT

DEVIL WITH PITCHFORK

emerging power will take over the existing symbols and degrade them over time in an attempt to erase their meaning. In the battle between the pagan symbols and Christian symbols, the pagans lost; Poseidon's trident became the devil's pitchfork, the wise crone's pointed hat became the symbol of a witch, and Venus's pentacle became a sign of the devil." Langdon paused. "Unfortunately, the United States military has also perverted the pentacle; it's now our foremost symbol of war. We paint it on all our fighter jets and hang it on the shoulders of all our generals." *So much for the goddess of love and beauty.*

"Interesting." Fache nodded toward the spread-eagle corpse. "And the positioning of the body? What do you make of that?"

Langdon shrugged. "The position simply reinforces the reference to the pentacle and sacred feminine."

Fache's expression clouded. "I beg your pardon?"

"Replication. Repeating a symbol is the simplest way to strengthen its meaning. Jacques Saunière positioned himself in the shape of a five-pointed star." *If one pentacle is good, two is better.*

Fache's eyes followed the five points of Saunière's arms, legs, and head as he again ran a hand across his slick hair. "Interesting analysis." He paused. "And the *nudity?*" He grumbled as he spoke the word, sounding repulsed by the sight of an aging male body. "Why did he remove his clothing?"

Damned good question, Langdon thought. He'd been wondering the same thing ever since he first saw the Polaroid. His best guess was that a naked human form was yet another endorsement of Venus—the goddess of human sexuality. Although modern culture had erased much of Venus's association with the male/female physical union, a sharp etymological eye could still spot a vestige of Venus's original meaning in the word *venereal.* Langdon decided not to go there.

"Mr. Fache, I obviously can't tell you why Mr. Saunière drew that symbol on himself or placed himself in this way, but I *can* tell you that a man like Jacques Saunière would consider the pentacle a sign of the female deity. The correlation between this symbol and the sacred feminine is widely known by art historians and symbologists."

"Fine. And the use of his own blood as ink?"

"Obviously he had nothing else to write with."

Fache was silent a moment. "Actually, I believe he used blood such that the police would follow certain forensic procedures."

"I'm sorry?"

"Look at his left hand."

Langdon's eyes traced the length of the curator's pale arm to his left hand but saw nothing. Uncertain, he circled the corpse and crouched down, now noting with surprise that the curator was clutching a large, felt-tipped marker.

"Saunière was holding it when we found him," Fache said, leaving Langdon and moving several yards to a portable table covered with investigation tools, cables, and assorted electronic gear. "As I told you," he said, rummaging around the table, "we have touched nothing. Are you familiar with this kind of pen?"

Langdon knelt down farther to see the pen's label.

STYLO DE LUMIÈRE NOIRE.

He glanced up in surprise.

The black-light pen or watermark stylus was a specialized felt-tipped marker originally designed by museums, restorers, and forgery police to place invisible marks on items. The stylus wrote in a noncorrosive, alcohol-based fluorescent ink that was visible only under black light. Nowadays, museum maintenance staffs carried these markers on their daily rounds to place invisible "tick marks" on the frames of paintings that needed restoration.

As Langdon stood up, Fache walked over to the spotlight and turned it off. The gallery plunged into sudden darkness.

Momentarily blinded, Langdon felt a rising uncertainty. Fache's silhouette appeared, illuminated in bright purple. He approached carrying a portable light source, which shrouded him in a violet haze.

"As you may know," Fache said, his eyes luminescing in the violet glow, "police use black-light illumination to search crime scenes for blood and other forensic evidence. So you can imagine our surprise . . ." Abruptly, he pointed the light down at the corpse.

Langdon looked down and jumped back in shock.

His heart pounded as he took in the bizarre sight now glowing before him on the parquet floor. Scrawled in luminescent handwriting, the curator's final words glowed purple beside his corpse. As Langdon stared at the shimmering text, he felt the fog that had surrounded this entire night growing thicker.

Langdon read the message again and looked up at Fache. "What the hell does this mean!"

Fache's eyes shone white. "*That,* monsieur, is precisely the question you are here to answer."

NOT FAR AWAY, inside Saunière's office, Lieutenant Collet had returned to the Louvre and was huddled over an audio console set up on the curator's enormous desk. With the exception of the eerie, robot-like doll of a medieval knight that seemed to be staring at him from the corner of Saunière's desk, Collet was comfortable. He adjusted his AKG headphones and checked the input levels on the hard-disk recording system. All systems were go. The microphones were functioning flawlessly, and the audio feed was crystal clear.

Le moment de vérité, he mused.

Smiling, he closed his eyes and settled in to enjoy the rest of the conversation now being taped inside the Grand Gallery.

Chapter 9

*T*HE MODEST DWELLING within the Church of Saint-Sulpice was located on the second floor of the church itself, to the left of the choir balcony. A two-room suite with a stone floor and minimal furnishings, it had been home to Sister Sandrine Bieil for over a decade. The nearby convent was her formal residence, if anyone asked, but she preferred the quiet of the church and had made herself quite comfortable upstairs with a bed, phone, and hot plate.

As the church's *conservatrice d'affaires,* Sister Sandrine was responsible for overseeing all nonreligious aspects of church operations—general maintenance, hiring support staff and guides, securing the building after hours, and ordering supplies like communion wine and wafers.

Tonight, asleep in her small bed, she awoke to the shrill of her telephone. Tiredly, she lifted the receiver.

"*Soeur Sandrine. Église Saint-Sulpice.*"

"Hello, Sister," the man said in French.

Sister Sandrine sat up. *What time is it?* Although she recognized her boss's voice, in fifteen years she had never been awoken by him. The abbé was a deeply pious man who went home to bed immediately after mass.

"I apologize if I have awoken you, Sister," the abbé said, his own voice sounding groggy and on edge. "I have a favor to ask of you. I just received a call from an influential American bishop. Perhaps you know him? Manuel Aringarosa?"

"The head of Opus Dei?" *Of course I know of him. Who in the Church doesn't?* Aringarosa's conservative prelature had grown powerful in recent years. Their ascension to grace was jump-started in 1982 when Pope John Paul II unexpectedly elevated them to a "personal prelature of the Pope," officially sanctioning all of their practices. Suspiciously, Opus Dei's elevation occurred the same year the wealthy sect allegedly had transferred almost one billion dollars into the Vatican's Institute for Religious Works—commonly known as the Vatican Bank—bailing it out of an embarrassing bankruptcy. In a second maneuver that raised eyebrows, the Pope placed the founder of Opus Dei on the "fast track" for sainthood, accelerating an often century-long waiting period for canonization to a mere twenty years. Sister Sandrine could not help but feel that Opus Dei's good standing in Rome was suspect, but one did not argue with the Holy See.

"Bishop Aringarosa called to ask me a favor," the abbé told her, his voice nervous. "One of his numeraries is in Paris tonight. . . ."

As Sister Sandrine listened to the odd request, she felt a deepening confusion. "I'm sorry, you say this visiting Opus Dei numerary cannot wait until morning?"

"I'm afraid not. His plane leaves very early. He has always dreamed of seeing Saint-Sulpice."

"But the church is far more interesting by day. The sun's rays through the oculus, the graduated shadows on the gnomon, *this* is what makes Saint-Sulpice unique."

"Sister, I agree, and yet I would consider it a personal favor if you could let him in tonight. He can be there at . . . say one o'clock? That's in twenty minutes."

Sister Sandrine frowned. "Of course. It would be my pleasure."

The abbé thanked her and hung up.

Puzzled, Sister Sandrine remained a moment in the warmth of her bed, trying to shake off the cobwebs of sleep. Her sixty-year-old body did not awake as fast as it used to, although tonight's phone call had certainly roused her senses. Opus Dei had always made her uneasy. Beyond the prelature's adherence to the arcane ritual of corporal mortification, their views on women were medieval at best. She had been shocked to learn that female numeraries were forced to clean the men's residence halls for no pay while the men were at mass; women slept on hardwood floors, while the men had straw mats; and women were forced to endure additional requirements of corporal mortification . . . all as added penance for original sin. It seemed Eve's bite from the apple of knowledge was a debt women were doomed to pay for eternity. Sadly, while most of the Catholic Church was gradually moving in the right direction with respect to women's rights, Opus Dei threatened to reverse the progress. Even so, Sister Sandrine had her orders.

Swinging her legs off the bed, she stood slowly, chilled by the cold stone on the soles of her bare feet. As the chill rose through her flesh, she felt an unexpected apprehension.

Women's intuition?

A follower of God, Sister Sandrine had learned to find peace in the calming voices of her own soul. Tonight, however, those voices were as silent as the empty church around her.

Chapter 8

ANGDON COULDN'T tear his eyes from the glowing purple text scrawled across the parquet floor. Jacques Saunière's final communication seemed as unlikely a departing message as any Langdon could imagine.

The message read:

13-3-2-21-1-1-8-5
O, Draconian devil!
Oh, lame saint!

Although Langdon had not the slightest idea what it meant, he did understand Fache's instinct that the pentacle had something to do with devil worship.

O, Draconian devil!

Saunière had left a literal reference to the devil. Equally as bizarre was the series of numbers. "Part of it looks like a numeric cipher."

"Yes," Fache said. "Our cryptographers are already working on it. We believe these numbers may be the key to who killed him. Maybe a telephone exchange or some kind of social identification. Do the numbers have any symbolic meaning to you?"

Langdon looked again at the digits, sensing it would take him hours to extract any symbolic meaning. *If Saunière had even intended any.* To Langdon, the numbers looked totally random. He was accustomed to symbolic progressions that made some semblance of sense, but everything here—the pentacle, the text, the numbers—seemed disparate at the most fundamental level.

"You alleged earlier," Fache said, "that Saunière's actions here were all in an effort to send some sort of message . . . goddess worship or something in that vein? How does this message fit in?"

Langdon knew the question was rhetorical. This bizarre communiqué obviously did not fit Langdon's scenario of goddess worship at all.

O, Draconian devil? Oh, lame saint?

Fache said, "This text appears to be an accusation of some sort. Wouldn't you agree?"

Langdon tried to imagine the curator's final minutes trapped alone in the Grand Gallery, knowing he was about to die. It seemed logical. "An accusation against his murderer makes sense, I suppose."

"My job, of course, is to put a name to that person. Let me ask you this, Mr. Langdon. To your eye, beyond the numbers, what about this message is most strange?"

Most strange? A dying man had barricaded himself in the gallery, drawn a pentacle on himself, and scrawled a mysterious accusation on the floor. What about the scenario *wasn't* strange?

"The word *Draconian*?" he ventured, offering the first thing that came to mind. Langdon was fairly certain that a reference to Draco—the ruthless seventh-century B.C. politician—was an unlikely dying thought. " 'Draconian devil' seems an odd choice of vocabulary."

"*Draconian?*" Fache's tone came with a tinge of impatience now. "Saunière's choice of vocabulary hardly seems the primary issue here."

Langdon wasn't sure what issue Fache had in mind, but he was starting to suspect that Draco and Fache would have gotten along well.

"Saunière was a Frenchman," Fache said flatly. "He lived in Paris. And yet he chose to write this message . . ."

"In English," Langdon said, now realizing the captain's meaning.

Fache nodded. "*Précisément.* Any idea why?"

Langdon knew Saunière spoke impeccable English, and yet the reason he had chosen English as the language in which to write his final words escaped Langdon. He shrugged.

Fache motioned back to the pentacle on Saunière's abdomen. "Nothing to do with devil worship? Are you still certain?"

Langdon was certain of nothing anymore. "The symbology and text don't seem to coincide. I'm sorry I can't be of more help."

"Perhaps this will clarify." Fache backed away from the body and raised the black light again, letting the beam spread out in a wider angle. "And now?"

To Langdon's amazement, a rudimentary circle glowed around the curator's body. Saunière had apparently lain down and swung the pen around himself in several long arcs, essentially inscribing himself inside a circle.

In a flash, the meaning became clear.

"The *Vitruvian Man,*" Langdon gasped. Saunière had created a life-sized replica of Leonardo da Vinci's most famous sketch.

Considered the most anatomically correct drawing of its day, Da Vinci's *Vitruvian Man* had become a modern-day icon of culture, appearing on posters, mouse pads, and T-shirts around the world. The celebrated sketch consisted of a perfect circle in which was inscribed a nude male . . . his arms and legs outstretched in a naked spread eagle.

Da Vinci. Langdon felt a shiver of amazement. The clarity of Saunière's intentions could not be denied. In his final moments of life, the curator had stripped off his clothing and arranged his body in a clear image of Leonardo da Vinci's *Vitruvian Man.*

The circle had been the missing critical element. A feminine symbol of protection, the circle around the naked man's body completed Da Vinci's intended message—male and female harmony. The question now, though, was *why* Saunière would imitate a famous drawing.

"Mr. Langdon," Fache said, "certainly a man like yourself is aware that Leonardo da Vinci had a tendency toward the darker arts."

Langdon was surprised by Fache's knowledge of Da Vinci, and it certainly went a long way toward explaining the captain's suspicions about devil worship. Da Vinci had always been an awkward subject for historians, especially in the Christian tradition. Despite the visionary's genius, he was a flamboyant homosexual and worshipper of Nature's divine order, both of which placed him in a perpetual state of sin against God. Moreover, the artist's eerie eccentricities projected an admittedly demonic aura: Da Vinci exhumed corpses to study human anatomy; he kept mysterious journals in illegible reverse handwriting; he believed he possessed the alchemic power to turn lead into gold and even cheat God by creating an elixir to postpone death; and his inventions included horrific, never-before-imagined weapons of war and torture.

Misunderstanding breeds distrust, Langdon thought.

Even Da Vinci's enormous output of breathtaking Christian art only furthered the artist's reputation for spiritual hypocrisy. Accepting hundreds of lucrative Vatican commissions, Da Vinci painted Christian themes not as an expression of his own beliefs but rather as a commercial venture—a means of funding a lavish lifestyle. Unfortunately, Da Vinci was a prankster who often amused himself by quietly gnawing at the hand that fed him. He incorporated in many of his Christian paintings hidden symbolism that was anything but Christian—tributes to his own beliefs and a subtle thumbing of his nose at the Church. Langdon had even given a

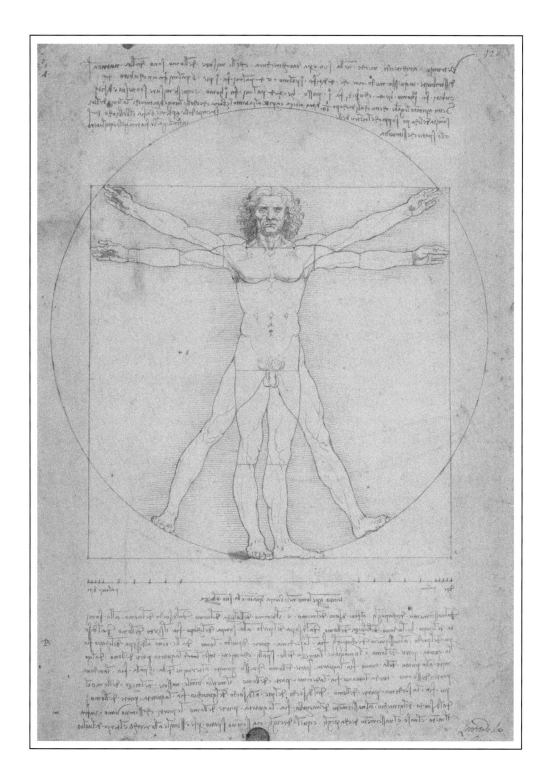

VITRUVIAN MAN BY LEONARDO DA VINCI

lecture once at the National Gallery in London entitled: "The Secret Life of Leonardo: Pagan Symbolism in Christian Art."

"I understand your concerns," Langdon now said, "but Da Vinci never really practiced any dark arts. He was an exceptionally spiritual man, albeit one in constant conflict with the Church." As Langdon said this, an odd thought popped into his mind. He glanced down at the message on the floor again. *O, Draconian devil! Oh, lame saint!*

"Yes?" Fache said.

Langdon weighed his words carefully. "I was just thinking that Saunière shared a lot of spiritual ideologies with Da Vinci, including a concern over the Church's elimination of the sacred feminine from modern religion. Maybe, by imitating a famous Da Vinci drawing, Saunière was simply echoing some of their shared frustrations with the modern Church's demonization of the goddess."

Fache's eyes hardened. "You think Saunière is calling the Church a lame saint and a Draconian devil?"

Langdon had to admit it seemed far-fetched, and yet the pentacle seemed to endorse the idea on some level. "All I am saying is that Mr. Saunière dedicated his life to studying the history of the goddess, and nothing has done more to erase that history than the Catholic Church. It seems reasonable that Saunière might have chosen to express his disappointment in his final good-bye."

"Disappointment?" Fache demanded, sounding hostile now. "This message sounds more *enraged* than disappointed, wouldn't you say?"

Langdon was reaching the end of his patience. "Captain, you asked for my instincts as to what Saunière is trying to say here, and that's what I'm giving you."

"That this is an indictment of the Church?" Fache's jaw tightened as he spoke through clenched teeth. "Mr. Langdon, I have seen a lot of death in my work, and let me tell you something. When a man is murdered by another man, I do not believe his final thoughts are to write an obscure spiritual statement that no one will understand. I believe he is thinking of one thing only." Fache's whispery voice sliced the air. "*La vengeance.* I believe Saunière wrote this note to tell us who killed him."

Langdon stared. "But that makes no sense whatsoever."

"No?"

"No," he fired back, tired and frustrated. "You told me Saunière was attacked in his office by someone he had apparently invited in."

"Yes."

"So it seems reasonable to conclude that the curator *knew* his attacker."

Fache nodded. "Go on."

LEONARDO DA VINCI, ENGRAVING

"So if Saunière *knew* the person who killed him, what kind of indictment is this?" He pointed at the floor. "Numeric codes? Lame saints? Draconian devils? Pentacles on his stomach? It's all too cryptic."

Fache frowned as if the idea had never occurred to him. "You have a point."

"Considering the circumstances," Langdon said, "I would assume that if Saunière wanted to tell you who killed him, he would have written down somebody's *name*."

As Langdon spoke those words, a smug smile crossed Fache's lips for the first time all night. *"Précisément,"* Fache said. *"Précisément."*

I AM WITNESSING the work of a master, mused Lieutenant Collet as he tweaked his audio gear and listened to Fache's voice coming through the headphones. The *agent supérieur* knew it was moments like these that had lifted the captain to the pinnacle of French law enforcement.

Fache will do what no one else dares.

The delicate art of *cajoler* was a lost skill in modern law enforcement, one that required exceptional poise under pressure. Few men possessed the necessary sangfroid for this kind of operation, but Fache seemed born for it. His restraint and patience bordered on the robotic.

Fache's sole emotion this evening seemed to be one of intense resolve, as if this arrest were somehow personal to him. Fache's briefing of his agents an hour ago had been unusually succinct and assured. *I know who murdered Jacques Saunière,* Fache had said. *You know what to do. No mistakes tonight.*

And so far, no mistakes had been made.

Collet was not yet privy to the evidence that had cemented Fache's certainty of their suspect's guilt, but he knew better than to question the instincts of the Bull. Fache's intuition seemed almost supernatural at times. *God whispers in his ear,* one agent had insisted after a particularly impressive display of Fache's sixth sense. Collet had to admit, if there was a God, Bezu Fache would be on His A-list. The captain attended mass and confession with zealous regularity—far more than the requisite holiday attendance fulfilled by other officials in the name of good public relations. When the Pope visited Paris a few years back, Fache had used all his muscle to obtain the honor of an audience. A photo of Fache with the Pope now hung in his office. *The Papal Bull,* the agents secretly called it.

Collet found it ironic that one of Fache's rare popular public stances in recent years had been his outspoken reaction to the Catholic pedophilia scandal. *These priests should be hanged twice!* Fache had declared. *Once for their crimes against children. And once for shaming the good name of the Catholic Church.* Collet had the odd sense it was the latter that angered Fache more.

Turning now to his laptop computer, Collet attended to the other half of his responsibilities here tonight—the GPS tracking system. The image onscreen revealed a detailed floor plan of the Denon Wing, a structural schematic uploaded from the Louvre Security Office. Letting his eyes trace the maze of galleries and hallways, Collet found what he was looking for.

Deep in the heart of the Grand Gallery blinked a tiny red dot.

La marque.

Fache was keeping his prey on a very tight leash tonight. Wisely so. Robert Langdon had proven himself one cool customer.

*T*O ENSURE his conversation with Mr. Langdon would not be interrupted, Bezu Fache had turned off his cellular phone. Unfortunately, it was an expensive model equipped with a two-way radio feature, which, contrary to his orders, was now being used by one of his agents to page him.

"Capitaine?" The phone crackled like a walkie-talkie.

Fache felt his teeth clench in rage. He could imagine nothing important enough that Collet would interrupt this *surveillance cachée*—especially at this critical juncture.

He gave Langdon a calm look of apology. "One moment please." He pulled the phone from his belt and pressed the radio transmission button. *"Oui?"*

"Capitaine, un agent du Département de Cryptographie est arrivé."

Fache's anger stalled momentarily. *A cryptographer?* Despite the lousy timing, this was probably good news. Fache, after finding Saunière's cryptic text on the floor, had uploaded photographs of the entire crime scene to the Cryptography Department in hopes someone there could tell him what the hell Saunière was trying to say. If a code breaker had now arrived, it most likely meant someone had decrypted Saunière's message.

"I'm busy at the moment," Fache radioed back, leaving no doubt in his tone that a line had been crossed. "Ask the cryptographer to wait at the command post. I'll speak to him when I'm done."

"Her," the voice corrected. "It's Agent Neveu."

Fache was becoming less amused with this call every passing moment. Sophie Neveu was one of DCPJ's biggest mistakes. A young Parisian *déchiffreuse* who had studied cryptography in England at the Royal Holloway, Sophie Neveu had been foisted on Fache two years ago as part of the ministry's attempt to incorporate more women into the police force. The ministry's ongoing foray into political correctness, Fache argued, was weakening the department. Women not only lacked the physicality necessary for police work, but their mere presence posed a dangerous distraction to the men in the field. As Fache had feared, Sophie Neveu was proving far more distracting than most.

At thirty-two years old, she had a dogged determination that bordered on obstinate. Her eager espousal of Britain's new cryptologic methodology continually exasperated the veteran French cryptographers above her. And by far the most troubling to Fache was the inescapable universal truth that in an office of middle-aged men, an attractive young woman always drew eyes away from the work at hand.

The man on the radio said, "Agent Neveu insisted on speaking to you immediately, Captain. I tried to stop her, but she's on her way into the gallery."

Fache recoiled in disbelief. "Unacceptable! I made it very clear—"

FOR A MOMENT, Robert Langdon thought Bezu Fache was suffering a stroke. The captain was mid-sentence when his jaw stopped moving and his eyes bulged. His blistering gaze seemed fixated on something over Langdon's shoulder. Before Langdon could turn to see what it was, he heard a woman's voice chime out behind him.

"Excusez-moi, messieurs."

Langdon turned to see a young woman approaching. She was moving down the corridor toward them with long, fluid strides . . . a haunting certainty to her gait. Dressed casually in a knee-length, cream-colored Irish sweater over black leggings, she was attractive and looked to be about thirty. Her thick burgundy hair fell unstyled to her shoulders, framing the warmth of her face. Unlike the waifish, cookie-cutter blondes that adorned Harvard dorm room walls, this woman was healthy with an unembellished beauty and genuineness that radiated a striking personal confidence.

To Langdon's surprise, the woman walked directly up to him and extended a polite hand. "Monsieur Langdon, I am Agent Neveu from DCPJ's Cryptology Department." Her words curved richly around her muted Anglo-Franco accent. "It is a pleasure to meet you."

Langdon took her soft palm in his and felt himself momentarily fixed in her strong gaze. Her eyes were olive-green—incisive and clear.

Fache drew a seething inhalation, clearly preparing to launch into a reprimand.

"Captain," she said, turning quickly and beating him to the punch, "please excuse the interruption, but—"

"Ce n'est pas le moment!" Fache sputtered.

"I tried to phone you." Sophie continued in English, as if out of courtesy to Langdon. "But your cell phone was turned off."

"I turned it off for a reason," Fache hissed. "I am speaking to Mr. Langdon."

"I've deciphered the numeric code," she said flatly.

Langdon felt a pulse of excitement. *She broke the code?*

Fache looked uncertain how to respond.

"Before I explain," Sophie said, "I have an urgent message for Mr. Langdon."

Fache's expression turned to one of deepening concern. "For Mr. Langdon?"

She nodded, turning back to Langdon. "You need to contact the U.S. Embassy, Mr. Langdon. They have a message for you from the States."

Langdon reacted with surprise, his excitement over the code giving way to a sudden ripple of concern. *A message from the States?* He tried to imagine who could be trying to reach him. Only a few of his colleagues knew he was in Paris.

Fache's broad jaw had tightened with the news. "The U.S. Embassy?" he demanded, sounding suspicious. "How would they know to find Mr. Langdon *here?*"

Sophie shrugged. "Apparently they called Mr. Langdon's hotel, and the concierge told them Mr. Langdon had been collected by a DCPJ agent."

Fache looked troubled. "And the embassy contacted DCPJ *Cryptography?*"

"No, sir," Sophie said, her voice firm. "When I called the DCPJ switchboard in an attempt to contact you, they had a message waiting for Mr. Langdon and asked me to pass it along if I got through to you."

Fache's brow furrowed in apparent confusion. He opened his mouth to speak, but Sophie had already turned back to Langdon.

"Mr. Langdon," she declared, pulling a small slip of paper from her pocket, "this is the number for your embassy's messaging service. They asked that you phone in as soon as possible." She handed him the paper with an intent gaze. "While I explain the code to Captain Fache, you need to make this call."

Langdon studied the slip. It had a Paris phone number and extension on it. "Thank you," he said, feeling worried now. "Where do I find a phone?"

Sophie began to pull a cell phone from her sweater pocket, but Fache waved her off. He now looked like Mount Vesuvius about to erupt. Without taking his eyes off Sophie, he produced his own cell phone and held it out. "This line is secure, Mr. Langdon. You may use it."

Langdon felt mystified by Fache's anger with the young woman. Feeling uneasy, he accepted the captain's phone. Fache immediately marched Sophie several steps away and began chastising her in hushed tones. Disliking the captain more and more, Langdon turned away from the odd confrontation and switched on the cell phone. Checking the slip of paper Sophie had given him, Langdon dialed the number.

The line began to ring.

One ring . . . two rings . . . three rings . . .

Finally the call connected.

Langdon expected to hear an embassy operator, but he found himself instead listening to an answering machine. Oddly, the voice on the tape was familiar. It was that of Sophie Neveu.

"Bonjour, vous êtes bien chez Sophie Neveu," the woman's voice said. *"Je suis absente pour le moment, mais . . ."*

Confused, Langdon turned back toward Sophie. "I'm sorry, Ms. Neveu? I think you may have given me—"

"No, that's the right number," Sophie interjected quickly, as if anticipating Langdon's confusion. "The embassy has an automated message system. You have to dial an access code to pick up your messages."

Langdon stared. "But—"

"It's the three-digit code on the paper I gave you."

Langdon opened his mouth to explain the bizarre error, but Sophie flashed him a silencing glare that lasted only an instant. Her green eyes sent a crystal-clear message.

Don't ask questions. Just do it.

Bewildered, Langdon punched in the extension on the slip of paper: 454.

Sophie's outgoing message immediately cut off, and Langdon heard an electronic voice announce in French: "You have *one* new message." Apparently, 454 was Sophie's remote access code for picking up her messages while away from home.

I'm picking up this woman's messages?

Langdon could hear the tape rewinding now. Finally, it stopped, and the machine engaged. Langdon listened as the message began to play. Again, the voice on the line was Sophie's.

"Mr. Langdon," the message began in a fearful whisper. "Do *not* react to this message. Just listen calmly. You are in danger right now. Follow my directions very closely."

Chapter 10

ILAS SAT behind the wheel of the black Audi the Teacher had arranged for him and gazed out at the great Church of Saint-Sulpice. Lit from beneath by banks of floodlights, the church's two bell towers rose like stalwart sentinels above the building's long body. On either flank, a shadowy row of sleek buttresses jutted out like the ribs of a beautiful beast.

The heathens used a house of God to conceal their keystone. Again the brotherhood had confirmed their legendary reputation for illusion and deceit. Silas was looking forward to finding the keystone and giving it to the Teacher so they could recover what the brotherhood had long ago stolen from the faithful.

How powerful that will make Opus Dei.

Parking the Audi on the deserted Place Saint-Sulpice, Silas exhaled, telling himself to clear his mind for the task at hand. His broad back still ached from the corporal mortification he had endured earlier today, and yet the pain was inconsequential compared with the anguish of his life before Opus Dei had saved him.

Still, the memories haunted his soul.

Release your hatred, Silas commanded himself. *Forgive those who trespassed against you.*

Looking up at the stone towers of Saint-Sulpice, Silas fought that familiar undertow . . . that force that often dragged his mind back in time, locking him once again in the prison that had been his world as a young man. The memories of purgatory came as they always did, like a tempest to his senses . . . the reek of rotting cabbage, the stench of death, human urine and feces. The cries of hopelessness against the howling wind of the Pyrenees and the soft sobs of forgotten men.

Andorra, he thought, feeling his muscles tighten.

Incredibly, it was in that barren and forsaken suzerain between Spain and France, shivering in his stone cell, wanting only to die, that Silas had been saved.

SOUTH TOWER, SAINT–SULPICE

He had not realized it at the time.

The light came long after the thunder.

His name was not Silas then, although he didn't recall the name his parents had given him. He had left home when he was seven. His drunken father, a burly dock-worker, enraged by the arrival of an albino son, beat his mother regularly, blaming her for the boy's embarrassing condition. When the boy tried to defend her, he too was badly beaten.

One night, there was a horrific fight, and his mother never got up. The boy stood over his lifeless mother and felt an unbearable upwelling of guilt for permitting it to happen.

This is my fault!

As if some kind of demon were controlling his body, the boy walked to the kitchen and grasped a butcher knife. Hypnotically, he moved to the bedroom where his father lay on the bed in a drunken stupor. Without a word, the boy stabbed him in the back. His father cried out in pain and tried to roll over, but his son stabbed him again, over and over until the apartment fell quiet.

The boy fled home but found the streets of Marseilles equally unfriendly. His strange appearance made him an outcast among the other young runaways, and he was forced to live alone in the basement of a dilapidated factory, eating stolen fruit and raw fish from the dock. His only companions were tattered magazines he found in the trash, and he taught himself to read them. Over time, he grew strong. When he was twelve, another drifter—a girl twice his age—mocked him on the streets and attempted to steal his food. The girl found herself pummeled to within inches of her life. When the authorities pulled the boy off her, they gave him an ultimatum—leave Marseilles or go to juvenile prison.

The boy moved down the coast to Toulon. Over time, the looks of pity on the streets turned to looks of fear. The boy had grown to a powerful young man. When people passed by, he could hear them whispering to one another. *A ghost,* they would say, their eyes wide with fright as they stared at his white skin. *A ghost with the eyes of a devil!*

And he felt like a ghost . . . transparent . . . floating from seaport to seaport.

People seemed to look right through him.

At eighteen, in a port town, while attempting to steal a case of cured ham from a cargo ship, he was caught by a pair of crewmen. The two sailors who began to beat him smelled of beer, just as his father had. The memories of fear and hatred surfaced like a monster from the deep. The young man broke the first sailor's neck with his bare hands, and only the arrival of the police saved the second sailor from a similar fate.

Two months later, in shackles, he arrived at a prison in Andorra.

You are as white as a ghost, the inmates ridiculed as the guards marched him in, naked and cold. *Mira el espectro! Perhaps the ghost will pass right through these walls!*

Over the course of twelve years, his flesh and soul withered until he knew he had become transparent.

I am a ghost.

I am weightless.

Yo soy un espectro . . . pálido como un fantasma . . . caminando este mundo a solas.

One night the ghost awoke to the screams of other inmates. He didn't know what invisible force was shaking the floor on which he slept, nor what mighty hand was trembling the mortar of his stone cell, but as he jumped to his feet, a large boulder toppled onto the very spot where he had been sleeping. Looking up to see where the stone had come from, he saw a hole in the trembling wall, and beyond it, a vision he had not seen in over ten years. The moon.

Even while the earth still shook, the ghost found himself scrambling through a narrow tunnel, staggering out into an expansive vista, and tumbling down a barren mountainside into the woods. He ran all night, always downward, delirious with hunger and exhaustion.

Skirting the edges of consciousness, he found himself at dawn in a clearing where train tracks cut a swath across the forest. Following the rails, he moved on as if dreaming. Seeing an empty freight car, he crawled in for shelter and rest. When he awoke the train was moving. *How long? How far?* A pain was growing in his gut. *Am I dying?* He slept again. This time he awoke to someone yelling, beating him, throwing him out of the freight car. Bloody, he wandered the outskirts of a small village looking in vain for food. Finally, his body too weak to take another step, he lay down by the side of the road and slipped into unconsciousness.

The light came slowly, and the ghost wondered how long he had been dead. *A day? Three days?* It didn't matter. His bed was soft like a cloud, and the air around him smelled sweet with candles. Jesus was there, staring down at him. *I am here,* Jesus said. *The stone has been rolled aside, and you are born again.*

He slept and awoke. Fog shrouded his thoughts. He had never believed in heaven, and yet Jesus was watching over him. Food appeared beside his bed, and the ghost ate it, almost able to feel the flesh materializing on his bones. He slept again. When he awoke, Jesus was still smiling down, speaking. *You are saved, my son. Blessed are those who follow my path.*

Again, he slept.

It was a scream of anguish that startled the ghost from his slumber. His body leapt out of bed, staggered down a hallway toward the sounds of shouting. He entered into a kitchen and saw a large man beating a smaller man. Without knowing why, the ghost grabbed the large man and hurled him backward against a wall. The man fled, leaving the ghost standing over the body of a young man in priest's robes. The priest had a badly shattered nose. Lifting the bloody priest, the ghost carried him to a couch.

"Thank you, my friend," the priest said in awkward French. "The offertory money is tempting for thieves. You speak French in your sleep. Do you also speak Spanish?"

The ghost shook his head.

"What is your name?" he continued in broken French.

The ghost could not remember the name his parents had given him. All he heard were the taunting gibes of the prison guards.

The priest smiled. "*No hay problema.* My name is Manuel Aringarosa. I am a missionary from Madrid. I was sent here to build a church for the Obra de Dios."

"Where am I?" His voice sounded hollow.

"Oviedo. In the north of Spain."

"How did I get here?"

"Someone left you on my doorstep. You were ill. I fed you. You've been here many days."

The ghost studied his young caretaker. Years had passed since anyone had shown any kindness. "Thank you, Father."

The priest touched his bloody lip. "It is I who am thankful, my friend."

When the ghost awoke in the morning, his world felt clearer. He gazed up at the crucifix on the wall above his bed. Although it no longer spoke to him, he felt a comforting aura in its presence. Sitting up, he was surprised to find a newspaper clipping on his bedside table. The article was in French, a week old. When he read the story, he filled with fear. It told of an earthquake in the mountains that had destroyed a prison and freed many dangerous criminals.

His heart began pounding. *The priest knows who I am!* The emotion he felt was one he had not felt for some time. Shame. Guilt. It was accompanied by the fear of being caught. He jumped from his bed. *Where do I run?*

"The Book of Acts," a voice said from the door.

The ghost turned, frightened.

The young priest was smiling as he entered. His nose was awkwardly bandaged, and he was holding out an old Bible. "I found one in French for you. The chapter is marked."

Uncertain, the ghost took the Bible and looked at the chapter the priest had marked.

Acts 16.

The verses told of a prisoner named Silas who lay naked and beaten in his cell, singing hymns to God. When the ghost reached Verse 26, he gasped in shock.

"*. . . And suddenly, there was a great earthquake, so that the foundations of the prison were shaken, and all the doors fell open.*"

His eyes shot up at the priest.

 ACTS 16:25–26

25 And at midnight Paul and Silas prayed, and sang praises unto God: and the prisoners heard them.
26 And suddenly, there was a great earthquake, so that the foundations of the prison were shaken, and all the doors fell open.

THE DA VINCI CODE

The priest smiled warmly. "From now on, my friend, if you have no other name, I shall call you Silas."

The ghost nodded blankly. *Silas.* He had been given flesh. *My name is Silas.*

"It's time for breakfast," the priest said. "You will need your strength if you are to help me build this church."

TWENTY THOUSAND FEET above the Mediterranean, Alitalia flight 1618 bounced in turbulence, causing passengers to shift nervously. Bishop Aringarosa barely noticed. His thoughts were with the future of Opus Dei. Eager to know how plans in Paris were progressing, he wished he could phone Silas. But he could not. The Teacher had seen to that.

"It is for your own safety," the Teacher had explained, speaking in English with a French accent. "I am familiar enough with electronic communications to know they can be intercepted. The results could be disastrous for you."

Aringarosa knew he was right. The Teacher seemed an exceptionally careful man. He had not revealed his own identity to Aringarosa, and yet he had proven himself a man well worth obeying. After all, he had somehow obtained very secret information. *The names of the brotherhood's four top members!* This had been one of the coups that convinced the bishop the Teacher was truly capable of delivering the astonishing prize he claimed he could unearth.

"Bishop," the Teacher had told him, "I have made all the arrangements. For my plan to succeed, you must allow Silas to answer *only* to me for several days. The two of you will not speak. I will communicate with him through secure channels."

"You will treat him with respect?"

"A man of faith deserves the highest."

"Excellent. Then I understand. Silas and I shall not speak until this is over."

"I do this to protect your identity, Silas's identity, and my investment."

"Your investment?"

"Bishop, if your own eagerness to keep abreast of progress puts you in jail, then you will be unable to pay me my fee."

The bishop smiled. "A fine point. Our desires are in accord. Godspeed."

Twenty million euro, the bishop thought, now gazing out the plane's window. The sum was approximately the same number of U.S. dollars. *A pittance for something so powerful.*

He felt a renewed confidence that the Teacher and Silas would not fail. Money and faith were powerful motivators.

*"*U*NE PLAISANTERIE NUMÉRIQUE?"* Bezu Fache was livid, glaring at Sophie Neveu in disbelief. *A numeric joke?* "Your professional assessment of Saunière's code is that it is some kind of mathematical prank?"

Fache was in utter incomprehension of this woman's gall. Not only had she just barged in on Fache without permission, but she was now trying to convince him that Saunière, in his final moments of life, had been inspired to leave a mathematical gag?

"This code," Sophie explained in rapid French, "is simplistic to the point of absurdity. Jacques Saunière must have known we would see through it immediately." She pulled a scrap of paper from her sweater pocket and handed it to Fache. "Here is the decryption."

Fache looked at the card.

1-1-2-3-5-8-13-21

"This is it?" he snapped. "All you did was put the numbers in increasing order!"

Sophie actually had the nerve to give a satisfied smile. "Exactly."

Fache's tone lowered to a guttural rumble. "Agent Neveu, I have no idea where the hell you're going with this, but I suggest you get there fast." He shot an anxious glance at Langdon, who stood nearby with the phone pressed to his ear, apparently still listening to his phone message from the U.S. Embassy. From Langdon's ashen expression, Fache sensed the news was bad.

"Captain," Sophie said, her tone dangerously defiant, "the sequence of numbers you have in your hand happens to be one of the most famous mathematical progressions in history."

Fache was not aware there even existed a mathematical progression that qualified as famous, and he certainly didn't appreciate Sophie's offhanded tone.

"This is the Fibonacci sequence," she declared, nodding toward the piece of paper in Fache's hand. "A progression in which each term is equal to the sum of the two preceding terms."

Fache studied the numbers. Each term was indeed the sum of the two previous, and yet Fache could not imagine what the relevance of all this was to Saunière's death.

"Mathematician Leonardo Fibonacci created this succession of numbers in the thirteenth century. Obviously there can be no coincidence that *all* of the numbers Saunière wrote on the floor belong to Fibonacci's famous sequence."

Fache stared at the young woman for several moments. "Fine, if there is no coincidence, would you tell me *why* Jacques Saunière chose to do this? What is he saying? What does this *mean?*"

She shrugged. "Absolutely nothing. That's the point. It's a simplistic cryptographic joke. Like taking the words of a famous poem and shuffling them at random to see if anyone recognizes what all the words have in common."

Fache took a menacing step forward, placing his face only inches from Sophie's. "I certainly hope you have a much more satisfying explanation than *that.*"

Sophie's soft features grew surprisingly stern as she leaned in. "Captain, considering what you have at stake here tonight, I thought you might appreciate knowing that Jacques Saunière might be playing games with you. Apparently not. I'll inform the director of Cryptography you no longer need our services."

With that, she turned on her heel, and marched off the way she had come.

Stunned, Fache watched her disappear into the darkness. *Is she out of her mind?* Sophie Neveu had just redefined *le suicide professionnel.*

Fache turned to Langdon, who was still on the phone, looking more concerned than before, listening intently to his phone message. *The U.S. Embassy.* Bezu Fache despised many things . . . but few drew more wrath than the U.S. Embassy.

Fache and the ambassador locked horns regularly over shared affairs of state—their most common battleground being law enforcement for visiting Americans. Almost daily, DCPJ arrested American exchange students in possession of drugs, U.S. businessmen for soliciting underage prostitutes, American tourists for shoplifting or destruction of property. Legally, the U.S. Embassy could intervene and extradite guilty citizens back to the United States, where they received nothing more than a slap on the wrist.

And the embassy invariably did just that.

L'émasculation de la Police Judiciaire, Fache called it. *Paris-Match* had run a cartoon recently depicting Fache as a police dog, trying to bite an American criminal, but unable to reach because it was chained to the U.S. Embassy.

Not tonight, Fache told himself. *There is far too much at stake.*

By the time Robert Langdon hung up the phone, he looked ill.

"Is everything all right?" Fache asked.

Weakly, Langdon shook his head.

Bad news from home, Fache sensed, noticing Langdon was sweating slightly as Fache took back his cell phone.

"An accident," Langdon stammered, looking at Fache with a strange expression. "A friend . . ." He hesitated. "I'll need to fly home first thing in the morning."

Fache had no doubt the shock on Langdon's face was genuine, and yet he sensed another emotion there too, as if a distant fear were suddenly simmering in the American's eyes. "I'm sorry to hear that," Fache said, watching Langdon closely. "Would you like to sit down?" He motioned toward one of the viewing benches in the gallery.

Langdon nodded absently and took a few steps toward the bench. He paused, looking more confused with every moment. "Actually, I think I'd like to use the rest room."

Fache frowned inwardly at the delay. "The rest room. Of course. Let's take a break for a few minutes." He motioned back down the long hallway in the direction they had come from. "The rest rooms are back toward the curator's office."

Langdon hesitated, pointing in the other direction toward the far end of the Grand Gallery corridor. "I believe there's a much closer rest room at the end."

Fache realized Langdon was right. They were two-thirds of the way down, and the Grand Gallery dead-ended at a pair of rest rooms. "Shall I accompany you?"

Langdon shook his head, already moving deeper into the gallery. "Not necessary. I think I'd like a few minutes alone."

Fache was not wild about the idea of Langdon wandering alone down the remaining length of corridor, but he took comfort in knowing the Grand Gallery was a dead end whose only exit was at the other end—the gate under which they had entered. Although French fire regulations required several emergency stairwells for a space this large, those stairwells had been sealed automatically when Saunière tripped the security system. Granted, that system had now been reset, unlocking the stairwells, but it didn't matter—the external doors, if opened, would set off fire alarms and were guarded outside by DCPJ agents. Langdon could not possibly leave without Fache knowing about it.

"I need to return to Mr. Saunière's office for a moment," Fache said. "Please come find me directly, Mr. Langdon. There is more we need to discuss."

Langdon gave a quiet wave as he disappeared into the darkness.

Turning, Fache marched angrily in the opposite direction. Arriving at the gate, he slid under, exited the Grand Gallery, marched down the hall, and stormed into the command center at Saunière's office.

"Who gave the approval to let Sophie Neveu into this building!" Fache bellowed.

Collet was the first to answer. "She told the guards outside she'd broken the code."

Fache looked around. "Is she gone?"

"She's not with you?"

"She left." Fache glanced out at the darkened hallway. Apparently Sophie had been in no mood to stop by and chat with the other officers on her way out.

For a moment, Fache considered radioing the guards in the entresol and telling them to stop Sophie and drag her back up here before she could leave the premises. He thought better of it. That was only his pride talking . . . wanting the last word. He'd had enough distractions tonight.

Deal with Agent Neveu later, he told himself, already looking forward to firing her.

Pushing Sophie from his mind, Fache stared for a moment at the miniature knight standing on Saunière's desk. Then he turned back to Collet. "Do you have him?"

Collet gave a curt nod and spun the laptop toward Fache. The red dot was clearly visible on the floor plan overlay, blinking methodically in a room marked TOILETTES PUBLIQUES.

"Good," Fache said, lighting a cigarette and stalking into the hall. "I've got a phone call to make. Be damned sure the rest room is the only place Langdon goes."

ROBERT LANGDON felt light-headed as he trudged toward the end of the Grand Gallery. Sophie's phone message played over and over in his mind. At the end of the corridor, illuminated signs bearing the international stick-figure symbols for rest rooms guided him through a maze-like series of dividers displaying Italian drawings and hiding the rest rooms from sight.

Finding the men's room door, Langdon entered and turned on the lights.

The room was empty.

Walking to the sink, he splashed cold water on his face and tried to wake up. Harsh fluorescent lights glared off the stark tile, and the room smelled of ammonia. As he toweled off, the rest room's door creaked open behind him. He spun.

Sophie Neveu entered, her green eyes flashing fear. "Thank God you came. We don't have much time."

Langdon stood beside the sinks, staring in bewilderment at DCPJ cryptographer Sophie Neveu. Only minutes ago, Langdon had listened to her phone message, thinking the newly arrived cryptographer must be insane. And yet, the more he listened, the more he sensed Sophie Neveu was speaking in earnest. *Do not react to this message. Just listen calmly. You are in danger right now. Follow my directions very closely.* Filled with uncertainty, Langdon had decided to do exactly as Sophie advised. He told Fache that the phone message was regarding an injured friend back home. Then he had asked to use the rest room at the end of the Grand Gallery.

Sophie stood before him now, still catching her breath after doubling back to the rest room. In the fluorescent lights, Langdon was surprised to see that her strong air actually radiated from unexpectedly soft features. Only her gaze was sharp, and the juxtaposition conjured images of a multilayered Renoir portrait . . . veiled but distinct, with a boldness that somehow retained its shroud of mystery.

"I wanted to warn you, Mr. Langdon . . ." Sophie began, still catching her breath, "that you are *sous surveillance cachée*. Under a guarded observation." As she spoke, her accented English resonated off the tile walls, giving her voice a hollow quality.

"But . . . why?" Langdon demanded. Sophie had already given him an explanation on the phone, but he wanted to hear it from her lips.

"Because," she said, stepping toward him, "Fache's primary suspect in this murder is *you*."

Langdon was braced for the words, and yet they still sounded utterly ridiculous. According to Sophie, Langdon had been called to the Louvre tonight not as a symbologist but rather as a *suspect* and was currently the unwitting target of one of DCPJ's favorite interrogation methods—*surveillance cachée*—a deft deception in which the police calmly invited a suspect to a crime scene and interviewed him in hopes he would get nervous and mistakenly incriminate himself.

"Look in your jacket's left pocket," Sophie said. "You'll find proof they are watching you."

Langdon felt his apprehension rising. *Look in my pocket?* It sounded like some kind of cheap magic trick.

"Just look."

Bewildered, Langdon reached his hand into his tweed jacket's left pocket—one he never used. Feeling around inside, he found nothing. *What the devil did you expect?* He began wondering if Sophie might just be insane after all. Then his fingers brushed something unexpected. Small and hard. Pinching the tiny object between his fingers, Langdon pulled it out and stared in astonishment. It was a metallic, button-shaped disk, about the size of a watch battery. He had never seen it before. "What the . . . ?"

"GPS tracking dot," Sophie said. "Continuously transmits its location to a Global Positioning System satellite that DCPJ can monitor. We use them to monitor people's locations. It's accurate within two feet anywhere on the globe. They have you on an electronic leash. The agent who picked you up at the hotel slipped it inside your pocket before you left your room."

Langdon flashed back to the hotel room . . . his quick shower, getting dressed, the DCPJ agent politely holding out Langdon's tweed coat as they left the room. *It's cool outside, Mr. Langdon,* the agent had said. *Spring in Paris is not all your song boasts.* Langdon had thanked him and donned the jacket.

Sophie's olive gaze was keen. "I didn't tell you about the tracking dot earlier because I didn't want you checking your pocket in front of Fache. He can't know you've found it."

Langdon had no idea how to respond.

"They tagged you with GPS because they thought you might run." She paused. "In fact, they *hoped* you would run; it would make their case stronger."

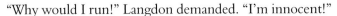

"Why would I run!" Langdon demanded. "I'm innocent!"

"Fache feels otherwise."

Angrily, Langdon stalked toward the trash receptacle to dispose of the tracking dot.

"No!" Sophie grabbed his arm and stopped him. "Leave it in your pocket. If you throw it out, the signal will stop moving, and they'll know you found the dot. The only reason Fache left you alone is because he can monitor where you are. If he thinks you've discovered what he's doing . . ." Sophie did not finish the thought. Instead, she pried the metallic disk from Langdon's hand and slid it back into the pocket of his tweed coat. "The dot stays with you. At least for the moment."

Langdon felt lost. "How the hell could Fache actually believe I killed Jacques Saunière!"

"He has some fairly persuasive reasons to suspect you." Sophie's expression was grim. "There is a piece of evidence here that you have not yet seen. Fache has kept it carefully hidden from you."

Langdon could only stare.

"Do you recall the three lines of text that Saunière wrote on the floor?"

Langdon nodded. The numbers and words were imprinted on Langdon's mind.

Sophie's voice dropped to a whisper now. "Unfortunately, what you saw was not the entire message. There was a *fourth* line that Fache photographed and then wiped clean before you arrived."

Although Langdon knew the soluble ink of a watermark stylus could easily be wiped away, he could not imagine why Fache would erase evidence.

"The last line of the message," Sophie said, "was something Fache did not want you to know about." She paused. "At least not until he was done with you."

Sophie produced a computer printout of a photo from her sweater pocket and began unfolding it. "Fache uploaded images of the crime scene to the Cryptology Department earlier tonight in hopes we could figure out what Saunière's message was trying to say. This is a photo of the complete message." She handed the page to Langdon.

Bewildered, Langdon looked at the image. The close-up photo revealed the glowing message on the parquet floor. The final line hit Langdon like a kick in the gut.

13-3-2-21-1-1-8-5
O, Draconian devil!
Oh, lame saint!
P.S. Find Robert Langdon

*F*OR SEVERAL SECONDS, Langdon stared in wonder at the photograph of Saunière's postscript. *P.S. Find Robert Langdon.* He felt as if the floor were tilting beneath his feet. *Saunière left a postscript with my name on it?* In his wildest dreams, Langdon could not fathom why.

"Now do you understand," Sophie said, her eyes urgent, "why Fache ordered you here tonight, and why you are his primary suspect?"

The only thing Langdon understood at the moment was why Fache had looked so smug when Langdon suggested Saunière would have accused his killer by name.

Find Robert Langdon.

"Why would Saunière write this?" Langdon demanded, his confusion now giving way to anger. "Why would I want to kill Jacques Saunière?"

"Fache has yet to uncover a motive, but he has been recording his entire conversation with you tonight in hopes you might reveal one."

Langdon opened his mouth, but still no words came.

"He's fitted with a miniature microphone," Sophie explained. "It's connected to a transmitter in his pocket that radios the signal back to the command post."

"This is impossible," Langdon stammered. "I have an alibi. I went directly back to my hotel after my lecture. You can ask the hotel desk."

"Fache already did. His report shows you retrieving your room key from the concierge at about ten-thirty. Unfortunately, the time of the murder was closer to eleven. You easily could have left your hotel room unseen."

"This is insanity! Fache has no evidence!"

Sophie's eyes widened as if to say: *No evidence?* "Mr. Langdon, your name is written on the floor beside the body, and Saunière's date book says you were with him at approximately the time of the murder." She paused. "Fache has more than enough evidence to take you into custody for questioning."

Langdon suddenly sensed that he needed a lawyer. "I didn't do this."

Sophie sighed. "This is not American television, Mr. Langdon. In France, the laws protect the police, not criminals. Unfortunately, in this case, there is also the media consideration. Jacques Saunière was a very prominent and well-loved figure in Paris, and his murder will be news in the morning. Fache will be under immediate pressure to make a statement, and he looks a lot better having a suspect in custody already. Whether or not you are guilty, you most certainly will be held by DCPJ until they can figure out what really happened."

Langdon felt like a caged animal. "Why are you telling me all this?"

"Because, Mr. Langdon, I believe you are innocent." Sophie looked away for a moment and then back into his eyes. "And also because it is partially *my* fault that you're in trouble."

"I'm sorry? It's *your* fault Saunière is trying to frame me?"

"Saunière wasn't trying to frame you. It was a mistake. That message on the floor was meant for me."

Langdon needed a minute to process that one. "I beg your pardon?"

"That message wasn't for the police. He wrote it for *me*. I think he was forced to do everything in such a hurry that he just didn't realize how it would look to the police." She paused. "The numbered code is meaningless. Saunière wrote it to make sure the investigation included cryptographers, ensuring that *I* would know as soon as possible what had happened to him."

Langdon felt himself losing touch fast. Whether or not Sophie Neveu had lost her mind was at this point up for grabs, but at least Langdon now understood why she was trying to help him. *P.S. Find Robert Langdon.* She apparently believed the curator had left her a cryptic postscript telling her to find Langdon. "But why do you think his message was for you?"

"The *Vitruvian Man,*" she said flatly. "That particular sketch has always been my favorite Da Vinci work. Tonight he used it to catch my attention."

"Hold on. You're saying the curator *knew* your favorite piece of art?"

She nodded. "I'm sorry. This is all coming out of order. Jacques Saunière and I . . ."

Sophie's voice caught, and Langdon heard a sudden melancholy there, a painful past, simmering just below the surface. Sophie and Jacques Saunière apparently had some kind of special relationship. Langdon studied the beautiful young woman before him, well aware that aging men in France often took young mistresses. Even so, Sophie Neveu as a "kept woman" somehow didn't seem to fit.

"We had a falling-out ten years ago," Sophie said, her voice a whisper now.

"We've barely spoken since. Tonight, when Crypto got the call that he had been murdered, and I saw the images of his body and text on the floor, I realized he was trying to send me a message."

"Because of *The Vitruvian Man*?"

"Yes. And the letters P.S."

"Post Script?"

She shook her head. "P.S. are my initials."

"But your name is Sophie Neveu."

She looked away. "P.S. is the nickname he called me when I lived with him." She blushed. "It stood for *Princesse Sophie*."

Langdon had no response.

"Silly, I know," she said. "But it was years ago. When I was a little girl."

"You knew him when you were a little *girl*?"

"Quite well," she said, her eyes welling now with emotion. "Jacques Saunière was my grandfather."

"WHERE'S LANGDON?" Fache demanded, exhaling the last of a cigarette as he paced back into the command post.

"Still in the men's room, sir." Lieutenant Collet had been expecting the question.

Fache grumbled, "Taking his time, I see."

The captain eyed the GPS dot over Collet's shoulder, and Collet could almost hear the wheels turning. Fache was fighting the urge to go check on Langdon. Ideally, the subject of an observation was allowed the most time and freedom possible, lulling him into a false sense of security. Langdon needed to return of his own volition. Still, it had been almost ten minutes.

Too long.

"Any chance Langdon is on to us?" Fache asked.

Collet shook his head. "We're still seeing small movements inside the men's room, so the GPS dot is obviously still on him. Perhaps he feels ill? If he had found the dot, he would have removed it and tried to run."

Fache checked his watch. "Fine."

Still Fache seemed preoccupied. All evening, Collet had sensed an atypical intensity in his captain. Usually detached and cool under pressure, Fache tonight seemed emotionally engaged, as if this were somehow a personal matter for him.

Not surprising, Collet thought. *Fache needs this arrest desperately.* Recently the Board of Ministers and the media had become more openly critical of Fache's aggressive tactics, his clashes with powerful foreign embassies, and his gross overbudgeting on new technologies. Tonight, a high-tech, high-profile arrest of an American would go a long way to silence Fache's critics, helping him secure the job a few more years until he could retire with the lucrative pension. *God knows he needs the pension,* Collet thought. Fache's zeal for technology had hurt him both professionally and personally. Fache was rumored to have invested his entire savings in the technology craze a few years back and lost his shirt. *And Fache is a man who wears only the finest shirts.*

Tonight, there was still plenty of time. Sophie Neveu's odd interruption, though unfortunate, had been only a minor wrinkle. She was gone now, and Fache still had cards to play. He had yet to inform Langdon that his name had been scrawled on the floor by the victim. *P.S. Find Robert Langdon.* The American's reaction to that little bit of evidence would be telling indeed.

"Captain?" one of the DCPJ agents now called from across the office. "I think you better take this call." He was holding out a telephone receiver, looking concerned.

"Who is it?" Fache said.

The agent frowned. "It's the director of our Cryptology Department."

"And?"

"It's about Sophie Neveu, sir. Something is not quite right."

*I*T WAS TIME.

Silas felt strong as he stepped from the black Audi, the nighttime breeze rustling his loose-fitting robe. *The winds of change are in the air.* He knew the task before him would require more finesse than force, and he left his handgun in the car. The thirteen-round Heckler and Koch USP 40 had been provided by the Teacher.

A weapon of death has no place in a house of God.

The plaza before the great church was deserted at this hour, the only visible souls on the far side of Place Saint-Sulpice a couple of teenage hookers showing their wares to the late-night tourist traffic. Their nubile bodies sent a familiar longing to Silas's loins. His thigh flexed instinctively, causing the barbed *cilice* belt to cut painfully into his flesh.

The lust evaporated instantly. For ten years now, Silas had faithfully denied himself all sexual indulgence, even self-administered. It was *The Way.* He knew he had sacrificed much to follow Opus Dei, but he had received much more in return. A vow of celibacy and the relinquishment of all personal assets hardly seemed a sacrifice. Considering the poverty from which he had come and the sexual horrors he had endured in prison, celibacy was a welcome change.

Now, having returned to France for the first time since being arrested and shipped to prison in Andorra, Silas could feel his homeland testing him, dragging violent memories from his redeemed soul. *You have been reborn,* he reminded himself. His service to God today had required the sin of murder, and it was a sacrifice Silas knew he would have to hold silently in his heart for all eternity.

The measure of your faith is the measure of the pain you can endure, the Teacher had told him. Silas was no stranger to pain and felt eager to prove himself to the Teacher, the one who had assured him his actions were ordained by a higher power.

"Hago la obra de Dios," Silas whispered, moving now toward the church entrance.

Pausing in the shadow of the massive doorway, he took a deep breath. It was not until this instant that he truly realized what he was about to do, and what awaited him inside.

The keystone. It will lead us to our final goal.

He raised his ghost-white fist and banged three times on the door.

Moments later, the bolts of the enormous wooden portal began to move.

ENTRANCE TO SAINT-SULPICE

*S*OPHIE WONDERED how long it would take Fache to figure out she had not left the building. Seeing that Langdon was clearly overwhelmed, Sophie questioned whether she had done the right thing by cornering him here in the men's room.

What else was I supposed to do?

She pictured her grandfather's body, naked and spread-eagle on the floor. There was a time when he had meant the world to her, yet tonight, Sophie was surprised to feel almost no sadness for the man. Jacques Saunière was a stranger to her now. Their relationship had evaporated in a single instant one March night when she was twenty-two. *Ten years ago.* Sophie had come home a few days early from graduate university in England and mistakenly witnessed her grandfather engaged in something Sophie was obviously not supposed to see. It was an image she barely could believe to this day.

If I hadn't seen it with my own eyes . . .

Too ashamed and stunned to endure her grandfather's pained attempts to explain, Sophie immediately moved out on her own, taking money she had saved, and getting a small flat with some roommates. She vowed never to speak to anyone about what she had seen. Her grandfather tried desperately to reach her, sending cards and letters, begging Sophie to meet him so he could explain. *Explain how!?* Sophie never responded except once—to forbid him ever to call her or try to meet her in public. She was afraid his explanation would be more terrifying than the incident itself.

Incredibly, Saunière had never given up on her, and Sophie now possessed a decade's worth of correspondence unopened in a dresser drawer. To her grandfather's credit, he had never once disobeyed her request and phoned her.

Until this afternoon.

"Sophie?" His voice had sounded startlingly old on her answering machine. "I have abided by your wishes for so long . . . and it pains me to call, but I must speak to you. Something terrible has happened."

Standing in the kitchen of her Paris flat, Sophie felt a chill to hear him again after all these years. His gentle voice brought back a flood of fond childhood memories.

"Sophie, please listen." He was speaking English to her, as he always did when she was a little girl. *Practice French at school. Practice English at home.* "You cannot be mad forever. Have you not read the letters that I've sent all these years? Do you not yet understand?" He paused. "We must speak at once. Please grant your grandfather this one wish. Call me at the Louvre. Right away. I believe you and I are in grave danger."

Sophie stared at the answering machine. *Danger?* What was he talking about?

"Princess . . ." Her grandfather's voice cracked with an emotion Sophie could not place. "I know I've kept things from you, and I know it has cost me your love. But it was for your own safety. Now you must know the truth. Please, I must tell you the truth about your family."

Sophie suddenly could hear her own heart. *My family?* Sophie's parents had died when she was only four. Their car went off a bridge into fast-moving water. Her grandmother and younger brother had also been in the car, and Sophie's entire family had been erased in an instant. She had a box of newspaper clippings to confirm it.

His words had sent an unexpected surge of longing through her bones. *My family!* In that fleeting instant, Sophie saw images from the dream that had awoken her countless times when she was a little girl: *My family is alive! They are coming home!* But, as in her dream, the pictures evaporated into oblivion.

Your family is dead, Sophie. They are not coming home.

"Sophie . . ." her grandfather said on the machine. "I have been waiting for years to tell you. Waiting for the right moment, but now time has run out. Call me at the Louvre. As soon as you get this. I'll wait here all night. I fear we both may be in danger. There's so much you need to know."

The message ended.

In the silence, Sophie stood trembling for what felt like minutes. As she considered her grandfather's message, only one possibility made sense, and his true intent dawned.

It was bait.

Obviously, her grandfather wanted desperately to see her. He was trying anything. Her disgust for the man deepened. Sophie wondered if maybe he had fallen terminally ill and had decided to attempt any ploy he could think of to get Sophie to visit him one last time. If so, he had chosen wisely.

My family.

Now, standing in the darkness of the Louvre men's room, Sophie could hear the echoes of this afternoon's phone message. *Sophie, we both may be in danger. Call me.*

She had not called him. Nor had she planned to. Now, however, her skepticism had been deeply challenged. Her grandfather lay murdered inside his own museum. And he had written a code on the floor.

A code for *her*. Of this, she was certain.

Despite not understanding the meaning of his message, Sophie was certain its cryptic nature was additional proof that the words were intended for her. Sophie's passion and aptitude for cryptography were a product of growing up with Jacques Saunière—a fanatic himself for codes, word games, and puzzles. *How many Sundays did we spend doing the cryptograms and crosswords in the newspaper?*

At the age of twelve, Sophie could finish the *Le Monde* crossword without any help, and her grandfather graduated her to crosswords in English, mathematical puzzles, and substitution ciphers. Sophie devoured them all. Eventually she turned her passion into a profession by becoming a codebreaker for the Judicial Police.

Tonight, the cryptographer in Sophie was forced to respect the efficiency with which her grandfather had used a simple code to unite two total strangers—Sophie Neveu and Robert Langdon.

The question was *why?*

Unfortunately, from the bewildered look in Langdon's eyes, Sophie sensed the American had no more idea than she did why her grandfather had thrown them together.

She pressed again. "You and my grandfather had planned to meet tonight. What about?"

Langdon looked truly perplexed. "His secretary set the meeting and didn't offer any specific reason, and I didn't ask. I assumed he'd heard I would be lecturing on the pagan iconography of French cathedrals, was interested in the topic, and thought it would be fun to meet for drinks after the talk."

Sophie didn't buy it. The connection was flimsy. Her grandfather knew more about pagan iconography than anyone else on earth. Moreover, he was an exceptionally private man, not someone prone to chatting with random American professors unless there were an important reason.

Sophie took a deep breath and probed further. "My grandfather called me this afternoon and told me he and I were in grave danger. Does *that* mean anything to you?"

Langdon's blue eyes now clouded with concern. "No, but considering what just happened . . ."

Sophie nodded. Considering tonight's events, she would be a fool not to be frightened. Feeling drained, she walked to the small plate-glass window at the far end of the bathroom and gazed out in silence through the mesh of alarm tape embedded in the glass. They were high up—forty feet at least.

Sighing, she raised her eyes and gazed out at Paris's dazzling landscape. On her left, across the Seine, the illuminated Eiffel Tower. Straight ahead, the Arc de Triomphe. And to the right, high atop the sloping rise of Montmartre, the graceful arabesque dome of Sacré-Coeur, its polished stone glowing white like a resplendent sanctuary.

Here at the westernmost tip of the Denon Wing, the north-south thoroughfare of Place du Carrousel ran almost flush with the building with only a narrow sidewalk separating it from the Louvre's outer wall. Far below, the usual caravan of the city's nighttime delivery trucks sat idling, waiting for the signals to change, their running lights seeming to twinkle mockingly up at Sophie.

"I don't know what to say," Langdon said, coming up behind her. "Your grandfather is obviously trying to tell us something. I'm sorry I'm so little help."

SACRÉ-COEUR, MONTMARTRE

Sophie turned from the window, sensing a sincere regret in Langdon's deep voice. Even with all the trouble around him, he obviously wanted to help her. *The teacher in him,* she thought, having read DCPJ's workup on their suspect. This was an academic who clearly despised not understanding.

We have that in common, she thought.

As a codebreaker, Sophie made her living extracting meaning from seemingly senseless data. Tonight, her best guess was that Robert Langdon, whether he knew it or not, possessed information that she desperately needed. *Princesse Sophie, Find Robert Langdon.* How much clearer could her grandfather's message be? Sophie needed more time with Langdon. Time to think. Time to sort out this mystery together. Unfortunately, time was running out.

Gazing up at Langdon, Sophie made the only play she could think of. "Bezu Fache will be taking you into custody at any minute. I can get you out of this museum. But we need to act now."

Langdon's eyes went wide. "You want me to *run?*"

"It's the smartest thing you could do. If you let Fache take you into custody now, you'll spend weeks in a French jail while DCPJ and the U.S. Embassy fight over which courts try your case. But if we get you out of here, and make it to your embassy, then your government will protect your rights while you and I prove you had nothing to do with this murder."

Langdon looked not even vaguely convinced. "Forget it! Fache has armed guards on every single exit! Even if we escape without being shot, running away only makes me look guilty. You need to tell Fache that the message on the floor was for *you,* and that my name is not there as an accusation."

"I *will* do that," Sophie said, speaking hurriedly, "but after you're safely inside the U.S. Embassy. It's only about a mile from here, and my car is parked just outside the museum. Dealing with Fache from here is too much of a gamble. Don't you see? Fache has made it his mission tonight to prove you are guilty. The only reason he postponed your arrest was to run this observance in hopes you did something that made his case stronger."

"Exactly. Like *running!*"

The cell phone in Sophie's sweater pocket suddenly began ringing. *Fache probably.* She reached in her sweater and turned off the phone.

"Mr. Langdon," she said hurriedly, "I need to ask you one last question." *And your entire future may depend on it.* "The writing on the floor is obviously not proof of your guilt, and yet Fache told our team he is *certain* you are his man. Can you think of any other reason he might be convinced you're guilty?"

Langdon was silent for several seconds. "None whatsoever."

Sophie sighed. *Which means Fache is lying.* Why, Sophie could not begin to imagine, but that was hardly the issue at this point. The fact remained that Bezu Fache was determined to put Robert Langdon behind bars tonight, at any cost. Sophie needed Langdon for herself, and it was this dilemma that left Sophie only one logical conclusion.

I need to get Langdon to the U.S. Embassy.

Turning toward the window, Sophie gazed through the alarm mesh embedded in the plate glass, down the dizzying forty feet to the pavement below. A leap from this height would leave Langdon with a couple of broken legs. At best.

Nonetheless, Sophie made her decision.

Robert Langdon was about to escape the Louvre, whether he wanted to or not.

HAT DO YOU MEAN she's not answering?" Fache looked incredulous. "You're calling her cell phone, right? I know she's carrying it."

Collet had been trying to reach Sophie now for several minutes. "Maybe her batteries are dead. Or her ringer's off."

Fache had looked distressed ever since talking to the director of Cryptology on the phone. After hanging up, he had marched over to Collet and demanded he get Agent Neveu on the line. Now Collet had failed, and Fache was pacing like a caged lion.

"Why did Crypto call?" Collet now ventured.

Fache turned. "To tell us they found no references to Draconian devils and lame saints."

"That's all?"

"No, also to tell us that they had just identified the numerics as Fibonacci numbers, but they suspected the series was meaningless."

Collet was confused. "But they already sent Agent Neveu to tell us that."

Fache shook his head. "They didn't send Neveu."

"What?"

"According to the director, at my orders he paged his entire team to look at the images I'd wired him. When Agent Neveu arrived, she took one look at the photos of Saunière and the code and left the office without a word. The director said he didn't question her behavior because she was understandably upset by the photos."

"Upset? She's never seen a picture of a dead body?"

Fache was silent a moment. "I was not aware of this, and it seems neither was the director until a coworker informed him, but apparently Sophie Neveu is Jacques Saunière's granddaughter."

Collet was speechless.

"The director said she never once mentioned Saunière to him, and he assumed it was because she probably didn't want preferential treatment for having a famous grandfather."

No wonder she was upset by the pictures. Collet could barely conceive of the unfortunate coincidence that called in a young woman to decipher a code written by a dead family member. Still, her actions made no sense. "But she obviously recognized the numbers as Fibonacci numbers because she came here and *told* us. I don't understand why she would leave the office without telling anyone she had figured it out."

Collet could think of only one scenario to explain the troubling developments: Saunière had written a numeric code on the floor in hopes Fache would involve cryptographers in the investigation, and therefore involve his own granddaughter. As for the rest of the message, was Saunière communicating in some way with his granddaughter? If so, what did the message tell her? And how did Langdon fit in?

Before Collet could ponder it any further, the silence of the deserted museum was shattered by an alarm. The bell sounded like it was coming from inside the Grand Gallery.

"Alarme!" one of the agents yelled, eyeing his feed from the Louvre security center. *"Grande Galerie! Toilettes Messieurs!"*

Fache wheeled to Collet. "Where's Langdon?"

"Still in the men's room!" Collet pointed to the blinking red dot on his laptop schematic. "He must have broken the window!" Collet knew Langdon wouldn't get far. Although Paris fire codes required windows above fifteen meters in public buildings be breakable in case of fire, exiting a Louvre second-story window without the help of a hook and ladder would be suicide. Furthermore, there were no trees or grass on the western end of the Denon Wing to cushion a fall. Directly

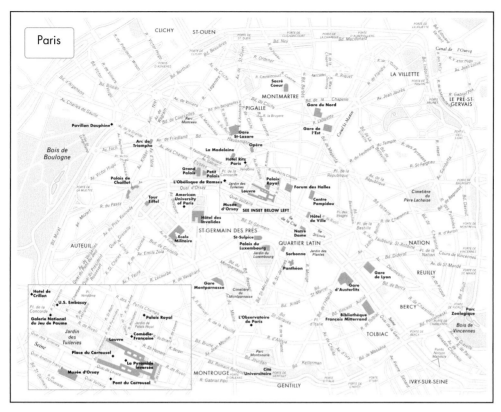

beneath that rest room window, the two-lane Place du Carrousel ran within a few feet of the outer wall. "My God," Collet exclaimed, eyeing the screen. "Langdon's moving to the window ledge!"

But Fache was already in motion. Yanking his Manurhin MR-93 revolver from his shoulder holster, the captain dashed out of the office.

Collet watched the screen in bewilderment as the blinking dot arrived at the window ledge and then did something utterly unexpected. The dot moved *outside* the perimeter of the building.

What's going on? he wondered. *Is Langdon out on a ledge or—*

"*Jesu!*" Collet jumped to his feet as the dot shot farther outside the wall. The signal seemed to shudder for a moment, and then the blinking dot came to an abrupt stop about ten yards outside the perimeter of the building.

Fumbling with the controls, Collet called up a Paris street map and recalibrated the GPS. Zooming in, he could now see the exact location of the signal.

It was no longer moving.

It lay at a dead stop in the middle of Place du Carrousel.

Langdon had jumped.

FACHE SPRINTED down the Grand Gallery as Collet's radio blared over the distant sound of the alarm.

"He jumped!" Collet was yelling. "I'm showing the signal out on Place du Carrousel! Outside the bathroom window! And it's not moving at all! Jesus, I think Langdon has just committed suicide!"

Fache heard the words, but they made no sense. He kept running. The hallway seemed never-ending. As he sprinted past Saunière's body, he set his sights on the partitions at the far end of the Denon Wing. The alarm was getting louder now.

"Wait!" Collet's voice blared again over the radio. "He's moving! My God, he's alive. Langdon's moving!"

Fache kept running, cursing the length of the hallway with every step.

"Langdon's moving faster!" Collet was still yelling on the radio. "He's running down Carrousel. Wait . . . he's picking up speed. He's moving too fast!"

Arriving at the partitions, Fache snaked his way through them, saw the rest room door, and ran for it.

The walkie-talkie was barely audible now over the alarm. "He must be in a car! I think he's in a car! I can't—"

Collet's words were swallowed by the alarm as Fache finally burst into the men's room with his gun drawn. Wincing against the piercing shrill, he scanned the area.

The stalls were empty. The bathroom deserted. Fache's eyes moved immediately to the shattered window at the far end of the room. He ran to the opening and looked over the edge. Langdon was nowhere to be seen. Fache could not imagine anyone risking a stunt like this. Certainly if he had dropped that far, he would be badly injured.

The alarm cut off finally, and Collet's voice became audible again over the walkie-talkie.

PLACE DU CARROUSEL, PASSING THROUGH THE LOUVRE MUSEUM

". . . moving south . . . faster . . . crossing the Seine on Pont du Carrousel!"

Fache turned to his left. The only vehicle on Pont du Carrousel was an enormous twin-bed Trailor delivery truck moving southward away from the Louvre. The truck's open-air bed was covered with a vinyl tarp, roughly resembling a giant hammock. Fache felt a shiver of apprehension. That truck, only moments ago, had probably been stopped at a red light directly beneath the rest room window.

An insane risk, Fache told himself. Langdon had no way of knowing what the truck was carrying beneath that tarp. What if the truck were carrying steel? Or cement? Or even garbage? A forty-foot leap? It was madness.

"The dot is turning!" Collet called. "He's turning right on Pont des Saints-Pères!"

Sure enough, the Trailor truck that had crossed the bridge was slowing down and making a right turn onto Pont des Saints-Pères. *So be it,* Fache thought. Amazed, he watched the truck disappear around the corner. Collet was already radioing the agents outside, pulling them off the Louvre perimeter and sending them to their patrol cars in pursuit, all the while broadcasting the truck's changing location like some kind of bizarre play-by-play.

It's over, Fache knew. His men would have the truck surrounded within minutes. Langdon was not going anywhere.

Stowing his weapon, Fache exited the rest room and radioed Collet. "Bring my car around. I want to be there when we make the arrest."

As Fache jogged back down the length of the Grand Gallery, he wondered if Langdon had even survived the fall.

Not that it mattered.

Langdon ran. Guilty as charged.

ONLY FIFTEEN YARDS from the rest room, Langdon and Sophie stood in the darkness of the Grand Gallery, their backs pressed to one of the large partitions that hid the bathrooms from the gallery. They had barely managed to hide themselves before Fache had darted past them, gun drawn, and disappeared into the bathroom.

The last sixty seconds had been a blur.

Langdon had been standing inside the men's room refusing to run from a crime he didn't commit, when Sophie began eyeing the plate-glass window and examining the alarm mesh running through it. Then she peered downward into the street, as if measuring the drop.

"With a little aim, you can get out of here," she said.

Aim? Uneasy, he peered out the rest room window.

Up the street, an enormous twin-bed eighteen-wheeler was headed for the stoplight beneath the window. Stretched across the truck's massive cargo bay was a blue vinyl tarp, loosely covering the truck's load. Langdon hoped Sophie was not thinking what she seemed to be thinking.

"Sophie, there's no way I'm jump—"

"Take out the tracking dot."

Bewildered, Langdon fumbled in his pocket until he found the tiny metallic disk. Sophie took it from him and strode immediately to the sink. She grabbed a thick bar of soap, placed the tracking dot on top of it, and used her thumb to push the disk down hard into the bar. As the disk sank into the soft surface, she pinched the hole closed, firmly embedding the device in the bar.

Handing the bar to Langdon, Sophie retrieved a heavy, cylindrical trash can from under the sinks. Before Langdon could protest, Sophie ran at the window, holding the can before her like a battering ram. Driving the bottom of the trash can into the center of the window, she shattered the glass.

Alarms erupted overhead at earsplitting decibel levels.

"Give me the soap!" Sophie yelled, barely audible over the alarm.

Langdon thrust the bar into her hand.

Palming the soap, she peered out the shattered window at the eighteen-wheeler idling below. The target was plenty big—an expansive, stationary tarp—and it was less than ten feet from the side of the building. As the traffic lights prepared to change, Sophie took a deep breath and lobbed the bar of soap out into the night.

The soap plummeted downward toward the truck, landing on the edge of the tarp, and sliding downward into the cargo bay just as the traffic light turned green.

"Congratulations," Sophie said, dragging him toward the door. "You just escaped from the Louvre."

Fleeing the men's room, they moved into the shadows just as Fache rushed past.

NOW, WITH THE FIRE alarm silenced, Langdon could hear the sounds of DCPJ sirens tearing away from the Louvre. *A police exodus.* Fache had hurried off as well, leaving the Grand Gallery deserted.

"There's an emergency stairwell about fifty meters back into the Grand Gallery," Sophie said. "Now that the guards are leaving the perimeter, we can get out of here."

Langdon decided not to say another word all evening. Sophie Neveu was clearly a hell of a lot smarter than he was.

Chapter 19

T HE C HURCH OF S AINT - S ULPICE , it is said, has the most eccentric history of any building in Paris. Built over the ruins of an ancient temple to the Egyptian goddess Isis, the church possesses an architectural footprint matching that of Notre Dame to within inches. The sanctuary has played host to the baptisms of the Marquis de Sade and Baudelaire, as well as the marriage of Victor Hugo. The attached seminary has a well-documented history of unorthodoxy and was once the clandestine meeting hall for numerous secret societies.

Tonight, the cavernous nave of Saint-Sulpice was as silent as a tomb, the only hint of life the faint smell of incense from mass earlier that evening. Silas sensed an uneasiness in Sister Sandrine's demeanor as she led him into the sanctuary. He was not surprised by this. Silas was accustomed to people being uncomfortable with his appearance.

"You're an American," she said.

"French by birth," Silas responded. "I had my calling in Spain, and I now study in the United States."

Sister Sandrine nodded. She was a small woman with quiet eyes. "And you have *never* seen Saint-Sulpice?"

"I realize this is almost a sin in itself."

[far left] MARQUIS DE SADE

CHARLES BAUDELAIRE

"She is more beautiful by day."

"I am certain. Nonetheless, I am grateful that you would provide me this opportunity tonight."

"The abbé requested it. You obviously have powerful friends."

You have no idea, Silas thought.

As he followed Sister Sandrine down the main aisle, Silas was surprised by the austerity of the sanctuary. Unlike Notre Dame with its colorful frescoes, gilded altar-work, and warm wood, Saint-Sulpice was stark and cold, conveying an almost barren quality reminiscent of the ascetic cathedrals of Spain. The lack of decor made the interior look even more expansive, and as Silas gazed up into the soaring ribbed vault of the ceiling, he imagined he was standing beneath the hull of an enormous overturned ship.

CEILING, SAINT-SULPICE

A fitting image, he thought. The brotherhood's ship was about to be capsized forever. Feeling eager to get to work, Silas wished Sister Sandrine would leave him. She was a small woman whom Silas could incapacitate easily, but he had vowed not to use force unless absolutely necessary. *She is a woman of the cloth, and it is not her fault the brotherhood chose her church as a hiding place for their keystone. She should not be punished for the sins of others.*

"I am embarrassed, Sister, that you were awoken on my behalf."

"Not at all. You are in Paris a short time. You should not miss Saint-Sulpice. Are your interests in the church more architectural or historical?"

"Actually, Sister, my interests are spiritual."

She gave a pleasant laugh. "That goes without saying. I simply wondered where to begin your tour."

Silas felt his eyes focus on the altar. "A tour is unnecessary. You have been more than kind. I can show myself around."

ALTAR, SAINT-SULPICE

"It is no trouble," she said. "After all, I am awake."

Silas stopped walking. They had reached the front pew now, and the altar was only fifteen yards away. He turned his massive body fully toward the small woman, and he could sense her recoil as she gazed up into his red eyes. "If it does not seem too rude, Sister, I am not accustomed to simply walking into a house of God and taking a tour. Would you mind if I took some time alone to pray before I look around?"

Sister Sandrine hesitated. "Oh, of course. I shall wait in the rear of the church for you."

Silas put a soft but heavy hand on her shoulder and peered down. "Sister, I feel guilty already for having awoken you. To ask you to stay awake is too much. Please, you should return to bed. I can enjoy your sanctuary and then let myself out."

She looked uneasy. "Are you sure you won't feel abandoned?"

"Not at all. Prayer is a solitary joy."

"As you wish."

Silas took his hand from her shoulder. "Sleep well, Sister. May the peace of the Lord be with you."

"And also with you." Sister Sandrine headed for the stairs. "Please be sure the door closes tightly on your way out."

"I will be sure of it." Silas watched her climb out of sight. Then he turned and knelt in the front pew, feeling the *cilice* cut into his leg.

Dear God, I offer up to you this work I do today. . . .

CROUCHING IN THE SHADOWS of the choir balcony high above the altar, Sister Sandrine peered silently through the balustrade at the cloaked monk kneeling alone. The sudden dread in her soul made it hard to stay still. For a fleeting instant, she wondered if this mysterious visitor could be the enemy they had warned her about, and if tonight she would have to carry out the orders she had been holding all these years. She decided to stay there in the darkness and watch his every move.

EMERGING FROM THE SHADOWS, Langdon and Sophie moved stealthily up the deserted Grand Gallery corridor toward the emergency exit stairwell.

As he moved, Langdon felt like he was trying to assemble a jigsaw puzzle in the dark. The newest aspect of this mystery was a deeply troubling one: *The captain of the Judicial Police is trying to frame me for murder.*

"Do you think," he whispered, "that maybe *Fache* wrote that message on the floor?"

Sophie didn't even turn. "Impossible."

Langdon wasn't so sure. "He seems pretty intent on making me look guilty. Maybe he thought writing my name on the floor would help his case?"

"The Fibonacci sequence? The P.S.? All the Da Vinci and goddess symbolism? That *had* to be my grandfather."

Langdon knew she was right. The symbolism of the clues meshed too perfectly— the pentacle, the *Vitruvian Man,* Da Vinci, the goddess, and even the Fibonacci sequence. *A coherent symbolic set,* as iconographers would call it. All inextricably tied.

"And his phone call to me this afternoon," Sophie added. "He said he had to tell me something. I'm certain his message at the Louvre was his final effort to tell me something important, something he thought you could help me understand."

Langdon frowned. *O, Draconian devil! Oh, lame saint!* He wished he could comprehend the message, both for Sophie's well-being and for his own. Things had definitely gotten worse since he first laid eyes on the cryptic words. His fake leap out the bathroom window was not going to help Langdon's popularity with Fache one bit. Somehow he doubted the captain of the French police would see the humor in chasing down and arresting a bar of soap.

"The doorway isn't much farther," Sophie said.

"Do you think there's a possibility that the *numbers* in your grandfather's message hold the key to understanding the other lines?" Langdon had once worked on a series of Baconian manuscripts that contained epigraphical ciphers in which certain lines of code were clues as to how to decipher the other lines.

"I've been thinking about the numbers all night. Sums, quotients, products. I don't see anything. Mathematically, they're arranged at random. Cryptographic gibberish."

"And yet they're all part of the Fibonacci sequence. That can't be coincidence."

"It's not. Using Fibonacci numbers was my grandfather's way of waving another flag at me—like writing the message in English, or arranging himself like my favorite piece of art, or drawing a pentacle on himself. All of it was to catch my attention."

"The pentacle has meaning to you?"

"Yes. I didn't get a chance to tell you, but the pentacle was a special symbol between my grandfather and me when I was growing up. We used to play Tarot cards for fun, and my indicator card *always* turned out to be from the suit of pentacles. I'm sure he stacked the deck, but pentacles got to be our little joke."

Langdon felt a chill. *They played Tarot?* The medieval Italian card game was so replete with hidden heretical symbolism that Langdon had dedicated an entire chapter in his new manuscript to the Tarot. The game's twenty-two cards bore names like *The Female Pope, The Empress,* and *The Star.* Originally, Tarot had been devised as a secret means to pass along ideologies banned by the Church. Now, Tarot's mystical qualities were passed on by modern fortune-tellers.

THE FEMALE POPE

THE STAR   THE FOOL

The Tarot indicator suit for feminine divinity is pentacles, Langdon thought, realizing that if Saunière had been stacking his granddaughter's deck for fun, pentacles was an apropos inside joke.

They arrived at the emergency stairwell, and Sophie carefully pulled open the door. No alarm sounded. Only the doors to the outside were wired. Sophie led Langdon down a tight set of switchback stairs toward the ground level, picking up speed as they went.

"Your grandfather," Langdon said, hurrying behind her, "when he told you about the pentacle, did he mention goddess worship or any resentment of the Catholic Church?"

Sophie shook her head. "I was more interested in the mathematics of it—the Divine Proportion, PHI, Fibonacci sequences, that sort of thing."

Langdon was surprised. "Your grandfather taught you about the number PHI?"

"Of course. The Divine Proportion." Her expression turned sheepish. "In fact, he used to joke that I was half divine . . . you know, because of the letters in my name."

Langdon considered it a moment and then groaned.

s-o-PHI-e.

Still descending, Langdon refocused on PHI. He was starting to realize that Saunière's clues were even more consistent than he had first imagined.

Da Vinci . . . Fibonacci numbers . . . the pentacle.

Incredibly, all of these things were connected by a single concept so fundamental to art history that Langdon often spent several class periods on the topic.

PHI.

He felt himself suddenly reeling back to Harvard, standing in front of his "Symbolism in Art" class, writing his favorite number on the chalkboard.

1.618

Langdon turned to face his sea of eager students. "Who can tell me what this number is?"

A long-legged math major in back raised his hand. "That's the number PHI." He pronounced it *fee*.

"Nice job, Stettner," Langdon said. "Everyone, meet PHI."

"Not to be confused with PI," Stettner added, grinning. "As we mathematicians like to say: PHI is one *H* of a lot cooler than PI!"

Langdon laughed, but nobody else seemed to get the joke.

Stettner slumped.

"This number PHI," Langdon continued, "one-point-six-one-eight, is a very important number in art. Who can tell me why?"

Stettner tried to redeem himself. "Because it's so pretty?"

Everyone laughed.

"Actually," Langdon said, "Stettner's right again. PHI is generally considered the most beautiful number in the universe."

The laughter abruptly stopped, and Stettner gloated.

As Langdon loaded his slide projector, he explained that the number PHI was derived from the Fibonacci sequence—a progression famous not only because the sum of adjacent terms equaled the next term, but because the *quotients* of adjacent terms possessed the astonishing property of approaching the number 1.618—PHI!

Despite PHI's seemingly mystical mathematical origins, Langdon explained, the truly mind-boggling aspect of PHI was its role as a fundamental building block in nature. Plants, animals, and even human beings all possessed dimensional properties that adhered with eerie exactitude to the ratio of PHI to 1.

"PHI's ubiquity in nature," Langdon said, killing the lights, "clearly exceeds coincidence, and so the ancients assumed the number PHI must have been preordained by the Creator of the universe. Early scientists heralded one-point-six-one-eight as the *Divine Proportion*."

"Hold on," said a young woman in the front row. "I'm a bio major and I've never seen this Divine Proportion in nature."

"No?" Langdon grinned. "Ever study the relationship between females and males in a honeybee community?"

"Sure. The female bees always outnumber the male bees."

"Correct. And did you know that if you divide the number of female bees by the number of male bees in any beehive in the world, you always get the same number?"

"You do?"

"Yup. PHI."

The girl gaped. "NO WAY!"

"Way!" Langdon fired back, smiling as he projected a slide of a spiral seashell. "Recognize this?"

"It's a nautilus," the bio major said. "A cephalopod mollusk that pumps gas into its chambered shell to adjust its buoyancy."

NAUTILUS

"Correct. And can you guess what the ratio is of each spiral's diameter to the next?"

The girl looked uncertain as she eyed the concentric arcs of the nautilus spiral.

Langdon nodded. "PHI. The Divine Proportion. One-point-six-one-eight to one."

The girl looked amazed.

Langdon advanced to the next slide—a close-up of a sunflower's seed head. "Sunflower seeds grow in opposing spirals. Can you guess the ratio of each rotation's diameter to the next?"

"PHI?" everyone said.

"Bingo." Langdon began racing through slides now—spiraled pinecone petals, leaf arrangement on plant stalks, insect segmentation—all displaying astonishing obedience to the Divine Proportion.

"This is amazing!" someone cried out.

"Yeah," someone else said, "but what does it have to do with *art?*"

"Aha!" Langdon said. "Glad you asked." He pulled up another slide—a pale yellow parchment displaying Leonardo da Vinci's famous male nude—*The Vitruvian Man*—named for Marcus Vitruvius, the brilliant Roman architect who praised the Divine Proportion in his text *De Architectura*.

"Nobody understood better than Da Vinci the divine structure of the human body. Da Vinci actually *exhumed* corpses to measure the exact proportions of human bone structure. He was the first to show that the human body is literally made of building blocks whose proportional ratios *always* equal PHI."

Everyone in class gave him a dubious look.

"Don't believe me?" Langdon challenged. "Next time you're in the shower, take a tape measure."

A couple of football players snickered.

"Not just you insecure jocks," Langdon prompted. "*All* of you. Guys and girls. Try it. Measure the distance from the tip of your head to the floor. Then divide that by the distance from your belly button to the floor. Guess what number you get."

"Not PHI!" one of the jocks blurted out in disbelief.

"Yes, PHI," Langdon replied. "One-point-six-one-eight. Want another example? Measure the distance from your shoulder to your fingertips, and then divide it by the distance from your elbow to your fingertips. PHI again. Another? Hip to floor divided by knee to floor. PHI again. Finger joints. Toes. Spinal divisions. PHI. PHI. PHI. My friends, each of you is a walking tribute to the Divine Proportion."

Even in the darkness, Langdon could see they were all astounded. He felt a familiar warmth inside. This is why he taught. "My friends, as you can see, the chaos of the world has an underlying order. When the ancients discovered PHI, they were certain they had stumbled across God's building block for the world, and they worshipped Nature because of that. And one can understand why. God's hand is evident in Nature, and even to this day there exist pagan, Mother Earth–revering religions. Many of us celebrate nature the way the pagans did, and don't even know it. May Day is a perfect example, the celebration of spring . . . the earth coming back to life to produce her bounty. The mysterious magic inherent in the Divine Proportion was written at the beginning of time. Man is simply playing by Nature's rules, and because *art* is man's attempt to imitate the beauty of the Creator's hand, you can imagine we might be seeing a lot of instances of the Divine Proportion in art this semester."

Over the next half hour, Langdon showed them slides of artwork by Michelangelo, Albrecht Dürer, Da Vinci, and many others, demonstrating each artist's intentional and rigorous adherence to the Divine Proportion in the layout of his compositions. Langdon unveiled PHI in the architectural dimensions of the

THE PARTHENON, GREECE

Greek Parthenon, the pyramids of Egypt, and even the United Nations Building in New York. PHI appeared in the organizational structures of Mozart's sonatas, Beethoven's Fifth Symphony, as well as the works of Bartók, Debussy, and Schubert. The number PHI, Langdon told them, was even used by Stradivarius to calculate the exact placement of the f-holes in the construction of his famous violins.

"In closing," Langdon said, walking to the chalkboard, "we return to *symbols*." He drew five intersecting lines that formed a five-pointed star. "This symbol is one of the most powerful images you will see this term. Formally known as a pentagram—or *pentacle,*

EGYPTIAN PYRAMIDS

as the ancients called it—this symbol is considered both divine and magical by many cultures. Can anyone tell me why that might be?"

Stettner, the math major, raised his hand. "Because if you draw a pentagram, the lines automatically divide themselves into segments according to the Divine Proportion."

Langdon gave the kid a proud nod. "Nice job. Yes, the ratios of line segments in a pentacle *all* equal PHI, making this symbol the *ultimate* expression of the Divine Proportion. For this reason, the five-pointed star has always been the symbol for beauty and perfection associated with the goddess and the sacred feminine."

The girls in class beamed.

"One note, folks. We've only touched on Da Vinci today, but we'll be seeing a lot more of him this semester. Leonardo was a well-documented devotee of the ancient ways of the goddess. Tomorrow, I'll show you his fresco *The Last Supper,* which is one of the most astonishing tributes to the sacred feminine you will ever see."

"You're kidding, right?" somebody said. "I thought *The Last Supper* was about Jesus!"

Langdon winked. "There are symbols hidden in places you would never imagine."

"COME ON," Sophie whispered. "What's wrong? We're almost there. Hurry!"

Langdon glanced up, feeling himself return from faraway thoughts. He realized he was standing at a dead stop on the stairs, paralyzed by sudden revelation.

O, Draconian devil! Oh, lame saint!

Sophie was looking back at him.

It can't be that simple, Langdon thought.

But he knew of course that it was.

There in the bowels of the Louvre . . . with images of PHI and Da Vinci swirling through his mind, Robert Langdon suddenly and unexpectedly deciphered Saunière's code.

"O, Draconian devil!" he said. "Oh, lame saint! It's the simplest kind of code!"

SOPHIE WAS STOPPED on the stairs below him, staring up in confusion. *A code?* She had been pondering the words all night and had not seen a code. Especially a simple one.

"You said it yourself." Langdon's voice reverberated with excitement. "Fibonacci numbers only have meaning in their proper order. Otherwise they're mathematical gibberish."

Sophie had no idea what he was talking about. *The Fibonacci numbers?* She was certain they had been intended as nothing more than a means to get the Cryptography Department involved tonight. *They have another purpose?* She plunged her hand into her pocket and pulled out the printout, studying her grandfather's message again.

13-3-2-21-1-1-8-5
O, Draconian devil!
Oh, lame saint!

What about the numbers?

"The scrambled Fibonacci sequence is a clue," Langdon said, taking the print-out. "The numbers are a hint as to how to decipher the rest of the message. He wrote the sequence out of order to tell us to apply the same concept to the text. O, Draconian devil? Oh, lame saint? Those lines mean nothing. They are simply *letters* written out of order."

Sophie needed only an instant to process Langdon's implication, and it seemed laughably simple. "You think this message is . . . *une anagramme?*" She stared at him. "Like a word jumble from a newspaper?"

Langdon could see the skepticism on Sophie's face and certainly understood. Few people realized that anagrams, despite being a trite modern amusement, had a rich history of sacred symbolism.

The mystical teachings of the Kabbala drew heavily on anagrams—rearranging the letters of Hebrew words to derive new meanings. French kings throughout the Renaissance were so convinced that anagrams held magic power that they appointed royal anagrammatists to help them make better decisions by analyzing words in important documents. The Romans actually referred to the study of anagrams as *ars magna*—"the great art."

Langdon looked up at Sophie, locking eyes with her now. "Your grandfather's meaning was right in front of us all along, and he left us more than enough clues to see it."

Without another word, Langdon pulled a pen from his jacket pocket and rearranged the letters in each line.

O, Draconian devil!
Oh, lame saint!

was a perfect anagram of . . .

Leonardo da Vinci!
The Mona Lisa!

THE MONA LISA.

For an instant, standing in the exit stairwell, Sophie forgot all about trying to leave the Louvre.

Her shock over the anagram was matched only by her embarrassment at not having deciphered the message herself. Sophie's expertise in complex cryptanalysis had caused her to overlook simplistic word games, and yet she knew she should have seen it. After all, she was no stranger to anagrams—especially in English.

When she was young, often her grandfather would use anagram games to hone her English spelling. Once he had written the English word "planets" and told Sophie that an astonishing ninety-two *other* English words of varying lengths could be formed using those same letters. Sophie had spent three days with an English dictionary until she found them all.

"I can't imagine," Langdon said, staring at the printout, "how your grandfather created such an intricate anagram in the minutes before he died."

Sophie knew the explanation, and the realization made her feel even worse. *I should have seen this!* She now recalled that her grandfather—a wordplay aficionado and art lover—had entertained himself as a young man by creating anagrams of famous works of art. In fact, one of his anagrams had gotten him in trouble once when Sophie was a little girl. While being interviewed by an American art magazine, Saunière had expressed his distaste for the modernist Cubist movement by noting that Picasso's masterpiece *Les Demoiselles d'Avignon* was a perfect anagram of *vile meaningless doodles.* Picasso fans were not amused.

"My grandfather probably created this *Mona Lisa* anagram long ago," Sophie said, glancing up at Langdon. *And tonight he was forced to use it as a makeshift code.* Her grandfather's voice had called out from beyond with chilling precision.

LES DEMOISELLES D'AVIGNON BY PABLO PICASSO

Leonardo da Vinci!

The Mona Lisa!

Why his final words to her referenced the famous painting, Sophie had no idea, but she could think of only one possibility. A disturbing one.

Those were not his final words. . . .

Was she supposed to visit the *Mona Lisa*? Had her grandfather left her a message there? The idea seemed perfectly plausible. After all, the famous painting hung in the Salle des États—a private viewing chamber accessible only from the Grand Gallery.

In fact, Sophie now realized, the doors that opened into the chamber were situated only twenty meters from where her grandfather had been found dead.

He easily could have visited the Mona Lisa before he died.

Sophie gazed back up the emergency stairwell and felt torn. She knew she should usher Langdon from the museum immediately, and yet instinct urged her to the contrary. As Sophie recalled her first childhood visit to the Denon Wing, she realized that if her grandfather had a secret to tell her, few places on earth made a more apt rendezvous than Da Vinci's *Mona Lisa.*

"SHE'S JUST A little bit farther," her grandfather had whispered, clutching Sophie's tiny hand as he led her through the deserted museum after hours.

Sophie was six years old. She felt small and insignificant as she gazed up at the enormous ceilings and down at the dizzying floor. The empty museum frightened her, although she was not about to let her grandfather know that. She set her jaw firmly and let go of his hand.

"Up ahead is the Salle des États," her grandfather said as they approached the Louvre's most famous room. Despite her grandfather's obvious excitement, Sophie wanted to go home. She had seen pictures of the *Mona Lisa* in books and didn't like it at all. She couldn't understand why everyone made such a fuss.

"*C'est ennuyeux,*" Sophie grumbled.

"Boring," he corrected. "French at school. English at home."

"*Le Louvre, c'est pas chez moi!*" she challenged.

He gave her a tired laugh. "Right you are. Then let's speak English just for fun."

Sophie pouted and kept walking. As they entered the Salle des États, her eyes scanned the narrow room and settled on the obvious spot of honor—the center of the right-hand wall, where a lone portrait hung behind a protective Plexiglas wall. Her grandfather paused in the doorway and motioned toward the painting.

"Go ahead, Sophie. Not many people get a chance to visit her alone."

Swallowing her apprehension, Sophie moved slowly across the room. After everything she'd heard about the *Mona Lisa,* she felt as if she were approaching royalty. Arriving in front of the protective Plexiglas, Sophie held her breath and looked up, taking it in all at once.

Sophie was not sure what she had expected to feel, but it most certainly was not this. No jolt of amazement. No instant of wonder. The famous face looked as it did in books. She stood in silence for what felt like forever, waiting for something to happen.

"So what do you think?" her grandfather whispered, arriving behind her. "Beautiful, yes?"

"She's too little."

Saunière smiled. "You're little and you're beautiful."

I am not beautiful, she thought. Sophie hated her red hair and freckles, and she was bigger than all the boys in her class. She looked back at the *Mona Lisa* and shook her head. "She's even worse than in the books. Her face is . . . *brumeux.*"

"Foggy," her grandfather tutored.

"Foggy," Sophie repeated, knowing the conversation would not continue until she repeated her new vocabulary word.

"That's called the *sfumato* style of painting," he told her, "and it's very hard to do. Leonardo da Vinci was better at it than anyone."

Sophie still didn't like the painting. "She looks like she knows something . . . like when kids at school have a secret."

Her grandfather laughed. "That's part of why she is so famous. People like to guess why she is smiling."

"Do *you* know why she's smiling?"

"Maybe." Her grandfather winked. "Someday I'll tell you all about it."

Sophie stamped her foot. "I told you I don't like secrets!"

"Princess," he smiled. "Life is filled with secrets. You can't learn them all at once."

"I'm going back up," Sophie declared, her voice hollow in the stairwell.

"To the *Mona Lisa*?" Langdon recoiled. *"Now?"*

Sophie considered the risk. "I'm not a murder suspect. I'll take my chances. I need to understand what my grandfather was trying to tell me."

"What about the embassy?"

Sophie felt guilty turning Langdon into a fugitive only to abandon him, but she saw no other option. She pointed down the stairs to a metal door. "Go through that door, and follow the illuminated exit signs. My grandfather used to bring me down here. The signs will lead you to a security turnstile. It's monodirectional and opens out." She handed Langdon her car keys. "Mine is the red SmartCar in the employee lot. Directly outside this bulkhead. Do you know how to get to the embassy?"

Langdon nodded, eyeing the keys in his hand.

"Listen," Sophie said, her voice softening. "I think my grandfather may have left me a message at the *Mona Lisa*—some kind of clue as to who killed him. Or why I'm in danger." *Or what happened to my family.* "I have to go see."

"But if he wanted to tell you why you were in danger, why wouldn't he simply write it on the floor where he died? Why this complicated word game?"

"Whatever my grandfather was trying to tell me, I don't think he wanted anyone else to hear it. Not even the police." Clearly, her grandfather had done everything in his power to send a confidential transmission directly to *her*. He had written it in code, included her secret initials, and told her to find Robert Langdon—a wise command, considering the American symbologist had deciphered his code. "As strange as it may sound," Sophie said, "I think he wants me to get to the *Mona Lisa* before anyone else does."

"I'll come."

"No! We don't know how long the Grand Gallery will stay empty. *You* have to go."

Langdon seemed hesitant, as if his own academic curiosity were threatening to override sound judgment and drag him back into Fache's hands.

"Go. Now." Sophie gave him a grateful smile. "I'll see you at the embassy, Mr. Langdon."

Langdon looked displeased. "I'll meet you there on *one* condition," he replied, his voice stern.

She paused, startled. "What's that?"

"That you stop calling me *Mr.* Langdon."

Sophie detected the faint hint of a lopsided grin growing across Langdon's face, and she felt herself smile back. "Good luck, Robert."

WHEN LANGDON reached the landing at the bottom of the stairs, the unmistakable smell of linseed oil and plaster dust assaulted his nostrils. Ahead, an illuminated SORTIE/EXIT displayed an arrow pointing down a long corridor.

Langdon stepped into the hallway.

To the right gaped a murky restoration studio out of which peered an army of statues in various states of repair. To the left, Langdon saw a suite of studios that resembled Harvard art classrooms—rows of easels, paintings, palettes, framing tools—an art assembly line.

As he moved down the hallway, Langdon wondered if at any moment he might awake with a start in his bed in Cambridge. The entire evening had felt like a bizarre dream. *I'm about to dash out of the Louvre . . . a fugitive.*

Saunière's clever anagrammatic message was still on his mind, and Langdon wondered what Sophie would find at the *Mona Lisa* . . . if anything. She had seemed certain her grandfather meant for her to visit the famous painting one more time. As plausible an interpretation as this seemed, Langdon felt haunted now by a troubling paradox.

P.S. Find Robert Langdon.

Saunière had written Langdon's name on the floor, commanding Sophie to find him. But why? Merely so Langdon could help her break an anagram?

It seemed quite unlikely.

After all, Saunière had no reason to think Langdon was especially skilled at anagrams. *We've never even met.* More important, Sophie had stated flat out that *she* should have broken the anagram on her own. It had been Sophie who spotted the Fibonacci sequence, and, no doubt, Sophie who, if given a little more time, would have deciphered the message with no help from Langdon.

Sophie was supposed to break that anagram on her own. Langdon was suddenly feeling more certain about this, and yet the conclusion left an obvious gaping lapse in the logic of Saunière's actions.

Why me? Langdon wondered, heading down the hall. *Why was Saunière's dying wish that his estranged granddaughter find me? What is it that Saunière thinks I know?*

With an unexpected jolt, Langdon stopped short. Eyes wide, he dug in his pocket and yanked out the computer printout. He stared at the last line of Saunière's message.

P.S. Find Robert Langdon.

He fixated on two letters.

P.S.

In that instant, Langdon felt Saunière's puzzling mix of symbolism fall into stark focus. Like a peal of thunder, a career's worth of symbology and history came crashing down around him. Everything Jacques Saunière had done tonight suddenly made perfect sense.

Langdon's thoughts raced as he tried to assemble the implications of what this all meant. Wheeling, he stared back in the direction from which he had come.

Is there time?

He knew it didn't matter.

Without hesitation, Langdon broke into a sprint back toward the stairs.

KNEELING IN the first pew, Silas pretended to pray as he scanned the layout of the sanctuary. Saint-Sulpice, like most churches, had been built in the shape of a giant Roman cross. Its long central section—the nave—led directly to the main altar, where it was transversely intersected by a shorter section, known as the transept. The intersection of nave and transept occurred directly beneath the main cupola and was considered the heart of the church . . . her most sacred and mystical point.

Not tonight, Silas thought. *Saint-Sulpice hides her secrets elsewhere.*

Turning his head to the right, he gazed into the south transept, toward the open area of floor beyond the end of the pews, to the object his victims had described.

There it is.

Embedded in the gray granite floor, a thin polished strip of brass glistened in the stone . . . a golden line slanting across the church's floor. The line bore graduated markings, like a ruler. It was a gnomon, Silas had been told, a pagan astronomical device like a sundial. Tourists, scientists, historians, and pagans from around the world came to Saint-Sulpice to gaze upon this famous line.

The Rose Line.

Slowly, Silas let his eyes trace the path of the brass strip as it made its way across the floor from his right to left, slanting in front of him at an awkward angle, entirely at odds with the symmetry of the church. Slicing across the main altar itself, the line looked to Silas like a slash wound across a beautiful face. The strip cleaved the communion rail in two and then crossed the entire width of the church, finally reaching the corner of the north transept, where it arrived at the base of a most unexpected structure.

A colossal Egyptian obelisk.

Here, the glistening Rose Line took a ninety-degree *vertical* turn and continued directly up the face of the obelisk itself, ascending thirty-three feet to the very tip of the pyramidical apex, where it finally ceased.

The Rose Line, Silas thought. *The brotherhood hid the keystone at the Rose Line.*

Earlier tonight, when Silas told the Teacher that the Priory keystone was hidden inside Saint-Sulpice, the Teacher had sounded doubtful. But when Silas added that the brothers had all given him a precise location, with relation to a brass line running through Saint-Sulpice, the Teacher had gasped with revelation. "You speak of the Rose Line!"

ROSE LINE, SAINT-SULPICE

The Teacher quickly told Silas of Saint-Sulpice's famed architectural oddity—a strip of brass that segmented the sanctuary on a perfect north-south axis. It was an ancient sundial of sorts, a vestige of the pagan temple that had once stood on this very spot. The sun's rays, shining through the oculus on the south wall, moved farther down the line every day, indicating the passage of time, from solstice to solstice.

The north-south stripe had been known as the Rose Line. For centuries, the symbol of the Rose had been associated with maps and guiding souls in the proper direction. The Compass Rose—drawn on almost every map—indicated North, East, South, and West. Originally known as the Wind Rose, it denoted the directions of the thirty-two winds, blowing from the directions of eight major winds, eight half-winds, and sixteen quarter-winds. When diagrammed inside a circle, these thirty-two points of the compass perfectly resembled a traditional thirty-two-petal rose bloom. To this day, the fundamental navigational tool was still known as a Compass Rose, its northernmost direction still marked by an arrowhead . . . or, more commonly, the symbol of the fleur-de-lis.

COMPASS ROSE

On a globe, a Rose Line—also called a meridian or longitude—was any imaginary line drawn from the North Pole to the South Pole. There were, of course, an infinite number of Rose Lines because every point on the globe could have a longitude drawn through it connecting north and south poles. The question for early navigators was *which* of these lines would be called *the* Rose Line—the zero longitude—the line from which all other longitudes on earth would be measured.

Today that line was in Greenwich, England.

But it had not always been.

Long before the establishment of Greenwich as the prime meridian, the zero longitude of the entire world had passed directly through Paris, and through the Church of Saint-Sulpice. The brass marker in Saint-Sulpice was a memorial to the world's first prime meridian, and although Greenwich had stripped Paris of the honor in 1888, the original Rose Line was still visible today.

"And so the legend is true," the Teacher had told Silas. "The Priory keystone has been said to lie 'beneath the Sign of the Rose.' "

Now, still on his knees in a pew, Silas glanced around the church and listened to make sure no one was there. For a moment, he thought he heard a rustling in the choir balcony. He turned and gazed up for several seconds. Nothing.

I am alone.

Standing now, he faced the altar and genuflected three times. Then he turned left and followed the brass line due north toward the obelisk.

AT THAT MOMENT, at Leonardo da Vinci International Airport in Rome, the jolt of tires hitting the runway startled Bishop Aringarosa from his slumber.

I drifted off, he thought, impressed he was relaxed enough to sleep.

"Benvenuto a Roma," the intercom announced.

Sitting up, Aringarosa straightened his black cassock and allowed himself a rare smile. This was one trip he had been happy to make. *I have been on the defensive for too long.* Tonight, however, the rules had changed. Only five months ago, Aringarosa had feared for the future of the Faith. Now, as if by the will of God, the solution had presented itself.

Divine intervention.

If all went as planned tonight in Paris, Aringarosa would soon be in possession of something that would make him the most powerful man in Christendom.

Chapter 23

SOPHIE ARRIVED BREATHLESS outside the large wooden doors of the Salle des États—the room that housed the *Mona Lisa.* Before entering, she gazed reluctantly farther down the hall, twenty yards or so, to the spot where her grandfather's body still lay under the spotlight.

The remorse that gripped her was powerful and sudden, a deep sadness laced with guilt. The man had reached out to her so many times over the past ten years, and yet Sophie had remained immovable—leaving his letters and packages unopened in a bottom drawer and denying his efforts to see her. *He lied to me! Kept appalling secrets! What was I supposed to do?* And so she had blocked him out. Completely.

Now her grandfather was dead, and he was talking to her from the grave.

The Mona Lisa.

She reached for the huge wooden doors, and pushed. The entryway yawned open. Sophie stood on the threshold a moment, scanning the large rectangular chamber beyond. It too was bathed in a soft red light. The Salle des États was one of this museum's rare *culs-de-sac*—a dead end and the only room off the middle of the Grand Gallery. This door, the chamber's sole point of entry, faced a dominating fifteen-foot Botticelli on the far wall. Beneath it, centered on the parquet floor, an immense octagonal viewing divan served as a welcome respite for thousands of visitors to rest their legs while they admired the Louvre's most valuable asset.

Even before Sophie entered, though, she knew she was missing something. *A black light.* She gazed down the hall at her grandfather under the lights in the distance, surrounded by electronic gear. If he had written anything in here, he almost certainly would have written it with the watermark stylus.

Taking a deep breath, Sophie hurried down to the well-lit crime scene. Unable to look at her grandfather, she focused solely on the PTS tools. Finding a small ultraviolet penlight, she slipped it in the pocket of her sweater and hurried back up the hallway toward the open doors of the Salle des États.

Sophie turned the corner and stepped over the threshold. Her entrance, however, was met by an unexpected sound of muffled footsteps racing toward her from inside the chamber. *There's someone in here!* A ghostly figure emerged suddenly from out of the reddish haze. Sophie jumped back.

"There you are!" Langdon's hoarse whisper cut the air as his silhouette slid to a stop in front of her.

Her relief was only momentary. "Robert, I told you to get out of here! If Fache—"

"Where were you?"

"I had to get the black light," she whispered, holding it up. "If my grandfather left me a message—"

"Sophie, listen." Langdon caught his breath as his blue eyes held her firmly. "The letters P.S. . . . do they mean anything else to you? Anything at all?"

Afraid their voices might echo down the hall, Sophie pulled him into the Salle des États and closed the enormous twin doors silently, sealing them inside. "I told you, the initials mean Princess Sophie."

"I know, but did you ever see them anywhere *else?* Did your grandfather ever use P.S. in any other way? As a monogram, or maybe on stationery or a personal item?"

The question startled her. *How would Robert know that?* Sophie had indeed seen the initials P.S. once before, in a kind of monogram. It was the day before her ninth birthday. She was secretly combing the house, searching for hidden birthday presents. Even then, she could not bear secrets kept from her. *What did Grand-père get for me this year?* She dug through cupboards and drawers. *Did he get me the doll I wanted? Where would he hide it?*

Finding nothing in the entire house, Sophie mustered the courage to sneak into her grandfather's bedroom. The room was off-limits to her, but her grandfather was downstairs asleep on the couch.

I'll just take a fast peek!

Tiptoeing across the creaky wood floor to his closet, Sophie peered on the shelves behind his clothing. Nothing. Next she looked under the bed. Still nothing. Moving to his bureau, she opened the drawers and one by one began pawing carefully through them. *There must be something for me here!* As she reached the bottom drawer, she still had not found any hint of a doll. Dejected, she opened the final drawer and pulled aside some black clothes she had never seen him wear. She was about to close the drawer when her eyes caught a glint of gold in the back of the drawer. It looked like a pocket watch chain, but she knew he didn't wear one. Her heart raced as she realized what it must be.

A necklace!

Sophie carefully pulled the chain from the drawer. To her surprise, on the end was a brilliant gold key. Heavy and shimmering. Spellbound, she held it up. It looked like no key she had ever seen. Most keys were flat with jagged teeth, but this one had a triangular column with little pockmarks all over it. Its large golden head was in the shape of a cross, but not a normal cross. This was an even-armed one, like a plus sign. Embossed in the middle of the cross was a strange symbol—two letters intertwined with some kind of flowery design.

"P.S.," she whispered, scowling as she read the letters. *Whatever could this be?*

"Sophie?" her grandfather spoke from the doorway.

Startled, she spun, dropping the key on the floor with a loud clang. She stared down at the key, afraid to look up at her grandfather's face. "I . . . was looking for my birthday present," she said, hanging her head, knowing she had betrayed his trust.

For what seemed like an eternity, her grandfather stood silently in the doorway. Finally, he let out a long troubled breath. "Pick up the key, Sophie."

Sophie retrieved the key.

Her grandfather walked in. "Sophie, you need to respect other people's privacy." Gently, he knelt down and took the key from her. "This key is very special. If you had lost it . . ."

Her grandfather's quiet voice made Sophie feel even worse. "I'm sorry, *Grand-père*. I really am." She paused. "I thought it was a necklace for my birthday."

He gazed at her for several seconds. "I'll say this once more, Sophie, because it's important. You need to learn to respect other people's privacy."

"Yes, *Grand-père.*"

"We'll talk about this some other time. Right now, the garden needs to be weeded."

Sophie hurried outside to do her chores.

The next morning, Sophie received no birthday present from her grandfather. She hadn't expected one, not after what she had done. But he didn't even wish her happy birthday all day. Sadly, she trudged up to bed that night. As she climbed in, though, she found a note card lying on her pillow. On the card was written a simple riddle. Even before she solved the riddle, she was smiling. *I know what this is!* Her grandfather had done this for her last Christmas morning.

A treasure hunt!

Eagerly, she pored over the riddle until she solved it. The solution pointed her to another part of the house, where she found another card and another riddle. She solved this one too, racing on to the next card. Running wildly, she darted back and forth across the house, from clue to clue, until at last she found a clue that directed her back to her own bedroom. Sophie dashed up the stairs, rushed into her room, and stopped in her tracks. There in the middle of the room sat a shining red bicycle with a ribbon tied to the handlebars. Sophie shrieked with delight.

"I know you asked for a doll," her grandfather said, smiling in the corner. "I thought you might like this even better."

The next day, her grandfather taught her to ride, running beside her down the walkway. When Sophie steered out over the thick lawn and lost her balance, they both went tumbling onto the grass, rolling and laughing.

"*Grand-père,*" Sophie said, hugging him. "I'm really sorry about the key."

"I know, sweetie. You're forgiven. I can't possibly stay mad at you. Grandfathers and granddaughters always forgive each other."

Sophie knew she shouldn't ask, but she couldn't help it. "What does it open? I never saw a key like that. It was very pretty."

Her grandfather was silent a long moment, and Sophie could see he was uncertain how to answer. *Grand-père never lies.* "It opens a box," he finally said. "Where I keep many secrets."

Sophie pouted. "I hate secrets!"

"I know, but these are important secrets. And someday, you'll learn to appreciate them as much as I do."

"I saw letters on the key, and a flower."

"Yes, that's my favorite flower. It's called a fleur-de-lis. We have them in the garden. The white ones. In English we call that kind of flower a lily."

"I know those! They're *my* favorite too!"

"Then I'll make a deal with you." Her grandfather's eyebrows raised the way they always did when he was about to give her a challenge. "If you can keep my key a secret, and *never* talk about it ever again, to me or anybody, then someday I will give it to you."

Sophie couldn't believe her ears. "You *will?*"

"I promise. When the time comes, the key will be yours. It has your name on it."

Sophie scowled. "No it doesn't. It said P.S. My name isn't P.S.!"

Her grandfather lowered his voice and looked around as if to make sure no one was listening. "Okay, Sophie, if you *must* know, P.S. is a code. It's your secret initials."

Her eyes went wide. "I have secret initials?"

"Of course. Granddaughters *always* have secret initials that only their grandfathers know."

"P.S.?"

He tickled her. *"Princesse Sophie."*

She giggled. "I'm not a princess!"

He winked. "You are to me."

From that day on, they never again spoke of the key. And she became his Princess Sophie.

INSIDE THE SALLE DES ÉTATS, Sophie stood in silence and endured the sharp pang of loss.

"The initials," Langdon whispered, eyeing her strangely. "Have you seen them?"

Sophie sensed her grandfather's voice whispering in the corridors of the museum. *Never speak of this key, Sophie. To me or to anyone.* She knew she had failed him in forgiveness, and she wondered if she could break his trust again. *P.S. Find Robert Langdon.* Her grandfather wanted Langdon to help. Sophie nodded. "Yes, I saw the initials P.S. once. When I was very young."

"Where?"

Sophie hesitated. "On something very important to him."

Langdon locked eyes with her. "Sophie, this is crucial. Can you tell me if the initials appeared with a symbol? A fleur-de-lis?"

Sophie felt herself staggering backward in amazement. "But . . . how could you possibly know that!"

Langdon exhaled and lowered his voice. "I'm fairly certain your grandfather was a member of a secret society. A very old covert brotherhood."

Sophie felt a knot tighten in her stomach. She was certain of it too. For ten years she had tried to forget the incident that had confirmed that horrifying fact for her. She had witnessed something unthinkable. *Unforgivable.*

"The fleur-de-lis," Langdon said, "combined with the initials P.S., that is the brotherhood's official device. Their coat of arms. Their logo."

"How do you know this?" Sophie was praying Langdon was not going to tell her that he *himself* was a member.

"I've written about this group," he said, his voice tremulous with excitement. "Researching the symbols of secret societies is a specialty of mine. They call themselves the *Prieuré de Sion*—the Priory of Sion. They're based here in France and attract powerful members from all over Europe. In fact, they are one of the oldest surviving secret societies on earth."

Sophie had never heard of them.

Langdon was talking in rapid bursts now. "The Priory's membership has included some of history's most cultured individuals: men like Botticelli, Sir Isaac Newton, Victor Hugo." He paused, his voice brimming now with academic zeal. "And, Leonardo da Vinci."

SIR ISAAC NEWTON

VICTOR HUGO

Sophie stared. "Da Vinci was in a secret society?"

"Da Vinci presided over the Priory between 1510 and 1519 as the brotherhood's Grand Master, which might help explain your grandfather's passion for Leonardo's work. The two men share a historical fraternal bond. And it all fits perfectly with their fascination for goddess iconology, paganism, feminine deities, and contempt for the Church. The Priory has a well-documented history of reverence for the sacred feminine."

"You're telling me this group is a pagan goddess worship cult?"

"More like *the* pagan goddess worship cult. But more important, they are known as the guardians of an ancient secret. One that made them immeasurably powerful."

Despite the total conviction in Langdon's eyes, Sophie's gut reaction was one of stark disbelief. *A secret pagan cult? Once headed by Leonardo da Vinci?* It all sounded utterly absurd. And yet, even as she dismissed it, she felt her mind reeling back ten years—to the night she had mistakenly surprised her grandfather and witnessed what she still could not accept. *Could that explain—?*

"The identities of living Priory members are kept extremely secret," Langdon said, "but the P.S. and fleur-de-lis that you saw as a child are proof. It could *only* have been related to the Priory."

Sophie realized now that Langdon knew far more about her grandfather than she had previously imagined. This American obviously had volumes to share with her, but this was not the place. "I can't afford to let them catch you, Robert. There's a lot we need to discuss. You need to go!"

LANGDON HEARD only the faint murmur of her voice. He wasn't going anywhere. He was lost in another place now. A place where ancient secrets rose to the surface. A place where forgotten histories emerged from the shadows.

Slowly, as if moving underwater, Langdon turned his head and gazed through the reddish haze toward the *Mona Lisa*.

The fleur-de-lis . . . the flower of Lisa . . . the Mona Lisa.

It was all intertwined, a silent symphony echoing the deepest secrets of the Priory of Sion and Leonardo da Vinci.

A FEW MILES AWAY, on the riverbank beyond Les Invalides, the bewildered driver of a twin-bed Trailor truck stood at gunpoint and watched as the captain of the Judicial Police let out a guttural roar of rage and heaved a bar of soap out into the turgid waters of the Seine.

Chapter 24

*S*ILAS GAZED upward at the Saint-Sulpice obelisk, taking in the length of the massive marble shaft. His sinews felt taut with exhilaration. He glanced around the church one more time to make sure he was alone. Then he knelt at the base of the structure, not out of reverence, but out of necessity.

The keystone is hidden beneath the Rose Line.

At the base of the Sulpice obelisk.

All the brothers had concurred.

On his knees now, Silas ran his hands across the stone floor. He saw no cracks or markings to indicate a movable tile, so he began rapping softly with his knuckles on the floor. Following the brass line closer to the obelisk, he knocked on each tile adjacent to the brass line. Finally, one of them echoed strangely.

There's a hollow area beneath the floor!

Silas smiled. His victims had spoken the truth.

Standing, he searched the sanctuary for something with which to break the floor tile.

BASE OF OBELISK, SAINT-SULPICE

THE DA VINCI CODE

HIGH ABOVE SILAS, in the balcony, Sister Sandrine stifled a gasp. Her darkest fears had just been confirmed. This visitor was not who he seemed. The mysterious Opus Dei monk had come to Saint-Sulpice for another purpose.

A secret purpose.

You are not the only one with secrets, she thought.

Sister Sandrine Bieil was more than the keeper of this church. She was a sentry. And tonight, the ancient wheels had been set in motion. The arrival of this stranger at the base of the obelisk was a signal from the brotherhood.

It was a silent call of distress.

THE U.S. EMBASSY in Paris is a compact complex on Avenue Gabriel, just north of the Champs-Élysées. The three-acre compound is considered U.S. soil, meaning all those who stand on it are subject to the same laws and protections as they would encounter standing in the United States.

The embassy's night operator was reading *Time* magazine's International Edition when the sound of her phone interrupted.

"U.S. Embassy," she answered.

"Good evening." The caller spoke English accented with French. "I need some assistance." Despite the politeness of the man's words, his tone sounded gruff and official. "I was told you had a phone message for me on your automated system. The name is Langdon. Unfortunately, I have forgotten my three-digit access code. If you could help me, I would be most grateful."

The operator paused, confused. "I'm sorry, sir. Your message must be quite old.

That system was removed two years ago for security precautions. Moreover, all the access codes were *five*-digit. Who told you we had a message for you?"

"You have *no* automated phone system?"

"No, sir. Any message for you would be handwritten in our services department. What was your name again?"

But the man had hung up.

Bezu Fache felt dumbstruck as he paced the banks of the Seine. He was certain he had seen Langdon dial a local number, enter a three-digit code, and then listen to a recording. *But if Langdon didn't phone the embassy, then who the hell did he call?*

It was at that moment, eyeing his cellular phone, that Fache realized the answers were in the palm of his hand. *Langdon used my phone to place that call.*

Keying into the cell phone's menu, Fache pulled up the list of recently dialed numbers and found the call Langdon had placed.

A Paris exchange, followed by the three-digit code 454.

Redialing the phone number, Fache waited as the line began ringing.

Finally a woman's voice answered. *"Bonjour, vous êtes bien chez Sophie Neveu,"* the recording announced. *"Je suis absente pour le moment, mais . . ."*

Fache's blood was boiling as he typed the numbers 4 . . . 5 . . . 4.

Chapter 26

Despite her monumental reputation, the *Mona Lisa* was a mere thirty-one inches by twenty-one inches—smaller even than the posters of her sold in the Louvre gift shop. She hung on the northwest wall of the Salle des Etats behind a two-inch-thick pane of protective Plexiglas. Painted on a poplar wood panel, her ethereal, mist-

MONA LISA BY LEONARDO DA VINCI

filled atmosphere was attributed to Da Vinci's mastery of the *sfumato* style, in which forms appear to evaporate into one another.

Since taking up residence in the Louvre, the *Mona Lisa*—or *La Joconde* as they call her in France—had been stolen twice, most recently in 1911, when she disappeared from the Louvre's *"salle impénétrable"*—Le Salon Carré. Parisians wept in the streets and wrote newspaper articles begging the thieves for the painting's return. Two years later, the *Mona Lisa* was discovered hidden in the false bottom of a trunk in a Florence hotel room.

Langdon, now having made it clear to Sophie that he had no intention of leaving, moved with her across the Salle des États. The *Mona Lisa* was still twenty yards ahead when Sophie turned on the black light, and the bluish crescent of penlight fanned out on the floor in front of them. She swung the beam back and forth across the floor like a minesweeper, searching for any hint of luminescent ink.

Walking beside her, Langdon was already feeling the tingle of anticipation that accompanied his face-to-face reunions with great works of art. He strained to see beyond the cocoon of purplish light emanating from the black light in Sophie's hand. To the left, the room's octagonal viewing divan emerged, looking like a dark island on the empty sea of parquet.

Langdon could now begin to see the panel of dark glass on the wall. Behind it, he knew, in the confines of her own private cell, hung the most celebrated painting in the world.

The *Mona Lisa*'s status as the most famous piece of art in the world, Langdon knew, had nothing to do with her enigmatic smile. Nor was it due to the mysterious interpretations attributed her by many art historians and conspiracy buffs. Quite simply, the *Mona Lisa* was famous because Leonardo da Vinci claimed she was his finest accomplishment. He carried the painting with him whenever he traveled and, if asked why, would reply that he found it hard to part with his most sublime expression of female beauty.

Even so, many art historians suspected Da Vinci's reverence for the *Mona Lisa* had nothing to do with its artistic mastery. In actuality, the painting was a surprisingly ordinary *sfumato* portrait. Da Vinci's veneration for this work, many claimed, stemmed from something far deeper: a hidden message in the layers of paint. The *Mona Lisa* was, in fact, one of the world's most documented inside jokes. The painting's well-documented collage of double entendres and playful allusions had been revealed in most art history tomes, and yet, incredibly, the public at large still considered her smile a great mystery.

No mystery at all, Langdon thought, moving forward and watching as the faint outline of the painting began to take shape. *No mystery at all.*

Most recently Langdon had shared the *Mona Lisa*'s secret with a rather unlikely group—a dozen inmates at the Essex County Penitentiary. Langdon's jail seminar was part of a Harvard outreach program attempting to bring education into the prison system—*Culture for Convicts,* as Langdon's colleagues liked to call it.

Standing at an overhead projector in a darkened penitentiary library, Langdon had shared the *Mona Lisa*'s secret with the prisoners attending class, men whom he found surprisingly engaged—rough, but sharp. "You may notice," Langdon told them, walking up to the projected image of the *Mona Lisa* on the library wall, "that the background behind her face is uneven." Langdon motioned to the glaring discrepancy. "Da Vinci painted the horizon line on the left significantly lower than the right."

"He screwed it up?" one of the inmates asked.

Langdon chuckled. "No. Da Vinci didn't do that too often. Actually, this is a little trick Da Vinci played. By lowering the countryside on the left, Da Vinci made Mona Lisa look much larger from the left side than from the right side. A little Da Vinci inside joke. Historically, the concepts of male and female have assigned sides—left is female, and right is male. Because Da Vinci was a big fan of feminine principles, he made Mona Lisa look more majestic from the *left* than the right."

"I heard he was a fag," said a small man with a goatee.

Langdon winced. "Historians don't generally put it quite that way, but yes, Da Vinci was a homosexual."

"Is that why he was into that whole feminine thing?"

"Actually, Da Vinci was in tune with the *balance* between male and female. He believed that a human soul could not be enlightened unless it had both male and female elements."

"You mean like chicks with dicks?" someone called.

This elicited a hearty round of laughs. Langdon considered offering an etymological sidebar about the word *hermaphrodite* and its ties to Hermes and Aphrodite, but something told him it would be lost on this crowd.

"Hey, Mr. Langford," a muscle-bound man said. "Is it true that the *Mona Lisa* is a picture of Da Vinci in drag? I heard that was true."

"It's quite possible," Langdon said. "Da Vinci was a prankster, and computerized analysis of the *Mona Lisa* and Da Vinci's self-portraits confirm some startling points of congruency in their faces. Whatever Da Vinci was up to," Langdon said, "his Mona Lisa is neither male nor female. It carries a subtle message of androgyny. It is a fusing of both."

"You sure that's not just some Harvard bullshit way of saying Mona Lisa is one ugly chick."

SELF-PORTRAIT BY LEONARDO DA VINCI

Now Langdon laughed. "You may be right. But actually Da Vinci left a big clue that the painting was supposed to be androgynous. Has anyone here ever heard of an Egyptian god named Amon?"

"Hell yes!" the big guy said. "God of masculine fertility!"

Langdon was stunned.

"It says so on every box of Amon condoms." The muscular man gave a wide

grin. "It's got a guy with a ram's head on the front and says he's the Egyptian god of fertility."

Langdon was not familiar with the brand name, but he was glad to hear the prophylactic manufacturers had gotten their hieroglyphs right. "Well done. Amon is indeed represented as a man with a ram's head, and his promiscuity and curved horns are related to our modern sexual slang 'horny.' "

"No shit!"

"No shit," Langdon said. "And do you know who Amon's counterpart was? The Egyptian *goddess* of fertility?"

The question met with several seconds of silence.

"It was Isis," Langdon told them, grabbing a grease pen. "So we have the male god, Amon." He wrote it down. "And the female goddess, Isis, whose ancient pictogram was once called L'ISA."

Langdon finished writing and stepped back from the projector.

AMON L'ISA

"Ring any bells?" he asked.

"Mona Lisa . . . holy crap," somebody gasped.

Langdon nodded. "Gentlemen, not only does the face of Mona Lisa look androgynous, but her name is an anagram of the divine union of male and female. And *that,* my friends, is Da Vinci's little secret, and the reason for Mona Lisa's knowing smile."

"MY GRANDFATHER was here," Sophie said, dropping suddenly to her knees, now only ten feet from the *Mona Lisa*. She pointed the black light tentatively to a spot on the parquet floor.

At first Langdon saw nothing. Then, as he knelt beside her, he saw a tiny droplet of dried liquid that was luminescing. *Ink?* Suddenly he recalled what black lights were actually used for. *Blood*. His senses tingled. Sophie was right. Jacques Saunière had indeed paid a visit to the *Mona Lisa* before he died.

"He wouldn't have come here without a reason," Sophie whispered, standing up. "I know he left a message for me here." Quickly striding the final few steps to the *Mona Lisa,* she illuminated the floor directly in front of the painting. She waved the light back and forth across the bare parquet.

"There's nothing here!"

At that moment, Langdon saw a faint purple glimmer on the protective glass before the *Mona Lisa*. Reaching down, he took Sophie's wrist and slowly moved the light up to the painting itself.

They both froze.

On the glass, six words glowed in purple, scrawled directly across the *Mona Lisa*'s face.

EATED AT SAUNIÈRE'S DESK, Lieutenant Collet pressed the phone to his ear in disbelief. *Did I hear Fache correctly?* "A bar of soap? But how could Langdon have known about the GPS dot?"

"Sophie Neveu," Fache replied. "She told him."

"What! Why?"

"Damned good question, but I just heard a recording that confirms she tipped him off."

Collet was speechless. *What was Neveu thinking?* Fache had proof that Sophie had interfered with a DCPJ sting operation? Sophie Neveu was not only going to be fired, she was also going to jail. "But, Captain . . . then where is Langdon *now?*"

"Have any fire alarms gone off there?"

"No, sir."

"And no one has come out under the Grand Gallery gate?"

"No. We've got a Louvre security officer on the gate. Just as you requested."

"Okay, Langdon must still be inside the Grand Gallery."

"Inside? But what is he doing?"

"Is the Louvre security guard armed?"

"Yes, sir. He's a senior warden."

"Send him in," Fache commanded. "I can't get my men back to the perimeter for a few minutes, and I don't want Langdon breaking for an exit." Fache paused. "And you'd better tell the guard Agent Neveu is probably in there with him."

"Agent Neveu left, I thought."

"Did you actually *see* her leave?"

"No, sir, but—"

"Well, nobody on the perimeter saw her leave either. They only saw her go in." Collet was flabbergasted by Sophie Neveu's bravado. *She's still inside the building?*

"Handle it," Fache ordered. "I want Langdon and Neveu at gunpoint by the time I get back."

As the Trailor truck drove off, Captain Fache rounded up his men. Robert Langdon had proven an elusive quarry tonight, and with Agent Neveu now helping him, he might be far harder to corner than expected.

Fache decided not to take any chances.

Hedging his bets, he ordered half of his men back to the Louvre perimeter. The other half he sent to guard the only location in Paris where Robert Langdon could find safe harbor.

*I*NSIDE THE Salle des États, Langdon stared in astonishment at the six words glowing on the Plexiglas. The text seemed to hover in space, casting a jagged shadow across Mona Lisa's mysterious smile.

"The Priory," Langdon whispered. "This proves your grandfather was a member!"

Sophie looked at him in confusion. "You *understand* this?"

"It's flawless," Langdon said, nodding as his thoughts churned. "It's a proclamation of one of the Priory's most fundamental philosophies!"

Sophie looked baffled in the glow of the message scrawled across the *Mona Lisa*'s face.

SO DARK THE CON OF MAN

"Sophie," Langdon said, "the Priory's tradition of perpetuating goddess worship is based on a belief that powerful men in the early Christian church 'conned' the world by propagating lies that devalued the female and tipped the scales in favor of the masculine."

Sophie remained silent, staring at the words.

"The Priory believes that Constantine and his male successors successfully converted the world from matriarchal paganism to patriarchal Christianity by waging a campaign of propaganda that demonized the sacred feminine, obliterating the goddess from modern religion forever."

Sophie's expression remained uncertain. "My grandfather sent me to this spot to find this. He must be trying to tell me more than *that*."

Langdon understood her meaning. *She thinks this is another code.* Whether a hidden meaning existed here or not, Langdon could not immediately say. His mind was still grappling with the bold clarity of Saunière's outward message.

So dark the con of man, he thought. *So dark indeed.*

Nobody could deny the enormous good the modern Church did in today's troubled world, and yet the Church had a deceitful and violent history. Their brutal crusade to "reeducate" the pagan and feminine-worshipping religions spanned three centuries, employing methods as inspired as they were horrific.

The Catholic Inquisition published the book that arguably could be called the most blood-soaked publication in human history. *Malleus Maleficarum*—or *The Witches' Hammer*—indoctrinated the world to "the dangers of freethinking women" and instructed the clergy how to locate, torture, and destroy them. Those deemed "witches" by the Church included all female scholars, priestesses, gypsies, mystics, nature lovers, herb gatherers, and any women "suspiciously attuned to the natural world." Midwives also were killed for their heretical practice of using medical knowledge to ease the pain of childbirth—a suffering, the Church claimed, that was God's rightful punishment for Eve's partaking of the Apple of Knowledge, thus giving birth to the idea of Original Sin. During three hundred years of witch hunts, the Church burned at the stake an astounding five *million* women.

The propaganda and bloodshed had worked.

Today's world was living proof.

Women, once celebrated as an essential half of spiritual enlightenment, had been banished from the temples of the world. There were no female Orthodox rabbis, Catholic priests, nor Islamic clerics. The once-hallowed act of Hieros Gamos—the natural sexual union between man and woman through which each became spiritually whole—had been recast as a shameful act. Holy men who had once required sexual union with their female counterparts to commune with God now feared their natural sexual urges as the work of the devil, collaborating with his favorite accomplice . . . *woman.*

Not even the feminine association with the *left-hand* side could escape the Church's defamation. In France and Italy, the words for "left"—*gauche* and *sinistra*—

came to have deeply negative overtones, while their right-hand counterparts rang of *right*eousness, dexterity, and correctness. To this day, radical thought was considered *left* wing, and anything evil was *sinister*.

The days of the goddess were over. The pendulum had swung. Mother Earth had become a *man's* world, and the gods of destruction and war were taking their toll. The male ego had spent two millennia running unchecked by its female counterpart. The Priory of Sion believed that it was this obliteration of the sacred feminine in modern life that had caused what the Hopi Native Americans called *koyanisquatsi*—"life out of balance"—an unstable situation marked by testosterone-fueled wars, a plethora of misogynistic societies, and a growing disrespect for Mother Earth.

MERMAID AS SYMBOL OF FEMININE POWER AND CRADLE OF LIFE

"Robert!" Sophie said, her whisper yanking him back. "Someone's coming!"

He heard the approaching footsteps out in the hallway.

"Over here!" Sophie extinguished the black light and seemed to evaporate before Langdon's eyes.

For an instant he felt totally blind. *Over where!* As his vision cleared he saw Sophie's silhouette racing toward the center of the room and ducking out of sight behind the octagonal viewing bench. He was about to dash after her when a boom-ing voice stopped him cold.

"*Arrêtez!*" a man commanded from the doorway.

The Louvre security agent advanced through the entrance to the Salle des États, his pistol outstretched, taking deadly aim at Langdon's chest.

Langdon felt his arms raise instinctively for the ceiling.

"*Couchez-vous!*" the guard commanded. "*Lie down!*"

Langdon was face first on the floor in a matter of seconds. The guard hurried over and kicked his legs apart, spreading Langdon out.

"*Mauvaise idée, Monsieur Langdon,*" he said, pressing the gun hard into Langdon's back. "*Mauvaise idée.*"

Face down on the parquet floor with his arms and legs spread wide, Langdon found little humor in the irony of his position. *The Vitruvian Man,* he thought. *Face down.*

*I*NSIDE SAINT-SULPICE, Silas carried the heavy iron votive candle holder from the altar back toward the obelisk. The shaft would do nicely as a battering ram. Eyeing the gray marble panel that covered the apparent hollow in the floor, he realized he could not possibly shatter the covering without making considerable noise.

Iron on marble. It would echo off the vaulted ceilings.

Would the nun hear him? She should be asleep by now. Even so, it was a chance Silas preferred not to take. Looking around for a cloth to wrap around the tip of the iron pole, he saw nothing except the altar's linen mantle, which he refused to defile. *My cloak,* he thought. Knowing he was alone in the great church, Silas untied his cloak and slipped it off his body. As he removed it, he felt a sting as the wool fibers stuck to the fresh wounds on his back.

CANDLESTICKS ON ALTAR, SAINT-SULPICE

Naked now, except for his loin swaddle, Silas wrapped his cloak over the end of the iron rod. Then, aiming at the center of the floor tile, he drove the tip into it. A muffled thud. The stone did not break. He drove the pole into it again. Again a dull thud, but this time accompanied by a crack. On the third swing, the covering finally shattered, and stone shards fell into a hollow area beneath the floor.

A compartment!

Quickly pulling the remaining pieces from the opening, Silas gazed into the void. His blood pounded as he knelt down before it. Raising his pale bare arm, he reached inside.

At first he felt nothing. The floor of the compartment was bare, smooth stone. Then, feeling deeper, reaching his arm in under the Rose Line, he touched something! A thick stone tablet. Getting his fingers around the edge, he gripped it and gently lifted the tablet out. As he stood and examined his find, he realized he was holding a rough-hewn stone slab with engraved words. He felt for an instant like a modern-day Moses.

As Silas read the words on the tablet, he felt surprise. He had expected the keystone to be a map, or a complex series of directions, perhaps even encoded. The keystone, however, bore the simplest of inscriptions.

Job 38:11

A Bible verse? Silas was stunned with the devilish simplicity. The secret location of that which they sought was revealed in a Bible verse? The brotherhood stopped at nothing to mock the righteous!

Job. Chapter thirty-eight. Verse eleven.

Although Silas did not recall the exact contents of verse eleven by heart, he knew the Book of Job told the story of a man whose faith in God survived repeated tests. *Appropriate,* he thought, barely able to contain his excitement.

Looking over his shoulder, he gazed down the shimmering Rose Line and couldn't help but smile. There atop the main altar, propped open on a gilded book stand, sat an enormous leather-bound Bible.

UP IN THE BALCONY, Sister Sandrine was shaking. Moments ago, she had been about to flee and carry out her orders, when the man below suddenly removed his cloak. When she saw his alabaster-white flesh, she was overcome with a horrified bewilderment. His broad, pale back was soaked with blood-red slashes. Even from here she could see the wounds were fresh.

This man has been mercilessly whipped!

She also saw the bloody *cilice* around his thigh, the wound beneath it dripping. *What kind of God would want a body punished this way?* The rituals of Opus Dei, Sister Sandrine knew, were not something she would ever understand. But that was hardly her concern at this instant. *Opus Dei is searching for the keystone.* How they knew of it, Sister Sandrine could not imagine, although she knew she did not have time to think.

The bloody monk was now quietly donning his cloak again, clutching his prize as he moved toward the altar, toward the Bible.

In breathless silence, Sister Sandrine left the balcony and raced down the hall to her quarters. Getting on her hands and knees, she reached beneath her wooden bed frame and retrieved the sealed envelope she had hidden there years ago.

Tearing it open, she found four Paris phone numbers.

Trembling, she began to dial.

DOWNSTAIRS, Silas laid the stone tablet on the altar and turned his eager hands to the leather Bible. His long white fingers were sweating now as he turned the pages. Flipping through the Old Testament, he found the Book of Job. He located chapter thirty-eight. As he ran his finger down the column of text, he anticipated the words he was about to read.

They will lead the way!

Finding verse number eleven, Silas read the text. It was only seven words. Confused, he read it again, sensing something had gone terribly wrong. The verse simply read:

HITHERTO SHALT THOU COME, BUT NO FURTHER.

SECURITY WARDEN Claude Grouard simmered with rage as he stood over his prostrate captive in front of the *Mona Lisa. This bastard killed Jacques Saunière!* Saunière had been like a well-loved father to Grouard and his security team.

Grouard wanted nothing more than to pull the trigger and bury a bullet in Robert Langdon's back. As senior warden, Grouard was one of the few guards who actually carried a loaded weapon. He reminded himself, however, that killing Langdon would be a generous fate compared to the misery about to be communicated by Bezu Fache and the French prison system.

Grouard yanked his walkie-talkie off his belt and attempted to radio for backup. All he heard was static. The additional electronic security in this chamber always wrought havoc with the guards' communications. *I have to move to the doorway*. Still aiming his weapon at Langdon, Grouard began backing slowly toward the entrance. On his third step, he spied something that made him stop short.

What the hell is that!

An inexplicable mirage was materializing near the center of the room. A silhouette. There was someone else in the room? A woman was moving through the darkness, walking briskly toward the far left wall. In front of her, a purplish beam of light swung back and forth across the floor, as if she were searching for something with a colored flashlight.

"Qui est là?" Grouard demanded, feeling his adrenaline spike for a second time in the last thirty seconds. He suddenly didn't know where to aim his gun or what direction to move.

"PTS," the woman replied calmly, still scanning the floor with her light.

Police Technique et Scientifique. Grouard was sweating now. *I thought all the agents were gone!* He now recognized the purple light as ultraviolet, consistent with a PTS team, and yet he could not understand why DCPJ would be looking for evidence in here.

"Votre nom!" Grouard yelled, instinct telling him something was amiss. *"Répondez!"*

"C'est moi," the voice responded in calm French. *"Sophie Neveu."*

Somewhere in the distant recesses of Grouard's mind, the name registered. *Sophie Neveu?* That was the name of Saunière's granddaughter, wasn't it? She used to come in here as a little kid, but that was years ago. *This couldn't possibly be her!* And even if it were Sophie Neveu, that was hardly a reason to trust her; Grouard had heard the rumors of the painful falling-out between Saunière and his grand-daughter.

"You know me," the woman called. "And Robert Langdon did not kill my grand-father. Believe me."

Warden Grouard was not about to take *that* on faith. *I need backup!* Trying his walkie-talkie again, he got only static. The entrance was still a good twenty yards behind him, and Grouard began backing up slowly, choosing to leave his gun trained on the man on the floor. As Grouard inched backward, he could see the woman across the room raising her UV light and scrutinizing a large painting that hung on the far side of the Salle des États, directly opposite the *Mona Lisa*.

Grouard gasped, realizing which painting it was.

What in the name of God is she doing?

Across the room, Sophie Neveu felt a cold sweat breaking across her forehead. Langdon was still spread-eagle on the floor. *Hold on, Robert. Almost there.* Knowing the guard would never actually shoot either of them, Sophie now turned her attention back to the matter at hand, scanning the entire area around one masterpiece in particular—another Da Vinci. But the UV light revealed nothing out of the ordinary. Not on the floor, on the walls, or even on the canvas itself.

There must be something here!

Sophie felt totally certain she had deciphered her grandfather's intentions correctly.

What else could he possibly intend?

The masterpiece she was examining was a five-foot-tall canvas. The bizarre scene Da Vinci had painted included an awkwardly posed Virgin Mary sitting with Baby Jesus, John the Baptist, and the Angel Uriel on a perilous outcropping of rocks. When Sophie was a little girl, no trip to the *Mona Lisa* had been complete without her grandfather dragging her across the room to see this second painting.

Grand-père, I'm here! But I don't see it!

Behind her, Sophie could hear the guard trying to radio again for help.

Think!

She pictured the message scrawled on the protective glass of the *Mona Lisa. So dark the con of man.* The painting before her had no protective glass on which to write a message, and Sophie knew her grandfather would never have defaced this masterpiece by writing on the painting itself. She paused. *At least not on the front.* Her eyes shot upward, climbing the long cables that dangled from the ceiling to support the canvas.

Could that be it? Grabbing the left side of the carved wood frame, she pulled it toward her. The painting was large and the backing flexed as she swung it away from the wall. Sophie slipped her head and shoulders in behind the painting and raised the black light to inspect the back.

It took only seconds to realize her instinct had been wrong. The back of the painting was pale and blank. There was no purple text here, only the mottled brown backside of aging canvas and—

Wait.

Sophie's eyes locked on an incongruous glint of lustrous metal lodged near the bottom edge of the frame's wooden armature. The object was small, partially wedged in the slit where the canvas met the frame. A shimmering gold chain dangled off it.

To Sophie's utter amazement, the chain was affixed to a familiar gold key. The broad, sculpted head was in the shape of a cross and bore an engraved seal she had not seen since she was nine years old. A fleur-de-lis with the initials P.S. In that instant, Sophie felt the ghost of her grandfather whispering in her ear. *When the time comes, the key will be yours.* A tightness gripped her throat as she realized that her grandfather, even in death, had kept his promise. *This key opens a box,* his voice was saying, *where I keep many secrets.*

Sophie now realized that the entire purpose of tonight's word game had been this key. Her grandfather had it with him when he was killed. Not wanting it to fall into the hands of the police, he hid it behind this painting. Then he devised an ingenious treasure hunt to ensure only Sophie would find it.

"Au secours!" the guard's voice yelled.

Sophie snatched the key from behind the painting and slipped it deep in her pocket along with the UV penlight. Peering out from behind the canvas, she could see the guard was still trying desperately to raise someone on the walkie-talkie. He was backing toward the entrance, still aiming the gun firmly at Langdon.

"Au secours!" he shouted again into his radio.

Static.

He can't transmit, Sophie realized, recalling that tourists with cell phones often got frustrated in here when they tried to call home to brag about seeing the *Mona Lisa*. The extra surveillance wiring in the walls made it virtually impossible to get a carrier unless you stepped out into the hall. The guard was backing quickly toward the exit now, and Sophie knew she had to act immediately.

Gazing up at the large painting behind which she was partially ensconced, Sophie realized that Leonardo da Vinci, for the second time tonight, was there to help.

ANOTHER FEW METERS, Grouard told himself, keeping his gun leveled.

"Arrêtez! Ou je la détruis!" the woman's voice echoed across the room.

Grouard glanced over and stopped in his tracks. *"Mon Dieu, non!"*

Through the reddish haze, he could see that the woman had actually lifted the large painting off its cables and propped it on the floor in front of her. At five feet tall, the canvas almost entirely hid her body. Grouard's first thought was to wonder why the painting's trip wires hadn't set off alarms, but of course the artwork cable sensors had yet to be reset tonight. *What is she doing!*

When he saw it, his blood went cold.

The canvas started to bulge in the middle, the fragile outlines of the Virgin Mary, Baby Jesus, and John the Baptist beginning to distort.

"Non!" Grouard screamed, frozen in horror as he watched the priceless Da Vinci stretching. The woman was pushing her knee into the center of the canvas from behind! *"NON!"*

Grouard wheeled and aimed his gun at her but instantly realized it was an empty threat. The canvas was only fabric, but it was utterly impenetrable—a six-million-dollar piece of body armor.

I can't put a bullet through a Da Vinci!

"Set down your gun and radio," the woman said in calm French, "or I'll put my knee through this painting. I think you know how my grandfather would feel about that."

Grouard felt dizzy. "Please . . . no. That's *Madonna of the Rocks*!" He dropped his gun and radio, raising his hands over his head.

"Thank you," the woman said. "Now do exactly as I tell you, and everything will work out fine."

MOMENTS LATER, Langdon's pulse was still thundering as he ran beside Sophie down the emergency stairwell toward the ground level. Neither of them had said a word since leaving the trembling Louvre guard lying in the Salle des États. The guard's pistol was now clutched tightly in Langdon's hands, and he couldn't wait to get rid of it. The weapon felt heavy and dangerously foreign.

Taking the stairs two at a time, Langdon wondered if Sophie had any idea how valuable a painting she had almost ruined. Her choice in art seemed eerily pertinent to tonight's adventure. The Da Vinci she had grabbed, much like the *Mona Lisa,* was notorious among art historians for its plethora of hidden pagan symbolism.

"You chose a valuable hostage," he said as they ran.

"Madonna of the Rocks," she replied. "But I didn't choose it, my grandfather did. He left me a little something behind the painting."

Langdon shot her a startled look. "What!? But how did you know which painting? Why *Madonna of the Rocks?"*

"So dark the con of man." She flashed a triumphant smile. "I missed the first two anagrams, Robert. I wasn't about to miss the third."

HEY'RE DEAD!" Sister Sandrine stammered into the telephone in her Saint-Sulpice residence. She was leaving a message on an answering machine. "Please pick up! They're all dead!"

The first three phone numbers on the list had produced terrifying results—a hysterical widow, a detective working late at a murder scene, and a somber priest consoling a bereaved family. All three contacts were dead. And now, as she called the fourth and final number—the number she was not supposed to call unless the first three could not be reached—she got an answering machine. The outgoing message offered no name but simply asked the caller to leave a message.

"The floor panel has been broken!" she pleaded as she left the message. "The other three are dead!"

Sister Sandrine did not know the identities of the four men she protected, but the private phone numbers stashed beneath her bed were for use on only one condition.

If that floor panel is ever broken, the faceless messenger had told her, *it means the upper echelon has been breached. One of us has been mortally threatened and been forced to tell a desperate lie. Call the numbers. Warn the others. Do not fail us in this.*

It was a silent alarm. Foolproof in its simplicity. The plan had amazed her when she first heard it. If the identity of one brother was compromised, he could tell a lie that would start in motion a mechanism to warn the others. Tonight, however, it seemed that more than one had been compromised.

"Please answer," she whispered in fear. "Where are you?"

"Hang up the phone," a deep voice said from the doorway.

Turning in terror, she saw the massive monk. He was clutching the heavy iron candle stand. Shaking, she set the phone back in the cradle.

"They are dead," the monk said. "All four of them. And they have played me for a fool. Tell me where the keystone is."

CEILING, SAINT-SULPICE

"I don't know!" Sister Sandrine said truthfully. "That secret is guarded by others." *Others who are dead!*

The man advanced, his white fists gripping the iron stand. "You are a sister of the Church, and yet you serve *them*?"

"Jesus had but one true message," Sister Sandrine said defiantly. "I cannot see that message in Opus Dei."

A sudden explosion of rage erupted behind the monk's eyes. He lunged, lashing out with the candle stand like a club. As Sister Sandrine fell, her last feeling was an overwhelming sense of foreboding.

All four are dead.

The precious truth is lost forever.

*T*HE SECURITY alarm on the west end of the Denon Wing sent the pigeons in the nearby Tuileries Gardens scattering as Langdon and Sophie dashed out of the bulkhead into the Paris night. As they ran across the plaza to Sophie's car, Langdon could hear police sirens wailing in the distance.

"That's it there," Sophie called, pointing to a red snub-nosed two-seater parked on the plaza.

She's kidding, right? The vehicle was easily the smallest car Langdon had ever seen.

"SmartCar," she said. "A hundred kilometers to the liter."

Langdon had barely thrown himself into the passenger seat before Sophie gunned the SmartCar up and over a curb onto a gravel divider. He gripped the dash as the car shot out across a sidewalk and bounced back down over into the small rotary at Carrousel du Louvre.

For an instant, Sophie seemed to consider taking the shortcut across the rotary by plowing straight ahead, through the median's perimeter hedge, and bisecting the large circle of grass in the center.

"No!" Langdon shouted, knowing the hedges around Carrousel du Louvre were there to hide the perilous chasm in the center—*La Pyramide Inversée*—the upside-down pyramid skylight he had seen earlier from inside the museum. It was large enough to swallow their SmartCar in a single gulp. Fortunately, Sophie decided on the more conventional route, jamming the wheel hard to the right, circling properly until she exited, cut left, and swung into the northbound lane, accelerating toward Rue de Rivoli.

The two-tone police sirens blared louder behind them, and Langdon could see the lights now in his side-view mirror. The SmartCar engine whined in protest as Sophie urged it faster away from the Louvre. Fifty yards ahead, the traffic light at

Rivoli turned red. Sophie cursed under her breath and kept racing toward it. Langdon felt his muscles tighten.

"Sophie?"

Slowing only slightly as they reached the intersection, Sophie flicked her head-lights and stole a quick glance both ways before flooring the accelerator again and carving a sharp left turn through the empty intersection onto Rivoli. Accelerating west for a quarter of a mile, Sophie banked to the right around a wide rotary. Soon they were shooting out the other side onto the wide avenue of Champs-Élysées.

As they straightened out, Langdon turned in his seat, craning his neck to look out the rear window toward the Louvre. The police did not seem to be chasing them. The sea of blue lights was assembling at the museum.

His heartbeat finally slowing, Langdon turned back around. "That was interesting."

Sophie didn't seem to hear. Her eyes remained fixed ahead down the long thoroughfare of Champs-Élysées, the two-mile stretch of posh storefronts that was often called the Fifth Avenue of Paris. The embassy was only about a mile away, and Langdon settled into his seat.

So dark the con of man.

Sophie's quick thinking had been impressive.

Madonna of the Rocks.

Sophie had said her grandfather left her something behind the painting. *A final message?* Langdon could not help but marvel over Saunière's brilliant hiding place; *Madonna of the Rocks* was yet another fitting link in the evening's chain of interconnected symbolism. Saunière, it seemed, at every turn, was reinforcing his fondness for the dark and mischievous side of Leonardo da Vinci.

Da Vinci's original commission for *Madonna of the Rocks* had come from an organization known as the Confraternity of the Immaculate Conception, which needed a painting for the centerpiece of an altar triptych in their church of San Francesco in Milan. The nuns gave Leonardo specific dimensions, and the desired theme for the painting—the Virgin Mary, baby John the Baptist, Uriel, and Baby Jesus sheltering in a cave. Although Da Vinci did as they requested, when he delivered the work, the group reacted with horror. He had filled the painting with explosive and disturbing details.

The painting showed a blue-robed Virgin Mary sitting with her arm around an infant child, presumably Baby Jesus. Opposite Mary sat Uriel, also with an infant, presumably baby John the Baptist. Oddly, though, rather than the usual Jesus-blessing-John scenario, it was baby *John* who was blessing Jesus . . . and Jesus was

THE MADONNA OF THE ROCKS BY LEONARDO DA VINCI   *THE VIRGIN OF THE ROCKS* BY LEONARDO DA VINCI

submitting to his authority! More troubling still, Mary was holding one hand high above the head of infant John and making a decidedly threatening gesture—her fingers looking like eagle's talons, gripping an invisible head. Finally, the most obvious and frightening image: Just below Mary's curled fingers, Uriel was making a cutting gesture with his hand—as if slicing the neck of the invisible head gripped by Mary's claw-like hand.

Langdon's students were always amused to learn that Da Vinci eventually mollified the confraternity by painting them a second, "watered-down" version of *Madonna of the Rocks* in which everyone was arranged in a more orthodox manner. The second version now hung in London's National Gallery under the name *Virgin of the Rocks,* although Langdon still preferred the Louvre's more intriguing original.

As Sophie gunned the car up Champs-Élysées, Langdon said, "The painting. What was behind it?"

Her eyes remained on the road. "I'll show you once we're safely inside the embassy."

"You'll *show* it to me?" Langdon was surprised. "He left you a physical object?"

Sophie gave a curt nod. "Embossed with a fleur-de-lis and the initials P.S."

Langdon couldn't believe his ears.

WE'RE GOING TO MAKE IT, Sophie thought as she swung the SmartCar's wheel to the right, cutting sharply past the luxurious Hôtel de Crillon into Paris's tree-lined diplomatic neighborhood. The embassy was less than a mile away now. She was finally feeling like she could breathe normally again.

Even as she drove, Sophie's mind remained locked on the key in her pocket, her memories of seeing it many years ago, the gold head shaped as an equal-armed cross, the triangular shaft, the indentations, the embossed flowery seal, and the letters P.S.

Although the key barely had entered Sophie's thoughts through the years, her work in the intelligence community had taught her plenty about security, and now the key's peculiar tooling no longer looked so mystifying. *A laser-tooled varying matrix. Impossible to duplicate.* Rather than teeth that moved tumblers, this key's complex series of laser-burned pockmarks was examined by an electric eye. If the eye determined that the hexagonal pockmarks were correctly spaced, arranged, and rotated, then the lock would open.

Sophie could not begin to imagine what a key like this opened, but she sensed Robert would be able to tell her. After all, he had described the key's embossed seal without ever seeing it. The cruciform on top implied the key belonged to some kind of Christian organization, and yet Sophie knew of no churches that used laser-tooled varying matrix keys.

Besides, my grandfather was no Christian. . . .

Sophie had witnessed proof of that ten years ago. Ironically, it had been another *key*—a far more normal one—that had revealed his true nature to her.

The afternoon had been warm when she landed at Charles de Gaulle Airport and hailed a taxi home. *Grand-père will be so surprised to see me,* she thought. Returning from graduate school in Britain for spring break a few days early, Sophie couldn't wait to see him and tell him all about the encryption methods she was studying.

When she arrived at their Paris home, however, her grandfather was not there. Disappointed, she knew he had not been expecting her and was probably working at the Louvre. *But it's Saturday afternoon,* she realized. He seldom worked on weekends. On weekends, he usually—

Grinning, Sophie ran out to the garage. Sure enough, his car was gone. It was the weekend. Jacques Saunière despised city driving and owned a car for one destination only—his vacation château in Normandy, north of Paris. Sophie, after months in the congestion of London, was eager for the smells of nature and to start her vacation right away. It was still early evening, and she decided to leave immediately and surprise him. Borrowing a friend's car, Sophie drove north, winding into the deserted moon-swept hills near Creully. She arrived just after ten o'clock, turning down the long private driveway toward her grandfather's retreat. The access road was over a mile long, and she was halfway down it before she could start to see the house through the trees—a mammoth, old stone château nestled in the woods on the side of a hill.

Sophie had half expected to find her grandfather asleep at this hour and was excited to see the house twinkling with lights. Her delight turned to surprise, however, when she arrived to find the driveway filled with parked cars—Mercedeses, BMWs, Audis, and a Rolls-Royce.

Sophie stared a moment and then burst out laughing. *My grand-père, the famous recluse!* Jacques Saunière, it seemed, was far less reclusive than he liked to pretend. Clearly he was hosting a party while Sophie was away at school, and from the looks of the automobiles, some of Paris's most influential people were in attendance.

Eager to surprise him, she hurried to the front door. When she got there, though, she found it locked. She knocked. Nobody answered. Puzzled, she walked around and tried the back door. It too was locked. No answer.

Confused, she stood a moment and listened. The only sound she heard was the cool Normandy air letting out a low moan as it swirled through the valley.

No music.

No voices.

Nothing.

In the silence of the woods, Sophie hurried to the side of the house and clambered up on a woodpile, pressing her face to the living room window. What she saw inside made no sense at all.

"Nobody's here!"

The entire first floor looked deserted.

Where are all the people?

Heart racing, Sophie ran to the woodshed and got the spare key her grandfather kept hidden under the kindling box. She ran to the front door and let herself in. As she stepped into the deserted foyer, the control panel for the security system started blinking red—a warning that the entrant had ten seconds to type the proper code before the security alarms went off.

He has the alarm on during a party?

Sophie quickly typed the code and deactivated the system.

Entering, she found the entire house uninhabited. Upstairs too. As she descended again to the deserted living room, she stood a moment in the silence, wondering what could possibly be happening.

It was then that Sophie heard it.

Muffled voices. And they seemed to be coming from underneath her. Sophie could not imagine. Crouching, she put her ear to the floor and listened. Yes, the sound was definitely coming from below. The voices seemed to be singing, or . . . *chanting*? She was frightened. Almost more eerie than the sound itself was the realization that this house did not even have a basement.

At least none I've ever seen.

Turning now and scanning the living room, Sophie's eyes fell to the only object in the entire house that seemed out of place—her grandfather's favorite antique, a sprawling Aubusson tapestry. It usually hung on the east wall beside the fireplace, but tonight it had been pulled aside on its brass rod, exposing the wall behind it.

Walking toward the bare wooden wall, Sophie sensed the chanting getting louder. Hesitant, she leaned her ear against the wood. The voices were clearer now. People were definitely chanting . . . intoning words Sophie could not discern.

The space behind this wall is hollow!

Feeling around the edge of the panels, Sophie found a recessed fingerhold. It was discreetly crafted. *A sliding door.* Heart pounding, she placed her finger in the slot and pulled it. With noiseless precision, the heavy wall slid sideways. From out of the darkness beyond, the voices echoed up.

Sophie slipped through the door and found herself on a rough-hewn stone staircase that spiraled downward. She'd been coming to this house since she was a child and yet had no idea this staircase even existed!

As she descended, the air grew cooler. The voices clearer. She heard men and women now. Her line of sight was limited by the spiral of the staircase, but the last step was now rounding into view. Beyond it, she could see a small patch of the basement floor—stone, illuminated by the flickering orange blaze of firelight.

Holding her breath, Sophie inched down another few steps and crouched down to look. It took her several seconds to process what she was seeing.

The room was a grotto—a coarse chamber that appeared to have been hollowed from the granite of the hillside. The only light came from torches on the walls. In the glow of the flames, thirty or so people stood in a circle in the center of the room.

I'm dreaming, Sophie told herself. *A dream. What else could this be?*

Everyone in the room was wearing a mask. The women were dressed in white gossamer gowns and golden shoes. Their masks were white, and in their hands they carried golden orbs. The men wore long black tunics, and their masks were black. They looked like pieces in a giant chess set. Everyone in the circle rocked back and forth and chanted in reverence to something on the floor before them . . . something Sophie could not see.

The chanting grew steady again. Accelerating. Thundering now. Faster. The participants took a step inward and knelt. In that instant, Sophie could finally see what they all were witnessing. Even as she staggered back in horror, she felt the image searing itself into her memory forever. Overtaken by nausea, Sophie spun, clutching at the stone walls as she clambered back up the stairs. Pulling the door closed, she fled the deserted house, and drove in a tearful stupor back to Paris.

That night, with her life shattered by disillusionment and betrayal, she packed her belongings and left her home. On the dining room table, she left a note.

I WAS THERE. DON'T TRY TO FIND ME.

Beside the note, she laid the old spare key from the château's woodshed.

"SOPHIE!" Langdon's voice intruded. "Stop! *Stop!*"

Emerging from the memory, Sophie slammed on the brakes, skidding to a halt. "What? What happened?!"

Langdon pointed down the long street before them.

When she saw it, Sophie's blood went cold. A hundred yards ahead, the intersection was blocked by a couple of DCPJ police cars, parked askew, their purpose obvious. *They've sealed off Avenue Gabriel!*

Langdon gave a grim sigh. "I take it the embassy is off-limits this evening?"

Down the street, the two DCPJ officers who stood beside their cars were now staring in their direction, apparently curious about the headlights that had halted so abruptly up the street from them.

Okay, Sophie, turn around very slowly.

Putting the SmartCar in reverse, she performed a composed three-point turn and reversed her direction. As she drove away, she heard the sound of squealing tires behind them. Sirens blared to life.

Cursing, Sophie slammed down the accelerator.

Chapter 35

*S*OPHIE'S SMARTCAR tore through the diplomatic quarter, weaving past embassies and consulates, finally racing out a side street and taking a right turn back onto the massive thoroughfare of Champs-Élysées.

Langdon sat white-knuckled in the passenger seat, twisted backward, scanning behind them for any signs of the police. He suddenly wished he had not decided to run. *You didn't,* he reminded himself. Sophie had made the decision for him when she threw the GPS dot out the bathroom window. Now, as they sped away from the embassy, serpentining through sparse traffic on Champs-Élysées, Langdon felt his options deteriorating. Although Sophie seemed to have lost the police, at least for the moment, Langdon doubted their luck would hold for long.

Behind the wheel Sophie was fishing in her sweater pocket. She removed a small metal object and held it out for him. "Robert, you'd better have a look at this. This is what my grandfather left me behind *Madonna of the Rocks.*"

Feeling a shiver of anticipation, Langdon took the object and examined it. It was heavy and shaped like a cruciform. His first instinct was that he was holding a funeral *pieu*—a miniature version of a memorial spike designed to be stuck into the ground at a gravesite. But then he noted the shaft protruding from the cruciform was prismatic and triangular. The shaft was also pockmarked with hundreds of tiny hexagons that appeared to be finely tooled and scattered at random.

"It's a laser-cut key," Sophie told him. "Those hexagons are read by an electric eye."

A key? Langdon had never seen anything like it.

"Look at the other side," she said, changing lanes and sailing through an intersection.

When Langdon turned the key, he felt his jaw drop. There, intricately embossed on the center of the cross, was a stylized fleur-de-lis with the initials P.S.! "Sophie," he said, "this is the seal I told you about! The official device of the Priory of Sion."

She nodded. "As I told you, I saw the key a long time ago. He told me never to speak of it again."

Langdon's eyes were still riveted on the embossed key. Its high-tech tooling and age-old symbolism exuded an eerie fusion of ancient and modern worlds.

"He told me the key opened a box where he kept many secrets."

Langdon felt a chill to imagine what kind of secrets a man like Jacques Saunière might keep. What an ancient brotherhood was doing with a futuristic key, Langdon had no idea. The Priory existed for the sole purpose of protecting a secret. A secret of incredible power. *Could this key have something to do with it?* The thought was overwhelming. "Do you know what it opens?"

Sophie looked disappointed. "I was hoping *you* knew."

Langdon remained silent as he turned the cruciform in his hand, examining it.

"It looks Christian," Sophie pressed.

Langdon was not so sure about that. The head of this key was not the traditional long-stemmed Christian cross but rather was a *square* cross—with four arms of equal length—which predated Christianity by fifteen hundred years. This kind of cross carried none of the Christian connotations of crucifixion associated with the longer-stemmed Latin cross, originated by Romans as a torture device. Langdon was always surprised how few Christians who gazed upon "the crucifix" realized their symbol's violent history was reflected in its very name: "cross" and "crucifix" came from the Latin verb *cruciare*—to torture.

EQUAL-ARMED
CROSS

"Sophie," he said, "all I can tell you is that equal-armed crosses like this one are considered *peaceful* crosses. Their square configurations make them impractical for use in crucifixion, and their balanced vertical and horizontal elements convey a natural union of male and female, making them symbolically consistent with Priory philosophy."

She gave him a weary look. "You have no idea, do you?"

Langdon frowned. "Not a clue."

"Okay, we have to get off the road." Sophie checked her rearview mirror. "We need a safe place to figure out what that key opens."

Langdon thought longingly of his comfortable room at the Ritz. Obviously, that was not an option. "How about my hosts at the American University of Paris?"

"Too obvious. Fache will check with them."

"You must know people. You live here."

"Fache will run my phone and e-mail records, talk to my coworkers. My contacts are compromised, and finding a hotel is no good because they all require identification."

Langdon wondered again if he might have been better off taking his chances letting Fache arrest him at the Louvre. "Let's call the embassy. I can explain the situation and have the embassy send someone to meet us somewhere."

"Meet us?" Sophie turned and stared at him as if he were crazy. "Robert, you're dreaming. Your embassy has no jurisdiction except on their own property. Sending someone to retrieve us would be considered aiding a fugitive of the French government. It won't happen. If you walk into your embassy and request temporary asylum, that's one thing, but asking them to take action against French law enforcement in the field?" She shook her head. "Call your embassy right now, and they are going to tell you to avoid further damage and turn yourself over to Fache. Then they'll promise to pursue diplomatic channels to get you a fair trial." She gazed up the line of elegant storefronts on Champs-Élysées. "How much cash do you have?"

Langdon checked his wallet. "A hundred dollars. A few euro. Why?"

"Credit cards?"

"Of course."

As Sophie accelerated, Langdon sensed she was formulating a plan. Dead ahead, at the end of Champs-Élysées, stood the Arc de Triomphe—Napoleon's 164-foot-

ARC DE TRIOMPHE

tall tribute to his own military potency—encircled by France's largest rotary, a nine-lane behemoth.

Sophie's eyes were on the rearview mirror again as they approached the rotary. "We lost them for the time being," she said, "but we won't last another five minutes if we stay in this car."

So steal a different one, Langdon mused, *now that we're criminals.* "What are you going to do?"

Sophie gunned the SmartCar into the rotary. "Trust me."

Langdon made no response. Trust had not gotten him very far this evening. Pulling back the sleeve of his jacket, he checked his watch—a vintage, collector's-edition Mickey Mouse wristwatch that had been a gift from his parents on his tenth birthday. Although its juvenile dial often drew odd looks, Langdon had never owned any other watch; Disney animations had been his first introduction to the magic of form and color, and Mickey now served as Langdon's daily reminder to stay young at heart. At the moment, however, Mickey's arms were skewed at an awkward angle, indicating an equally awkward hour.

2:51 A.M.

"Interesting watch," Sophie said, glancing at his wrist and maneuvering the SmartCar around the wide, counterclockwise rotary.

"Long story," he said, pulling his sleeve back down.

"I imagine it would have to be." She gave him a quick smile and exited the rotary, heading due north, away from the city center. Barely making two green lights, she reached the third intersection and took a hard right onto Boulevard Malesherbes. They'd left the rich, tree-lined streets of the diplomatic neighborhood and plunged into a darker industrial neighborhood. Sophie took a quick left, and a moment later, Langdon realized where they were.

Gare Saint-Lazare.

Ahead of them, the glass-roofed train terminal resembled the awkward offspring of an airplane hangar and a greenhouse. European train stations never slept. Even at this hour, a half-dozen taxis idled near the main entrance. Vendors manned carts of sandwiches and mineral water while grungy kids in backpacks emerged from the station rubbing their eyes, looking around as if trying to remember what city they were in now. Up ahead on the street, a couple of city policemen stood on the curb giving directions to some confused tourists.

Sophie pulled her SmartCar in behind the line of taxis and parked in a red zone despite plenty of legal parking across the street. Before Langdon could ask what was going on, she was out of the car. She hurried to the window of the taxi in front of them and began speaking to the driver.

LA GARE SAINT-LAZARE BY CLAUDE MONET

As Langdon got out of the SmartCar, he saw Sophie hand the taxi driver a big wad of cash. The taxi driver nodded and then, to Langdon's bewilderment, sped off without them.

"What happened?" Langdon demanded, joining Sophie on the curb as the taxi disappeared.

Sophie was already heading for the train station entrance. "Come on. We're buying two tickets on the next train out of Paris."

Langdon hurried along beside her. What had begun as a one-mile dash to the U.S. Embassy had now become a full-fledged evacuation from Paris. Langdon was liking this idea less and less.

THE DRIVER who collected Bishop Aringarosa from Leonardo da Vinci International Airport pulled up in a small, unimpressive black Fiat sedan. Aringarosa recalled a day when all Vatican transports were big luxury cars that sported grille-plate medallions and flags emblazoned with the seal of the Holy See. *Those days are gone.* Vatican cars were now less ostentatious and almost always unmarked. The Vatican claimed this was to cut costs to better serve their dioceses, but Aringarosa suspected it was more of a security measure. The world had gone mad, and in many parts of Europe, advertising your love of Jesus Christ was like painting a bull's-eye on the roof of your car.

Bundling his black cassock around himself, Aringarosa climbed into the back seat and settled in for the long drive to Castel Gandolfo. It would be the same ride he had taken five months ago.

Last year's trip to Rome, he sighed. *The longest night of my life.*

Five months ago, the Vatican had phoned to request Aringarosa's immediate presence in Rome. They offered no explanation. *Your tickets are at the airport.* The Holy See worked hard to retain a veil of mystery, even for its highest clergy.

The mysterious summons, Aringarosa suspected, was probably a photo opportunity for the Pope and other Vatican officials to piggyback on Opus Dei's recent public success—the completion of their National Headquarters in New York City. *Architectural Digest* had called Opus Dei's building "a shining beacon of Catholicism sublimely integrated with the modern landscape," and lately the Vatican seemed to be drawn to anything and everything that included the word "modern."

Aringarosa had no choice but to accept the invitation, albeit reluctantly. Not a fan of the current papal administration, Aringarosa, like most conservative clergy, had watched with grave concern as the new Pope settled into his first year in office. An unprecedented liberal, His Holiness had secured the papacy through one of the most controversial and unusual conclaves in Vatican history. Now, rather than being humbled by his unexpected rise to power, the Holy Father had wasted no time flexing all the muscle associated with the highest office in Christendom. Drawing on an unsettling tide of liberal support within the College of Cardinals, the Pope was now declaring his papal mission to be "rejuvenation of Vatican doctrine and updating Catholicism into the third millennium."

The translation, Aringarosa feared, was that the man was actually arrogant enough to think he could rewrite God's laws and win back the hearts of those who felt the demands of true Catholicism had become too inconvenient in a modern world.

Aringarosa had been using all of his political sway—substantial considering the size of the Opus Dei constituency and their bankroll—to persuade the Pope and his advisers that softening the Church's laws was not only faithless and cowardly, but political suicide. He reminded them that previous tempering of Church law—the Vatican II fiasco—had left a devastating legacy: Church attendance was now lower than ever, donations were drying up, and there were not even enough Catholic priests to preside over their churches.

People need structure and direction from the Church, Aringarosa insisted, *not coddling and indulgence!*

On that night, months ago, as the Fiat had left the airport, Aringarosa was surprised to find himself heading not toward Vatican City but rather eastward up a sinuous mountain road. "Where are we going?" he had demanded of his driver.

"Alban Hills," the man replied. "Your meeting is at Castel Gandolfo."

The Pope's summer residence? Aringarosa had never been, nor had he ever desired to see it. In addition to being the Pope's summer vacation home, the sixteenth-century citadel housed the Specula Vaticana—the Vatican Observatory—one of the most advanced astronomical observatories in Europe. Aringarosa had never been comfortable with the Vatican's historical need to dabble in science. What was the rationale for fusing science and faith? Unbiased science could not possibly be performed by a man who possessed faith in God. Nor did faith have any need for physical confirmation of its beliefs.

Nonetheless, there it is, he thought as Castel Gandolfo came into view, rising against a star-filled November sky. From the access road, Gandolfo resembled a great stone monster pondering a suicidal leap. Perched at the very edge of a cliff, the castle leaned out over the cradle of Italian civilization—the valley where the Curiazi and Orazi clans fought long before the founding of Rome.

Even in silhouette, Gandolfo was a sight to behold—an impressive example of

CASTEL GANDOLFO

tiered, defensive architecture, echoing the potency of this dramatic cliffside setting. Sadly, Aringarosa now saw, the Vatican had ruined the building by constructing two huge aluminum telescope domes atop the roof, leaving this once-dignified edifice looking like a proud warrior wearing a couple of party hats.

When Aringarosa got out of the car, a young Jesuit priest hurried out and greeted him. "Bishop, welcome. I am Father Mangano. An astronomer here."

Good for you. Aringarosa grumbled his hello and followed his host into the castle's foyer—a wide-open space whose decor was a graceless blend of Renaissance art and astronomy images. Following his escort up the wide travertine marble staircase, Aringarosa saw signs for conference centers, science lecture halls, and tourist information services. It amazed him to think the Vatican was failing at every turn to provide coherent, stringent guidelines for spiritual growth and yet somehow still found time to give astrophysics lectures to tourists.

"Tell me," Aringarosa said to the young priest, "when did the tail start wagging the dog?"

The priest gave him an odd look. "Sir?"

Aringarosa waved it off, deciding not to launch into that particular offensive again this evening. *The Vatican has gone mad.* Like a lazy parent who found it easier to acquiesce to the whims of a spoiled child than to stand firm and teach values, the Church just kept softening at every turn, trying to reinvent itself to accommodate a culture gone astray.

The top floor's corridor was wide, lushly appointed, and led in only one direction—toward a huge set of oak doors with a brass sign.

BIBLIOTECA ASTRONOMICA

Aringarosa had heard of this place—the Vatican's Astronomy Library—rumored to contain more than twenty-five thousand volumes, including rare works of Copernicus, Galileo, Kepler, Newton, and Secchi. Allegedly, it was also the place in which the Pope's highest officers held private meetings . . . those meetings they preferred not to hold within the walls of Vatican City.

Approaching the door, Bishop Aringarosa would never have imagined the shocking news he was about to receive inside, or the deadly chain of events it would put into motion. It was not until an hour later, as he staggered from the meeting, that the devastating implications settled in. *Six months from now!* he had thought. *God help us!*

Now, seated in the Fiat, Bishop Aringarosa realized his fists were clenched just thinking about that first meeting. He released his grip and forced a slow inhalation, relaxing his muscles.

Everything will be fine, he told himself as the Fiat wound higher into the mountains. Still, he wished his cell phone would ring. *Why hasn't the Teacher called me? Silas should have the keystone by now.*

Trying to ease his nerves, the bishop meditated on the purple amethyst in his ring. Feeling the textures of the mitre-crozier appliqué and the facets of the diamonds, he reminded himself that this ring was a symbol of power far less than that which he would soon attain.

THE INSIDE of Gare Saint-Lazare looked like every other train station in Europe, a gaping indoor-outdoor cavern dotted with the usual suspects—homeless men holding cardboard signs, collections of bleary-eyed college kids sleeping on backpacks and zoning out to their portable MP3 players, and clusters of blue-clad baggage porters smoking cigarettes.

Sophie raised her eyes to the enormous departure board overhead. The black and white tabs reshuffled, ruffling downward as the information refreshed. When the update was finished, Langdon eyed the offerings. The topmost listing read:

LILLE—RAPIDE—3:06

"I wish it left sooner," Sophie said, "but Lille will have to do."

Sooner? Langdon checked his watch 2:59 A.M. The train left in seven minutes and they didn't even have tickets yet.

Sophie guided Langdon toward the ticket window and said, "Buy us two tickets with your credit card."

"I thought credit card usage could be traced by—"

"Exactly."

Langdon decided to stop trying to keep ahead of Sophie Neveu. Using his Visa card, he purchased two coach tickets to Lille and handed them to Sophie.

Sophie guided him out toward the tracks, where a familiar tone chimed overhead and a P.A. announcer gave the final boarding call for Lille. Sixteen separate tracks spread out before them. In the distance to the right, at quay three, the train to Lille was belching and wheezing in preparation for departure, but Sophie already had her arm through Langdon's and was guiding him in the exact opposite direction. They hurried through a side lobby, past an all-night café, and finally out a side door onto a quiet street on the west side of the station.

A lone taxi sat idling by the doorway.

The driver saw Sophie and flicked his lights.

Sophie jumped in the back seat. Langdon got in after her.

As the taxi pulled away from the station, Sophie took out their newly purchased train tickets and tore them up.

Langdon sighed. *Seventy dollars well spent.*

It was not until their taxi had settled into a monotonous northbound hum on Rue de Clichy that Langdon felt they'd actually escaped. Out the window to his right, he could see Montmartre and the beautiful dome of Sacré-Coeur. The image was interrupted by the flash of police lights sailing past them in the opposite direction.

Langdon and Sophie ducked down as the sirens faded.

Sophie had told the cab driver simply to head out of the city, and from her firmly set jaw, Langdon sensed she was trying to figure out their next move.

Langdon examined the cruciform key again, holding it to the window, bringing it close to his eyes in an effort to find any markings on it that might indicate where the key had been made. In the intermittent glow of passing streetlights, he saw no markings except the Priory seal.

"It doesn't make sense," he finally said.

"Which part?"

"That your grandfather would go to so much trouble to give you a key that you wouldn't know what to do with."

"I agree."

"Are you sure he didn't write anything else on the back of the painting?"

"I searched the whole area. This is all there was. This key, wedged behind the painting. I saw the Priory seal, stuck the key in my pocket, then we left."

Langdon frowned, peering now at the blunt end of the triangular shaft. Nothing. Squinting, he brought the key close to his eyes and examined the rim of the head. Nothing there either. "I think this key was cleaned recently."

"Why?"

"It smells like rubbing alcohol."

She turned. "I'm sorry?"

"It smells like somebody polished it with a cleaner." Langdon held the key to his nose and sniffed. "It's stronger on the other side." He flipped it over. "Yes, it's alcohol-based, like it's been buffed with a cleaner or—" Langdon stopped.

"What?"

He angled the key to the light and looked at the smooth surface on the broad arm of the cross. It seemed to shimmer in places . . . like it was wet. "How well did you look at the back of this key before you put it in your pocket?"

"What? Not well. I was in a hurry."

Langdon turned to her. "Do you still have the black light?"

Sophie reached in her pocket and produced the UV penlight. Langdon took it and switched it on, shining the beam on the back of the key.

The back luminesced instantly. There was writing there. In penmanship that was hurried but legible.

"Well," Langdon said, smiling. "I guess we know what the alcohol smell was."

SOPHIE STARED in amazement at the purple writing on the back of the key.

24 Rue Haxo

An address! My grandfather wrote down an address!

"Where is this?" Langdon asked.

Sophie had no idea. Facing front again, she leaned forward and excitedly asked the driver, *"Connaissez-vous la Rue Haxo?"*

The driver thought a moment and then nodded. He told Sophie it was out near the tennis stadium on the western outskirts of Paris. She asked him to take them there immediately.

"Fastest route is through Bois de Boulogne," the driver told her in French. "Is that okay?"

Sophie frowned. She could think of far less scandalous routes, but tonight she was not going to be picky. "Oui." *We can shock the visiting American.*

Sophie looked back at the key and wondered what they would possibly find at 24 Rue Haxo. *A church? Some kind of Priory headquarters?*

Her mind filled again with images of the secret ritual she had witnessed in the basement grotto ten years ago, and she heaved a long sigh. "Robert, I have a lot of things to tell you." She paused, locking eyes with him as the taxi raced westward. "But first I want you to tell me everything you know about this Priory of Sion."

*O*UTSIDE THE Salle des États, Bezu Fache was fuming as Louvre warden Grouard explained how Sophie and Langdon had disarmed him. *Why didn't you just shoot the blessed painting!*

"Captain?" Lieutenant Collet loped toward them from the direction of the command post. "Captain, I just heard. They located Agent Neveu's car."

"Did she make the embassy?"

"No. Train station. Bought two tickets. Train just left."

Fache waved off warden Grouard and led Collet to a nearby alcove, addressing him in hushed tones. "What was the destination?"

"Lille."

"Probably a decoy." Fache exhaled, formulating a plan. "Okay, alert the next station, have the train stopped and searched, just in case. Leave her car where it is and put plainclothes on watch in case they try to come back to it. Send men to search the streets around the station in case they fled on foot. Are buses running from the station?"

"Not at this hour, sir. Only the taxi queue."

"Good. Question the drivers. See if they saw anything. Then contact the taxi company dispatcher with descriptions. I'm calling Interpol."

Collet looked surprised. "You're putting this on the *wire?*"

Fache regretted the potential embarrassment, but he saw no other choice.

Close the net fast, and close it tight.

The first hour was critical. Fugitives were predictable the first hour after escape. They always needed the same thing. *Travel. Lodging. Cash.* The Holy Trinity. Interpol had the power to make all three disappear in the blink of an eye. By broadcast-faxing photos of Langdon and Sophie to Paris travel authorities, hotels, and banks, Interpol would leave no options—no way to leave the city, no place to hide, and no way to withdraw cash without being recognized. Usually, fugitives panicked on the street and did something stupid. Stole a car. Robbed a store. Used a bank card in desperation. Whatever mistake they committed, they quickly made their whereabouts known to local authorities.

"Only *Langdon,* right?" Collet said. "You're not flagging Sophie Neveu. She's our own agent."

"Of course I'm flagging her!" Fache snapped. "What good is flagging Langdon if she can do all his dirty work? I plan to run Neveu's employment file—friends, family, personal contacts—anyone she might turn to for help. I don't know what she thinks she's doing out there, but it's going to cost her one hell of a lot more than her job!"

"Do you want me on the phones or in the field?"

"Field. Get over to the train station and coordinate the team. You've got the reins, but don't make a move without talking to me."

"Yes, sir." Collet ran out.

Fache felt rigid as he stood in the alcove. Outside the window, the glass pyramid shone, its reflection rippling in the windswept pools. *They slipped through my fingers.* He told himself to relax.

Even a trained field agent would be lucky to withstand the pressure that Interpol was about to apply.

A female cryptologist and a schoolteacher?

They wouldn't last till dawn.

T HE HEAVILY FORESTED park known as the Bois de Boulogne was called many things, but the Parisian cognoscenti knew it as "the Garden of Earthly Delights." The epithet, despite sounding flattering, was quite to the contrary. Anyone who had seen the lurid Bosch painting of the same name understood the jab; the painting, like the forest, was dark and twisted, a purgatory for freaks and fetishists. At night, the forest's winding

THE GARDEN OF EARTHLY DELIGHTS BY HIERONYMUS BOSCH

lanes were lined with hundreds of glistening bodies for hire, earthly delights to satisfy one's deepest unspoken desires—male, female, and everything in between.

As Langdon gathered his thoughts to tell Sophie about the Priory of Sion, their taxi passed through the wooded entrance to the park and began heading west on the cobblestone crossfare. Langdon was having trouble concentrating as a scattering of the park's nocturnal residents were already emerging from the shadows and flaunting their wares in the glare of the headlights. Ahead, two topless teenage girls shot smoldering gazes into the taxi. Beyond them, a well-oiled black man in a G-string turned and flexed his buttocks. Beside him, a gorgeous blond woman lifted her miniskirt to reveal that she was not, in fact, a woman.

Heaven help me! Langdon turned his gaze back inside the cab and took a deep breath.

"Tell me about the Priory of Sion," Sophie said.

Langdon nodded, unable to imagine a less congruous a backdrop for the legend he was about to tell. He wondered where to begin. The brotherhood's history spanned more than a millennium . . . an astonishing chronicle of secrets, black-mail, betrayal, and even brutal torture at the hands of an angry Pope.

"The Priory of Sion," he began, "was founded in Jerusalem in 1099 by a French king named Godefroi de Bouillon, immediately after he had conquered the city."

Sophie nodded, her eyes riveted on him.

"King Godefroi was allegedly the possessor of a powerful secret—a secret that had been in his family since the time of Christ. Fearing his secret might be lost when he died, he founded a secret brotherhood—the Priory of Sion—and charged them with protecting his secret by quietly passing it on from generation to generation. During their years in Jerusalem, the Priory learned of a stash of hidden documents buried beneath the ruins of Herod's temple, which had been built atop the earlier ruins of Solomon's Temple. These documents, they believed, corroborated Godefroi's powerful secret and were so explosive in nature that the Church would stop at nothing to get them."

Sophie looked uncertain.

"The Priory vowed that no matter how long it took, these documents must be recovered from the rubble beneath the temple and protected forever, so the truth would never die. In order to retrieve the documents from within the ruins, the Priory created a military arm—a group of nine knights called the Order of the Poor Knights of Christ and the Temple of Solomon." Langdon paused. "More commonly known as the Knights Templar."

Sophie glanced up with a surprised look of recognition.

Langdon had lectured often enough on the Knights Templar to know that almost everyone on earth had heard of them, at least abstractedly. For academics, the Templars' history was a precarious world where fact, lore, and misinformation had become so intertwined that extracting a pristine truth was almost impossible. Nowadays, Langdon hesitated even to mention the Knights Templar while lecturing because it invariably led to a barrage of convoluted inquiries into assorted conspiracy theories.

Sophie already looked troubled. "You're saying the Knights Templar were founded by the Priory of Sion to retrieve a collection of secret documents? I thought the Templars were created to protect the Holy Land."

"A common misconception. The idea of protection of pilgrims was the *guise* under which the Templars ran their mission. Their true goal in the Holy Land was to retrieve the documents from beneath the ruins of the temple."

"And did they find them?"

Langdon grinned. "Nobody knows for sure, but the one thing on which all academics agree is this: The Knights discovered *something* down there in the ruins . . .

something that made them wealthy and powerful beyond anyone's wildest imagination."

Langdon quickly gave Sophie the standard academic sketch of the accepted Knights Templar history, explaining how the Knights were in the Holy Land during the Second Crusade and told King Baldwin II that they were there to protect Christian pilgrims on the roadways. Although unpaid and sworn to poverty, the Knights told the king they required basic shelter and requested his permission to take up residence in the stables under the ruins of the temple. King Baldwin granted the soldiers' request, and the Knights took up their meager residence inside the devastated shrine.

The odd choice of lodging, Langdon explained, had been anything but random. The Knights believed the documents the Priory sought were buried deep under the ruins—beneath the Holy of Holies, a sacred chamber where God Himself was believed to reside. Literally, the very center of the Jewish faith. For almost a decade, the nine Knights lived in the ruins, excavating in total secrecy through solid rock.

Sophie looked over. "And you said they discovered something?"

"They certainly did," Langdon said, explaining how it had taken nine years, but the Knights had finally found what they had been searching for. They took the treasure from the temple and traveled to Europe, where their influence seemed to solidify overnight.

Nobody was certain whether the Knights had blackmailed the Vatican or whether the Church simply tried to buy the Knights' silence, but Pope Innocent II immediately issued an unprecedented papal bull that afforded the Knights Templar limitless power and declared them "a law unto themselves"—an autonomous army independent of all interference from kings and prelates, both religious and political.

With their new carte blanche from the Vatican, the Knights Templar expanded at a staggering rate, both in numbers and political force, amassing vast estates in over a dozen countries. They began extending credit to bankrupt royals and charging interest in return, thereby establishing modern banking and broadening their wealth and influence still further.

By the 1300s, the Vatican sanction had helped the Knights amass so much power that Pope Clement V decided that something had to be done. Working in concert with France's King Philippe IV, the Pope devised an ingeniously planned sting operation to quash the Templars and seize their treasure, thus taking control of the secrets held over the Vatican. In a military maneuver worthy of the CIA, Pope Clement issued secret sealed orders to be opened simultaneously by his soldiers all across Europe on Friday, October 13 of 1307.

At dawn on the thirteenth, the documents were unsealed and their appalling contents revealed. Clement's letter claimed that God had visited him in a vision and warned him that the Knights Templar were heretics guilty of devil worship, homosexuality, defiling the cross, sodomy, and other blasphemous behavior. Pope Clement had been asked by God to cleanse the earth by rounding up all the Knights and torturing them until they confessed their crimes against God. Clement's Machiavellian operation came off with clockwork precision. On that day, countless Knights were captured, tortured mercilessly, and finally burned at the stake as heretics. Echoes of the tragedy still resonated in modern culture; to this day, Friday the thirteenth was considered unlucky.

Sophie looked confused. "The Knights Templar were obliterated? I thought fraternities of Templars still exist today?"

"They do, under a variety of names. Despite Clement's false charges and best efforts to eradicate them, the Knights had powerful allies, and some managed to escape the Vatican purges. The Templars' potent treasure trove of documents, which had apparently been their source of power, was Clement's true objective, but it slipped through his fingers. The documents had long since been entrusted to the Templars'

TEMPLARS BURNED AT THE STAKE

shadowy architects, the Priory of Sion, whose veil of secrecy had kept them safely out of range of the Vatican's onslaught. As the Vatican closed in, the Priory smuggled their documents from a Paris preceptory by night onto Templar ships in La Rochelle."

"Where did the documents go?"

Langdon shrugged. "That mystery's answer is known only to the Priory of Sion. Because the documents remain the source of constant investigation and speculation even today, they are believed to have been moved and rehidden several times. Current speculation places the documents somewhere in the United Kingdom."

Sophie looked uneasy.

"For a thousand years," Langdon continued, "legends of this secret have been passed on. The entire collection of documents, its power, and the secret it reveals have become known by a single name—Sangreal. Hundreds of books have been written about it, and few mysteries have caused as much interest among historians as the Sangreal."

"The Sangreal? Does the word have anything to do with the French word *sang* or Spanish *sangre*—meaning 'blood'?"

Langdon nodded. Blood was the backbone of the Sangreal, and yet not in the way Sophie probably imagined. "The legend is complicated, but the important thing to remember is that the Priory guards the proof, and is purportedly awaiting the right moment in history to reveal the truth."

"What truth? What secret could possibly be that powerful?"

Langdon took a deep breath and gazed out at the underbelly of Paris leering in the shadows. "Sophie, the word *Sangreal* is an ancient word. It has evolved over the years into another term . . . a more modern name." He paused. "When I tell you its modern name, you'll realize you already know a lot about it. In fact, almost everyone on earth has heard the story of the Sangreal."

Sophie looked skeptical. "I've never heard of it."

"Sure you have." Langdon smiled. "You're just used to hearing it called by the name 'Holy Grail.' "

*S*OPHIE SCRUTINIZED Langdon in the back of the taxi. *He's joking.* "The Holy Grail?"

Langdon nodded, his expression serious. "Holy Grail is the literal meaning of Sangreal. The phrase derives from the French *Sangraal*, which evolved to Sangreal, and was eventually split into two words, *San Greal*."

Holy Grail. Sophie was surprised she had not spotted the linguistic ties immediately. Even so, Langdon's claim still made no sense to her. "I thought the Holy Grail was a *cup*. You just told me the Sangreal is a collection of documents that reveals some dark secret."

"Yes, but the Sangreal documents are only *half* of the Holy Grail treasure. They are buried with the Grail itself . . . and reveal its true meaning. The documents gave the Knights Templar so much power because the pages revealed the true nature of the Grail."

The true nature of the Grail? Sophie felt even more lost now. The Holy Grail, she had thought, was the cup that Jesus drank from at the Last Supper and with which Joseph of Arimathea later caught His blood at the crucifixion. "The Holy Grail is the Cup of Christ," she said. "How much simpler could it be?"

"Sophie," Langdon whispered, leaning toward her now, "according to the Priory of Sion, the Holy Grail is not a cup at all. They claim the Grail legend—that of a *chalice*—is actually an ingeniously conceived allegory. That is, that the Grail story uses the *chalice* as a metaphor for something else, something far more powerful." He paused. "Something that fits perfectly with everything your grandfather has been trying to tell us tonight, including all his symbologic references to the sacred feminine."

Still unsure, Sophie sensed in Langdon's patient smile that he empathized with her confusion, and yet his eyes remained earnest. "But if the Holy Grail is not a cup," she asked, "what is it?"

Langdon had known this question was coming, and yet he still felt uncertain exactly how to tell her. If he did not present the answer in the proper historical background, Sophie would be left with a vacant air of bewilderment—the exact expression Langdon had seen on his own editor's face a few months ago after Langdon handed him a draft of the manuscript he was working on.

"This manuscript claims *what?*" his editor had choked, setting down his wine-glass and staring across his half-eaten power lunch. "You can't be serious."

"Serious enough to have spent a year researching it."

Prominent New York editor Jonas Faukman tugged nervously at his goatee. Faukman no doubt had heard some wild book ideas in his illustrious career, but this one seemed to have left the man flabbergasted.

"Robert," Faukman finally said, "don't get me wrong. I love your work, and we've had a great run together. But if I agree to publish an idea like this, I'll have people picketing outside my office for months. Besides, it will kill your reputation. You're a Harvard historian, for God's sake, not a pop schlockmeister looking for a quick buck. Where could you possibly find enough credible evidence to support a theory like this?"

With a quiet smile Langdon pulled a piece of paper from the pocket of his tweed coat and handed it to Faukman. The page listed a bibliography of over fifty titles—books by well-known historians, some contemporary, some centuries old—many of them academic bestsellers. All the book titles suggested the same premise Langdon had just proposed. As Faukman read down the list, he looked like a man who had just discovered the earth was actually flat. "I *know* some of these authors. They're . . . real historians!"

Langdon grinned. "As you can see, Jonas, this is not only *my* theory. It's been around for a long time. I'm simply building on it. No book has yet explored the legend of the Holy Grail from a symbologic angle. The iconographic evidence I'm finding to support the theory is, well, staggeringly persuasive."

Faukman was still staring at the list. "My God, one of these books was written by Sir Leigh Teabing—a British Royal Historian."

"Teabing has spent much of his life studying the Holy Grail. I've met with him. He was actually a big part of my inspiration. He's a believer, Jonas, along with all of the others on that list."

"You're telling me all of these historians actually believe . . ." Faukman swallowed, apparently unable to say the words.

Langdon grinned again. "The Holy Grail is arguably the most sought-after treasure in human history. The Grail has spawned legends, wars, and lifelong quests. Does it make sense that it is merely a cup? If so, then certainly *other* relics should generate similar or greater interest—the Crown of Thorns, the True Cross of the Crucifixion, the Titulus—and yet, they do not. Throughout history, the Holy Grail has been the most special." Langdon grinned. "Now you know why."

Faukman was still shaking his head. "But with all these books written about it, why isn't this theory more widely known?"

"These books can't possibly compete with centuries of established history, especially when that history is endorsed by the ultimate bestseller of all time."

Faukman's eyes went wide. "Don't tell me *Harry Potter* is actually about the Holy Grail."

"I was referring to the Bible."

Faukman cringed. "I knew that."

"*LAISSEZ-LE!*" Sophie's shouts cut the air inside the taxi. "Put it down!"

Langdon jumped as Sophie leaned forward over the seat and yelled at the taxi driver. Langdon could see the driver was clutching his radio mouthpiece and speaking into it.

Sophie turned now and plunged her hand into the pocket of Langdon's tweed jacket. Before Langdon knew what had happened, she had yanked out the pistol, swung it around, and was pressing it to the back of the driver's head. The driver instantly dropped his radio, raising his one free hand overhead.

"Sophie!" Langdon choked. "What the hell—"

"*Arrêtez!*" Sophie commanded the driver.

Trembling, the driver obeyed, stopping the car and putting it in park.

It was then that Langdon heard the metallic voice of the taxi company's dispatcher coming from the dashboard. "*. . . qui s'appelle Agent Sophie Neveu . . .*" the radio crackled. "*Et un Américain, Robert Langdon . . .*"

Langdon's muscles turned rigid. *They found us already?*

"*Descendez,*" Sophie demanded.

The trembling driver kept his arms over his head as he got out of his taxi and took several steps backward.

Sophie had rolled down her window and now aimed the gun outside at the bewildered cabbie. "Robert," she said quietly, "take the wheel. You're driving."

Langdon was not about to argue with a woman wielding a gun. He climbed out of the car and jumped back in behind the wheel. The driver was yelling curses, his arms still raised over his head.

"Robert," Sophie said from the back seat, "I trust you've seen enough of our magic forest?"

He nodded. *Plenty.*

"Good. Drive us out of here."

Langdon looked down at the car's controls and hesitated. *Shit.* He groped for the stick shift and clutch. "Sophie? Maybe you—"

"Go!" she yelled.

Outside, several hookers were walking over to see what was going on. One woman was placing a call on her cell phone. Langdon depressed the clutch and jostled the stick into what he hoped was first gear. He touched the accelerator, testing the gas.

Langdon popped the clutch. The tires howled as the taxi leapt forward, fishtailing wildly and sending the gathering crowd diving for cover. The woman with the cell phone leapt into the woods, only narrowly avoiding being run down.

"Doucement!" Sophie said, as the car lurched down the road. "What are you doing?"

"I tried to warn you," he shouted over the sound of gnashing gears. "I drive an automatic!"

ALTHOUGH THE spartan room in the brownstone on Rue La Bruyère had witnessed a lot of suffering, Silas doubted anything could match the anguish now gripping his pale body. *I was deceived. Everything is lost.*

Silas had been tricked. The brothers had lied, choosing death instead of revealing their true secret. Silas did not have the strength to call the Teacher. Not only had Silas killed the only four people who knew where the keystone was hidden, he had killed a nun inside Saint-Sulpice. *She was working against God! She scorned the work of Opus Dei!*

A crime of impulse, the woman's death complicated matters greatly. Bishop Aringarosa had placed the phone call that got Silas into Saint-Sulpice; what would the abbé think when he discovered the nun was dead? Although Silas had placed her back in her bed, the wound on her head was obvious. Silas had attempted to replace the broken tiles in the floor, but that damage too was obvious. They would know someone had been there.

Silas had planned to hide within Opus Dei when his task here was complete. *Bishop Aringarosa will protect me.* Silas could imagine no more blissful existence than a life of meditation and prayer deep within the walls of Opus Dei's headquarters in New York City. He would never again set foot outside. Everything he needed was within that sanctuary. *Nobody will miss me.* Unfortunately, Silas knew, a prominent man like Bishop Aringarosa could not disappear so easily.

I have endangered the bishop. Silas gazed blankly at the floor and pondered taking his own life. After all, it had been Aringarosa who gave Silas life in the first place . . . in that small rectory in Spain, educating him, giving him purpose.

"My friend," Aringarosa had told him, "you were born an albino. Do not let others shame you for this. Do you not understand how special this makes you? Were you not aware that Noah himself was an albino?"

"Noah of the Ark?" Silas had never heard this.

Aringarosa was smiling. "Indeed, Noah of the Ark. An albino. Like you, he had skin white like an angel. Consider this. Noah saved all of life on the planet. You are destined for great things, Silas. The Lord has freed you for a reason. You have your calling. The Lord needs your help to do His work."

Over time, Silas learned to see himself in a new light. *I am pure. White. Beautiful. Like an angel.*

At the moment, though, in his room at the residence hall, it was his father's disappointed voice that whispered to him from the past.

Tu es un désastre. Un spectre.

Kneeling on the wooden floor, Silas prayed for forgiveness. Then, stripping off his robe, he reached again for the Discipline.

NOAH

*S*TRUGGLING WITH the gear shift, Langdon managed to maneuver the hijacked taxi to the far side of the Bois de Boulogne while stalling only twice. Unfortunately, the inherent humor in the situation was overshadowed by the taxi dispatcher repeatedly hailing their cab over the radio.

"Voiture cinq-six-trois. Où êtes-vous? Répondez!"

When Langdon reached the exit of the park, he swallowed his machismo and jammed on the brakes. "You'd better drive."

Sophie looked relieved as she jumped behind the wheel. Within seconds she had the car humming smoothly westward along Allée de Longchamp, leaving the Garden of Earthly Delights behind.

"Which way is Rue Haxo?" Langdon asked, watching Sophie edge the speedometer over a hundred kilometers an hour.

Sophie's eyes remained focused on the road. "The cab driver said it's adjacent to the Roland Garros tennis stadium. I know that area."

Langdon pulled the heavy key from his pocket again, feeling the weight in his palm. He sensed it was an object of enormous consequence. Quite possibly the key to his own freedom.

Earlier, while telling Sophie about the Knights Templar, Langdon had realized that this key, in addition to having the Priory seal embossed on it, possessed a more subtle tie to the Priory of Sion. The equal-armed cruciform was symbolic of balance and harmony but also of the Knights Templar. Everyone had seen the paintings of Knights Templar wearing white tunics emblazoned with red equal-armed crosses. Granted, the arms of the Templar cross were slightly flared at the ends, but they were still of equal length.

A square cross. Just like the one on this key.

Langdon felt his imagination starting to run wild as he fantasized about what they might find. *The Holy Grail*. He almost laughed out loud at the absurdity of it. The Grail was believed to be somewhere in England, buried in a hidden chamber beneath one of the many Templar churches, where it had been hidden since at least 1500.

The era of Grand Master Da Vinci.

The Priory, in order to keep their powerful documents safe, had been forced to move them many times in the early centuries. Historians now suspected as many as six different Grail relocations since its arrival in Europe from Jerusalem. The last Grail "sighting" had been in 1447 when numerous eyewitnesses described a fire that had broken out and almost engulfed the documents before they were carried to safety in four huge chests that each required six men to carry. After that, nobody claimed to see the Grail ever again. All that remained were occasional whisperings that it was hidden in Great Britain, the land of King Arthur and the Knights of the Round Table.

Wherever it was, two important facts remained:

Leonardo knew where the Grail resided during his lifetime.

That hiding place had probably not changed to this day.

For this reason, Grail enthusiasts still pored over Da Vinci's art and diaries in hopes of unearthing a hidden clue as to the Grail's current location. Some claimed the mountainous backdrop in *Madonna of the Rocks* matched the topography of a series of cave-ridden hills in Scotland. Others insisted that the suspicious placement of disciples in *The Last Supper* was some kind of code. Still others claimed that X rays of the *Mona Lisa* revealed she originally had been painted wearing a lapis lazuli pendant of Isis—a detail Da Vinci purportedly later decided to paint over. Langdon had never seen any evidence of the pendant, nor could he imagine how it could possibly reveal the Holy Grail, and yet Grail aficionados still discussed it ad nauseam on Internet bulletin boards and worldwide-web chat rooms.

Everyone loves a conspiracy.

And the conspiracies kept coming. Most recently, of course, had been the earth-shaking discovery that Da Vinci's famed *Adoration of the Magi* was hiding a dark secret beneath its layers of paint. Italian art diagnostician Maurizio Seracini had unveiled the unsettling truth, which the *New York Times Magazine* carried prominently in a story titled "The Leonardo Cover-Up."

Seracini had revealed beyond any doubt that while the *Adoration*'s gray-green sketched underdrawing was indeed Da Vinci's work, the painting itself was not. The truth was that some anonymous painter had filled in Da Vinci's sketch like a

THE ADORATION OF THE MAGI BY LEONARDO DA VINCI

paint-by-numbers years after Da Vinci's death. Far more troubling, however, was what lay *beneath* the impostor's paint. Photographs taken with infrared reflectography and X ray suggested that this rogue painter, while filling in Da Vinci's sketched study, had made suspicious departures from the underdrawing . . . as if to subvert Da Vinci's true intention. Whatever the true nature of the underdrawing, it had yet to be made public. Even so, embarrassed officials at Florence's Uffizi Gallery immediately banished the painting to a warehouse across the street. Visitors at the gallery's Leonardo Room now found a misleading and unapologetic plaque where the *Adoration* once hung.

THIS WORK IS UNDERGOING
DIAGNOSTIC TESTS IN PREPARATION
FOR RESTORATION.

In the bizarre underworld of modern Grail seekers, Leonardo da Vinci remained the quest's great enigma. His artwork seemed bursting to tell a secret, and yet whatever it was remained hidden, perhaps beneath a layer of paint, perhaps enciphered in plain view, or perhaps nowhere at all. Maybe Da Vinci's plethora of tantalizing clues was nothing but an empty promise left behind to frustrate the curious and bring a smirk to the face of his knowing Mona Lisa.

"Is it possible," Sophie asked, drawing Langdon back, "that the key you're holding unlocks the hiding place of the Holy Grail?"

Langdon's laugh sounded forced, even to him. "I really can't imagine. Besides, the Grail is believed to be hidden in the United Kingdom somewhere, not France." He gave her the quick history.

"But the Grail seems the only rational conclusion," she insisted. "We have an extremely secure key, stamped with the Priory of Sion seal, delivered to us by a member of the Priory of Sion—a brotherhood which, you just told me, are guardians of the Holy Grail."

Langdon knew her contention was logical, and yet intuitively he could not possibly accept it. Rumors existed that the Priory had vowed someday to bring the Grail back to France to a final resting place, but certainly no historical evidence existed to suggest that this indeed had happened. Even if the Priory had managed to bring the Grail back to France, the address 24 Rue Haxo near a tennis stadium hardly sounded like a noble final resting place. "Sophie, I really don't see how this key could have anything to do with the Grail."

"Because the Grail is supposed to be in England?"

"Not only that. The location of the Holy Grail is one of the best-kept secrets in history. Priory members wait decades proving themselves trustworthy before being elevated to the highest echelons of the fraternity and learning where the Grail is. That secret is protected by an intricate system of compartmentalized knowledge, and although the Priory brotherhood is very large, only *four* members at any given time know where the Grail is hidden—the Grand Master and his three *sénéchaux*.

The probability of your grandfather being one of those four top people is very slim."

My grandfather was one of them, Sophie thought, pressing down on the accelerator. She had an image stamped in her memory that confirmed her grandfather's status within the brotherhood beyond any doubt.

"And even if your grandfather *were* in the upper echelon, he would never be allowed to reveal anything to anyone outside the brotherhood. It is inconceivable that he would bring you into the inner circle."

I've already been there, Sophie thought, picturing the ritual in the basement. She wondered if this were the moment to tell Langdon what she had witnessed that night in the Normandy château. For ten years now, simple shame had kept her from telling a soul. Just thinking about it, she shuddered. Sirens howled somewhere in the distance, and she felt a thickening shroud of fatigue settling over her.

"There!" Langdon said, feeling excited to see the huge complex of the Roland Garros tennis stadium looming ahead.

Sophie snaked her way toward the stadium. After several passes, they located the intersection of Rue Haxo and turned onto it, driving in the direction of the lower numbers. The road became more industrial, lined with businesses.

We need number twenty-four, Langdon told himself, realizing he was secretly scanning the horizon for the spires of a church. *Don't be ridiculous. A forgotten Templar church in this neighborhood?*

"There it is," Sophie exclaimed, pointing.

Langdon's eyes followed to the structure ahead.

What in the world?

The building was modern. A squat citadel with a giant, neon equal-armed cross emblazoned atop its facade. Beneath the cross were the words:

DEPOSITORY BANK OF ZURICH

Langdon was thankful not to have shared his Templar church hopes with Sophie. A career hazard of symbologists was a tendency to extract hidden meaning from situations that had none. In this case, Langdon had entirely forgotten that the peaceful, equal-armed cross had been adopted as the perfect symbol for the flag of neutral Switzerland.

At least the mystery was solved.

Sophie and Langdon were holding the key to a Swiss bank deposit box.

O UTSIDE CASTEL GANDOLFO, an updraft of mountain air gushed over the top of the cliff and across the high bluff, sending a chill through Bishop Aringarosa as he stepped from the Fiat. *I should have worn more than this cassock,* he thought, fighting the reflex to shiver. The last thing he needed to appear tonight was weak or fearful.

The castle was dark save the windows at the very top of the building, which glowed ominously. *The library,* Aringarosa thought. *They are awake and waiting.* He ducked his head against the wind and continued on without so much as a glance toward the observatory domes.

The priest who greeted him at the door looked sleepy. He was the same priest who had greeted Aringarosa five months ago, albeit tonight he did so with much less hospitality. "We were worried about you, Bishop," the priest said, checking his watch and looking more perturbed than worried.

"My apologies. Airlines are so unreliable these days."

The priest mumbled something inaudible and then said, "They are waiting upstairs. I will escort you up."

The library was a vast square room with dark wood from floor to ceiling. On all sides, towering bookcases burgeoned with volumes. The floor was amber marble with black basalt trim, a handsome reminder that this building had once been a palace.

"Welcome, Bishop," a man's voice said from across the room.

Aringarosa tried to see who had spoken, but the lights were ridiculously low—much lower than they had been on his first visit, when everything was ablaze. *The night of stark awakening.* Tonight, these men sat in the shadows, as if they were somehow ashamed of what was about to transpire.

Aringarosa entered slowly, regally even. He could see the shapes of three men at a long table on the far side of the room. The silhouette of the man in the middle was immediately recognizable—the obese Secretariat Vaticana, overlord of all legal matters within Vatican City. The other two were high-ranking Italian cardinals.

Aringarosa crossed the library toward them. "My humble apologies for the hour. We're on different time zones. You must be tired."

"Not at all," the secretarius said, his hands folded on his enormous belly. "We are grateful you have come so far. The least we can do is be awake to meet you. Can we offer you some coffee or refreshments?"

"I'd prefer we don't pretend this is a social visit. I have another plane to catch. Shall we get to business?"

"Of course," the secretarius said. "You have acted more quickly than we imagined."

"Have I?"

"You still have a month."

"You made your concerns known five months ago," Aringarosa said. "Why should I wait?"

"Indeed. We are very pleased with your expediency."

Aringarosa's eyes traveled the length of the long table to a large black briefcase. "Is that what I requested?"

"It is." The secretarius sounded uneasy. "Although, I must admit, we are concerned with the request. It seems quite . . ."

"Dangerous," one of the cardinals finished. "Are you certain we cannot wire it to you somewhere? The sum is exorbitant."

Freedom is expensive. "I have no concerns for my own safety. God is with me."

The men actually looked doubtful.

"The funds are exactly as I requested?"

The secretarius nodded. "Large-denomination bearer bonds drawn on the Vatican Bank. Negotiable as cash anywhere in the world."

Aringarosa walked to the end of the table and opened the briefcase. Inside were two thick stacks of bonds, each embossed with the Vatican seal and the title *PORTATORE*, making the bonds redeemable to whoever was holding them.

The secretarius looked tense. "I must say, Bishop, all of us would feel less apprehensive if these funds were in *cash*."

I could not lift that much cash, Aringarosa thought, closing the case. "Bonds are negotiable as cash. You said so yourself."

The cardinals exchanged uneasy looks, and finally one said, "Yes, but these bonds are traceable directly to the Vatican Bank."

Aringarosa smiled inwardly. That was precisely the reason the Teacher suggested Aringarosa get the money in Vatican Bank bonds. It served as insurance. *We are all in this together now*. "This is a perfectly legal transaction," Aringarosa defended. "Opus Dei is a personal prelature of Vatican City, and His Holiness can disperse monies however he sees fit. No law has been broken here."

"True, and yet . . ." The secretarius leaned forward and his chair creaked under the burden. "We have no knowledge of what you intend to do with these funds, and if it is in any way illegal . . ."

"Considering what you are asking of me," Aringarosa countered, "what I do with this money is not your concern."

There was a long silence.

They know I'm right, Aringarosa thought. "Now, I imagine you have something for me to sign?"

They all jumped, eagerly pushing the paper toward him, as if they wished he would simply leave.

Aringarosa eyed the sheet before him. It bore the papal seal. "This is identical to the copy you sent me?"

"Exactly."

Aringarosa was surprised how little emotion he felt as he signed the document. The three men present, however, seemed to sigh in relief.

"Thank you, Bishop," the secretarius said. "Your service to the Church will never be forgotten."

Aringarosa picked up the briefcase, sensing promise and authority in its weight. The four men looked at one another for a moment as if there were something more to say, but apparently there was not. Aringarosa turned and headed for the door.

"Bishop?" one of the cardinals called out as Aringarosa reached the threshold.

Aringarosa paused, turning. "Yes?"

"Where will you go from here?"

Aringarosa sensed the query was more spiritual than geographical, and yet he had no intention of discussing morality at this hour. "Paris," he said, and walked out the door.

THE DEPOSITORY BANK OF ZURICH was a twenty-four-hour *Geldschrank* bank offering the full modern array of anonymous services in the tradition of the Swiss numbered account. Maintaining offices in Zurich, Kuala Lumpur, New York, and Paris, the bank had expanded its services in recent years to offer anonymous computer source code escrow services and faceless digitized backup.

The bread and butter of its operation was by far its oldest and simplest offering—the *anonyme Lager*—blind drop services, otherwise known as anonymous safe-deposit boxes. Clients wishing to store anything from stock certificates to valuable paintings could deposit their belongings anonymously, through a series of high-tech veils of privacy, withdrawing items at any time, also in total anonymity.

As Sophie pulled the taxi to a stop in front of their destination, Langdon gazed out at the building's uncompromising architecture and sensed the Depository Bank of Zurich was a firm with little sense of humor. The building was a windowless rectangle that seemed to be forged entirely of dull steel. Resembling an enormous metal brick, the edifice sat back from the road with a fifteen-foot-tall, neon, equilateral cross glowing over its facade.

Switzerland's reputation for secrecy in banking had become one of the country's most lucrative exports. Facilities like this had become controversial in the art community because they provided a perfect place for art thieves to hide stolen goods, for years if necessary, until the heat was off. Because deposits were protected from police inspection by privacy laws and were attached to numbered accounts rather than people's names, thieves could rest easily knowing their stolen goods were safe and could never be traced to them.

Sophie stopped the taxi at an imposing gate that blocked the bank's driveway—a cement-lined ramp that descended beneath the building. A video camera overhead was aimed directly at them, and Langdon had the feeling that this camera, unlike those at the Louvre, was authentic.

Sophie rolled down the window and surveyed the electronic podium on the driver's side. An LCD screen provided directions in seven languages. Topping the list was English.

INSERT KEY.

Sophie took the gold laser-pocked key from her pocket and turned her attention back to the podium. Below the screen was a triangular hole.

"Something tells me it will fit," Langdon said.

Sophie aligned the key's triangular shaft with the hole and inserted it, sliding it in until the entire shaft had disappeared. This key apparently required no turning. Instantly, the gate began to swing open. Sophie took her foot off the brake and coasted down to a second gate and podium. Behind her, the first gate closed, trapping them like a ship in a lock.

Langdon disliked the constricted sensation. *Let's hope this second gate works too.*

This second podium bore familiar directions.

INSERT KEY.

When Sophie inserted the key, the second gate immediately opened. Moments later they were winding down the ramp into the belly of the structure.

The private garage was small and dim, with spaces for about a dozen cars. At the far end, Langdon spied the building's main entrance. A red carpet stretched across the cement floor, welcoming visitors to a huge door that appeared to be forged of solid metal.

Talk about mixed messages, Langdon thought. *Welcome and keep out.*

Sophie pulled the taxi into a parking space near the entrance and killed the engine. "You'd better leave the gun here."

With pleasure, Langdon thought, sliding the pistol under the seat.

Sophie and Langdon got out and walked up the red carpet toward the slab of steel. The door had no handle, but on the wall beside it was another triangular keyhole. No directions were posted this time.

"Keeps out the slow learners," Langdon said.

Sophie laughed, looking nervous. "Here we go." She stuck the key in the hole, and the door swung inward with a low hum. Exchanging glances, Sophie and Langdon entered. The door shut with a thud behind them.

The foyer of the Depository Bank of Zurich employed as imposing a decor as any Langdon had ever seen. Where most banks were content with the usual polished marble and granite, this one had opted for wall-to-wall metal and rivets.

Who's their decorator? Langdon wondered. *Allied Steel?*

Sophie looked equally intimidated as her eyes scanned the lobby.

The gray metal was everywhere—the floor, walls, counters, doors, even the lobby chairs appeared to be fashioned of molded iron. Nonetheless, the effect was impressive. The message was clear: You are walking into a vault.

A large man behind the counter glanced up as they entered. He turned off the small television he was watching and greeted them with a pleasant smile. Despite his enormous muscles and visible sidearm, his diction chimed with the polished courtesy of a Swiss bellhop.

"*Bonsoir,*" he said. "How may I help you?"

The dual-language greeting was the newest hospitality trick of the European host. It presumed nothing and opened the door for the guest to reply in whichever language was more comfortable.

Sophie replied with neither. She simply laid the gold key on the counter in front of the man.

The man glanced down and immediately stood straighter. "Of course. Your elevator is at the end of the hall. I will alert someone that you are on your way."

Sophie nodded and took her key back. "Which floor?"

The man gave her an odd look. "Your key instructs the elevator which floor."

She smiled. "Ah, yes."

THE GUARD WATCHED as the two newcomers made their way to the elevators, inserted their key, boarded the lift, and disappeared. As soon as the door had closed, he grabbed the phone. He was not calling to alert anyone of their arrival; there was no need for that. A vault greeter already had been alerted automatically when the client's key was inserted outside in the entry gate.

Instead, the guard was calling the bank's night manager. As the line rang, the guard switched the television back on and stared at it. The news story he had been watching was just ending. It didn't matter. He got another look at the two faces on the television.

The manager answered. "*Oui?*"

"We have a situation down here."

"What's happening?" the manager demanded.

"The French police are tracking two fugitives tonight."

"So?"

"Both of them just walked into our bank."

The manager cursed quietly. "Okay. I'll contact Monsieur Vernet immediately."

The guard then hung up and placed a second call. This one to Interpol.

LANGDON WAS SURPRISED to feel the elevator dropping rather than climbing. He had no idea how many floors they had descended beneath the Depository Bank of Zurich before the door finally opened. He didn't care. He was happy to be out of the elevator.

Displaying impressive alacrity, a host was already standing there to greet them. He was elderly and pleasant, wearing a neatly pressed flannel suit that made him look oddly out of place—an old-world banker in a high-tech world.

"*Bonsoir,*" the man said. "Good evening. Would you be so kind as to follow me, *s'il vous plaît?*" Without waiting for a response, he spun on his heel and strode briskly down a narrow metal corridor.

Langdon walked with Sophie down a series of corridors, past several large rooms filled with blinking mainframe computers.

"*Voici,*" their host said, arriving at a steel door and opening it for them. "Here you are."

Langdon and Sophie stepped into another world. The small room before them looked like a lavish sitting room at a fine hotel. Gone were the metal and rivets, replaced with oriental carpets, dark oak furniture, and cushioned chairs. On the broad desk in the middle of the room, two crystal glasses sat beside an opened bottle of Perrier, its bubbles still fizzing. A pewter pot of coffee steamed beside it.

Clockwork, Langdon thought. *Leave it to the Swiss.*

The man gave a perceptive smile. "I sense this is your first visit to us?"

Sophie hesitated and then nodded.

"Understood. Keys are often passed on as inheritance, and our first-time users are invariably uncertain of the protocol." He motioned to the table of drinks. "This room is yours as long as you care to use it."

"You say keys are sometimes inherited?" Sophie asked.

"Indeed. Your key is like a Swiss numbered account, which are often willed through generations. On our gold accounts, the shortest safety-deposit box lease is fifty years. Paid in advance. So we see plenty of family turnover."

Langdon stared. "Did you say fifty *years*?"

"At a minimum," their host replied. "Of course, you can purchase much longer leases, but barring further arrangements, if there is no activity on an account for fifty years, the contents of that safe-deposit box are automatically destroyed. Shall I run through the process of accessing your box?"

Sophie nodded. "Please."

Their host swept an arm across the luxurious salon. "This is your private viewing room. Once I leave the room, you may spend all the time you need in here to review and modify the contents of your safe-deposit box, which arrives . . . over here." He walked them to the far wall where a wide conveyor belt entered the room in a graceful curve, vaguely resembling a baggage claim carousel. "You insert your key in that slot there. . . ." The man pointed to a large electronic podium facing the conveyor belt. The podium had a familiar triangular hole. "Once the computer confirms the markings on your key, you enter your account number, and your safe-deposit box will be retrieved robotically from the vault below for your inspection. When you are finished with your box, you place it back on the conveyor belt, insert your key again, and the process is reversed. Because everything is automated, your privacy is guaranteed, even from the staff of this bank. If you need anything at all, simply press the call button on the table in the center of the room."

Sophie was about to ask a question when a telephone rang. The man looked puzzled and embarrassed. "Excuse me, please." He walked over to the phone, which was sitting on the table beside the coffee and Perrier.

"*Oui?*" he answered.

His brow furrowed as he listened to the caller. "*Oui . . . oui . . . d'accord.*" He hung up, and gave them an uneasy smile. "I'm sorry, I must leave you now. Make yourselves at home." He moved quickly toward the door.

"Excuse me," Sophie called. "Could you clarify something before you go? You mentioned that we enter an *account* number?"

The man paused at the door, looking pale. "But of course. Like most Swiss banks, our safe-deposit boxes are attached to a *number*, not a name. You have a key and a personal account number known only to you. Your key is only half of your identification. Your personal account number is the other half. Otherwise, if you lost your key, anyone could use it."

Sophie hesitated. "And if my benefactor gave me no account number?"

The banker's heart pounded. *Then you obviously have no business here!* He gave them a calm smile. "I will ask someone to help you. He will be in shortly."

Leaving, the banker closed the door behind him and twisted a heavy lock, sealing them inside.

ACROSS TOWN, Collet was standing in the Gare du Nord train terminal when his phone rang.

It was Fache. "Interpol got a tip," he said. "Forget the train. Langdon and Neveu just walked into the Paris branch of the Depository Bank of Zurich. I want your men over there right away."

"Any leads yet on what Saunière was trying to tell Agent Neveu and Robert Langdon?"

Fache's tone was cold. "If you arrest them, Lieutenant Collet, then I can ask them personally."

Collet took the hint. "Twenty-four Rue Haxo. Right away, Captain." He hung up and radioed his men.

ANDRÉ VERNET—president of the Paris branch of the Depository Bank of Zurich—lived in a lavish flat above the bank. Despite his plush accommodations, he had always dreamed of owning a riverside apartment on the Île Saint-Louis, where he could rub shoulders with the true *cognoscenti,* rather than here, where he simply met the filthy rich.

When I retire, Vernet told himself, *I will fill my cellar with rare Bordeaux, adorn my salon with a Fragonard and perhaps a Boucher, and spend my days hunting for antique furniture and rare books in the Quartier Latin.*

Tonight, Vernet had been awake only six and a half minutes. Even so, as he hurried through the bank's underground corridor, he looked as if his personal tailor and hairdresser had polished him to a fine sheen. Impeccably dressed in a silk suit, Vernet sprayed some breath spray in his mouth and tightened his tie as he walked. No stranger to being awoken to attend to his international clients arriving from different time zones, Vernet modeled his sleep habits after the Maasai warriors—the African tribe famous for their ability to rise from the deepest sleep to a state of total battle readiness in a matter of seconds.

Battle ready, Vernet thought, fearing the comparison might be uncharacteristically apt tonight. The arrival of a gold-key client always required an extra flurry of attention, but the arrival of a gold-key client who was *wanted* by the Judicial Police would be an extremely delicate matter. The bank had enough battles with law enforcement over the privacy rights of their clients without proof that some of them were criminals.

Five minutes, Vernet told himself. *I need these people out of my bank before the police arrive.*

If he moved quickly, this impending disaster could be deftly sidestepped. Vernet could tell the police that the fugitives in question had indeed walked into his bank as reported, but because they were not clients and had no account number, they were turned away. He wished the damned watchman had not called Interpol. Discretion was apparently not part of the vocabulary of a 15-euro-per-hour watchman.

Stopping at the doorway, he took a deep breath and loosened his muscles. Then, forcing a balmy smile, he unlocked the door and swirled into the room like a warm breeze.

"Good evening," he said, his eyes finding his clients. "I am André Vernet. How can I be of serv—" The rest of the sentence lodged somewhere beneath his Adam's apple. The woman before him was as unexpected a visitor as Vernet had ever had.

"I'm sorry, do we know each other?" Sophie asked. She did not recognize the banker, but he for a moment looked as if he'd seen a ghost.

"No . . . ," the bank president fumbled. "I don't . . . believe so. Our services are anonymous." He exhaled and forced a calm smile. "My assistant tells me you have a gold key but no account number? Might I ask how you came by this key?"

"My grandfather gave it to me," Sophie replied, watching the man closely. His uneasiness seemed more evident now.

"Really? Your grandfather gave you the key but failed to give you the account number?"

"I don't think he had time," Sophie said. "He was murdered tonight."

Her words sent the man staggering backward. "Jacques Saunière is dead?" he demanded, his eyes filling with horror. "But . . . how?!"

Now it was Sophie who reeled, numb with shock. "You *knew* my grandfather?"

Banker André Vernet looked equally astounded, steadying himself by leaning on an end table. "Jacques and I were dear friends. When did this happen?"

"Earlier this evening. Inside the Louvre."

Vernet walked to a deep leather chair and sank into it. "I need to ask you both a very important question." He glanced up at Langdon and then back to Sophie. "Did either of you have anything to do with his death?"

"No!" Sophie declared. "Absolutely not."

Vernet's face was grim, and he paused, pondering. "Your pictures are being circulated by Interpol. This is how I recognized you. You're wanted for a murder."

Sophie slumped. *Fache ran an Interpol broadcast already?* It seemed the captain was more motivated than Sophie had anticipated. She quickly told Vernet who Langdon was and what had happened inside the Louvre tonight.

Vernet looked amazed. "And as your grandfather was dying, he left you a message telling you to find Mr. Langdon?"

"Yes. And this key." Sophie laid the gold key on the coffee table in front of Vernet, placing the Priory seal face down.

Vernet glanced at the key but made no move to touch it. "He left you only this key? Nothing else? No slip of paper?"

Sophie knew she had been in a hurry inside the Louvre, but she was certain she had seen nothing else behind *Madonna of the Rocks*. "No. Just the key."

Vernet gave a helpless sigh. "I'm afraid every key is electronically paired with a ten-digit account number that functions as a password. Without that number, your key is worthless."

Ten digits. Sophie reluctantly calculated the cryptographic odds. *Ten billion possible choices.* Even if she could bring in DCPJ's most powerful parallel processing computers, she still would need weeks to break the code. "Certainly, monsieur, considering the circumstances, you can help us."

"I'm sorry. I truly can do nothing. Clients select their own account numbers via a secure terminal, meaning account numbers are known only to the client and computer. This is one way we ensure anonymity. And the safety of our employees."

Sophie understood. Convenience stores did the same thing. EMPLOYEES DO NOT HAVE KEYS TO THE SAFE. This bank obviously did not want to risk someone stealing a key and then holding an employee hostage for the account number.

Sophie sat down beside Langdon, glanced down at the key and then up at Vernet. "Do you have any idea what my grandfather is storing in your bank?"

"None whatsoever. That is the definition of a *Geldschrank* bank."

"Monsieur Vernet," she pressed, "our time tonight is short. I am going to be very direct if I may." She reached out to the gold key and flipped it over, watching the man's eyes as she revealed the Priory of Sion seal. "Does the symbol on this key mean anything to you?"

Vernet glanced down at the fleur-de-lis seal and made no reaction. "No, but many of our clients emboss corporate logos or initials onto their keys."

Sophie sighed, still watching him carefully. "This seal is the symbol of a secret society known as the Priory of Sion."

Vernet again showed no reaction. "I know nothing of this. Your grandfather was a friend, but we spoke mostly of business." The man adjusted his tie, looking nervous now.

"Monsieur Vernet," Sophie pressed, her tone firm. "My grandfather called me tonight and told me he and I were in grave danger. He said he had to give me something. He gave me a key to your bank. Now he is dead. Anything you can tell us would be helpful."

Vernet broke a sweat. "We need to get out of the building. I'm afraid the police will arrive shortly. My watchman felt obliged to call Interpol."

Sophie had feared as much. She took one last shot. "My grandfather said he needed to tell me the truth about my family. Does that mean anything to you?"

"Mademoiselle, your family died in a car accident when you were young. I'm sorry. I know your grandfather loved you very much. He mentioned to me several times how much it pained him that you two had fallen out of touch."

Sophie was uncertain how to respond.

Langdon asked, "Do the contents of this account have anything to do with the Sangreal?"

Vernet gave him an odd look. "I have no idea what that is." Just then, Vernet's cell phone rang, and he snatched it off his belt. *"Oui?"* He listened a moment, his expression one of surprise and growing concern. *"La police? Si rapidement?"* He cursed, gave some quick directions in French, and said he would be up to the lobby in a minute.

Hanging up the phone, he turned back to Sophie. "The police have responded far more quickly than usual. They are arriving as we speak."

Sophie had no intention of leaving empty-handed. "Tell them we came and went already. If they want to search the bank, demand a search warrant. That will take them time."

"Listen," Vernet said, "Jacques was a friend, and my bank does not need this kind of press, so for those two reasons, I have no intention of allowing this arrest to be made on my premises. Give me a minute and I will see what I can do to help you leave the bank undetected. Beyond that, I cannot get involved." He stood up and hurried for the door. "Stay here. I'll make arrangements and be right back."

"But the safe-deposit box," Sophie declared. "We can't just leave."

"There's nothing I can do," Vernet said, hurrying out the door. "I'm sorry."

Sophie stared after him a moment, wondering if maybe the account number was buried in one of the countless letters and packages her grandfather had sent her over the years and which she had left unopened.

Langdon stood suddenly, and Sophie sensed an unexpected glimmer of contentment in his eyes.

"Robert? You're smiling."

"Your grandfather was a genius."

"I'm sorry?"

"Ten digits?"

Sophie had no idea what he was talking about.

"The account number," he said, a familiar lopsided grin now crossing his face. "I'm pretty sure he left it for us after all."

"Where?"

Langdon produced the printout of the crime-scene photo and spread it out on the coffee table. Sophie needed only to read the first line to know Langdon was correct.

13-3-2-21-1-1-8-5

O, Draconian devil!

Oh, lame saint!

P.S. Find Robert Langdon

Chapter 44

"T EN DIGITS," Sophie said, her cryptologic senses tingling as she studied the printout.

13-3-2-21-1-1-8-5

Grand-père wrote his account number on the Louvre floor!

When Sophie had first seen the scrambled Fibonacci sequence on the parquet, she had assumed its sole purpose was to encourage DCPJ to call in their cryptographers and get Sophie *involved*. Later, she realized the numbers were also a clue as to how to decipher the other lines—*a sequence out of order . . . a numeric anagram*. Now, utterly amazed, she saw the numbers had a more important meaning still. They were almost certainly the final key to opening her grandfather's mysterious safe-deposit box.

"He was the master of double-entendres," Sophie said, turning to Langdon. "He loved anything with multiple layers of meaning. Codes within codes."

Langdon was already moving toward the electronic podium near the conveyor belt. Sophie grabbed the computer printout and followed.

The podium had a keypad similar to that of a bank ATM terminal. The screen displayed the bank's cruciform logo. Beside the keypad was a triangular hole. Sophie wasted no time inserting the shaft of her key into the hole.

The screen refreshed instantly.

ACCOUNT NUMBER:

_ _ _ _ _ _ _ _ _ _

The cursor blinked. Waiting.

Ten digits. Sophie read the numbers off the printout, and Langdon typed them in.

<pre>
         ACCOUNT NUMBER:
          1332211185
</pre>

When he had typed the last digit, the screen refreshed again. A message in several languages appeared. English was on top.

<pre>
            CAUTION:
Before you strike the enter key, please check
    the accuracy of your account number.
For your own security, if the computer does not recognize
    your account number, this system will
          automatically shut down.
</pre>

"Fonction terminer," Sophie said, frowning. "Looks like we only get one try." Standard ATM machines allowed users *three* attempts to type a PIN before confiscating their bank card. This was obviously no ordinary cash machine.

"The number looks right," Langdon confirmed, carefully checking what they had typed and comparing it to the printout. He motioned to the ENTER key. "Fire away."

Sophie extended her index finger toward the keypad, but hesitated, an odd thought now hitting her.

"Go ahead," Langdon urged. "Vernet will be back soon."

"No." She pulled her hand away. "This isn't the right account number."

"Of course it is! Ten digits. What else would it be?"

"It's too random."

Too random? Langdon could not have disagreed more. Every bank advised its customers to choose PINs at random so nobody could guess them. Certainly clients *here* would be advised to choose their account numbers at random.

Sophie deleted everything they had just typed in and looked up at Langdon, her gaze self-assured. "It's far too coincidental that this supposedly *random* account number could be rearranged to form the Fibonacci sequence."

Langdon realized she had a point. Earlier, Sophie had rearranged this account number into the Fibonacci sequence. What were the odds of being able to do that?

Sophie was at the keypad again, entering a different number, as if from memory. "Moreover, with my grandfather's love of symbolism and codes, it seems to follow that he would have chosen an account number that had meaning to him, something he could easily remember." She finished typing the entry and gave a sly smile. "Something that appeared random . . . but was *not*."

Langdon looked at the screen.

ACCOUNT NUMBER:
1123581321

It took him an instant, but when Langdon spotted it, he knew she was right.
The Fibonacci sequence.
1-1-2-3-5-8-13-21
When the Fibonacci sequence was melded into a single ten-digit number, it became virtually unrecognizable. *Easy to remember, and yet seemingly random.* A brilliant ten-digit code that Saunière would never forget. Furthermore, it perfectly explained why the scrambled numbers on the Louvre floor could be rearranged to form the famous progression.

Sophie reached down and pressed the ENTER key.

Nothing happened.

At least nothing they could detect.

AT THAT MOMENT, beneath them, in the bank's cavernous subterranean vault, a robotic claw sprang to life. Sliding on a double-axis transport system attached to the ceiling, the claw headed off in search of the proper coordinates. On the cement floor below, hundreds of identical plastic crates lay aligned on an enormous grid . . . like rows of small coffins in an underground crypt.

Whirring to a stop over the correct spot on the floor, the claw dropped down, an electric eye confirming the bar code on the box. Then, with computer precision, the claw grasped the heavy handle and hoisted the crate vertically. New gears engaged, and the claw transported the box to the far side of the vault, coming to a stop over a stationary conveyor belt.

Gently now, the retrieval arm set down the crate and retracted.

Once the arm was clear, the conveyor belt whirred to life. . . .

UPSTAIRS, Sophie and Langdon exhaled in relief to see the conveyor belt move. Standing beside the belt, they felt like weary travelers at baggage claim awaiting a mysterious piece of luggage whose contents were unknown.

The conveyor belt entered the room on their right through a narrow slit beneath a retractable door. The metal door slid up, and a huge plastic box appeared, emerging from the depths on the inclined conveyor belt. The box was black, heavy molded plastic, and far larger than she imagined. It looked like an air-freight pet transport crate without any airholes.

The box coasted to a stop directly in front of them.

Langdon and Sophie stood there, silent, staring at the mysterious container.

Like everything else about this bank, this crate was industrial—metal clasps, a bar code sticker on top, and molded heavy-duty handle. Sophie thought it looked like a giant toolbox.

Wasting no time, Sophie unhooked the two buckles facing her. Then she glanced over at Langdon. Together, they raised the heavy lid and let it fall back.

Stepping forward, they peered down into the crate.

At first glance, Sophie thought the crate was empty. Then she saw something. Sitting at the bottom of the crate. A lone item.

The polished wooden box was about the size of a shoebox and had ornate hinges. The wood was a lustrous deep purple with a strong grain. *Rosewood,* Sophie realized. Her grandfather's favorite. The lid bore a beautiful inlaid design of a rose. She and Langdon exchanged puzzled looks. Sophie leaned in and grabbed the box, lifting it out.

My God, it's heavy!

She carried it gingerly to a large receiving table and set it down. Langdon stood beside her, both of them staring at the small treasure chest her grandfather apparently had sent them to retrieve.

Langdon stared in wonderment at the lid's hand-carved inlay—a five-petal rose. He had seen this type of rose many times. "The five-petal rose," he whispered, "is a Priory symbol for the Holy Grail."

Sophie turned and looked at him. Langdon could see what she was thinking, and he was thinking it too. The dimensions of the box, the apparent weight of its contents, and a Priory symbol for the Grail all seemed to imply one unfathomable conclusion. *The Cup of Christ is in this wooden box.* Langdon again told himself it was impossible.

"It's a perfect size," Sophie whispered, "to hold . . . a chalice."

It can't be a chalice.

Sophie pulled the box toward her across the table, preparing to open it. As she moved it, though, something unexpected happened. The box let out an odd gurgling sound.

Langdon did a double take. *There's liquid inside?*

Sophie looked equally confused. "Did you just hear . . . ?"

Langdon nodded, lost. "Liquid."

Reaching forward, Sophie slowly unhooked the clasp and raised the lid.

The object inside was unlike anything Langdon had ever seen. One thing was immediately clear to both of them, however. This was definitely *not* the Cup of Christ.

*T*HE POLICE are blocking the street," André Vernet said, walking into the waiting room. "Getting you out will be difficult." As he closed the door behind him, Vernet saw the heavy-duty plastic case on the conveyor belt and halted in his tracks. *My God! They accessed Saunière's account?*

Sophie and Langdon were at the table, huddling over what looked to be a large wooden jewelry box. Sophie immediately closed the lid and looked up. "We had the account number after all," she said.

Vernet was speechless. This changed everything. He respectfully diverted his eyes from the box and tried to figure out his next move. *I have to get them out of the bank!* But with the police already having set up a roadblock, Vernet could imagine only one way to do that. "Mademoiselle Neveu, if I can get you safely out of the bank, will you be taking the item with you or returning it to the vault before you leave?"

Sophie glanced at Langdon and then back to Vernet. "We need to take it."

Vernet nodded. "Very well. Then whatever the item is, I suggest you wrap it in your jacket as we move through the hallways. I would prefer nobody else see it."

As Langdon shed his jacket, Vernet hurried over to the conveyor belt, closed the now empty crate, and typed a series of simple commands. The conveyor belt began moving again, carrying the plastic container back down to the vault. Pulling the gold key from the podium, he handed it to Sophie.

"This way please. Hurry."

When they reached the rear loading dock, Vernet could see the flash of police lights filtering through the underground garage. He frowned. They were probably blocking the ramp. *Am I really going to try to pull this off?* He was sweating now.

Vernet motioned to one of the bank's small armored trucks. *Transport sûr* was another service offered by the Depository Bank of Zurich. "Get in the cargo hold," he said, heaving open the massive rear door and motioning to the glistening steel compartment. "I'll be right back."

As Sophie and Langdon climbed in, Vernet hurried across the loading dock to the dock overseer's office, let himself in, collected the keys for the truck, and found a driver's uniform jacket and cap. Shedding his own suit coat and tie, he began to put on the driver's jacket. Reconsidering, he donned a shoulder holster beneath the uniform. On his way out, he grabbed a driver's pistol from the rack, put in a clip, and stuffed it in the holster, buttoning his uniform over it. Returning to the truck, Vernet pulled the driver's cap down low and peered in at Sophie and Langdon, who were standing inside the empty steel box.

"You'll want this on," Vernet said, reaching inside and flicking a wall switch to illuminate the lone courtesy bulb on the hold's ceiling. "And you'd better sit down. Not a sound on our way out the gate."

Sophie and Langdon sat down on the metal floor. Langdon cradled the treasure wadded in his tweed jacket. Swinging the heavy doors closed, Vernet locked them inside. Then he got in behind the wheel and revved the engine.

As the armored truck lumbered toward the top of the ramp, Vernet could feel the sweat already collecting beneath his driver's cap. He could see there were far more police lights in front than he had imagined. As the truck powered up the ramp, the interior gate swung inward to let him pass. Vernet advanced and waited while the gate behind him closed before pulling forward and tripping the next sensor. The second gate opened, and the exit beckoned.

Except for the police car blocking the top of the ramp.

Vernet dabbed his brow and pulled forward.

A lanky officer stepped out and waved him to a stop a few meters from the road-block. Four patrol cars were parked out front.

Vernet stopped. Pulling his driver's cap down farther, he effected as rough a facade as his cultured upbringing would allow. Not budging from behind the wheel, he opened the door and gazed down at the agent, whose face was stern and sallow.

"*Qu'est-ce qui se passe?*" Vernet asked, his tone rough.

"Je suis Jérôme Collet," the agent said. *"Lieutenant Police Judiciaire."* He motioned to the truck's cargo hold. *"Qu'est-ce qu'il y a là-dedans?"*

"Hell if I know," Vernet replied in crude French. "I'm only a driver."

Collet looked unimpressed. "We're looking for two criminals."

Vernet laughed. "Then you came to the right spot. Some of these bastards I drive for have so much money they must be criminals."

The agent held up a passport picture of Robert Langdon. "Was this man in your bank tonight?"

Vernet shrugged. "No clue. I'm a dock rat. They don't let us anywhere near the clients. You need to go in and ask the front desk."

"Your bank is demanding a search warrant before we can enter."

Vernet put on a disgusted look. "Administrators. Don't get me started."

"Open your truck, please." Collet motioned toward the cargo hold.

Vernet stared at the agent and forced an obnoxious laugh. "Open the truck? You think I have keys? You think they trust us? You should see the crap wages I get paid."

The agent's head tilted to one side, his skepticism evident. "You're telling me you don't have keys to your own truck?"

Vernet shook his head. "Not the cargo area. Ignition only. These trucks get sealed by overseers on the loading dock. Then the truck sits in dock while someone drives the cargo keys to the drop-off. Once we get the call that the cargo keys are with the recipient, then I get the okay to drive. Not a second before. I never know what the hell I'm lugging."

"When was *this* truck sealed?"

"Must have been hours ago. I'm driving all the way up to Saint-Thurial tonight. Cargo keys are already up there."

The agent made no response, his eyes probing as if trying to read Vernet's mind.

A drop of sweat was preparing to slide down Vernet's nose. "You mind?" he said, wiping his nose with his sleeve and motioning to the police car blocking his way. "I'm on a tight schedule."

"Do all the drivers wear Rolexes?" the agent asked, pointing to Vernet's wrist.

Vernet glanced down and saw the glistening band of his absurdly expensive watch peeking out from beneath the sleeve of his jacket. *Merde.* "This piece of shit? Bought it for twenty euro from a Taiwanese street vendor in Saint-Germain-des-Prés. I'll sell it to you for forty."

The agent paused and finally stepped aside. "No thanks. Have a safe trip."

Vernet did not breathe again until the truck was a good fifty meters down the street. And now he had another problem. His cargo. *Where do I take them?*

*S*ILAS LAY PRONE on the canvas mat in his room, allowing the lash wounds on his back to clot in the air. Tonight's second session with the Discipline had left him dizzy and weak. He had yet to remove the *cilice* belt, and he could feel the blood trickling down his inner thigh. Still, he could not justify removing the strap.

I have failed the Church.

Far worse, I have failed the bishop.

Tonight was supposed to be Bishop Aringarosa's salvation. Five months ago, the bishop had returned from a meeting at the Vatican Observatory, where he had learned something that left him deeply changed. Depressed for weeks, Aringarosa had finally shared the news with Silas.

"But this is impossible!" Silas had cried out. "I cannot accept it!"

"It is true," Aringarosa said. "Unthinkable, but true. In only six months."

The bishop's words terrified Silas. He prayed for deliverance, and even in those dark days, his trust in God and *The Way* never wavered. It was only a month later that the clouds parted miraculously and the light of possibility shone through.

Divine intervention, Aringarosa had called it.

The bishop had seemed hopeful for the first time. "Silas," he whispered, "God has bestowed upon us an opportunity to protect *The Way*. Our battle, like all battles, will take sacrifice. Will you be a soldier of God?"

Silas fell to his knees before Bishop Aringarosa—the man who had given him a new life—and he said, "I am a lamb of God. Shepherd me as your heart commands."

When Aringarosa described the opportunity that had presented itself, Silas knew it could only be the hand of God at work. *Miraculous fate!* Aringarosa put Silas in contact with the man who had proposed the plan—a man who called himself the Teacher. Although the Teacher and Silas never met face-to-face, each time they spoke by phone, Silas was awed, both by the profundity of the Teacher's faith and by the scope of his power. The Teacher seemed to be a man who knew all, a man with eyes and ears in all places. How the Teacher gathered his information, Silas did not know, but Aringarosa had placed enormous trust in the Teacher, and he had told Silas to do the same. "Do as the Teacher commands you," the bishop told Silas. "And we will be victorious."

Victorious. Silas now gazed at the bare floor and feared victory had eluded them. The Teacher had been tricked. The keystone was a devious dead end. And with the deception, all hope had vanished.

Silas wished he could call Bishop Aringarosa and warn him, but the Teacher had removed all their lines of direct communication tonight. *For our safety.*

Finally, overcoming enormous trepidation, Silas crawled to his feet and found his robe, which lay on the floor. He dug his cell phone from the pocket. Hanging his head in shame, he dialed.

"Teacher," he whispered, "all is lost." Silas truthfully told the man how he had been tricked.

"You lose your faith too quickly," the Teacher replied. "I have just received news. Most unexpected and welcome. The secret lives. Jacques Saunière transferred information before he died. I will call you soon. Our work tonight is not yet done."

RIDING INSIDE the dimly lit cargo hold of the armored truck was like being transported inside a cell for solitary confinement. Langdon fought the all-too-familiar anxiety that haunted him in confined spaces. *Vernet said he would take us a safe distance out of the city. Where? How far?*

Langdon's legs had gotten stiff from sitting cross-legged on the metal floor, and he shifted his position, wincing to feel the blood pouring back into his lower body. In his arms, he still clutched the bizarre treasure they had extricated from the bank.

"I think we're on the highway now," Sophie whispered.

Langdon sensed the same thing. The truck, after an unnerving pause atop the bank ramp, had moved on, snaking left and right for a minute or two, and was now accelerating to what felt like top speed. Beneath them, the bulletproof tires hummed on smooth pavement. Forcing his attention to the rosewood box in his arms, Langdon laid the precious bundle on the floor, unwrapped his jacket, and extracted the box, pulling it toward him. Sophie shifted her position so they were sitting side by side. Langdon suddenly felt like they were two kids huddled over a Christmas present.

In contrast to the warm colors of the rosewood box, the inlaid rose had been crafted of a pale wood, probably ash, which shone clearly in the dim light. *The Rose.* Entire armies and religions had been built on this symbol, as had secret societies. *The Rosicrucians. The Knights of the Rosy Cross.*

"Go ahead," Sophie said. "Open it."

Langdon took a deep breath. Reaching for the lid, he stole one more admiring glance at the intricate woodwork and then, unhooking the clasp, he opened the lid, revealing the object within.

Langdon had harbored several fantasies about what they might find inside this box, but clearly he had been wrong on every account. Nestled snugly inside the box's heavily padded interior of crimson silk lay an object Langdon could not even begin to comprehend.

Crafted of polished white marble, it was a stone cylinder approximately the dimensions of a tennis ball can. More complicated than a simple column of stone, however, the cylinder appeared to have been assembled in many pieces. Five doughnut-sized disks of marble had been stacked and affixed to one another within a delicate brass framework. It looked like some kind of tubular, multi-wheeled kaleidoscope. Each end of the cylinder was affixed with an end cap, also marble, making it impossible to see inside. Having heard liquid within, Langdon assumed the cylinder was hollow.

As mystifying as the construction of the cylinder was, however, it was the engravings around the tube's circumference that drew Langdon's primary focus. Each of the five disks had been carefully carved with the same unlikely series of let-ters—the entire alphabet. The lettered cylinder reminded Langdon of one of his childhood toys—a rod threaded with lettered tumblers that could be rotated to spell different words.

THE ROSY CROSS

"Amazing, isn't it?" Sophie whispered.

Langdon glanced up. "I don't know. What the hell is it?"

Now there was a glint in Sophie's eye. "My grandfather used to craft these as a hobby. They were invented by Leonardo da Vinci."

Even in the diffuse light, Sophie could see Langdon's surprise.

"Da Vinci?" he muttered, looking again at the canister.

"Yes. It's called a *cryptex*. According to my grandfather, the blueprints come from one of Da Vinci's secret diaries."

"What is it for?"

Considering tonight's events, Sophie knew the answer might have some interesting implications. "It's a vault," she said. "For storing secret information."

Langdon's eyes widened further.

Sophie explained that creating models of Da Vinci's inventions was one of her grandfather's best-loved hobbies. A talented craftsman who spent hours in his wood and metal shop, Jacques Saunière enjoyed imitating master craftsmen—Fabergé, assorted cloisonné artisans, and the less artistic, but far more practical, Leonardo da Vinci.

Even a cursory glance through Da Vinci's journals revealed why the luminary was as notorious for his lack of follow-through as he was famous for his brilliance. Da Vinci had drawn up blueprints for hundreds of inventions he had never built. One of Jacques Saunière's favorite pastimes was bringing Da Vinci's more obscure brainstorms to life—timepieces, water pumps, cryptexes, and even a fully articulated model of a medieval French knight, which now stood proudly on the desk in his office. Designed by Da Vinci in 1495 as an outgrowth of his earliest anatomy and kinesiology studies, the internal mechanism of the robot knight possessed accurate joints and tendons, and was designed to sit up, wave its arms, and move its head via a flexible neck while opening and closing an anatomically correct jaw. This armor-clad knight, Sophie had always believed, was the most beautiful object her grandfather had ever built . . . that was, until she had seen the cryptex in this rosewood box.

"He made me one of these when I was little," Sophie said. "But I've never seen one so ornate and large."

Langdon's eyes had never left the box. "I've never heard of a cryptex."

Sophie was not surprised. Most of Leonardo's unbuilt inventions had never been studied or even named. The term *cryptex* possibly had been her grandfather's creation, an apt title for this device that used the science of *cryptology* to protect information written on the contained scroll or *codex*.

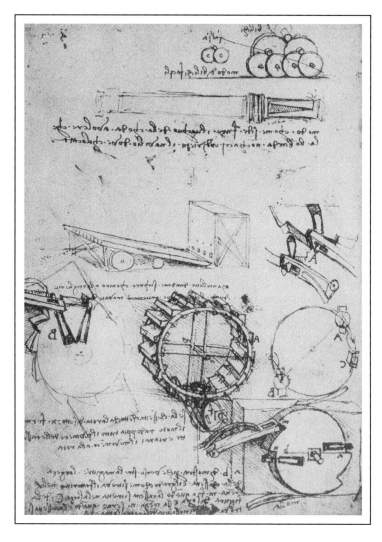

SKETCH OF BOMBARD AND WATER MECHANISM
BY LEONARDO DA VINCI

Da Vinci had been a cryptology pioneer, Sophie knew, although he was seldom given credit. Sophie's university instructors, while presenting computer encryption methods for securing data, praised modern cryptologists like Zimmerman and Schneier but failed to mention that it was Leonardo who had invented one of the first rudimentary forms of public key encryption centuries ago. Sophie's grandfather, of course, had been the one to tell her all about that.

As their armored truck roared down the highway, Sophie explained to Langdon that the cryptex had been Da Vinci's solution to the dilemma of sending secure messages over long distances. In an era without telephones or e-mail, anyone wanting to convey private information to someone far away had no option but to write it down and then trust a messenger to carry the letter. Unfortunately, if a messenger suspected the letter might contain valuable information, he could make far more money selling the information to adversaries than he could delivering the letter properly.

Many great minds in history had invented cryptologic solutions to the challenge of data protection: Julius Caesar devised a code-writing scheme called the Caesar Box; Mary, Queen of Scots created a substitution cipher and sent secret communiqués from prison; and the brilliant Arab scientist Abu Yusuf Ismail al-Kindi protected his secrets with an ingeniously conceived polyalphabetic substitution cipher.

Da Vinci, however, eschewed mathematics and cryptology for a *mechanical* solution. The cryptex. A portable container that could safeguard letters, maps, diagrams, anything at all. Once information was sealed inside the cryptex, only the individual with the proper password could access it.

"We require a password," Sophie said, pointing out the lettered dials. "A cryptex works much like a bicycle's combination lock. If you align the dials in the proper position, the lock slides open. This cryptex has five lettered dials. When you rotate them to their proper sequence, the tumblers inside align, and the entire cylinder slides apart."

"And inside?"

"Once the cylinder slides apart, you have access to a hollow central compartment, which can hold a scroll of paper on which is the information you want to keep private."

Code:
TIARHSEBIASOSCAX

Broken into four equal lines:

T I A R
H S E B
I A S O
S C A X

Each column read vertically:

T | I | A | R
H | S | E | B
I | S | S | O
S | C | A | X

Deciphered code:
THIS IS A CAESAR BOX

CAESAR BOX CODES

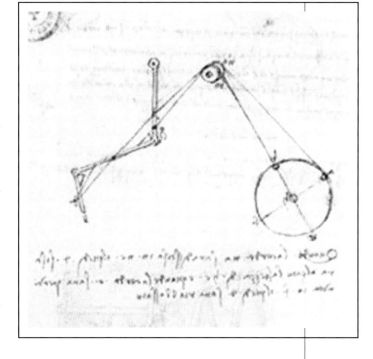

Langdon looked incredulous. "And you say your grandfather built these for you when you were younger?"

"Some smaller ones, yes. A couple times for my birthday, he gave me a cryptex and told me a riddle. The answer to the riddle was the password to the cryptex, and once I figured it out, I could open it up and find my birthday card."

"A lot of work for a card."

"No, the cards always contained another riddle or clue. My grandfather loved creating elaborate treasure hunts around our house, a string of clues that eventually led to my real gift. Each treasure hunt was a test of character and merit, to ensure I earned my rewards. And the tests were never simple."

Langdon eyed the device again, still looking skeptical. "But why not just pry it apart? Or smash it? The metal looks delicate, and marble is a soft rock."

Sophie smiled. "Because Da Vinci is too smart for that. He designed the cryptex so that if you try to force it open in any way, the information self-destructs. Watch." Sophie reached into the box and carefully lifted out the cylinder. "Any information to be inserted is first written on a papyrus scroll."

"Not vellum?"

Sophie shook her head. "Papyrus. I know sheep's vellum was more durable and more common in those days, but it had to be papyrus. The thinner the better."

"Okay."

"Before the papyrus was inserted into the cryptex's compartment, it was rolled around a delicate glass vial." She tipped the cryptex, and the liquid inside gurgled. "A vial of liquid."

"Liquid *what?*"

Sophie smiled. "Vinegar."

Langdon hesitated a moment and then began nodding. "Brilliant."

Vinegar and papyrus, Sophie thought. If someone attempted to force open the cryptex, the glass vial would break, and the vinegar would quickly dissolve the papyrus. By the time anyone extracted the secret message, it would be a glob of meaningless pulp.

"As you can see," Sophie told him, "the only way to access the information inside is to know the proper five-letter password. And with five dials, each with twenty-six letters, that's twenty-six to the fifth power." She quickly estimated the permutations. "Approximately twelve million possibilities."

"If you say so," Langdon said, looking like he had approximately twelve million questions running through his head. "What information do you think is inside?"

"Whatever it is, my grandfather obviously wanted very badly to keep it secret." She paused, closing the box lid and eyeing the five-petal Rose inlaid on it. Something was bothering her. "Did you say earlier that the Rose is a symbol for the Grail?"

"Exactly. In Priory symbolism, the Rose and the Grail are synonymous."

Sophie furrowed her brow. "That's strange, because my grandfather always told me the Rose meant *secrecy*. He used to hang a rose on his office door at home when he was having a confidential phone call and didn't want me to disturb him. He encouraged me to do the same." *Sweetie,* her grandfather said, *rather than lock each other out, we can each hang a rose—la fleur des secrets—on our door when we need privacy. This way we learn to respect and trust each other. Hanging a rose is an ancient Roman custom.*

"*Sub rosa,*" Langdon said. "The Romans hung a rose over meetings to indicate the meeting was confidential. Attendees understood that whatever was said *under the rose—or sub rosa—*had to remain a secret."

Langdon quickly explained that the Rose's overtone of secrecy was not the only reason the Priory used it as a symbol for the Grail. *Rosa rugosa,* one of the oldest species of rose, had five petals and pentagonal symmetry, just like the guiding star of Venus, giving the Rose strong iconographic ties to *womanhood.* In addition, the Rose had close ties to the concept of "true direction" and navigating one's way. The Compass Rose helped travelers navigate, as did Rose Lines, the longitudinal lines on maps. For this reason, the Rose was a symbol that spoke of the Grail on many levels—secrecy, womanhood, and guidance—the feminine chalice and guiding star that led to secret truth.

As Langdon finished his explanation, his expression seemed to tighten suddenly.

"Robert? Are you okay?"

His eyes were riveted to the rosewood box. *"Sub . . . rosa,"* he choked, a fearful bewilderment sweeping across his face. "It can't be."

"What?"

Langdon slowly raised his eyes. "Under the sign of the Rose," he whispered. "This cryptex . . . I think I know what it is."

LANGDON COULD scarcely believe his own supposition, and yet, considering *who* had given this stone cylinder to them, *how* he had given it to them, and now, the inlaid Rose on the container, Langdon could formulate only one conclusion.

I am holding the Priory keystone.

The legend was specific.

The keystone is an encoded stone that lies beneath the sign of the Rose.

"Robert?" Sophie was watching him. "What's going on?"

Langdon needed a moment to gather his thoughts. "Did your grandfather ever speak to you of something called *la clef de voûte?*"

"The key to the vault?" Sophie translated.

"No, that's the literal translation. *Clef de voûte* is a common architectural term. *Voûte* refers not to a bank vault, but to a *vault* in an archway. Like a *vaulted* ceiling."

"But vaulted ceilings don't have keys."

"Actually they do. Every stone archway requires a central, wedge-shaped stone at the top which locks the pieces together and carries all the weight. This stone is, in an architectural sense, the key to the vault. In English we call it a *keystone.*" Langdon watched her eyes for any spark of recognition.

Sophie shrugged, glancing down at the cryptex. "But this obviously is not a keystone."

Langdon didn't know where to begin. Keystones as a masonry technique for

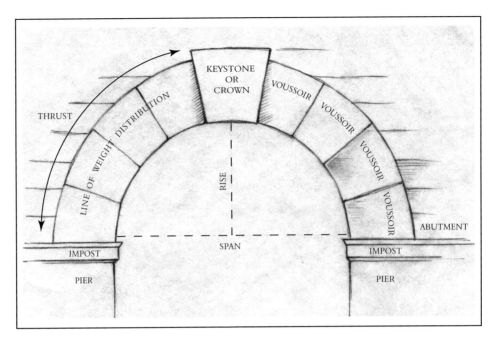

KEYSTONE ARCH

building stone archways had been one of the best-kept secrets of the early Masonic brotherhood. *The Royal Arch Degree. Architecture. Keystones.* It was all interconnected. The secret knowledge of how to use a wedged keystone to build a vaulted archway was part of the wisdom that had made the Masons such wealthy craftsmen, and it was a secret they guarded carefully. Keystones had always had a tradition of secrecy. And yet, the stone cylinder in the rosewood box was obviously something quite different. The Priory keystone—if this was indeed what they were holding— was not at all what Langdon had imagined.

"The Priory keystone is not my specialty," Langdon admitted. "My interest in the Holy Grail is primarily symbologic, so I tend to ignore the plethora of lore regarding how to actually find it."

Sophie's eyebrows arched. "*Find* the Holy Grail?"

Langdon gave an uneasy nod, speaking his next words carefully. "Sophie, according to Priory lore, the keystone is an encoded map . . . a map that reveals the hiding place of the Holy Grail."

Sophie's face went blank. "And you think this is it?"

Langdon didn't know what to say. Even to him it sounded unbelievable, and yet the keystone was the only logical conclusion he could muster. *An encrypted stone, hidden beneath the sign of the Rose.*

The idea that the cryptex had been designed by Leonardo da Vinci—former Grand Master of the Priory of Sion—shone as another tantalizing indicator that this was indeed the Priory keystone. *A former Grand Master's blueprint . . . brought to life centuries later by another Priory member.* The bond was too palpable to dismiss.

For the last decade, historians had been searching for the keystone in French churches. Grail seekers, familiar with the Priory's history of cryptic double-talk,

ROSE WINDOW, CHARTRES CATHEDRAL

had concluded *la clef de voûte* was a literal keystone—an architectural wedge—an engraved, encrypted stone, inserted into a vaulted archway in a church. *Beneath the sign of the Rose.* In architecture, there was no shortage of roses. *Rose windows. Rosette reliefs.* And, of course, an abundance of *cinquefoils*—the five-petaled decorative flowers often found at the top of archways, directly over the keystone. The hiding place seemed diabolically simple. The map to the Holy Grail was incorporated high in an archway of some forgotten church, mocking the blind churchgoers who wandered beneath it.

"This cryptex *can't* be the keystone," Sophie argued. "It's not old enough. I'm certain my grandfather made this. It can't be part of any ancient Grail legend."

"Actually," Langdon replied, feeling a tingle of excitement ripple through him, "the keystone is believed to have been created by the Priory sometime in the past couple of decades."

Sophie's eyes flashed disbelief. "But if this cryptex reveals the hiding place of the Holy Grail, why would my grandfather give it to *me*? I have no idea how to open it or what to do with it. I don't even know what the Holy Grail *is!*"

Langdon realized to his surprise that she was right. He had not yet had a chance to explain to Sophie the true nature of the Holy Grail. That story would have to wait. At the moment, they were focused on the keystone.

If that is indeed what this is. . . .

Against the hum of the bulletproof wheels beneath them, Langdon quickly explained to Sophie everything he had heard about the keystone. Allegedly, for centuries, the Priory's biggest secret—the location of the Holy Grail—was never written down. For security's sake, it was verbally transferred to each new rising *sénéchal* at a clandestine ceremony. However, at some point during the last century, whisperings began to surface that the Priory policy had changed. Perhaps it was on account of new electronic eavesdropping capabilities, but the Priory vowed never again even to *speak* the location of the sacred hiding place.

"But then how could they pass on the secret?" Sophie asked.

"That's where the keystone comes in," Langdon explained. "When one of the top four members died, the remaining three would choose from the lower echelons the next candidate to ascend as *sénéchal*. Rather than *telling* the new *sénéchal* where the Grail was hidden, they gave him a test through which he could prove he was worthy."

Sophie looked unsettled by this, and Langdon suddenly recalled her mentioning how her grandfather used to make treasure hunts for her—*preuves de mérite*. Admittedly, the keystone was a similar concept. Then again, tests like this were extremely common in secret societies. The best known was the Masons', wherein members ascended to higher degrees by proving they could keep a secret and by performing rituals and various tests of merit over many years. The tasks became progressively harder until they culminated in a successful candidate's induction as thirty-second-degree Mason.

"So the keystone is a *preuve de mérite*," Sophie said. "If a rising Priory *sénéchal* can open it, he proves himself worthy of the information it holds."

Langdon nodded. "I forgot you'd had experience with this sort of thing."

"Not only with my grandfather. In cryptology, that's called a 'self-authorizing language.' That is, if you're smart enough to read it, you're permitted to know what is being said."

Langdon hesitated a moment. "Sophie, you realize that if this is indeed the keystone, your grandfather's access to it implies he was exceptionally powerful within the Priory of Sion. He would have to have been one of the highest four members."

Sophie sighed. "He was powerful in a secret society. I'm certain of it. I can only assume it was the Priory."

Langdon did a double take. "You *knew* he was in a secret society?"

"I saw some things I wasn't supposed to see ten years ago. We haven't spoken since." She paused. "My grandfather was not only a ranking top member of the group . . . I believe he was *the* top member."

Langdon could not believe what she had just said. "Grand Master? But . . . there's no way you could know that!"

"I'd rather not talk about it." Sophie looked away, her expression as determined as it was pained.

Langdon sat in stunned silence. *Jacques Saunière? Grand Master?* Despite the astonishing repercussions if it were true, Langdon had the eerie sensation it almost made perfect sense. After all, previous Priory Grand Masters had *also* been distinguished public figures with artistic souls. Proof of that fact had been uncovered

ÉTPACTUMESTEUMIN
SABBATOSECUNdAPRIMO A
bIREPERSCCETESAISGIPULIAUTEMILLIRISCOE
PERUNTUELLERESPICASETFRICANTESMANTbUS + MANdU
CAbANTQUIdAMAUTEMdEFARISAEISdT
CEbANTEIECCEQVIAFACIUNTdISCIPVLITVISAb
bATIS + QUOdNONLICETRESPONdENSAUTEMINS
SÉTXTTAdEQSNUMQUAMbOC
LECISTISQVOdFECITdAUTdQVANdO
ESURVTIPSEETQVICUMEOERAI + INTROIbITINdAMVM
dEIEXPANESPROPOSITIONIS   REdIS
MANdVCAUITETdEdITETQVI   bIES
CVMERANTUXĞ QUIbVSNO
NILICEbATMANdVCARESINON   SOLIS SACERdOTIbVS

LES DOSSIERS SECRETS

years ago in Paris's Bibliothèque Nationale in papers that became known as *Les Dossiers Secrets*.

Every Priory historian and Grail buff had read the *Dossiers*. Cataloged under Number 4° lm¹ 249, the *Dossiers Secrets* had been authenticated by many specialists and incontrovertibly confirmed what historians had suspected for a long time: Priory Grand Masters included Leonardo da Vinci, Botticelli, Sir Isaac Newton, Victor Hugo, and, more recently, Jean Cocteau, the famous Parisian artist.

Why not Jacques Saunière?

Langdon's incredulity intensified with the realization that he had been slated to *meet* Saunière tonight. *The Priory Grand Master called a meeting with me. Why? To make artistic small talk?* It suddenly seemed unlikely. After all, if Langdon's instincts were correct, the Grand Master of the Priory of Sion had just transferred the brotherhood's legendary keystone to his granddaughter and simultaneously commanded her to find Robert Langdon.

Inconceivable!

Langdon's imagination could conjure no set of circumstances that would explain Saunière's behavior. Even if Saunière feared his own death, there were three *sénéchaux* who also possessed the secret and therefore guaranteed the Priory's security. Why would Saunière take such an enormous risk giving his granddaughter the

![Les Dossiers Secrets illustration]

LES DOSSIERS SECRETS

keystone, especially when the two of them didn't get along? And why involve Langdon . . . a total stranger?

A piece of this puzzle is missing, Langdon thought.

The answers were apparently going to have to wait. The sound of the slowing engine caused them both to look up. Gravel crunched beneath the tires. *Why is he pulling over already?* Langdon wondered. Vernet had told them he would take them well outside the city to safety. The truck decelerated to a crawl and made its way over unexpectedly rough terrain. Sophie shot Langdon an uneasy look, hastily closing the cryptex box and latching it. Langdon slipped his jacket back on.

When the truck came to a stop, the engine remained idling as the locks on the rear doors began to turn. When the doors swung open, Langdon was surprised to see they were parked in a wooded area, well off the road. Vernet stepped into view, a strained look in his eye. In his hand, he held a pistol.

"I'm sorry about this," he said. "I really have no choice."

ANDRÉ VERNET looked awkward with a pistol, but his eyes shone with a determination that Langdon sensed would be unwise to test.

"I'm afraid I must insist," Vernet said, training the weapon on the two of them in the back of the idling truck. "Set the box down."

Sophie clutched the box to her chest. "You said you and my grandfather were friends."

"I have a duty to protect your grandfather's assets," Vernet replied. "And that is exactly what I am doing. Now set the box on the floor."

"My grandfather entrusted this to me!" Sophie declared.

"Do it," Vernet commanded, raising the gun.

Sophie set the box at her feet.

Langdon watched the gun barrel swing now in his direction.

"Mr. Langdon," Vernet said, "you will bring the box over to me. And be aware that I'm asking you because *you* I would not hesitate to shoot."

Langdon stared at the banker in disbelief. "Why are you doing this?"

"Why do you imagine?" Vernet snapped, his accented English terse now. "To protect my client's assets."

"*We* are your clients now," Sophie said.

Vernet's visage turned ice-cold, an eerie transformation. "Mademoiselle Neveu, I don't know *how* you got that key and account number tonight, but it seems obvious that foul play was involved. Had I known the extent of your crimes, I would never have helped you leave the bank."

"I told you," Sophie said, "we had nothing to do with my grandfather's death!"

Vernet looked at Langdon. "And yet the radio claims you are wanted not only for the murder of Jacques Saunière but for those of three *other* men as well?"

"What!" Langdon was thunderstruck. *Three more murders?* The coincidental number hit him harder than the fact that he was the prime suspect. It seemed too unlikely to be a coincidence. *The three sénéchaux?* Langdon's eyes dropped to the rosewood box. *If the sénéchaux were murdered, Saunière had no options. He had to transfer the keystone to someone.*

"The police can sort that out when I turn you in," Vernet said. "I have gotten my bank involved too far already."

Sophie glared at Vernet. "You obviously have no intention of turning us in. You would have driven us back to the bank. And instead you bring us out here and hold us at gunpoint?"

"Your grandfather hired me for one reason—to keep his possessions both safe and private. Whatever this box contains, I have no intention of letting it become a piece of cataloged evidence in a police investigation. Mr. Langdon, bring me the box."

Sophie shook her head. "Don't do it."

A gunshot roared, and a bullet tore into the wall above him. The reverberation shook the back of the truck as a spent shell clinked onto the cargo floor.

Shit! Langdon froze.

Vernet spoke more confidently now. "Mr. Langdon, pick up the box."

Langdon lifted the box.

"Now bring it over to me." Vernet was taking dead aim, standing on the ground behind the rear bumper, his gun outstretched into the cargo hold now.

Box in hand, Langdon moved across the hold toward the open door.

I've got to do something! Langdon thought. *I'm about to hand over the Priory keystone!* As Langdon moved toward the doorway, his position of higher ground became more pronounced, and he began wondering if he could somehow use it to his advantage. Vernet's gun, though raised, was at Langdon's knee level. *A well-placed kick perhaps?* Unfortunately, as Langdon neared, Vernet seemed to sense the dangerous dynamic developing, and he took several steps back, repositioning himself six feet away. Well out of reach.

Vernet commanded, "Place the box beside the door."

Seeing no options, Langdon knelt down and set the rosewood box at the edge of the cargo hold, directly in front of the open doors.

"Now stand up."

Langdon began to stand up but paused, spying the small, spent pistol shell on the floor beside the truck's precision-crafted doorsill.

"Stand up, and step away from the box."

Langdon paused a moment longer, eyeing the metal threshold. Then he stood. As he did, he discreetly brushed the shell over the edge onto the narrow ledge that was the door's lower sill. Fully upright now, Langdon stepped backward.

"Return to the back wall and turn around."

Langdon obeyed.

VERNET COULD FEEL his own heart pounding. Aiming the gun with his right hand, he reached now with his left for the wooden box. He discovered that it was far too heavy. *I need two hands.* Turning his eyes back to his captives, he calculated the risk. Both were a good fifteen feet away, at the far end of the cargo hold, facing away from him. Vernet made up his mind. Quickly, he laid down the gun on the bumper, lifted the box with two hands, and set it on the ground, immediately grabbing the gun again and aiming it back into the hold. Neither of his prisoners had moved.

Perfect. Now all that remained was to close and lock the door. Leaving the box on the ground for the moment, he grabbed the metal door and began to heave it closed. As the door swung past him, Vernet reached up to grab the single bolt that needed to be slid into place. The door closed with a thud, and Vernet quickly grabbed the bolt, pulling it to the left. The bolt slid a few inches and crunched to an unexpected halt, not lining up with its sleeve. *What's going on?* Vernet pulled again, but the bolt wouldn't lock. The mechanism was not properly aligned. *The door isn't fully closed!* Feeling a surge of panic, Vernet shoved hard against the outside of the door, but it refused to budge. *Something is blocking it!* Vernet turned to throw full shoulder into the door, but this time the door exploded outward, striking Vernet in the face and sending him reeling backward onto the ground, his nose shattering in pain. The gun flew as Vernet reached for his face and felt the warm blood running from his nose.

Robert Langdon hit the ground somewhere nearby, and Vernet tried to get up, but he couldn't see. His vision blurred and he fell backward again. Sophie Neveu was shouting. Moments later, Vernet felt a cloud of dirt and exhaust billowing over him. He heard the crunching of tires on gravel and sat up just in time to see the truck's wide wheelbase fail to navigate a turn. There was a crash as the front bumper clipped a tree. The engine roared, and the tree bent. Finally, it was the bumper that gave, tearing half off. The armored car lurched away, its front bumper dragging. When the truck reached the paved access road, a shower of sparks lit up the night, trailing the truck as it sped away.

Vernet turned his eyes back to the ground where the truck had been parked. Even in the faint moonlight he could see there was nothing there.

The wooden box was gone.

THE UNMARKED FIAT sedan departing Castel Gandolfo snaked downward through the Alban Hills into the valley below. In the back seat, Bishop Aringarosa smiled, feeling the weight of the bearer bonds in the briefcase on his lap and wondering how long it would be before he and the Teacher could make the exchange.

Twenty million euro.

The sum would buy Aringarosa power far more valuable than that.

As his car sped back toward Rome, Aringarosa again found himself wondering why the Teacher had not yet contacted him. Pulling his cell phone from his cassock pocket, he checked the carrier signal. Extremely faint.

"Cell service is intermittent up here," the driver said, glancing at him in the rearview mirror. "In about five minutes, we'll be out of the mountains, and service improves."

"Thank you." Aringarosa felt a sudden surge of concern. *No service in the mountains?* Maybe the Teacher had been trying to reach him all this time. Maybe something had gone terribly wrong.

Quickly, Aringarosa checked the phone's voice mail. Nothing. Then again, he realized, the Teacher never would have left a recorded message; he was a man who took enormous care with his communications. Nobody understood better than the Teacher the perils of speaking openly in this modern world. Electronic eavesdropping had played a major role in how he had gathered his astonishing array of secret knowledge.

For this reason, he takes extra precautions.

Unfortunately, the Teacher's protocols for caution included a refusal to give Aringarosa any kind of contact number. *I alone will initiate contact,* the Teacher had informed him. *So keep your phone close.* Now that Aringarosa realized his phone might not have been working properly, he feared what the Teacher might think if he had been repeatedly phoning with no answer.

He'll think something is wrong.

Or that I failed to get the bonds.

The bishop broke a light sweat.

Or worse . . . that I took the money and ran!

Chapter 51

EVEN AT A MODEST sixty kilometers an hour, the dangling front bumper of the armored truck grated against the deserted suburban road with a grinding roar, spraying sparks up onto the hood.

We've got to get off the road, Langdon thought.

He could barely even see where they were headed. The truck's lone working headlight had been knocked off-center and was casting a skewed sidelong beam into the woods beside the country highway. Apparently the *armor* in this "armored truck" referred only to the cargo hold and not the front end.

Sophie sat in the passenger seat, staring blankly at the rosewood box on her lap.

"Are you okay?" Langdon asked.

Sophie looked shaken. "Do you believe him?"

"About the three additional murders? Absolutely. It answers a lot of questions—the issue of your grandfather's desperation to pass on the keystone, as well as the intensity with which Fache is hunting me."

"No, I meant about Vernet trying to protect his bank."

Langdon glanced over. "As opposed to?"

"Taking the keystone for himself."

Langdon had not even considered it. "How would he even know what this box contains?"

"His bank stored it. He knew my grandfather. Maybe he knew things. He might have decided he wanted the Grail for himself."

Langdon shook his head. Vernet hardly seemed the type. "In my experience, there are only two reasons people seek the Grail. Either they are naive and believe they are searching for the long-lost Cup of Christ . . ."

"Or?"

"Or they know the truth and are threatened by it. Many groups throughout history have sought to destroy the Grail."

The silence between them accentuated the sound of the scraping bumper. They had driven a few kilometers now, and as Langdon watched the cascade of sparks coming off the front of the truck, he wondered if it was dangerous. Either way, if they passed another car, it would certainly draw attention. Langdon made up his mind.

"I'm going to see if I can bend this bumper back."

Pulling onto the shoulder, he brought the truck to a stop.

Silence at last.

As Langdon walked toward the front of the truck, he felt surprisingly alert. Staring into the barrel of yet another gun tonight had given him a second wind. He took a deep breath of nighttime air and tried to get his wits about him. Accompanying the gravity of being a hunted man, Langdon was starting to feel the ponderous weight of responsibility, the prospect that he and Sophie might actually be holding an encrypted set of directions to one of the most enduring mysteries of all time.

As if this burden were not great enough, Langdon now realized that any possibility of finding a way to return the keystone to the Priory had just evaporated. News of the three additional murders had dire implications. *The Priory has been infiltrated. They are compromised.* The brotherhood was obviously being watched, or there was a mole within the ranks. It seemed to explain why Saunière might have transferred the keystone to Sophie and Langdon—people *outside* the brotherhood, people he knew were not compromised. *We can't very well give the keystone back to the brotherhood.* Even if Langdon had any idea how to find a Priory member, chances were good that whoever stepped forward to take the keystone could be the enemy himself. For the moment, at least, it seemed the keystone was in Sophie and Langdon's hands, whether they wanted it or not.

The truck's front end looked worse than Langdon had imagined. The left head-light was gone, and the right one looked like an eyeball dangling from its socket. Langdon straightened it, and it dislodged again. The only good news was that the front bumper had been torn almost clean off. Langdon gave it a hard kick and sensed he might be able to break it off entirely.

As he repeatedly kicked the twisted metal, Langdon recalled his earlier conversation with Sophie. *My grandfather left me a phone message,* Sophie had told him. *He said he needed to tell me the truth about my family.* At the time it had meant nothing, but now, knowing the Priory of Sion was involved, Langdon felt a startling new possibility emerge.

The bumper broke off suddenly with a crash. Langdon paused to catch his breath. At least the truck would no longer look like a Fourth of July sparkler. He grabbed the bumper and began dragging it out of sight into the woods, wondering where they should go next. They had no idea how to open the cryptex, or why Saunière had given it to them. Unfortunately, their survival tonight seemed to depend on getting answers to those very questions.

We need help, Langdon decided. *Professional help.*

In the world of the Holy Grail and the Priory of Sion, that meant only one man. The challenge, of course, would be selling the idea to Sophie.

INSIDE THE ARMORED CAR, while Sophie waited for Langdon to return, she could feel the weight of the rosewood box on her lap and resented it. *Why did my grandfather give this to me?* She had not the slightest idea what to do with it.

Think, Sophie! Use your head. Grand-père is trying to tell you something!

Opening the box, she eyed the cryptex's dials. *A proof of merit.* She could feel her grandfather's hand at work. *The keystone is a map that can be followed only by the worthy.* It sounded like her grandfather to the core.

Lifting the cryptex out of the box, Sophie ran her fingers over the dials. *Five letters.* She rotated the dials one by one. The mechanism moved smoothly. She aligned the disks such that her chosen letters lined up between the cryptex's two brass alignment arrows on either end of the cylinder. The dials now spelled a five-letter word that Sophie knew was absurdly obvious.

G-R-A-I-L.

Gently, she held the two ends of the cylinder and pulled, applying pressure slowly. The cryptex didn't budge. She heard the vinegar inside gurgle and stopped pulling. Then she tried again.

V-I-N-C-I

Again, no movement.

V-O-U-T-E

Nothing. The cryptex remained locked solid.

Frowning, she replaced it in the rosewood box and closed the lid. Looking outside at Langdon, Sophie felt grateful he was with her tonight. *P.S. Find Robert Langdon.* Her grandfather's rationale for including him was now clear. Sophie was not equipped to understand her grandfather's intentions, and so he had assigned Robert Langdon as her guide. A tutor to oversee her education. Unfortunately for Langdon, he had turned out to be far more than a tutor tonight. He had become the target of Bezu Fache . . . and some unseen force intent on possessing the Holy Grail.

Whatever the Grail turns out to be.

Sophie wondered if finding out was worth her life.

As the armored truck accelerated again, Langdon was pleased how much more smoothly it drove. "Do you know how to get to Versailles?"

Sophie eyed him. "Sightseeing?"

"No, I have a plan. There's a religious historian I know who lives near Versailles. I can't remember exactly where, but we can look it up. I've been to his estate a few times. His name is Leigh Teabing. He's a former British Royal Historian."

"And he lives in Paris?"

"Teabing's life passion is the Grail. When whisperings of the Priory keystone surfaced about fifteen years ago, he moved to France to search churches in hopes of finding it. He's written some books on the keystone and the Grail. He may be able to help us figure out how to open it and what to do with it."

Sophie's eyes were wary. "Can you trust him?"

"Trust him to what? Not steal the information?"

"And not to turn us in."

"I don't intend to tell him we're wanted by the police. I'm hoping he'll take us in until we can sort all this out."

"Robert, has it occurred to you that every television in France is probably getting ready to broadcast our pictures? Bezu Fache always uses the media to his advantage. He'll make it impossible for us to move around without being recognized."

Terrific, Langdon thought. *My French TV debut will be on "Paris's Most Wanted."* At least Jonas Faukman would be pleased; every time Langdon made the news, his book sales jumped.

"Is this man a good enough friend?" Sophie asked.

Langdon doubted Teabing was someone who watched television, especially at this hour, but still the question deserved consideration. Instinct told Langdon that Teabing would be totally trustworthy. An ideal safe harbor. Considering the circumstances, Teabing would probably trip over himself to help them as much as possible. Not only did he owe Langdon a favor, but Teabing was a Grail researcher, and Sophie claimed her grandfather was the actual *Grand Master* of the Priory of Sion. If Teabing heard *that,* he would salivate at the thought of helping them figure this out.

"Teabing could be a powerful ally," Langdon said. *Depending on how much you want to tell him.*

"Fache probably will be offering a monetary reward."

Langdon laughed. "Believe me, money is the last thing this guy needs." Leigh Teabing was wealthy in the way small countries were wealthy. A descendant of Britain's First Duke of Lancaster, Teabing had gotten his money the old-fashioned way—he'd inherited it. His estate outside of Paris was a seventeenth-century palace with two private lakes.

Langdon had first met Teabing several years ago through the British Broadcasting Corporation. Teabing had approached the BBC with a proposal for a historical documentary in which he would expose the explosive history of the Holy Grail to a mainstream television audience. The BBC producers loved Teabing's hot premise, his research, and his credentials, but they had concerns that the concept was so shocking and hard to swallow that the network might end up tarnishing its reputation for quality journalism. At Teabing's suggestion, the BBC solved its credibility fears by soliciting three cameos from respected historians from around the world, all of whom corroborated the stunning nature of the Holy Grail secret with their own research.

Langdon had been among those chosen.

The BBC had flown Langdon to Teabing's Paris estate for the filming. He sat before cameras in Teabing's opulent drawing room and shared his story, admitting his initial skepticism on hearing of the alternate Holy Grail story, then describing how years of research had persuaded him that the story was true. Finally, Langdon offered some of his own research—a series of symbologic connections that strongly supported the seemingly controversial claims.

When the program aired in Britain, despite its ensemble cast and well-documented evidence, the premise rubbed so hard against the grain of popular

Christian thought that it instantly confronted a firestorm of hostility. It never aired in the States, but the repercussions echoed across the Atlantic. Shortly afterward, Langdon received a postcard from an old friend—the Catholic Bishop of Philadelphia. The card simply read: *Et tu, Robert?*

"Robert," Sophie asked, "you're *certain* we can trust this man?"

"Absolutely. We're colleagues, he doesn't need money, and I happen to know he despises the French authorities. The French government taxes him at absurd rates because he bought a historic landmark. He'll be in no hurry to cooperate with Fache."

Sophie stared out at the dark roadway. "If we go to him, how much do you want to tell him?"

Langdon looked unconcerned. "Believe me, Leigh Teabing knows more about the Priory of Sion and the Holy Grail than anyone on earth."

Sophie eyed him. "More than my grandfather?"

"I meant more than anyone *outside* the brotherhood."

"How do you know Teabing isn't a member of the brotherhood?"

"Teabing has spent his life trying to broadcast the truth about the Holy Grail. The Priory's oath is to keep its true nature hidden."

"Sounds to me like a conflict of interest."

Langdon understood her concerns. Saunière had given the cryptex directly to Sophie, and although she didn't know what it contained or what she was supposed to do with it, she was hesitant to involve a total stranger. Considering the information potentially enclosed, the instinct was probably a good one. "We don't need to tell Teabing about the keystone immediately. Or at all, even. His house will give us a place to hide and think, and maybe when we talk to him about the Grail, you'll start to have an idea why your grandfather gave this to you."

"*Us,*" Sophie reminded.

Langdon felt a humble pride and wondered yet again why Saunière had included him.

"Do you know more or less where Mr. Teabing lives?" Sophie asked.

"His estate is called Château Villette."

Sophie turned with an incredulous look. "*The* Château Villette?"

"That's the one."

"Nice friends."

"You know the estate?"

"I've passed it. It's in the castle district. Twenty minutes from here."

Langdon frowned. "That far?"

"Yes, which will give you enough time to tell me what the Holy Grail *really* is."

Langdon paused. "I'll tell you at Teabing's. He and I specialize in different areas of the legend, so between the two of us, you'll get the full story." Langdon smiled. "Besides, the Grail has been Teabing's life, and hearing the story of the Holy Grail from Leigh Teabing will be like hearing the theory of relativity from Einstein himself."

"Let's hope Leigh doesn't mind late-night visitors."

"For the record, it's *Sir* Leigh." Langdon had made that mistake only once. "Teabing is quite a character. He was knighted by the Queen several years back after composing an extensive history on the House of York."

Sophie looked over. "You're kidding, right? We're going to visit a *knight?*"

Langdon gave an awkward smile. "We're on a Grail quest, Sophie. Who better to help us than a knight?"

THE SPRAWLING 185-acre estate of Château Villette was located twenty-five minutes northwest of Paris in the environs of Versailles. Designed by François Mansart in 1668 for the Count of Aufflay, it was one of Paris's most significant historical châteaux. Complete with two rectangular lakes and gardens designed by Le Nôtre, Château Villette was more of a modest castle than a mansion. The estate fondly had become known as *la Petite Versailles.*

Langdon brought the armored truck to a shuddering stop at the foot of the mile-long driveway. Beyond the imposing security gate, Sir Leigh Teabing's residence rose on a meadow in the distance. The sign on the gate was in English: PRIVATE PROPERTY. NO TRESPASSING.

As if to proclaim his home a British Isle unto itself, Teabing had not only posted his signs in English, but he had installed his gate's intercom entry system on the

CHÂTEAU VILLETTE

right-hand side of the truck—the passenger's side everywhere in Europe except England.

Sophie gave the misplaced intercom an odd look. "And if someone arrives without a passenger?"

"Don't ask." Langdon had already been through that with Teabing. "He prefers things the way they are at home."

Sophie rolled down her window. "Robert, you'd better do the talking."

Langdon shifted his position, leaning out across Sophie to press the intercom button. As he did, an alluring whiff of Sophie's perfume filled his nostrils, and he realized how close they were. He waited there, awkwardly prone, while a telephone began ringing over the small speaker.

Finally, the intercom crackled and an irritated French accent spoke. "Château Villette. Who is calling?"

"This is Robert Langdon," Langdon called out, sprawled across Sophie's lap. "I'm a friend of Sir Leigh Teabing. I need his help."

"My master is sleeping. As was I. What is your business with him?"

"It is a private matter. One of great interest to him."

"Then I'm sure he will be pleased to receive you in the morning."

Langdon shifted his weight. "It's quite important."

"As is Sir Leigh's sleep. If you are a friend, then you are aware he is in poor health."

Sir Leigh Teabing had suffered from polio as a child and now wore leg braces and walked with crutches, but Langdon had found him such a lively and colorful man on his last visit that it hardly seemed an infirmity. "If you would, please tell him I have uncovered new information about the Grail. Information that cannot wait until morning."

There was a long pause.

Langdon and Sophie waited, the truck idling loudly.

A full minute passed.

Finally, someone spoke. "My good man, I daresay you are still on Harvard Standard Time." The voice was crisp and light.

Langdon grinned, recognizing the thick British accent. "Leigh, my apologies for waking you at this obscene hour."

"My manservant tells me that not only are you in Paris, but you speak of the Grail."

"I thought that might get you out of bed."

"And so it has."

"Any chance you'd open the gate for an old friend?"

"Those who seek the truth are more than friends. They are brothers."

Langdon rolled his eyes at Sophie, well accustomed to Teabing's predilection for dramatic antics.

"Indeed I will open the gate," Teabing proclaimed, "but first I must confirm your heart is true. A test of your honor. You will answer three questions."

Langdon groaned, whispering at Sophie. "Bear with me here. As I mentioned, he's something of a character."

"Your first question," Teabing declared, his tone Herculean. "Shall I serve you coffee, or tea?"

Langdon knew Teabing's feelings about the American phenomenon of coffee. "Tea," he replied. "Earl Grey."

"Excellent. Your second question. Milk or sugar?"

Langdon hesitated.

"Milk," Sophie whispered in his ear. "I think the British take milk."

"Milk," Langdon said.

Silence.

"Sugar?"

Teabing made no reply.

Wait! Langdon now recalled the bitter beverage he had been served on his last visit and realized this question was a trick. *"Lemon!"* he declared. "Earl Grey with *lemon.*"

"Indeed." Teabing sounded deeply amused now. "And finally, I must make the most grave of inquiries." Teabing paused and then spoke in a solemn tone. "In which year did a Harvard sculler last outrow an Oxford man at Henley?"

Langdon had no idea, but he could imagine only one reason the question had been asked. "Surely such a travesty has never occurred."

The gate clicked open. "Your heart is true, my friend. You may pass."

*M*ONSIEUR *VERNET!"* The night manager of the Depository Bank of Zurich felt relieved to hear the bank president's voice on the phone. "Where did you go, sir? The police are here, everyone is waiting for you!"

"I have a little problem," the bank president said, sounding distressed. "I need your help right away."

You have more than a little problem, the manager thought. The police had entirely surrounded the bank and were threatening to have the DCPJ captain himself show up with the warrant the bank had demanded. "How can I help you, sir?"

"Armored truck number three. I need to find it."

Puzzled, the manager checked his delivery schedule. "It's here. Downstairs at the loading dock."

"Actually, no. The truck was stolen by the two individuals the police are tracking."

"What? How did they drive out?"

"I can't go into the specifics on the phone, but we have a situation here that could potentially be extremely unfortunate for the bank."

"What do you need me to do, sir?"

"I'd like you to activate the truck's emergency transponder."

The night manager's eyes moved to the LoJack control box across the room. Like many armored cars, each of the bank's trucks had been equipped with a radio-controlled homing device, which could be activated remotely from the bank. The manager had only used the emergency system once, after a hijacking, and it had worked flawlessly—locating the truck and transmitting the coordinates to the authorities automatically. Tonight, however, the manager had the impression the president was hoping for a bit more prudence. "Sir, you are aware that if I activate the LoJack system, the transponder will simultaneously inform the authorities that we have a problem."

Vernet was silent for several seconds. "Yes, I know. Do it anyway. Truck number three. I'll hold. I need the exact location of that truck the instant you have it."

"Right away, sir."

THIRTY SECONDS LATER, forty kilometers away, hidden in the undercarriage of the armored truck, a tiny transponder blinked to life.

Chapter 54

*A*s LANGDON and Sophie drove the armored truck up the winding, poplar-lined driveway toward the house, Sophie could already feel her muscles relaxing. It was a relief to be off the road, and she could think of few safer places to get their feet under them than this private, gated estate owned by a good-natured foreigner.

They turned into the sweeping circular driveway, and Château Villette came into view on their right. Three stories tall and at least sixty meters long, the edifice had gray stone facing illuminated by outside spotlights. The coarse facade stood in stark juxtaposition to the immaculately landscaped gardens and glassy pond.

The inside lights were just now coming on.

Rather than driving to the front door, Langdon pulled into a parking area nestled in the evergreens. "No reason to risk being spotted from the road," he said. "Or having Leigh wonder why we arrived in a wrecked armored truck."

Sophie nodded. "What do we do with the cryptex? We probably shouldn't leave it out here, but if Leigh sees it, he'll certainly want to know what it is."

"Not to worry," Langdon said, removing his jacket as he stepped out of the car. He wrapped the tweed coat around the box and held the bundle in his arms like a baby.

Sophie looked dubious. "Subtle."

"Teabing never answers his own door; he prefers to make an entrance. I'll find somewhere inside to stash this before he joins us." Langdon paused. "Actually, I should probably warn you before you meet him. Sir Leigh has a sense of humor that people often find a bit . . . strange."

Sophie doubted anything tonight would strike her as strange anymore.

The pathway to the main entrance was hand-laid cobblestone. It curved to a door of carved oak and cherry with a brass knocker the size of a grapefruit. Before Sophie could grasp the knocker, the door swung open from within.

A prim and elegant butler stood before them, making final adjustments on the white tie and tuxedo he had apparently just donned. He looked to be about fifty, with refined features and an austere expression that left little doubt he was unamused by their presence here.

"Sir Leigh will be down presently," he declared, his accent thick French. "He is dressing. He prefers not to greet visitors while wearing only a nightshirt. May I take your coat?" He scowled at the bunched-up tweed in Langdon's arms.

"Thank you, I'm fine."

"Of course you are. Right this way, please."

The butler guided them through a lush marble foyer into an exquisitely adorned drawing room, softly lit by tassel-draped Victorian lamps. The air inside smelled antediluvian, regal somehow, with traces of pipe tobacco, tea leaves, cooking sherry, and the earthen aroma of stone architecture. Against the far wall, flanked between two glistening suits of chain mail armor, was a rough-hewn fireplace large enough to roast an ox. Walking to the hearth, the butler knelt and touched a match to a pre-laid arrangement of oak logs and kindling. A fire quickly crackled to life.

The man stood, straightening his jacket. "His master requests that you make yourselves at home." With that, he departed, leaving Langdon and Sophie alone.

Sophie wondered which of the fireside antiques she was supposed to sit on—the Renaissance velvet divan, the rustic eagle-claw rocker, or the pair of stone pews that looked like they'd been lifted from some Byzantine temple.

Langdon unwrapped the cryptex from his coat, walked to the velvet

INTERIOR MARBLE STAIRCASE, CHÂTEAU VILLETTE

divan, and slid the wooden box deep underneath it, well out of sight. Then, shaking out his jacket, he put it back on, smoothed the lapels, and smiled at Sophie as he sat down directly over the stashed treasure.

The divan it is, Sophie thought, taking a seat beside him.

As she stared into the growing fire, enjoying the warmth, Sophie had the sensation that her grandfather would have loved this room. The dark wood paneling was bedecked with Old Master paintings, one of which Sophie recognized as a Poussin, her grandfather's second-favorite painter. On the mantel above the fireplace, an alabaster bust of Isis watched over the room.

Beneath the Egyptian goddess, inside the fireplace, two stone gargoyles served as andirons, their mouths gaping to reveal their menacing hollow throats. Gargoyles had always terrified Sophie as a child; that was, until her grandfather cured her of the fear by taking her atop Notre Dame Cathedral in a rainstorm. "Princess, look at these silly creatures," he had told her, pointing to the gargoyle rainspouts with their mouths gushing water. "Do you hear that funny sound in their throats?" Sophie nodded, having to smile at the burping sound of the water gurgling through their throats. "They're *gargling*," her grandfather told her. "*Gargariser!* And that's where they get the silly name 'gargoyles.' " Sophie had never again been afraid.

GARGOYLE AT NOTRE DAME CATHEDRAL, PARIS

The fond memory caused Sophie a pang of sadness as the harsh reality of the murder gripped her again. *Grand-père is gone.* She pictured the cryptex under the divan and wondered if Leigh Teabing would have any idea how to open it. *Or if we even should ask him.* Sophie's grandfather's final words had instructed her to find Robert Langdon. He had said nothing about involving anyone else. *We needed somewhere to hide,* Sophie said, deciding to trust Robert's judgment.

"Sir Robert!" a voice bellowed somewhere behind them. "I see you travel with a maiden."

Langdon stood up. Sophie jumped to her feet as well. The voice had come from the top of a curled staircase that snaked up to the shadows of the second floor. At the top of the stairs, a form moved in the shadows, only his silhouette visible.

"Good evening," Langdon called up. "Sir Leigh, may I present Sophie Neveu."

"An honor." Teabing moved into the light.

"Thank you for having us," Sophie said, now seeing the man wore metal leg braces and used crutches. He was coming down one stair at a time. "I realize it's quite late."

"It is so late, my dear, it's early." He laughed. *"Vous n'êtes pas Américaine?"*

Sophie shook her head. *"Parisienne."*

"Your English is superb."

"Thank you. I studied at the Royal Holloway."

"So then, that explains it." Teabing hobbled lower through the shadows. "Perhaps Robert told you I schooled just down the road at Oxford." Teabing fixed Langdon with a devilish smile. "Of course, I also applied to Harvard as my safety school."

Their host arrived at the bottom of the stairs, appearing to Sophie no more like a knight than Sir Elton John. Portly and ruby-faced, Sir Leigh Teabing had bushy red hair and jovial hazel eyes that seemed to twinkle as he spoke. He wore pleated pants and a roomy silk shirt under a paisley vest. Despite the aluminum braces on his legs, he carried himself with a resilient, vertical dignity that seemed more a by-product of noble ancestry than any kind of conscious effort.

Teabing arrived and extended a hand to Langdon. "Robert, you've lost weight."

Langdon grinned. "And you've found some."

Teabing laughed heartily, patting his rotund belly. "Touché. My only carnal pleasures these days seem to be culinary." Turning now to Sophie, he gently took her hand, bowing his head slightly, breathing lightly on her fingers, and diverting his eyes. "M'lady."

Sophie glanced at Langdon, uncertain whether she'd stepped back in time or into a nuthouse.

The butler who had answered the door now entered carrying a tea service, which he arranged on a table in front of the fireplace.

"This is Rémy Legaludec," Teabing said, "my manservant."

The slender butler gave a stiff nod and disappeared yet again.

"Rémy is *Lyonnais,*" Teabing whispered, as if it were an unfortunate disease. "But he does sauces quite nicely."

Langdon looked amused. "I would have thought you'd import an English staff?"

"Good heavens, no! I would not wish a British chef on anyone except the French tax collectors." He glanced over at Sophie. "*Pardonnez-moi,* Mademoiselle Neveu. Please be assured that my distaste for the French extends only to politics and the soccer pitch. Your government steals my money, and your football squad recently humiliated us."

Sophie offered an easy smile.

Teabing eyed her a moment and then looked at Langdon. "Something has happened. You both look shaken."

Langdon nodded. "We've had an interesting night, Leigh."

"No doubt. You arrive on my doorstep unannounced in the middle of the night speaking of the Grail. Tell me, is this indeed about the Grail, or did you simply say that because you know it is the lone topic for which I would rouse myself in the middle of the night?"

A little of both, Sophie thought, picturing the cryptex hidden beneath the couch.

"Leigh," Langdon said, "we'd like to talk to you about the Priory of Sion."

Teabing's bushy eyebrows arched with intrigue. "The keepers. So this is indeed about the Grail. You say you come with information? Something new, Robert?"

"Perhaps. We're not quite sure. We might have a better idea if we could get some information from you first."

Teabing wagged his finger. "Ever the wily American. A game of quid pro quo. Very well. I am at your service. What is it I can tell you?"

Langdon sighed. "I was hoping you would be kind enough to explain to Ms. Neveu the true nature of the Holy Grail."

Teabing looked stunned. "She doesn't *know?*"

Langdon shook his head.

The smile that grew on Teabing's face was almost obscene. "Robert, you've brought me a *virgin?*"

Langdon winced, glancing at Sophie. "*Virgin* is the term Grail enthusiasts use to describe anyone who has never heard the true Grail story."

Teabing turned eagerly to Sophie. "How much do you know, my dear?"

Sophie quickly outlined what Langdon had explained earlier—the Priory of Sion, the Knights Templar, the Sangreal documents, and the Holy Grail, which many claimed was not a cup . . . but rather something far more powerful.

"That's *all?*" Teabing fired Langdon a scandalous look. "Robert, I thought you were a gentleman. You've robbed her of the climax!"

"I know, I thought perhaps you and I could . . ." Langdon apparently decided the unseemly metaphor had gone far enough.

Teabing already had Sophie locked in his twinkling gaze. "You are a Grail virgin, my dear. And trust me, you will never forget your first time."

EATED ON the divan beside Langdon, Sophie drank her tea and ate a scone, feeling the welcome effects of caffeine and food. Sir Leigh Teabing was beaming as he awkwardly paced before the open fire, his leg braces clicking on the stone hearth.

"The Holy Grail," Teabing said, his voice sermonic. "Most people ask me only *where* it is. I fear that is a question I may never answer." He turned and looked directly at Sophie. "However . . . the far more relevant question is this: *What* is the Holy Grail?"

Sophie sensed a rising air of academic anticipation now in both of her male companions.

"To fully understand the Grail," Teabing continued, "we must first understand the Bible. How well do you know the New Testament?"

Sophie shrugged. "Not at all, really. I was raised by a man who worshipped Leonardo da Vinci."

Teabing looked both startled and pleased. "An enlightened soul. Superb! Then you must be aware that Leonardo was one of the keepers of the secret of the Holy Grail. And he hid clues in his art."

"Robert told me as much, yes."

"And Da Vinci's views on the New Testament?"

"I have no idea."

Teabing's eyes turned mirthful as he motioned to the bookshelf across the room. "Robert, would you mind? On the bottom shelf. *La Storia di Leonardo.*"

Langdon went across the room, found a large art book, and brought it back, setting it down on the table between them. Twisting the book to face Sophie, Teabing flipped open the heavy cover and pointed inside the rear cover to a series of quotations. "From Da Vinci's notebook on polemics and speculation," Teabing said, indicating one quote in particular. "I think you'll find this relevant to our discussion."

Sophie read the words.

> *Many have made a trade of delusions*
> *and false miracles, deceiving the stupid multitude.*
> —LEONARDO DA VINCI

"Here's another," Teabing said, pointing to a different quote.

> *Blinding ignorance does mislead us.*
> *O! Wretched mortals, open your eyes!*
> —LEONARDO DA VINCI

Sophie felt a little chill. "Da Vinci is talking about the Bible?"

Teabing nodded. "Leonardo's feelings about the Bible relate directly to the Holy Grail. In fact, Da Vinci painted the true Grail, which I will show you momentarily, but first we must speak of the Bible." Teabing smiled. "And everything you need to know about the Bible can be summed up by the great canon doctor Martyn Percy." Teabing cleared his throat and declared, "The Bible did not arrive by fax from heaven."

"I beg your pardon?"

"The Bible is a product of *man,* my dear. Not of God. The Bible did not fall magically from the clouds. Man created it as a historical record of tumultuous times, and it has evolved through countless translations, additions, and revisions. History has never had a definitive version of the book."

"Okay."

"Jesus Christ was a historical figure of staggering influence, perhaps the most enigmatic and inspirational leader the world has ever seen. As the prophesied

EGYPTIAN SUN DISKS AND SAINTS' HALOS

Messiah, Jesus toppled kings, inspired millions, and founded new philosophies. As a descendant of the lines of King Solomon and King David, Jesus possessed a rightful claim to the throne of the King of the Jews. Understandably, His life was recorded by thousands of followers across the land." Teabing paused to sip his tea and then placed the cup back on the mantel. "More than *eighty* gospels were considered for the New Testament, and yet only a relative few were chosen for inclusion—Matthew, Mark, Luke, and John among them.

"Who chose which gospels to include?" Sophie asked.

"Aha!" Teabing burst in with enthusiasm. "The fundamental irony of Christianity! The Bible, as we know it today, was collated by the pagan Roman emperor Constantine the Great."

"I thought Constantine was a Christian," Sophie said.

"Hardly," Teabing scoffed. "He was a lifelong pagan who was baptized on his deathbed, too weak to protest. In Constantine's day, Rome's official religion was sun worship—the cult of *Sol Invictus,* or the Invincible Sun—and Constantine was its head priest. Unfortunately for him, a growing religious turmoil was gripping Rome. Three centuries after the crucifixion of Jesus Christ, Christ's followers had

ISIS NURSING HORUS   MARY NURSING JESUS

multiplied exponentially. Christians and pagans began warring, and the conflict grew to such proportions that it threatened to rend Rome in two. Constantine decided something had to be done. In 325 A.D., he decided to unify Rome under a single religion. Christianity."

Sophie was surprised. "Why would a pagan emperor choose *Christianity* as the official religion?"

Teabing chuckled. "Constantine was a very good businessman. He could see that Christianity was on the rise, and he simply backed the winning horse. Historians still marvel at the brilliance with which Constantine converted the sun-worshipping pagans to Christianity. By fusing pagan symbols, dates, and rituals into the growing Christian tradition, he created a kind of hybrid religion that was acceptable to both parties."

"Transmogrification," Langdon said. "The vestiges of pagan religion in Christian symbology are undeniable. Egyptian sun disks became the halos of Catholic saints. Pictograms of Isis nursing her miraculously conceived son Horus became the blueprint for our modern images of the Virgin Mary nursing Baby Jesus. And virtually all the elements of the Catholic ritual—the miter, the altar, the doxology, and communion, the act of "God-eating"—were taken directly from earlier pagan mystery religions."

Teabing groaned. "Don't get a symbologist started on Christian icons. Nothing in Christianity is original. The pre-Christian God Mithras—called *the Son of God* and *the Light of the World*—was born on December 25, died, was buried in a rock tomb, and then resurrected in three days. By the way, December 25 is also the birthday of Osiris, Adonis, and Dionysus. The newborn Krishna was presented with gold, frankincense, and myrrh. Even Christianity's weekly holy day was stolen from the pagans."

"What do you mean?"

"Originally," Langdon said, "Christianity honored the Jewish Sabbath of Saturday, but Constantine shifted it to coincide with the pagan's veneration day of the sun." He paused, grinning. "To this day, most churchgoers attend services on Sunday morning with no idea that they are there on account of the pagan sun god's weekly tribute—*Sun*day."

Sophie's head was spinning. "And all of this relates to the Grail?"

"Indeed," Teabing said. "Stay with me. During this fusion of religions, Constantine needed to strengthen the new Christian tradition, and held a famous ecumenical gathering known as the Council of Nicaea."

MITHRA AND SIGNS OF THE ZODIAC

Sophie had heard of it only insofar as its being the birthplace of the Nicene Creed.

"At this gathering," Teabing said, "many aspects of Christianity were debated and voted upon—the date of Easter, the role of the bishops, the administration of sacraments, and, of course, the *divinity* of Jesus."

"I don't follow. His divinity?"

"My dear," Teabing declared, "until *that* moment in history, Jesus was viewed by His followers as a mortal prophet . . . a great and powerful man, but a *man* nonetheless. A mortal."

"Not the Son of God?"

"Right," Teabing said. "Jesus' establishment as 'the Son of God' was officially proposed and voted on by the Council of Nicaea."

"Hold on. You're saying Jesus' divinity was the result of a *vote?*"

"A relatively close vote at that," Teabing added. "Nonetheless, establishing Christ's divinity was critical to the further unification of the Roman empire and to the new Vatican power base. By officially endorsing Jesus as the Son of God, Constantine turned Jesus into a deity who existed beyond the scope of the human world, an entity whose power was unchallengeable. This not only precluded further pagan challenges to Christianity, but now the followers of Christ were able to redeem themselves *only* via the established sacred channel—the Roman Catholic Church."

Sophie glanced at Langdon, and he gave her a soft nod of concurrence.

"It was all about power," Teabing continued. "Christ as Messiah was critical to the functioning of Church and state. Many scholars claim that the early Church literally *stole* Jesus from His original followers, hijacking His human message, shrouding it in an impenetrable cloak of divinity, and using it to expand their own power. I've written several books on the topic."

"And I assume devout Christians send you hate mail on a daily basis?"

"Why would they?" Teabing countered. "The vast majority of educated Christians know the history of their faith. Jesus was indeed a great and powerful man. Constantine's underhanded political maneuvers don't diminish the majesty of Christ's life. Nobody is saying Christ was a fraud, or denying that He walked the earth and inspired millions to better lives. All we are saying is that Constantine took advantage of Christ's substantial influence and importance. And in doing so, he shaped the face of Christianity as we know it today."

Sophie glanced at the art book before her, eager to move on and see the Da Vinci painting of the Holy Grail.

"The twist is this," Teabing said, talking faster now. "Because Constantine upgraded Jesus' status almost four centuries *after* Jesus' death, thousands of documents already existed chronicling His life as a *mortal* man. To rewrite the history books, Constantine knew he would need a bold stroke. From this sprang the most profound moment in Christian history." Teabing paused, eyeing Sophie. "Constantine commissioned and financed a new Bible, which omitted those gospels that spoke of Christ's *human* traits and embellished those gospels that made Him godlike. The earlier gospels were outlawed, gathered up, and burned."

"An interesting note," Langdon added. "Anyone who chose the forbidden gospels over Constantine's version was deemed a heretic. The word *heretic* derives from that moment in history. The Latin word *haereticus* means 'choice.' Those who 'chose' the original history of Christ were the world's first *heretics*."

"Fortunately for historians," Teabing said, "some of the gospels that Constantine attempted to eradicate managed to survive. The Dead Sea Scrolls were found in the 1950s hidden in a cave near Qumran in the Judean desert. And, of course, the

THE CAVES AT QUMRAN

Coptic Scrolls in 1945 at Nag Hammadi. In addition to telling the true Grail story, these documents speak of Christ's ministry in very human terms. Of course, the Vatican, in keeping with their tradition of misinformation, tried very hard to suppress the release of these scrolls. And why wouldn't they? The scrolls highlight glaring historical discrepancies and fabrications, clearly confirming that the modern Bible was compiled and edited by men who possessed a political agenda—to promote the divinity of the man Jesus Christ and use His influence to solidify their own power base."

"And yet," Langdon countered, "it's important to remember that the modern Church's desire to suppress these documents comes from a sincere belief in their established view of Christ. The Vatican is made up of deeply pious men who truly believe these contrary documents could only be false testimony."

Teabing chuckled as he eased himself into a chair opposite Sophie. "As you can see, our professor has a far softer heart for Rome than I do. Nonetheless, he is correct about the modern clergy believing these opposing documents are false testimony. That's understandable. Constantine's Bible has been their truth for ages. Nobody is more indoctrinated than the indoctrinator."

"What he means," Langdon said, "is that we worship the gods of our fathers."

"What I mean," Teabing countered, "is that almost everything our fathers taught us about Christ is *false*. As are the stories about the Holy Grail."

Sophie looked again at the Da Vinci quote before her. *Blinding ignorance does mislead us. O! Wretched mortals, open your eyes!*

Teabing reached for the book and flipped toward the center. "And finally, before I show you Da Vinci's paintings of the Holy Grail, I'd like you to take a quick look at this." He opened the book to a colorful graphic that spanned both full pages. "I assume you recognize this fresco?"

He's kidding, right? Sophie was staring at the most famous fresco of all time—*The Last Supper*—Da Vinci's legendary painting from the wall of Santa Maria delle Grazie in Milan. The decaying fresco portrayed Jesus and His disciples at the moment that Jesus announced one of them would betray Him. "I know the fresco, yes."

"Then perhaps you would indulge me this little game? Close your eyes if you would."

Uncertain, Sophie closed her eyes.

"Where is Jesus sitting?" Teabing asked.

"In the center."

"Good. And what food are He and His disciples breaking and eating?"

"Bread." *Obviously*.

"Superb. And what drink?"

"Wine. They drank wine."

"Great. And one final question. How many wineglasses are on the table?"

Sophie paused, realizing it was the trick question. *And after dinner, Jesus took the cup of wine, sharing it with His disciples.* "One cup," she said. "The chalice." *The Cup of Christ. The Holy Grail.* "Jesus passed a single chalice of wine, just as modern Christians do at communion."

Teabing sighed. "Open your eyes."

She did. Teabing was grinning smugly. Sophie looked down at the painting, seeing to her astonishment that *everyone* at the table had a glass of wine, including Christ. Thirteen cups. Moreover, the cups were tiny, stemless, and made of glass. There was no chalice in the painting. No Holy Grail.

Teabing's eyes twinkled. "A bit strange, don't you think, considering that both the Bible and our standard Grail legend celebrate this moment as the definitive arrival of the Holy Grail. Oddly, Da Vinci appears to have forgotten to paint the Cup of Christ."

"Surely art scholars must have noted that."

"You will be shocked to learn what anomalies Da Vinci included here that most scholars either do not see or simply choose to ignore. This fresco, in fact, is the entire key to the Holy Grail mystery. Da Vinci lays it all out in the open in *The Last Supper*."

Sophie scanned the work eagerly. "Does this fresco tell us *what* the Grail really is?"

"Not *what* it is," Teabing whispered. "But rather *who* it is. The Holy Grail is not a thing. It is, in fact . . . a *person*."

SOPHIE STARED at Teabing a long moment and then turned to Langdon. "The Holy Grail is a person?"

Langdon nodded. "A woman, in fact." From the blank look on Sophie's face, Langdon could tell they had already lost her. He recalled having a similar reaction the first time he heard the statement. It was not until he understood the *symbology* behind the Grail that the feminine connection became clear.

Teabing apparently had a similar thought. "Robert, perhaps this is the moment for the symbologist to clarify?" He went to a nearby end table, found a piece of paper, and laid it in front of Langdon.

Langdon pulled a pen from his pocket. "Sophie, are you familiar with the modern icons for male and female?" He drew the common male symbol ♂ and female symbol ♀.

"Of course," she said.

"These," he said quietly, "are not the original symbols for male and female. Many people incorrectly assume the male symbol is derived from a shield and spear, while the female symbol represents a mirror reflecting beauty. In fact, the symbols originated as ancient astronomical symbols for the planet-god Mars and planet-goddess Venus. The original symbols are far simpler." Langdon drew another icon on the paper.

"This symbol is the original icon for *male,*" he told her. "A rudimentary phallus."

"Quite to the point," Sophie said.

"As it were," Teabing added.

Langdon went on. "This icon is formally known as the *blade,* and it represents aggression and manhood. In fact, this exact phallus symbol is still used today on modern military uniforms to denote rank."

"Indeed." Teabing grinned. "The more penises you have, the higher your rank. Boys will be boys."

Langdon winced. "Moving on, the female symbol, as you might imagine, is the exact opposite." He drew another symbol on the page. "This is called the *chalice*."

Sophie glanced up, looking surprised.

Langdon could see she had made the connection. "The chalice," he said, "resembles a cup or vessel, and more important, it resembles the shape of a woman's womb. This symbol communicates femininity, womanhood, and fertility." Langdon looked directly at her now. "Sophie, legend tells us the Holy Grail is a chalice—a cup. But the Grail's description as a *chalice* is actually an allegory to protect the true nature of the Holy Grail. That is to say, the legend uses the chalice as a *metaphor* for something far more important."

"A woman," Sophie said.

"Exactly." Langdon smiled. "The Grail is literally the ancient symbol for womanhood, and the *Holy* Grail represents the sacred feminine and the goddess, which of course has now been lost, virtually eliminated by the Church. The power of the female and her ability to produce life was once very sacred, but it posed a threat to the rise of the predominantly male Church, and so the sacred feminine was demonized and called unclean. It was *man,* not God, who created the concept of 'original sin,' whereby Eve tasted of the apple and caused the downfall of the human race. Woman, once the sacred giver of life, was now the enemy."

"I should add," Teabing chimed, "that this concept of woman as life-bringer was the foundation of ancient religion. Childbirth was mystical and powerful. Sadly, Christian philosophy decided to embezzle the female's creative power by ignoring biological truth and making *man* the Creator. Genesis tells us that Eve was created from Adam's rib. Woman became an offshoot of man. And a sinful one at that. Genesis was the beginning of the end for the goddess."

"The Grail," Langdon said, "is symbolic of the lost goddess. When Christianity came along, the old pagan religions did not die easily. Legends of chivalric quests for the lost Grail were in fact stories of forbidden quests to find the lost sacred feminine. Knights who claimed to be "searching for the chalice" were speaking in code as a way to protect themselves from a Church that had subjugated women,

EVE TEMPTED BY JOHN STANHOPE

banished the Goddess, burned nonbelievers, and forbidden the pagan reverence for the sacred feminine."

Sophie shook her head. "I'm sorry, when you said the Holy Grail was a person, I thought you meant it was an actual person."

"It is," Langdon said.

"And not just *any* person," Teabing blurted, clambering excitedly to his feet. "A woman who carried with her a secret so powerful that, if revealed, it threatened to devastate the very foundation of Christianity!"

Sophie looked overwhelmed. "Is this woman well known in history?"

"Quite." Teabing collected his crutches and motioned down the hall. "And if we adjourn to the study, my friends, it would be my honor to show you Da Vinci's painting of her."

TWO ROOMS AWAY, in the kitchen, manservant Rémy Legaludec stood in silence before a television. The news station was broadcasting photos of a man and woman . . . the same two individuals to whom Rémy had just served tea.

STANDING AT the roadblock outside the Depository Bank of Zurich, Lieutenant Collet wondered what was taking Fache so long to come up with the search warrant. The bankers were obviously hiding something. They claimed Langdon and Neveu had arrived earlier and were turned away from the bank because they did not have proper account identification.

So why won't they let us inside for a look?

Finally, Collet's cellular phone rang. It was the command post at the Louvre. "Do we have a search warrant yet?" Collet demanded.

"Forget about the bank, Lieutenant," the agent told him. "We just got a tip. We have the exact location where Langdon and Neveu are hiding."

Collet sat down hard on the hood of his car. "You're kidding."

"I have an address in the suburbs. Somewhere near Versailles."

"Does Captain Fache know?"

"Not yet. He's busy on an important call."

"I'm on my way. Have him call as soon as he's free." Collet took down the address and jumped in his car. As he peeled away from the bank, Collet realized he had forgotten to ask *who* had tipped DCPJ off to Langdon's location. Not that it mattered. Collet had been blessed with a chance to redeem his skepticism and earlier blunders. He was about to make the most high-profile arrest of his career.

Collet radioed the five cars accompanying him. "No sirens, men. Langdon can't know we're coming."

FORTY KILOMETERS AWAY, a black Audi pulled off a rural road and parked in the shadows on the edge of a field. Silas got out and peered through the rungs of the wrought-iron fence that encircled the vast compound before him. He gazed up the long moonlit slope to the château in the distance.

The downstairs lights were all ablaze. *Odd for this hour,* Silas thought, smiling. The information the Teacher had given him was obviously accurate. *I will not leave this house without the keystone,* he vowed. *I will not fail the bishop and the Teacher.*

Checking the thirteen-round clip in his Heckler and Koch, Silas pushed it through the bars and let it fall onto the mossy ground inside the compound. Then, gripping the top of the fence, he heaved himself up and over, dropping to the ground on the other side. Ignoring the slash of pain from his *cilice,* Silas retrieved his gun and began the long trek up the grassy slope.

TEABING'S "STUDY" was like no study Sophie had ever seen. Six or seven times larger than even the most luxurious of office spaces, the knight's *cabinet de travail* resembled an ungainly hybrid of science laboratory, archival library, and indoor flea market. Lit by three overhead chandeliers, the boundless tile floor was dotted with clustered islands of worktables buried beneath books, artwork, artifacts, and a surprising amount of electronic gear—computers, projectors, microscopes, copy machines, and flatbed scanners.

"I converted the ballroom," Teabing said, looking sheepish as he shuffled into the room. "I have little occasion to dance."

Sophie felt as if the entire night had become some kind of twilight zone where nothing was as she expected. "This is all for your work?"

"Learning the truth has become my life's love," Teabing said. "And the Sangreal is my favorite mistress."

The Holy Grail is a woman, Sophie thought, her mind a collage of interrelated ideas that seemed to make no sense. "You said you have a *picture* of this woman who you claim is the Holy Grail."

"Yes, but it is not I who *claim* she is the Grail. Christ Himself made that claim."

"Which one is the painting?" Sophie asked, scanning the walls.

"Hmmm . . ." Teabing made a show of seeming to have forgotten. "The Holy Grail. The Sangreal. The Chalice." He wheeled suddenly and pointed to the far wall. On it hung an eight-foot-long print of *The Last Supper,* the same exact image Sophie had just been looking at. "There she is!"

Sophie was certain she had missed something. "That's the same painting you just showed me."

He winked. "I know, but the enlargement is so much more exciting. Don't you think?"

Sophie turned to Langdon for help. "I'm lost."

THE LAST SUPPER
BY LEONARDO
DA VINCI

Langdon smiled. "As it turns out, the Holy Grail *does* indeed make an appearance in *The Last Supper*. Leonardo included her prominently."

"Hold on," Sophie said. "You told me the Holy Grail is a *woman*. *The Last Supper* is a painting of thirteen men."

"Is it?" Teabing arched his eyebrows. "Take a closer look."

Uncertain, Sophie made her way closer to the painting, scanning the thirteen figures—Jesus Christ in the middle, six disciples on His left, and six on His right. "They're all men," she confirmed.

"Oh?" Teabing said. "How about the one seated in the place of honor, at the right hand of the Lord?"

Sophie examined the figure to Jesus' immediate right, focusing in. As she studied the person's face and body, a wave of astonishment rose within her. The individual had flowing red hair, delicate folded hands, and the hint of a bosom. It was, without a doubt . . . female.

"That's a woman!" Sophie exclaimed.

Teabing was laughing. "Surprise, surprise. Believe me, it's no mistake. Leonardo was skilled at painting the difference between the sexes."

Sophie could not take her eyes from the woman beside Christ. *The Last Supper is supposed to be thirteen men. Who is this woman?* Although Sophie had seen this classic image many times, she had not once noticed this glaring discrepancy.

"Everyone misses it," Teabing said. "Our preconceived notions of this scene are so powerful that our mind blocks out the incongruity and overrides our eyes."

"It's known as *scotoma*," Langdon added. "The brain does it sometimes with powerful symbols."

"Another reason you might have missed the woman," Teabing said, "is that many of the photographs in art books were taken before 1954, when the details were still hidden beneath layers of grime and several restorative repaintings done by clumsy hands in the eighteenth century. Now, at last, the fresco has been cleaned down to Da Vinci's original layer of paint." He motioned to the photograph. "*Et voilà!*"

Sophie moved closer to the image. The woman to Jesus' right was young and pious-looking, with a demure face, beautiful red hair, and hands folded quietly. *This is the woman who singlehandedly could crumble the Church?*

"Who is she?" Sophie asked.

"That, my dear," Teabing replied, "is Mary Magdalene."

Sophie turned. "The prostitute?"

Teabing drew a short breath, as if the word had injured him personally. "Magdalene was no such thing. That unfortunate misconception is the legacy of

DETAIL OF *THE LAST SUPPER* BY LEONARDO DA VINCI

a smear campaign launched by the early Church. The Church needed to defame Mary Magdalene in order to cover up her dangerous secret—her role as the Holy Grail."

"Her *role?*"

"As I mentioned," Teabing clarified, "the early Church needed to convince the world that the mortal prophet Jesus was a *divine* being. Therefore, any gospels that described *earthly* aspects of Jesus' life had to be omitted from the Bible. Unfortunately for the early editors, one particularly troubling earthly theme kept recurring in the gospels. Mary Magdalene." He paused. "More specifically, her marriage to Jesus Christ."

"I beg your pardon?" Sophie's eyes moved to Langdon and then back to Teabing.

"It's a matter of historical record," Teabing said, "and Da Vinci was certainly aware of that fact. *The Last Supper* practically shouts at the viewer that Jesus and Magdalene were a pair."

Sophie glanced back to the fresco.

"Notice that Jesus and Magdalene are clothed as mirror images of one another." Teabing pointed to the two individuals in the center of the fresco.

Sophie was mesmerized. Sure enough, their clothes were inverse colors. Jesus wore a red robe and blue cloak; Mary Magdalene wore a blue robe and red cloak. *Yin and yang.*

"Venturing into the more bizarre," Teabing said, "note that Jesus and His bride appear to be joined at the hip and are leaning away from one another as if to create this clearly delineated negative space between them."

Even before Teabing traced the contour for her, Sophie saw it—the indisputable ∨ shape at the focal point of the painting. It was the same symbol Langdon had drawn earlier for the Grail, the chalice, and the female womb.

"Finally," Teabing said, "if you view Jesus and Magdalene as compositional elements rather than as people, you will see another obvious shape leap out at you." He paused. "A *letter* of the alphabet."

Sophie saw it at once. To say the letter leapt out at her was an understatement. The letter was suddenly all Sophie could see. Glaring in the center of the painting was the unquestionable outline of an enormous, flawlessly formed letter M.

"A bit too perfect for coincidence, wouldn't you say?" Teabing asked.

Sophie was amazed. "Why is it there?"

Teabing shrugged. "Conspiracy theorists will tell you it stands for *Matrimonio* or *Mary Magdalene*. To be honest, nobody is certain. The only certainty is that the hidden M is no mistake. Countless Grail-related works contain the hidden letter M—whether as watermarks, underpaintings, or compositional allusions. The most blatant M, of course, is emblazoned on the altar at Our Lady of Paris in London, which was designed by a former Grand Master of the Priory of Sion, Jean Cocteau."

Sophie weighed the information. "I'll admit, the hidden M's are intriguing, although I assume nobody is claiming they are proof of Jesus' marriage to Magdalene."

[top] JEAN COCTEAU MURAL AT OUR LADY OF PARIS, LONDON
[bottom] "M ALTAR" IN FRONT OF COCTEAU MURAL

"No, no," Teabing said, going to a nearby table of books. "As I said earlier, the marriage of Jesus and Mary Magdalene is part of the historical record." He began pawing through his book collection. "Moreover, Jesus as a married man makes infinitely more sense than our standard biblical view of Jesus as a bachelor."

"Why?" Sophie asked.

"Because Jesus was a Jew," Langdon said, taking over while Teabing searched for his book, "and the social decorum during that time virtually forbade a Jewish man to be unmarried. According to Jewish custom, celibacy was condemned, and the obligation for a Jewish father was to find a suitable wife for his son. If Jesus were not married, at least one of the Bible's gospels would have mentioned it and offered some explanation for His unnatural state of bachelorhood."

Teabing located a huge book and pulled it toward him across the table. The leather-bound edition was poster-sized, like a huge atlas. The cover read: *The Gnostic Gospels.* Teabing heaved it open, and Langdon and Sophie joined him. Sophie could see it contained photographs of what appeared to be magnified passages of ancient documents—tattered papyrus with handwritten text. She did not recognize the ancient language, but the facing pages bore typed translations.

"These are photocopies of the Nag Hammadi and Dead Sea Scrolls, which I mentioned earlier," Teabing said. "The earliest Christian records. Troublingly, they do not match up with the gospels in the Bible." Flipping toward the middle of the book, Teabing pointed to a passage. "The Gospel of Philip is always a good place to start."

Sophie read the passage:

And the companion of the Saviour is Mary Magdalene. Christ loved her more than all the disciples and used to kiss her often on her mouth. The rest of the disciples were offended by it and expressed disapproval. They said to him, "Why do you love her more than all of us?"

The words surprised Sophie, and yet they hardly seemed conclusive. "It says nothing of marriage."

"Au contraire." Teabing smiled, pointing to the first line. "As any Aramaic scholar will tell you, the word *companion,* in those days, literally meant *spouse.*"

Langdon concurred with a nod.

Sophie read the first line again. *And the companion of the Saviour is Mary Magdalene.*

Teabing flipped through the book and pointed out several other passages that, to Sophie's surprise, clearly suggested Magdalene and Jesus had a romantic relationship. As she read the passages, Sophie recalled an angry priest who had banged on her grandfather's door when she was a schoolgirl.

"Is this the home of Jacques Saunière?" the priest had demanded, glaring down at young Sophie when she pulled open the door. "I want to talk to him about this editorial he wrote." The priest held up a newspaper.

Sophie summoned her grandfather, and the two men disappeared into his study and closed the door. *My grandfather wrote something in the paper?* Sophie immediately ran to the kitchen and flipped through that morning's paper. She found her grandfather's name on an article on the second page. She read it. Sophie didn't understand all of what was said, but it sounded like the French government, under pressure from priests, had agreed to ban an American movie called *The Last Temptation of Christ,* which was about Jesus having sex with a lady called Mary Magdalene. Her grandfather's article said the Church was arrogant and wrong to ban it.

No wonder the priest is mad, Sophie thought.

"It's pornography! Sacrilege!" the priest yelled, emerging from the study and storming to the front door. "How can you possibly endorse that! This American Martin Scorsese is a blasphemer, and the Church will permit him no pulpit in France!" The priest slammed the door on his way out.

When her grandfather came into the kitchen, he saw Sophie with the paper and frowned. "You're quick."

Sophie said, "You think Jesus Christ had a girlfriend?"

"No, dear, I said the Church should not be allowed to tell us what notions we can and can't entertain."

"Did Jesus have a girlfriend?"

Her grandfather was silent for several moments. "Would it be so bad if He did?"

Sophie considered it and then shrugged. "I wouldn't mind."

SIR LEIGH TEABING was still talking. "I shan't bore you with the countless references to Jesus and Magdalene's union. That has been explored ad nauseam by modern historians. I would, however, like to point out the following." He motioned to another passage. "This is from the Gospel of Mary Magdalene."

Sophie had not known a gospel existed in Magdalene's words. She read the text:

And Peter said, "Did the Saviour really speak with a woman without our knowledge? Are we to turn about and all listen to her? Did he prefer her to us?"

And Levi answered, "Peter, you have always been hot-tempered. Now I see you contending against the woman like an adversary. If the Saviour made her worthy, who are you indeed to reject her? Surely the Saviour knows her very well. That is why he loved her more than us."

"The woman they are speaking of," Teabing explained, "is Mary Magdalene. Peter is jealous of her."

"Because Jesus preferred Mary?"

"Not only that. The stakes were far greater than mere affection. At this point in the gospels, Jesus suspects He will soon be captured and crucified. So He gives Mary Magdalene instructions on how to carry on His Church after He is gone. As

THREE DEPICTIONS OF THE LAST SUPPER,
SHOWING JESUS WITH A WOMAN

THE LAST SUPPER
(GERMANY, 13TH CENTURY)

THE LAST SUPPER BY JEAN FOUQUET
(C. 1415–1481)

THE LAST SUPPER BY ALBRECHT DÜRER, WOODCUT

a result, Peter expresses his discontent over playing second fiddle to a woman. I daresay Peter was something of a sexist."

Sophie was trying to keep up. "This is *Saint* Peter. The rock on which Jesus built His Church."

"The same, except for one catch. According to these unaltered gospels, it was not *Peter* to whom Christ gave directions with which to establish the Christian Church. It was *Mary Magdalene*."

Sophie looked at him. "You're saying the Christian Church was to be carried on by a *woman?*"

"That was the plan. Jesus was the original feminist. He intended for the future of His Church to be in the hands of Mary Magdalene."

"And Peter had a problem with that," Langdon said, pointing to *The Last Supper*. "That's Peter there. You can see that Da Vinci was well aware of how Peter felt about Mary Magdalene."

Again, Sophie was speechless. In the painting, Peter was leaning menacingly toward Mary Magdalene and slicing his blade-like hand across her neck. The same threatening gesture as in *Madonna of the Rocks*!

"And here too," Langdon said, pointing now to the crowd of disciples near Peter. "A bit ominous, no?"

Sophie squinted and saw a hand emerging from the crowd of disciples. "Is that hand wielding a *dagger?*"

"Yes. Stranger still, if you count the arms, you'll see that this hand belongs to . . . no one at all. It's disembodied. Anonymous."

Sophie was starting to feel overwhelmed. "I'm sorry, I still don't understand how all of this makes Mary Magdalene the Holy Grail."

"Aha!" Teabing exclaimed again. "Therein lies the rub!" He turned once more to the table and pulled out a large chart, spreading it out for her. It was an elaborate genealogy. "Few people realize that Mary Magdalene, in addition to being Christ's right hand, was a powerful woman already."

DISEMBODIED HAND,
THE LAST SUPPER

Sophie could now see the title of the family tree.

THE TRIBE OF BENJAMIN

"Mary Magdalene is here," Teabing said, pointing near the top of the genealogy.
Sophie was surprised. "She was of the House of Benjamin?"

"Indeed," Teabing said. "Mary Magdalene was of royal descent."

"But I was under the impression Magdalene was poor."

Teabing shook his head. "Magdalene was recast as a whore in order to erase evidence of her powerful family ties."

Sophie found herself again glancing at Langdon, who again nodded. She turned back to Teabing. "But why would the early Church *care* if Magdalene had royal blood?"

The Briton smiled. "My dear child, it was not Mary Magdalene's royal blood that concerned the Church so much as it was her consorting with Christ, who *also* had royal blood. As you know, the Book of Matthew tells us that Jesus was of the House of David. A descendant of King Solomon—King of the Jews. By marrying into the powerful House of Benjamin, Jesus fused two royal bloodlines, creating a potent political union with the potential of making a legitimate claim to the throne and restoring the line of kings as it was under Solomon."

Sophie sensed he was at last coming to his point.

Teabing looked excited now. "The legend of the Holy Grail is a legend about royal blood. When Grail legend speaks of 'the chalice that held the blood of Christ' . . . it speaks, in fact, of Mary Magdalene—the female womb that carried Jesus' royal bloodline."

The words seemed to echo across the ballroom and back before they fully registered in Sophie's mind. *Mary Magdalene carried the royal bloodline of Jesus Christ?* "But how could Christ have a bloodline unless . . . ?" She paused and looked at Langdon.

Langdon smiled softly. "Unless they had a child."

Sophie stood transfixed.

"Behold," Teabing proclaimed, "the greatest cover-up in human history. Not only was Jesus Christ married, but He was a father. My dear, Mary Magdalene was the Holy Vessel. She was the chalice that bore the royal bloodline of Jesus Christ. She was the womb that bore the lineage, and the vine from which the sacred fruit sprang forth!"

Sophie felt the hairs stand up on her arms. "But how could a secret *that* big be kept quiet all of these years?"

"Heavens!" Teabing said. "It has been anything but *quiet!* The royal bloodline of Jesus Christ is the source of the most enduring legend of all time—the Holy Grail. Magdalene's story has been shouted from the rooftops for centuries in all kinds of metaphors and languages. Her story is everywhere once you open your eyes."

"And the Sangreal documents?" Sophie said. "They allegedly contain proof that Jesus had a royal bloodline?"

"They do."

"So the entire Holy Grail legend is all about royal blood?"

"Quite literally," Teabing said. "The word *Sangreal* derives from *San Greal*—or Holy Grail. But in its most ancient form, the word *Sangreal* was divided in a different spot." Teabing wrote on a piece of scrap paper and handed it to her.

She read what he had written.

Sang Real

Instantly, Sophie recognized the translation.
Sang Real literally meant *Royal Blood*.

THE MALE receptionist in the lobby of the Opus Dei headquarters on Lexington Avenue in New York City was surprised to hear Bishop Aringarosa's voice on the line. "Good evening, sir."

"Have I had any messages?" the bishop demanded, sounding unusually anxious.

"Yes, sir. I'm very glad you called in. I couldn't reach you in your apartment. You had an urgent phone message about half an hour ago."

"Yes?" He sounded relieved by the news. "Did the caller leave a name?"

"No, sir, just a number." The operator relayed the number.

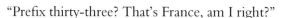

"Prefix thirty-three? That's France, am I right?"

"Yes, sir. Paris. The caller said it was critical you contact him immediately."

"Thank you. I have been waiting for that call." Aringarosa quickly severed the connection.

As the receptionist hung up the receiver, he wondered why Aringarosa's phone connection sounded so crackly. The bishop's daily schedule showed him in New York this weekend, and yet he sounded a world away. The receptionist shrugged it off. Bishop Aringarosa had been acting very strangely the last few months.

MY CELLULAR PHONE must not have been receiving, Aringarosa thought as the Fiat approached the exit for Rome's Ciampino Charter Airport. *The Teacher was trying to reach me.* Despite Aringarosa's concern at having missed the call, he felt encouraged that the Teacher felt confident enough to call Opus Dei headquarters directly.

Things must have gone well in Paris tonight.

As Aringarosa began dialing the number, he felt excited to know he would soon be in Paris. *I'll be on the ground before dawn.* Aringarosa had a chartered turboprop awaiting him here for the short flight to France. Commercial carriers were not an option at this hour, especially considering the contents of his briefcase.

The line began to ring.

A female voice answered. *"Direction Centrale Police Judiciaire."*

Aringarosa felt himself hesitate. This was unexpected. "Ah, yes . . . I was asked to call this number?"

"Qui êtes-vous?" the woman said. "Your name?"

Aringarosa was uncertain if he should reveal it. *The French Judicial Police?*

"Your *name,* monsieur?" the woman pressed.

"Bishop Manuel Aringarosa."

"Un moment." There was a click on the line.

After a long wait, another man came on, his tone gruff and concerned. "Bishop, I am glad I finally reached you. You and I have much to discuss."

*S*ANGREAL . . . *Sang Real . . . San Greal . . . Royal Blood . . . Holy Grail.*

It was all intertwined.

The Holy Grail is Mary Magdalene . . . the mother of the royal bloodline of Jesus Christ. Sophie felt a new wave of disorientation as she stood in the silence of the ballroom and stared at Robert Langdon. The more pieces Langdon and Teabing laid on the table tonight, the more unpredictable this puzzle became.

"As you can see, my dear," Teabing said, hobbling toward a bookshelf, "Leonardo is not the only one who has been trying to tell the world the truth about the Holy Grail. The royal bloodline of Jesus Christ has been chronicled in exhaustive detail by scores of historians." He ran a finger down a row of several dozen books.

Sophie tilted her head and scanned the list of titles:

THE TEMPLAR REVELATION:
Secret Guardians of the True Identity of Christ

THE WOMAN WITH THE ALABASTER JAR:
Mary Magdalene and the Holy Grail

THE GODDESS IN THE GOSPELS:
Reclaiming the Sacred Feminine

"Here is perhaps the best-known tome," Teabing said, pulling a tattered hard-cover from the stack and handing it to her.

The cover read:

HOLY BLOOD, HOLY GRAIL
The Acclaimed International Bestseller

Sophie glanced up. "An international bestseller? I've never heard of it."

"You were young. This caused quite a stir back in the nineteen eighties. To my taste, the authors made some dubious leaps of faith in their analysis, but their fundamental premise is sound, and to their credit, they finally brought the idea of Christ's bloodline into the mainstream."

"What was the Church's reaction to the book?"

"Outrage, of course. But that was to be expected. After all, this was a secret the Vatican had tried to bury in the fourth century. That's part of what the Crusades were about. Gathering and destroying information. The threat Mary Magdalene posed to the men of the early Church was potentially ruinous. Not only was she the woman to whom Jesus had assigned the task of founding the Church, but she also had physical proof that the Church's newly proclaimed *deity* had spawned a mortal bloodline. The Church, in order to defend itself against the Magdalene's power, perpetuated her image as a whore and buried evidence of Christ's marriage to her, thereby defusing any potential claims that Christ had a surviving bloodline and was a mortal prophet."

Sophie glanced at Langdon, who nodded. "Sophie, the historical evidence supporting this is substantial."

"I admit," Teabing said, "the assertions are dire, but you must understand the Church's powerful motivations to conduct such a cover-up. They could never have survived public knowledge of a bloodline. A child of Jesus would undermine the critical notion of Christ's divinity and therefore the Christian Church, which declared itself the sole vessel through which humanity could access the divine and gain entrance to the kingdom of heaven."

"The five-petal rose," Sophie said, pointing suddenly to the spine of one of Teabing's books. *The same exact design inlaid on the rosewood box.*

Teabing glanced at Langdon and grinned. "She has a good eye." He turned back to Sophie. "That is the Priory symbol for the Grail. Mary Magdalene. Because her name was forbidden by the Church, Mary Magdalene became secretly known by many pseudonyms—the Chalice, the Holy Grail, and the Rose." He paused. "The Rose has ties to the five-pointed pentacle of Venus and the guiding Compass Rose. By the way, the word *rose* is identical in English, French, German, and many other languages."

"Rose," Langdon added, "is also an anagram of Eros, the Greek god of sexual love."

Sophie gave him a surprised look as Teabing plowed on.

"The Rose has always been the premiere symbol of female sexuality. In primitive goddess cults, the five petals represented the five stations of female life—birth, menstruation, motherhood, menopause, and death. And in modern times, the flowering rose's ties to womanhood are considered more visual." He glanced at Robert. "Perhaps the symbologist could explain?"

Robert hesitated. A moment too long.

"Oh, heavens!" Teabing huffed. "You Americans are such prudes." He looked back at Sophie. "What Robert is fumbling with is the fact that the blossoming flower resembles the female genitalia, the sublime blossom from which all mankind enters the world. And if you've ever seen any paintings by Georgia O'Keeffe, you'll know exactly what I mean."

"The point here," Langdon said, motioning back to the bookshelf, "is that all of these books substantiate the same historical claim."

"That Jesus was a father." Sophie was still uncertain.

"Yes," Teabing said. "And that Mary Magdalene was the womb that carried His royal lineage. The Priory of Sion, to this day, still worships Mary Magdalene as the Goddess, the Holy Grail, the Rose, and the Divine Mother."

Sophie again flashed on the ritual in the basement.

"According to the Priory," Teabing continued, "Mary Magdalene was pregnant at the time of the crucifixion. For the safety of Christ's unborn child, she had no choice but to flee the Holy Land. With the help of Jesus' trusted uncle, Joseph of Arimathea, Mary Magdalene secretly traveled to France, then known as Gaul. There she found safe refuge in the Jewish community. It was here in France that she gave birth to a daughter. Her name was Sarah."

Sophie glanced up. "They actually know the child's *name?*"

"Far more than that. Magdalene's and Sarah's lives were scrutinously chronicled by their Jewish protectors. Remember that Magdalene's child belonged to the lineage of Jewish kings—David and Solomon. For this reason, the Jews in France considered Magdalene sacred royalty and revered her as the progenitor of the royal line of kings. Countless scholars of that era chronicled Mary Magdalene's days in France, including the birth of Sarah and the subsequent family tree."

Sophie was startled. "There exists a *family tree* of Jesus Christ?"

"Indeed. And it is purportedly one of the cornerstones of the Sangreal documents. A complete genealogy of the early descendants of Christ."

"But what good is a documented genealogy of Christ's bloodline?" Sophie asked. "It's not proof. Historians could not possibly confirm its authenticity."

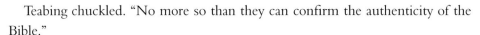

Teabing chuckled. "No more so than they can confirm the authenticity of the Bible."

"Meaning?"

"Meaning that history is always written by the winners. When two cultures clash, the loser is obliterated, and the winner writes the history books—books which glorify their own cause and disparage the conquered foe. As Napoleon once said, 'What is history, but a fable agreed upon?' " He smiled. "By its very nature, history is always a one-sided account."

Sophie had never thought of it that way.

"The Sangreal documents simply tell the *other* side of the Christ story. In the end, which side of the story you believe becomes a matter of faith and personal exploration, but at least the information has survived. The Sangreal documents include tens of thousands of pages of information. Eyewitness accounts of the Sangreal treasure describe it as being carried in four enormous trunks. In those trunks are reputed to be the *Purist Documents*—thousands of pages of unaltered, pre-Constantine documents, written by the early followers of Jesus, revering Him as a wholly human teacher and prophet. Also rumored to be part of the treasure is the legendary '*Q' Document*—a manuscript that even the Vatican admits they believe exists. Allegedly, it is a book of Jesus' teachings, possibly written in His own hand."

"Writings by Christ Himself?"

"Of course," Teabing said. "Why wouldn't Jesus have kept a chronicle of His ministry? Most people did in those days. Another explosive document believed to be in the treasure is a manuscript called *The Magdalene Diaries*—Mary Magdalene's personal account of her relationship with Christ, His crucifixion, and her time in France."

Sophie was silent for a long moment. "And these four chests of documents were the treasure that the Knights Templar found under Solomon's Temple?"

"Exactly. The documents that made the Knights so powerful. The documents that have been the object of countless Grail quests throughout history."

"But you said the Holy Grail was *Mary Magdalene*. If people are searching for documents, why would you call it a search for the Holy Grail?"

Teabing eyed her, his expression softening. "Because the hiding place of the Holy Grail includes a sarcophagus."

Outside, the wind howled in the trees.

Teabing spoke more quietly now. "The quest for the Holy Grail is literally the quest to kneel before the bones of Mary Magdalene. A journey to pray at the feet of the outcast one, the lost sacred feminine."

Sophie felt an unexpected wonder. "The hiding place of the Holy Grail is actually . . . a *tomb?*"

Teabing's hazel eyes got misty. "It is. A tomb containing the body of Mary Magdalene and the documents that tell the true story of her life. At its heart, the quest for the Holy Grail has always been a quest for the Magdalene—the wronged Queen, entombed with proof of her family's rightful claim to power."

Sophie waited a moment as Teabing gathered himself. So much about her grandfather was still not making sense. "Members of the Priory," she finally said, "all these years have answered the charge of protecting the Sangreal documents and the tomb of Mary Magdalene?"

"Yes, but the brotherhood had another, more important duty as well—to protect the *bloodline* itself. Christ's lineage was in perpetual danger. The early Church feared that if the lineage were permitted to grow, the secret of Jesus and Magdalene would eventually surface and challenge the fundamental Catholic doctrine—that of a divine Messiah who did not consort with women or engage in sexual union." He paused. "Nonetheless, Christ's line grew quietly under cover in France until making a bold move in the fifth century, when it intermarried with French royal blood and created a lineage known as the Merovingian bloodline."

This news surprised Sophie. Merovingian was a term learned by every student in France. "The Merovingians founded Paris."

"Yes. That's one of the reasons the Grail legend is so rich in France. Many of the Vatican's Grail quests here were in fact stealth missions to erase members of the royal bloodline. Have you heard of King Dagobert?"

Sophie vaguely recalled the name from a grisly tale in history class. "Dagobert was a Merovingian king, wasn't he? Stabbed in the eye while sleeping?"

"Exactly. Assassinated by the Vatican in collusion with Pepin d'Heristal. Late seventh century. With Dagobert's murder, the Merovingian bloodline was almost exterminated. Fortunately, Dagobert's son, Sigisbert, secretly escaped the attack and carried on the lineage, which later included Godefroi de Bouillon—founder of the Priory of Sion."

"The same man," Langdon said, "who ordered the Knights Templar to recover the Sangreal documents from beneath Solomon's Temple and thus provide the Merovingians proof of their hereditary ties to Jesus Christ."

Teabing nodded, heaving a ponderous sigh. "The modern Priory of Sion has a momentous duty. Theirs is a threefold charge. The brotherhood must protect the Sangreal documents. They must protect the tomb of Mary Magdalene. And, of course, they must nurture and protect the bloodline of Christ—those few members of the royal Merovingian bloodline who have survived into modern times."

GODEFROI DE BOUILLON

The words hung in the huge space, and Sophie felt an odd vibration, as if her bones were reverberating with some new kind of truth. *Descendants of Jesus who survived into modern times.* Her grandfather's voice again was whispering in her ear. *Princess, I must tell you the truth about your family.*

A chill raked her flesh.

Royal blood.

She could not imagine.

Princess Sophie.

"Sir Leigh?" The manservant's words crackled through the intercom on the wall, and Sophie jumped. "If you could join me in the kitchen a moment?"

Teabing scowled at the ill-timed intrusion. He went over to the intercom and pressed the button. "Rémy, as you know, I am busy with my guests. If we need anything else from the kitchen tonight, we will help ourselves. Thank you and good night."

"A word with you before I retire, sir. If you would."

Teabing grunted and pressed the button. "Make it quick, Rémy."

"It is a household matter, sir, hardly fare for guests to endure."

Teabing looked incredulous. "And it cannot wait until morning?"

"No, sir. My question won't take a minute."

Teabing rolled his eyes and looked at Langdon and Sophie. "Sometimes I wonder who is serving whom?" He pressed the button again. "I'll be right there, Rémy. Can I bring you anything when I come?"

"Only freedom from oppression, sir."

"Rémy, you realize your *steak au poivre* is the only reason you still work for me."

"So you tell me, sir. So you tell me."

*P*RINCESS SOPHIE.

Sophie felt hollow as she listened to the clicking of Teabing's crutches fade down the hallway. Numb, she turned and faced Langdon in the deserted ballroom. He was already shaking his head as if reading her mind.

"No, Sophie," he whispered, his eyes reassuring. "The same thought crossed my mind when I realized your grandfather was in the Priory, and you said he wanted to tell you a secret about your family. But it's impossible." Langdon paused. "Saunière is not a Merovingian name."

Sophie wasn't sure whether to feel relieved or disappointed. Earlier, Langdon had asked an unusual passing question about Sophie's mother's maiden name. Chauvel. The question now made sense. "And Chauvel?" she asked, anxious.

Again he shook his head. "I'm sorry. I know that would have answered some questions for you. Only two direct lines of Merovingians remain. Their family names are Plantard and Saint-Clair. Both families live in hiding, probably protected by the Priory."

Sophie repeated the names silently in her mind and then shook her head. There was no one in her family named Plantard or Saint-Clair. A weary undertow was pulling at her now. She realized she was no closer than she had been at the Louvre to understanding what truth her grandfather had wanted to reveal to her. Sophie wished her grandfather had never mentioned her family this afternoon. He had torn open old wounds that felt as painful now as ever. *They are dead, Sophie. They are not coming back.* She thought of her mother singing her to sleep at night, of her father giving her rides on his shoulders, and of her grandmother and younger brother smiling at her with their fervent green eyes. All that was stolen. And all she had left was her grandfather.

And now he is gone too. I am alone.

Sophie turned quietly back to *The Last Supper* and gazed at Mary Magdalene's long red hair and quiet eyes. There was something in the woman's expression that echoed the loss of a loved one. Sophie could feel it too.

"Robert?" she said softly.

He stepped closer.

"I know Leigh said the Grail story is all around us, but tonight is the first time I've ever heard any of this."

Langdon looked as if he wanted to put a comforting hand on her shoulder, but he refrained. "You've heard her story before, Sophie. Everyone has. We just don't realize it when we hear it."

"I don't understand."

"The Grail story is everywhere, but it is hidden. When the Church outlawed speaking of the shunned Mary Magdalene, her story and importance had to be passed on through more discreet channels . . . channels that supported metaphor and symbolism."

"Of course. The arts."

Langdon motioned to *The Last Supper*. "A perfect example. Some of today's most enduring art, literature, and music secretly tell the history of Mary Magdalene and Jesus."

Langdon quickly told her about works by Da Vinci, Botticelli, Poussin, Bernini, Mozart, and Victor Hugo that all whispered of the quest to

SELF-PORTRAIT BY NICOLAS POUSSIN

restore the banished sacred feminine. Enduring legends like Sir Gawain and the Green Knight, King Arthur, and Sleeping Beauty were Grail allegories. Victor Hugo's *Hunchback of Notre Dame* and Mozart's *Magic Flute* were filled with Masonic symbolism and Grail secrets.

"Once you open your eyes to the Holy Grail," Langdon said, "you see her everywhere. Paintings. Music. Books. Even in cartoons, theme parks, and popular movies."

Langdon held up his Mickey Mouse watch and told her that Walt Disney had made it his quiet life's work to pass on the Grail story to future generations. Throughout his entire life, Disney had been hailed as "the Modern-Day Leonardo da Vinci." Both men were generations ahead of their times, uniquely gifted artists, members of secret societies, and, most notably, avid pranksters. Like Leonardo, Walt Disney loved infusing hidden messages and symbolism in his art. For the trained symbologist, watching an early Disney movie was like being barraged by an avalanche of allusion and metaphor.

Most of Disney's hidden messages dealt with religion, pagan myth, and stories of the subjugated goddess. It was no mistake that Disney retold tales like *Cinderella, Sleeping Beauty,* and *Snow White*—all of which dealt with the incarceration of the sacred feminine. Nor did one need a background in symbolism to understand that Snow White—a princess who fell from grace after partaking of a poisoned apple— was a clear allusion to the downfall of Eve in the Garden of Eden. Or that *Sleeping Beauty*'s Princess Aurora—code-named "Rose" and hidden deep in the forest to protect her from the clutches of the evil witch—was the Grail story for children.

Despite its corporate image, Disney still had a savvy, playful element among its employees, and their artists still amused themselves by inserting hidden symbolism in Disney products. Langdon would never forget one of his students bringing in a DVD of *The Lion King* and pausing the film to reveal a freeze-frame in which they thought they saw the letters SEX spelled out by floating dust particles over Simba's head. Although Langdon suspected this was more of a cartoonist's sophomoric prank than any kind of enlightened allusion to pagan human sexuality, he had learned not to underestimate Disney's grasp of symbolism. *The Little Mermaid* was a spellbinding tapestry of spiritual symbols so specifically goddess-related that they could not be coincidence.

When Langdon had first seen *The Little Mermaid,* he had actually gasped aloud when he noticed that the painting in Ariel's underwater home was none other than seventeenth-century artist Georges de la Tour's *The Penitent Magdalene*—a famous homage to the banished Mary Magdalene—fitting decor considering the movie turned out to be a ninety-minute collage of blatant symbolic references to the lost

IMAGE FROM DISNEY'S *THE LITTLE MERMAID,* SHOWING GEORGES DE LA TOUR'S
THE PENITENT MAGDALENE

sanctity of Isis, Eve, Pisces the fish goddess, and, repeatedly, Mary Magdalene. The Little Mermaid's name, Ariel, possessed powerful ties to the sacred feminine and, in the Book of Isaiah, was synonymous with "the Holy City besieged." Of course, the Little Mermaid's flowing red hair was certainly no coincidence either.

The clicking of Teabing's crutches approached in the hallway, his pace unusually brisk. When their host entered the study, his expression was stern.

"You'd better explain yourself, Robert," he said coldly. "You have not been honest with me."

I'M BEING FRAMED, Leigh," Langdon said, trying to stay calm. *You know me. I wouldn't kill anyone.*

Teabing's tone did not soften. "Robert, you're on television, for Christ's sake. Did you know you were wanted by the authorities?"

"Yes."

"Then you abused my trust. I'm astonished you would put me at risk by coming here and asking me to ramble on about the Grail so you could hide out in my home."

"I didn't kill anyone."

"Jacques Saunière is dead, and the police say you did it." Teabing looked saddened. "Such a contributor to the arts . . ."

"Sir?" The manservant had appeared now, standing behind Teabing in the study doorway, his arms crossed. "Shall I show them out?"

"Allow me." Teabing hobbled across the study, unlocked a set of wide glass doors, and swung them open onto a side lawn. "Please find your car, and leave."

Sophie did not move. "We have information about the *clef de voûte. The Priory keystone.*"

Teabing stared at her for several seconds and scoffed derisively. "A desperate ploy. Robert knows how I've sought it."

"She's telling the truth," Langdon said. "That's why we came to you tonight. To talk to you about the keystone."

The manservant intervened now. "Leave, or I shall call the authorities."

"Leigh," Langdon whispered, "we know where it is."

Teabing's balance seemed to falter a bit.

Rémy now marched stiffly across the room. "Leave at once! Or I will forcibly—"

"Rémy!" Teabing spun, snapping at his servant. "Excuse us for a moment."

The servant's jaw dropped. "Sir? I must protest. These people are—"

"I'll handle this." Teabing pointed to the hallway.

After a moment of stunned silence, Rémy skulked out like a banished dog.

In the cool night breeze coming through the open doors, Teabing turned back to Sophie and Langdon, his expression still wary. "This better be good. What do you know of the keystone?"

IN THE THICK BRUSH outside Teabing's study, Silas clutched his pistol and gazed through the glass doors. Only moments ago, he had circled the house and seen Langdon and the woman talking in the large study. Before he could move in, a man on crutches entered, yelled at Langdon, threw open the doors, and demanded his guests leave. *Then the woman mentioned the keystone, and everything changed.* Shouts turned to whispers. Moods softened. And the glass doors were quickly closed.

Now, as he huddled in the shadows, Silas peered through the glass. *The keystone is somewhere inside the house.* Silas could feel it.

Staying in the shadows, he inched closer to the glass, eager to hear what was being said. He would give them five minutes. If they did not reveal where they had placed the keystone, Silas would have to enter and persuade them with force.

INSIDE THE STUDY, Langdon could sense their host's bewilderment.

"Grand Master?" Teabing choked, eyeing Sophie. "Jacques Saunière?"

Sophie nodded, seeing the shock in his eyes.

"But you could not possibly know that!"

"Jacques Saunière was my grandfather."

Teabing staggered back on his crutches, shooting a glance at Langdon, who nodded. Teabing turned back to Sophie. "Miss Neveu, I am speechless. If this is true, then I am truly sorry for your loss. I should admit, for my research, I have kept lists of men in Paris whom I thought might be good candidates for involvement in the Priory. Jacques Saunière was on that list along with many others. But Grand Master, you say? It's hard to fathom." Teabing was silent a moment and then shook his head. "But it still makes no sense. Even if your grandfather *were* the Priory Grand Master and created the keystone himself, he would *never* tell you how to find it. The keystone reveals the pathway to the brotherhood's ultimate treasure. Granddaughter or not, you are not eligible to receive such knowledge."

"Mr. Saunière was dying when he passed on the information," Langdon said. "He had limited options."

"He didn't *need* options," Teabing argued. "There exist three *sénéchaux* who also know the secret. That is the beauty of their system. One will rise to Grand Master and they will induct a new *sénéchal* and share the secret of the keystone."

"I guess you didn't see the entire news broadcast," Sophie said. "In addition to my grandfather, *three* other prominent Parisians were murdered today. All in similar ways. All looked like they had been interrogated."

Teabing's jaw fell. "And you think they were . . ."

"The *sénéchaux,*" Langdon said.

"But how? A murderer could not possibly learn the identities of *all* four top members of the Priory of Sion! Look at *me,* I have been researching them for decades, and I can't even name *one* Priory member. It seems inconceivable that all three *sénéchaux* and the Grand Master could be discovered and killed in one day."

"I doubt the information was gathered in a single day," Sophie said. "It sounds like a well-planned *décapiter.* It's a technique we use to fight organized crime syndicates. If DCPJ wants to move on a certain group, they will silently listen and watch for months, identify all the main players, and then move in and take them all at the same moment. Decapitation. With no leadership, the group falls into chaos and divulges other information. It's possible someone patiently watched the Priory and then attacked, hoping the top people would reveal the location of the keystone."

Teabing looked unconvinced. "But the brothers would never talk. They are sworn to secrecy. Even in the face of death."

"Exactly," Langdon said. "Meaning, if they never divulged the secret, *and* they were killed . . ."

Teabing gasped. "Then the location of the keystone would be lost forever!"

"And with it," Langdon said, "the location of the Holy Grail."

Teabing's body seemed to sway with the weight of Langdon's words. Then, as if too tired to stand another moment, he flopped in a chair and stared out the window.

Sophie walked over, her voice soft. "Considering my grandfather's predicament, it seems possible that in total desperation he tried to pass the secret on to someone outside the brotherhood. Someone he thought he could trust. Someone in his family."

Teabing was pale. "But someone capable of such an attack . . . of discovering so much about the brotherhood . . ." He paused, radiating a new fear. "It could only be one force. This kind of infiltration could only have come from the Priory's oldest enemy."

Langdon glanced up. "The Church."

"Who else? Rome has been seeking the Grail for centuries."

Sophie was skeptical. "You think the *Church* killed my grandfather?"

Teabing replied, "It would not be the first time in history the Church has killed to protect itself. The documents that accompany the Holy Grail are explosive, and the Church has wanted to destroy them for years."

Langdon was having trouble buying Teabing's premise that the Church would blatantly murder people to obtain these documents. Having met the new Pope and many of the cardinals, Langdon knew they were deeply spiritual men who would never condone assassination. *Regardless of the stakes.*

Sophie seemed to be having similar thoughts. "Isn't it possible that these Priory members were murdered by someone *outside* the Church? Someone who didn't understand what the Grail really is? The Cup of Christ, after all, would be quite an enticing treasure. Certainly treasure hunters have killed for less."

"In my experience," Teabing said, "men go to far greater lengths to avoid what they fear than to obtain what they desire. I sense a desperation in this assault on the Priory."

"Leigh," Langdon said, "the argument is paradoxical. Why would members of the Catholic clergy *murder* Priory members in an effort to find and destroy documents they believe are false testimony anyway?"

Teabing chuckled. "The ivory towers of Harvard have made you soft, Robert. Yes, the clergy in Rome are blessed with potent faith, and because of this, their beliefs can weather any storm, including documents that contradict everything they hold dear. But what about the rest of the world? What about those who are not blessed with absolute certainty? What about those who look at the cruelty in the world and say, where is God today? Those who look at Church scandals and ask, who *are* these men who claim to speak the truth about Christ and yet lie to cover up the sexual abuse of children by their own priests?" Teabing paused. "What happens to *those* people, Robert, if persuasive scientific evidence comes out that the Church's version of the Christ story is inaccurate, and that the greatest story ever told is, in fact, the greatest story ever *sold*."

Langdon did not respond.

"I'll tell you what happens if the documents get out," Teabing said. "The Vatican faces a crisis of faith unprecedented in its two-millennium history."

After a long silence, Sophie said, "But if it *is* the Church who is responsible for this attack, why would they act now? After all these years? The Priory keeps the Sangreal documents hidden. They pose no immediate threat to the Church."

Teabing heaved an ominous sigh and glanced at Langdon. "Robert, I assume you are familiar with the Priory's final charge?"

Langdon felt his breath catch at the thought. "I am."

"Miss Neveu," Teabing said, "the Church and the Priory have had a tacit understanding for years. That is, the Church does not attack the Priory, and the Priory keeps the Sangreal documents hidden." He paused. "However, part of the Priory history has always included a plan to unveil the secret. With the arrival of a specific date in history, the brotherhood plans to break the silence and carry out its ultimate triumph by unveiling the Sangreal documents to the world and shouting the true story of Jesus Christ from the mountaintops."

Sophie stared at Teabing in silence. Finally, she too sat down. "And you think that date is approaching? And the Church knows it?"

"A speculation," Teabing said, "but it would certainly provide the Church motivation for an all-out attack to find the documents before it was too late."

Langdon had the uneasy feeling that Teabing was making good sense. "Do you think the Church would actually be capable of uncovering hard evidence of the Priory's date?"

"Why not—if we're assuming the Church was able to uncover the identities of the Priory members, then certainly they could have learned of their plans. And even if they don't have the exact date, their superstitions may be getting the best of them."

"Superstitions?" Sophie asked.

"In terms of prophecy," Teabing said, "we are currently in an epoch of enormous change. The millennium has recently passed, and with it has ended the two-thousand-year-long astrological Age of Pisces—the fish, which is also the sign of Jesus. As any astrological symbologist will tell you, the Piscean ideal believes that man must be *told* what to do by higher powers because man is incapable of thinking for himself. Hence it has been a time of fervent religion. Now, however, we are entering the Age of Aquarius—the water bearer—whose ideals claim that man will learn the *truth* and be able to think for himself. The ideological shift is enormous, and it is occurring right now."

Langdon felt a shiver. Astrological prophecy never held much interest or credibility for him, but he knew there were those in the Church who followed it very closely. "The Church calls this transitional period the End of Days."

Sophie looked skeptical. "As in the end of the world? The Apocalypse?"

PISCES   THE WATER BEARER (AQUARIUS)

"No," Langdon replied. "That's a common misconception. Many religions speak of the End of Days. It refers not to the end of the world, but rather the end of our current age—Pisces, which began at the time of Christ's birth, spanned two thousand years, and waned with the passing of the millennium. Now that we've passed into the Age of Aquarius, the End of Days has arrived."

"Many Grail historians," Teabing added, "believe that *if* the Priory is indeed planning to release this truth, *this* point in history would be a symbolically apt time. Most Priory academics, myself included, anticipated the brotherhood's release would coincide precisely with the millennium. Obviously, it did not. Admittedly, the Roman calendar does not mesh perfectly with astrological markers, so there is some gray area in the prediction. Whether the Church now has inside information that an exact date is looming, or whether they are just getting nervous on account of astrological prophecy, I don't know. Anyway, it's immaterial. Either scenario explains how the Church might be motivated to launch a preemptive attack against the Priory." Teabing frowned. "And believe me, if the Church finds the Holy Grail, they will destroy it. The documents and the relics of the blessed Mary Magdalene as well." His eyes grew heavy. "Then, my dear, with the Sangreal documents gone, all evidence will be lost. The Church will have won their age-old war to rewrite history. The past will be erased forever."

Slowly, Sophie pulled the cruciform key from her sweater pocket and held it out to Teabing.

Teabing took the key and studied it. "My goodness. The Priory seal. Where did you get this?"

"My grandfather gave it to me tonight before he died."

Teabing ran his fingers across the cruciform. "A key to a church?"

She drew a deep breath. "This key provides access to the keystone."

Teabing's head snapped up, his face wild with disbelief. "Impossible! What church did I miss? I've searched every church in France!"

"It's not in a church," Sophie said. "It's in a Swiss depository bank."

Teabing's look of excitement waned. "The keystone is in a bank?"

"A vault," Langdon offered.

"A *bank* vault?" Teabing shook his head violently. "That's impossible. The keystone is supposed to be hidden beneath the sign of the Rose."

"It is," Langdon said. "It was stored in a rosewood box inlaid with a five-petal Rose."

Teabing looked thunderstruck. "You've *seen* the keystone?"

Sophie nodded. "We visited the bank."

Teabing came over to them, his eyes wild with fear. "My friends, we must do something. The keystone is in danger! We have a duty to protect it. What if there are other keys? Perhaps stolen from the murdered *sénéchaux*? If the Church can gain access to the bank as you have—"

"Then they will be too late," Sophie said. "We removed the keystone."

"What! You removed the keystone from its hiding place?"

"Don't worry," Langdon said. "The keystone is well hidden."

"*Extremely* well hidden, I hope!"

"Actually," Langdon said, unable to hide his grin, "that depends on how often you dust under your couch."

THE WIND OUTSIDE Château Villette had picked up, and Silas's robe danced in the breeze as he crouched near the window. Although he had been unable to hear much of the conversation, the word *keystone* had sifted through the glass on numerous occasions.

It is inside.

The Teacher's words were fresh in his mind. *Enter Château Villette. Take the keystone. Hurt no one.*

Now, Langdon and the others had adjourned suddenly to another room, extinguishing the study lights as they went. Feeling like a panther stalking prey, Silas crept to the glass doors. Finding them unlocked, he slipped inside and closed the doors silently behind him. He could hear muffled voices from another room. Silas pulled the pistol from his pocket, turned off the safety, and inched down the hallway.

LIEUTENANT COLLET stood alone at the foot of Leigh Teabing's driveway and gazed up at the massive house. *Isolated. Dark. Good ground cover.* Collet watched his half-dozen agents spreading silently out along the length of the fence. They could be over it and have the house surrounded in a matter of minutes. Langdon could not have chosen a more ideal spot for Collet's men to make a surprise assault.

Collet was about to call Fache himself when at last his phone rang.

Fache sounded not nearly as pleased with the developments as Collet would have imagined. "Why didn't someone tell me we had a lead on Langdon?"

"You were on a phone call and—"

"Where exactly are you, Lieutenant Collet?"

Collet gave him the address. "The estate belongs to a British national named Teabing. Langdon drove a fair distance to get here, and the vehicle is inside the security gate, with no signs of forced entry, so chances are good that Langdon knows the occupant."

"I'm coming out," Fache said. "Don't make a move. I'll handle this personally."

Collet's jaw dropped. "But Captain, you're twenty minutes away! We should act immediately. I have him staked out. I'm with eight men total. Four of us have field rifles and the others have sidearms."

"Wait for me."

"Captain, what if Langdon has a hostage in there? What if he sees us and decides to leave on foot? We need to move *now!* My men are in position and ready to go."

"Lieutenant Collet, you will wait for me to arrive before taking action. That is an order." Fache hung up.

Stunned, Lieutenant Collet switched off his phone. *Why the hell is Fache asking me to wait?* Collet knew the answer. Fache, though famous for his instinct, was notorious for his pride. *Fache wants credit for the arrest.* After putting the American's face all over the television, Fache wanted to be sure his own face got equal time. Collet's job was simply to hold down the fort until the boss showed up to save the day.

As he stood there, Collet flashed on a second possible explanation for this delay. *Damage control.* In law enforcement, hesitating to arrest a fugitive only occurred when uncertainty had arisen regarding the suspect's guilt. *Is Fache having second thoughts that Langdon is the right man?* The thought was frightening. Captain Fache had gone out on a limb tonight to arrest Robert Langdon—*surveillance cachée,* Interpol, and now television. Not even the great Bezu Fache would survive the political fallout if he had mistakenly splashed a prominent American's face all over French television, claiming he was a murderer. If Fache now realized he'd made a mistake, then it made perfect sense that he would tell Collet not to make a move. The last thing Fache needed was for Collet to storm an innocent Brit's private estate and take Langdon at gunpoint.

Moreover, Collet realized, if Langdon were innocent, it explained one of this case's strangest paradoxes: Why had Sophie Neveu, the *granddaughter* of the victim, helped the alleged killer escape? Unless Sophie knew Langdon was falsely charged. Fache had posited all kinds of explanations tonight to explain Sophie's odd behavior, including that Sophie, as Saunière's sole heir, had persuaded her secret lover Robert Langdon to kill off Saunière for the inheritance money. Saunière, if he had suspected this, might have left the police the message *P.S. Find Robert Langdon.* Collet was fairly certain something else was going on here. Sophie Neveu seemed far too solid of character to be mixed up in something that sordid.

"Lieutenant?" One of the field agents came running over. "We found a car."

Collet followed the agent about fifty yards past the driveway. The agent pointed to a wide shoulder on the opposite side of the road. There, parked in the brush, almost out of sight, was a black Audi. It had rental plates. Collet felt the hood. Still warm. Hot even.

"That must be how Langdon got here," Collet said. "Call the rental company. Find out if it's stolen."

"Yes, sir."

Another agent waved Collet back over in the direction of the fence. "Lieutenant, have a look at this." He handed Collet a pair of night vision binoculars. "The grove of trees near the top of the driveway."

Collet aimed the binoculars up the hill and adjusted the image intensifier dials. Slowly, the greenish shapes came into focus. He located the curve of the driveway and slowly followed it up, reaching the grove of trees. All he could do was stare. There, shrouded in the greenery, was an armored truck. A truck identical to the one Collet had permitted to leave the Depository Bank of Zurich earlier tonight. He prayed this was some kind of bizarre coincidence, but he knew it could not be.

"It seems obvious," the agent said, "that this truck is how Langdon and Neveu got away from the bank."

Collet was speechless. He thought of the armored truck driver he had stopped at the roadblock. The Rolex. His impatience to leave. *I never checked the cargo hold*.

Incredulous, Collet realized that someone in the bank had actually lied to DCPJ about Langdon and Sophie's whereabouts and then helped them escape. *But who? And why?* Collet wondered if maybe *this* were the reason Fache had told him not to take action yet. Maybe Fache realized there were more people involved tonight than just Langdon and Sophie. *And if Langdon and Neveu arrived in the armored truck, then who drove the Audi?*

HUNDREDS OF MILES to the south, a chartered Beechcraft Baron 58 raced northward over the Tyrrhenian Sea. Despite calm skies, Bishop Aringarosa clutched an airsickness bag, certain he could be ill at any moment. His conversation with Paris had not at all been what he had imagined.

Alone in the small cabin, Aringarosa twisted the gold ring on his finger and tried to ease his overwhelming sense of fear and desperation. *Everything in Paris has gone terribly wrong.* Closing his eyes, Aringarosa said a prayer that Bezu Fache would have the means to fix it.

Chapter 69

TEABING SAT on the divan, cradling the wooden box on his lap and admiring the lid's intricate inlaid Rose. *Tonight has become the strangest and most magical night of my life.*

"Lift the lid," Sophie whispered, standing over him, beside Langdon.

Teabing smiled. *Do not rush me.* Having spent over a decade searching for this keystone, he wanted to savor every millisecond of this moment. He ran a palm across the wooden lid, feeling the texture of the inlaid flower.

"The Rose," he whispered. *The Rose is Magdalene is the Holy Grail. The Rose is the compass that guides the way.* Teabing felt foolish. For years he had traveled to cathedrals and churches all over France, paying for special access, examining hundreds of archways beneath rose windows, searching for an encrypted keystone. *La clef de voûte—a stone key beneath the sign of the Rose.*

Teabing slowly unlatched the lid and raised it.

As his eyes finally gazed upon the contents, he knew in an instant it could only be the keystone. He was staring at a stone cylinder, crafted of interconnecting lettered dials. The device seemed surprisingly familiar to him.

"Designed from Da Vinci's diaries," Sophie said. "My grandfather made them as a hobby."

Of course, Teabing realized. He had seen the sketches and blueprints. *The key to finding the Holy Grail lies inside this stone.* Teabing lifted the heavy cryptex from the box, holding it gently. Although he had no idea how to open the cylinder, he sensed his own destiny lay inside. In moments of failure, Teabing had questioned whether his life's quest would ever be rewarded. Now those doubts were gone forever. He could hear the ancient words . . . the foundation of the Grail legend:

Vous ne trouvez pas le Saint-Graal, c'est le Saint-Graal qui vous trouve.

You do not find the Grail, the Grail finds you.

And tonight, incredibly, the key to finding the Holy Grail had walked right through his front door.

MARY MAGDALENE AT THE ROCK

WHILE SOPHIE AND TEABING sat with the cryptex and talked about the vinegar, the dials, and what the password might be, Langdon carried the rosewood box across the room to a well-lit table to get a better look at it. Something Teabing had just said was now running through Langdon's mind.

The key to the Grail is hidden beneath the sign of the Rose.

Langdon held the wooden box up to the light and examined the inlaid symbol of the Rose. Although his familiarity with art did not include woodworking or inlaid furniture, he had just recalled the famous tiled ceiling of the Spanish monastery outside of Madrid, where, three centuries after its construction, the ceiling tiles began to fall out, revealing sacred texts scrawled by monks on the plaster beneath.

Langdon looked again at the Rose.

Beneath the Rose.

Sub Rosa.

Secret.

A bump in the hallway behind him made Langdon turn. He saw nothing but shadows. Teabing's manservant most likely had passed through. Langdon turned back to the box. He ran his finger over the smooth edge of the inlay, wondering if he could pry the Rose out, but the craftsmanship was perfect. He doubted even a razor blade could fit in between the inlaid Rose and the carefully carved depression into which it was seated.

Opening the box, he examined the inside of the lid. It was smooth. As he shifted its position, though, the light caught what appeared to be a small hole on the underside of the lid, positioned in the exact center. Langdon closed the lid and examined the inlaid symbol from the top. No hole.

It doesn't pass through.

Setting the box on the table, he looked around the room and spied a stack of papers with a paper clip on it. Borrowing the clip, he returned to the box, opened it, and studied the hole again. Carefully, he unbent the paper clip and inserted one end into the hole. He gave a gentle push. It took almost no effort. He heard something clatter quietly onto the table. Langdon closed the lid to look. It was a small piece of wood, like a puzzle piece. The wooden Rose had popped out of the lid and fallen onto the desk.

Speechless, Langdon stared at the bare spot on the lid where the Rose had been. There, engraved in the wood, written in an immaculate hand, were four lines of text in a language he had never seen.

The characters look vaguely Semitic, Langdon thought to himself, *and yet I don't recognize the language!*

A sudden movement behind him caught his attention. Out of nowhere, a crushing blow to the head knocked Langdon to his knees.

As he fell, he thought for a moment he saw a pale ghost hovering over him, clutching a gun. Then everything went black.

*S*OPHIE NEVEU, despite working in law enforcement, had never found herself at gunpoint until tonight. Almost inconceivably, the gun into which she was now staring was clutched in the pale hand of an enormous albino with long white hair. He looked at her with red eyes that radiated a frightening, disembodied quality. Dressed in a wool robe with a rope tie, he resembled a medieval cleric. Sophie could not imagine who he was, and yet she was feeling a sudden newfound respect for Teabing's suspicions that the Church was behind this.

"You know what I have come for," the monk said, his voice hollow.

Sophie and Teabing were seated on the divan, arms raised as their attacker had commanded. Langdon lay groaning on the floor. The monk's eyes fell immediately to the keystone on Teabing's lap.

Teabing's tone was defiant. "You will not be able to open it."

"My Teacher is very wise," the monk replied, inching closer, the gun shifting between Teabing and Sophie.

Sophie wondered where Teabing's manservant was. *Didn't he hear Robert fall?*

"Who is your teacher?" Teabing asked. "Perhaps we can make a financial arrangement."

"The Grail is priceless." He moved closer.

"You're bleeding," Teabing noted calmly, nodding to the monk's right ankle where a trickle of blood had run down his leg. "And you're limping."

"As do you," the monk replied, motioning to the metal crutches propped beside Teabing. "Now, hand me the keystone."

"You know of the keystone?" Teabing said, sounding surprised.

"Never mind what I know. Stand up slowly, and give it to me."

"Standing is difficult for me."

"Precisely. I would prefer nobody attempt any quick moves."

Teabing slipped his right hand through one of his crutches and grasped the keystone in his left. Lurching to his feet, he stood erect, palming the heavy cylinder in his left hand, and leaning unsteadily on his crutch with his right.

The monk closed to within a few feet, keeping the gun aimed directly at Teabing's head. Sophie watched, feeling helpless as the monk reached out to take the cylinder.

"You will not succeed," Teabing said. "Only the worthy can unlock this stone."

GOD ALONE *judges the worthy,* Silas thought.

"It's quite heavy," the man on crutches said, his arm wavering now. "If you don't take it soon, I'm afraid I shall drop it!" He swayed perilously.

Silas stepped quickly forward to take the stone, and as he did, the man on crutches lost his balance. The crutch slid out from under him, and he began to topple sideways to his right. *No!* Silas lunged to save the stone, lowering his weapon in the process. But the keystone was moving away from him now. As the man fell to his right, his left hand swung backward, and the cylinder tumbled from his palm onto the couch. At the same instant, the metal crutch that had been sliding out from under the man seemed to accelerate, cutting a wide arc through the air toward Silas's leg.

Splinters of pain tore up Silas's body as the crutch made perfect contact with his *cilice,* crushing the barbs into his already raw flesh. Buckling, Silas crumpled to his knees, causing the belt to cut deeper still. The pistol discharged with a deafening roar, the bullet burying itself harmlessly in the floorboards as Silas fell. Before he could raise the gun and fire again, the woman's foot caught him square beneath the jaw.

AT THE BOTTOM of the driveway, Collet heard the gunshot. The muffled pop sent panic through his veins. With Fache on the way, Collet had already relinquished any hopes of claiming personal credit for finding Langdon tonight. But Collet would be damned if Fache's ego landed him in front of a Ministerial Review Board for negligent police procedure.

A weapon was discharged inside a private home! And you waited at the bottom of the driveway?

Collet knew the opportunity for a stealth approach had long since passed. He also knew if he stood idly by for another second, his entire career would be history by morning. Eyeing the estate's iron gate, he made his decision.

"Tie on, and pull it down."

IN THE DISTANT RECESSES of his groggy mind, Robert Langdon had heard the gunshot. He'd also heard a scream of pain. His own? A jackhammer was boring a hole into the back of his cranium. Somewhere nearby, people were talking.

"Where the devil were you?" Teabing was yelling.

The manservant hurried in. "What happened? Oh my God! Who is that? I'll call the police!"

"Bloody hell! Don't call the police. Make yourself useful and get us something with which to restrain this monster."

"And some ice!" Sophie called after him.

Langdon drifted out again. More voices. Movement. Now he was seated on the divan. Sophie was holding an ice pack to his head. His skull ached. As Langdon's vision finally began to clear, he found himself staring at a body on the floor. *Am I hallucinating?* The massive body of an albino monk lay bound and gagged with duct tape. His chin was split open, and the robe over his right thigh was soaked with blood. He too appeared to be just now coming to.

Langdon turned to Sophie. "Who is that? What . . . happened?"

Teabing hobbled over. "You were rescued by a knight brandishing an Excalibur made by Acme Orthopedic."

Huh? Langdon tried to sit up.

Sophie's touch was shaken but tender. "Just give yourself a minute, Robert."

"I fear," Teabing said, "that I've just demonstrated for your lady friend the unfortunate benefit of my condition. It seems everyone underestimates you."

From his seat on the divan, Langdon gazed down at the monk and tried to imagine what had happened.

"He was wearing a *cilice,*" Teabing explained.

"A what?"

Teabing pointed to a bloody strip of barbed leather that lay on the floor. "A Discipline belt. He wore it on his thigh. I took careful aim."

Langdon rubbed his head. He knew of Discipline belts. "But how . . . did you know?"

Teabing grinned. "Christianity is my field of study, Robert, and there are certain sects who wear their hearts on their sleeves." He pointed his crutch at the blood soaking through the monk's cloak. "As it were."

"Opus Dei," Langdon whispered, recalling recent media coverage of several prominent Boston businessmen who were members of Opus Dei. Apprehensive coworkers had falsely and publicly accused the men of wearing *cilice* belts beneath their three-piece suits. In fact, the three men did no such thing. Like many members of Opus Dei, these businessmen were at the "supernumerary" stage and practiced no corporal mortification at all. They were devout Catholics, caring fathers to their children, and deeply dedicated members of the community. Not surprisingly, the media spotlighted their spiritual commitment only briefly before moving on to the shock value of the sect's more stringent "numerary" members . . . members like the monk now lying on the floor before Langdon.

Teabing was looking closely at the bloody belt. "But why would Opus Dei be trying to find the Holy Grail?"

Langdon was too groggy to consider it.

"Robert," Sophie said, walking to the wooden box. "What's this?" She was holding the small Rose inlay he had removed from the lid.

"It covered an engraving on the box. I think the text might tell us how to open the keystone."

Before Sophie and Teabing could respond, a sea of blue police lights and sirens erupted at the bottom of the hill and began snaking up the half-mile driveway.

Teabing frowned. "My friends, it seems we have a decision to make. And we'd better make it fast."

$\mathcal{C}$OLLET AND his agents burst through the front door of Sir Leigh Teabing's estate with their guns drawn. Fanning out, they began searching all the rooms on the first level. They found a bullet hole in the drawing room floor, signs of a struggle, a small amount of blood, a strange, barbed leather belt, and a partially used roll of duct tape. The entire level seemed deserted.

Just as Collet was about to divide his men to search the basement and grounds behind the house, he heard voices on the level above them.

"They're upstairs!"

Rushing up the wide staircase, Collet and his men moved room by room through the huge home, securing darkened bedrooms and hallways as they closed in on the sounds of voices. The sound seemed to be coming from the last bedroom on an exceptionally long hallway. The agents inched down the corridor, sealing off alternate exits.

As they neared the final bedroom, Collet could see the door was wide open. The voices had stopped suddenly, and had been replaced by an odd rumbling, like an engine.

Sidearm raised, Collet gave the signal. Reaching silently around the door frame, he found the light switch and flicked it on. Spinning into the room with men pouring in after him, Collet shouted and aimed his weapon at . . . nothing.

An empty guest bedroom. Pristine.

The rumbling sounds of an automobile engine poured from a black electronic panel on the wall beside the bed. Collet had seen these elsewhere in the house. Some kind of intercom system. He raced over. The panel had about a dozen labeled buttons:

STUDY . . . KITCHEN . . . LAUNDRY . . . CELLAR . . .

So where the hell do I hear a car?

MASTER BEDROOM . . . SUN ROOM . . . BARN . . . LIBRARY . . .

Barn! Collet was downstairs in seconds, running toward the back door, grabbing one of his agents on the way. The men crossed the rear lawn and arrived breathless at the front of a weathered gray barn. Even before they entered, Collet could hear the fading sounds of a car engine. He drew his weapon, rushed in, and flicked on the lights.

The right side of the barn was a rudimentary workshop—lawnmowers, automotive tools, gardening supplies. A familiar intercom panel hung on the wall nearby. One of its buttons was flipped down, transmitting.

GUEST BEDROOM II.

Collet wheeled, anger brimming. *They lured us upstairs with the intercom!* Searching the other side of the barn, he found a long line of horse stalls. No horses. Apparently the owner preferred a different kind of horsepower; the stalls had been converted into an impressive automotive parking facility. The collection was astonishing—a black Ferrari, a pristine Rolls-Royce, an antique Aston Martin sports coupe, a vintage Porsche 356.

The last stall was empty.

Collet ran over and saw oil stains on the stall floor. *They can't get off the compound.* The driveway and gate were barricaded with two patrol cars to prevent this very situation.

"Sir?" The agent pointed down the length of the stalls.

The barn's rear slider was wide open, giving way to a dark, muddy slope of rugged fields that stretched out into the night behind the barn. Collet ran to the door, trying to see out into the darkness. All he could make out was the faint shadow of a forest in the distance. No headlights. This wooded valley was probably crisscrossed by dozens of unmapped fire roads and hunting trails, but Collet was confident his quarry would never make the woods. "Get some men spread out down there. They're probably already stuck somewhere nearby. These fancy sports cars can't handle terrain."

"Um, sir?" The agent pointed to a nearby pegboard on which hung several sets of keys. The labels above the keys bore familiar names.

DAIMLER ... ROLLS-ROYCE ...
ASTON MARTIN ... PORSCHE ...

The last peg was empty.

When Collet read the label above the empty peg, he knew he was in trouble.

HE RANGE ROVER was Java Black Pearl, four-wheel drive, standard transmission, with high-strength polypropylene lamps, rear light cluster fittings, and the steering wheel on the right.

Langdon was pleased he was not driving.

Teabing's manservant Rémy, on orders from his master, was doing an impressive job of maneuvering the vehicle across the moonlit fields behind Château Villette. With no headlights, he had crossed an open knoll and was now descending a long slope, moving farther away from the estate. He seemed to be heading toward a jagged silhouette of wooded land in the distance.

Langdon, cradling the keystone, turned in the passenger seat and eyed Teabing and Sophie in the back seat.

"How's your head, Robert?" Sophie asked, sounding concerned.

Langdon forced a pained smile. "Better, thanks." It was killing him.

Beside her, Teabing glanced over his shoulder at the bound and gagged monk lying in the cramped luggage area behind the back seat. Teabing had the monk's gun on his lap and looked like an old photo of a British safari chap posing over his kill.

"So glad you popped in this evening, Robert," Teabing said, grinning as if he were having fun for the first time in years.

"Sorry to get you involved in this, Leigh."

"Oh, please, I've waited my entire life to be involved." Teabing looked past Langdon out the windshield at the shadow of a long hedgerow. He tapped Rémy on the shoulder from behind. "Remember, no brake lights. Use the emergency brake if you need it. I want to get into the woods a bit. No reason to risk them seeing us from the house."

Rémy coasted to a crawl and guided the Range Rover through an opening in the hedge. As the vehicle lurched onto an overgrown pathway, almost immediately the trees overhead blotted out the moonlight.

I can't see a thing, Langdon thought, straining to distinguish any shapes at all in front of them. It was pitch black. Branches rubbed against the left side of the vehicle, and Rémy corrected in the other direction. Keeping the wheel more or less straight now, he inched ahead about thirty yards.

"You're doing beautifully, Rémy," Teabing said. "That should be far enough. Robert, if you could press that little blue button just below the vent there. See it?"

Langdon found the button and pressed it.

A muted yellow glow fanned out across the path in front of them, revealing thick underbrush on either side of the pathway. *Fog lights,* Langdon realized. They gave off just enough light to keep them on the path, and yet they were deep enough into the woods now that the lights would not give them away.

"Well, Rémy," Teabing chimed happily. "The lights are on. Our lives are in your hands."

"Where are we going?" Sophie asked.

"This trail continues about three kilometers into the forest," Teabing said. "Cutting across the estate and then arching north. Provided we don't hit any standing water or fallen trees, we shall emerge unscathed on the shoulder of highway five."

Unscathed. Langdon's head begged to differ. He turned his eyes down to his own lap, where the keystone was safely stowed in its wooden box. The inlaid Rose on the lid was back in place, and although his head felt muddled, Langdon was eager to remove the inlay again and examine the engraving beneath more closely. He unlatched the lid and began to raise it when Teabing laid a hand on his shoulder from behind.

"Patience, Robert," Teabing said. "It's bumpy and dark. God save us if we break anything. If you didn't recognize the language in the light, you won't do any better in the dark. Let's focus on getting away in one piece, shall we? There will be time for that very soon."

Langdon knew Teabing was right. With a nod, he relatched the box.

The monk in back was moaning now, struggling against his trusses. Suddenly, he began kicking wildly.

Teabing spun around and aimed the pistol over the seat. "I can't imagine your complaint, sir. You trespassed in my home and planted a nasty welt on the skull of a dear friend. I would be well within my rights to shoot you right now and leave you to rot in the woods."

The monk fell silent.

"Are you sure we should have brought him?" Langdon asked.

"Bloody well positive!" Teabing exclaimed. "You're wanted for murder, Robert. This scoundrel is your ticket to freedom. The police apparently want you badly enough to have tailed you to my home."

"My fault," Sophie said. "The armored car probably had a transmitter."

"Not the point," Teabing said. "I'm not surprised the *police* found you, but I *am* surprised that this Opus Dei character found you. From all you've told me, I can't imagine how this man could have tailed you to my home unless he had a contact either within the Judicial Police or within the Zurich Depository."

Langdon considered it. Bezu Fache certainly seemed intent on finding a scapegoat for tonight's murders. And Vernet had turned on them rather suddenly, although considering Langdon was being charged with four murders, the banker's change of heart seemed understandable.

"This monk is not working alone, Robert," Teabing said, "and until you learn *who* is behind all this, you both are in danger. The good news, my friend, is that you are now in the position of power. This monster behind me holds that information, and whoever is pulling his strings has got to be quite nervous right now."

Rémy was picking up speed, getting comfortable with the trail. They splashed through some water, climbed a small rise, and began descending again.

"Robert, could you be so kind as to hand me that phone?" Teabing pointed to the car phone on the dash. Langdon handed it back, and Teabing dialed a number. He waited for a very long time before someone answered. "Richard? Did I wake you? Of course, I did. Silly question. I'm sorry. I have a small problem. I'm feeling a bit off. Rémy and I need to pop up to the Isles for my treatments. Well, right away, actually. Sorry for the short notice. Can you have Elizabeth ready in about twenty minutes? I know, do the best you can. See you shortly." He hung up.

"Elizabeth?" Langdon said.

"My plane. She cost me a Queen's ransom."

Langdon turned full around and looked at him.

"What?" Teabing demanded. "You two can't expect to stay in France with the entire Judicial Police after you. London will be much safer."

Sophie had turned to Teabing as well. "You think we should leave the country?"

"My friends, I am far more influential in the civilized world than here in France. Furthermore, the Grail is believed to be in Great Britain. If we unlock the keystone, I am certain we will discover a map that indicates we have moved in the proper direction."

"You're running a big risk," Sophie said, "by helping us. You won't make any friends with the French police."

Teabing gave a wave of disgust. "I am finished with France. I moved here to find the keystone. That work is now done. I shan't care if I ever again see Château Villette."

Sophie sounded uncertain. "How will we get through airport security?"

Teabing chuckled. "I fly from Le Bourget—an executive airfield not far from here. French doctors make me nervous, so every fortnight, I fly north to take my treatments in England. I pay for certain special privileges at both ends. Once we're airborne, you can make a decision as to whether or not you'd like someone from the U.S. Embassy to meet us."

Langdon suddenly didn't want anything to do with the embassy. All he could think of was the keystone, the inscription, and whether it would all lead to the Grail. He wondered if Teabing was right about Britain. Admittedly most modern legends placed the Grail somewhere in the United Kingdom. Even King Arthur's mythical, Grail-rich Isle of Avalon was now believed to be none other than Glastonbury, England. Wherever the Grail lay, Langdon never imagined he would actually be looking for it. *The Sangreal documents. The true history of Jesus Christ. The tomb of Mary Magdalene.* He suddenly felt as if he were living in some kind of limbo tonight . . . a bubble where the real world could not reach him.

"Sir?" Rémy said. "Are you truly thinking of returning to England for good?"

"Rémy, you needn't worry," Teabing assured. "Just because I am returning to the Queen's realm does not mean I intend to subject my palate to bangers and mash for the rest of my days. I expect you will join me there permanently. I'm planning to buy a splendid

THE RUINS OF GLASTONBURY ABBEY

villa in Devonshire, and we'll have all your things shipped up immediately. An adventure, Rémy. I say, an adventure!"

Langdon had to smile. As Teabing railed on about his plans for a triumphant return to Britain, Langdon felt himself caught up in the man's infectious enthusiasm.

Gazing absently out the window, Langdon watched the woods passing by, ghostly pale in the yellow blush of the fog lights. The side mirror was tipped inward, brushed askew by branches, and Langdon saw the reflection of Sophie sitting quietly in the back seat. He watched her for a long while and felt an unexpected upwelling of contentment. Despite his troubles tonight, Langdon was thankful to have landed in such good company.

After several minutes, as if suddenly sensing his eyes on her, Sophie leaned forward and put her hands on his shoulders, giving him a quick rub. "You okay?"

"Yeah," Langdon said. "Somehow."

Sophie sat back in her seat, and Langdon saw a quiet smile cross her lips. He realized that he too was now grinning.

WEDGED in the back of the Range Rover, Silas could barely breathe. His arms were wrenched backward and heavily lashed to his ankles with kitchen twine and duct tape. Every bump in the road sent pain shooting through his twisted shoulders. At least his captors had removed the *cilice.* Unable to inhale through the strip of tape over his mouth, he could only breathe through his nostrils, which were slowly clogging up due to the dusty rear cargo area into which he had been crammed. He began coughing.

"I think he's choking," the French driver said, sounding concerned.

The British man who had struck Silas with his crutch now turned and peered over the seat, frowning coldly at Silas. "Fortunately for you, we British judge man's civility not by his compassion for his friends, but by his compassion for his enemies." The Brit reached down and grabbed the duct tape on Silas's mouth. In one fast motion, he tore it off.

Silas felt as if his lips had just caught fire, but the air pouring into his lungs was sent from God.

"Whom do you work for?" the British man demanded.

"I do the work of God," Silas spat back through the pain in his jaw where the woman had kicked him.

"You belong to Opus Dei," the man said. It was not a question.

"You know nothing of who I am."

"Why does Opus Dei want the keystone?"

Silas had no intention of answering. The keystone was the link to the Holy Grail, and the Holy Grail was the key to protecting the faith.

I do the work of God. The Way is in peril.

Now, in the Range Rover, struggling against his bonds, Silas feared he had failed the Teacher and the bishop forever. He had no way even to contact them and tell them the terrible turn of events. *My captors have the keystone! They will reach the Grail before we do!* In the stifling darkness, Silas prayed. He let the pain of his body fuel his supplications.

A miracle, Lord. I need a miracle. Silas had no way of knowing that hours from now, he would get one.

"ROBERT?" Sophie was still watching him. "A funny look just crossed your face."

Langdon glanced back at her, realizing his jaw was firmly set and his heart was racing. An incredible notion had just occurred to him. *Could it really be that simple an explanation?* "I need to use your cell phone, Sophie."

"Now?"

"I think I just figured something out."

"What?"

"I'll tell you in a minute. I need your phone."

Sophie looked wary. "I doubt Fache is tracing, but keep it under a minute just in case." She gave him her phone.

"How do I dial the States?"

"You need to reverse the charges. My service doesn't cover transatlantic."

Langdon dialed zero, knowing that the next sixty seconds might answer a question that had been puzzling him all night.

Chapter 68

$\mathcal{N}$EW YORK editor Jonas Faukman had just climbed into bed for the night when the telephone rang. *A little late for callers,* he grumbled, picking up the receiver.

An operator's voice asked him, "Will you accept charges for a collect call from Robert Langdon?"

Puzzled, Jonas turned on the light. "Uh . . . sure, okay."

The line clicked. "Jonas?"

"Robert? You wake me up *and* you charge me for it?"

"Jonas, forgive me," Langdon said. "I'll keep this very short. I really need to know. The manuscript I gave you. Have you—"

"Robert, I'm sorry, I know I said I'd send the edits out to you this week, but I'm swamped. Next Monday. I promise."

"I'm not worried about the edits. I need to know if you sent any copies out for blurbs without telling me?"

Faukman hesitated. Langdon's newest manuscript—an exploration of the history of goddess worship—included several sections about Mary Magdalene that were going to raise some eyebrows. Although the material was well documented and had been covered by others, Faukman had no intention of printing Advance Reading Copies of Langdon's book without at least a few endorsements from serious historians and art luminaries. Jonas had chosen ten big names in the art world and sent them all sections of the manuscript along with a polite letter asking if they would be willing to write a short endorsement for the jacket. In Faukman's experience, most people jumped at the opportunity to see their name in print.

"Jonas?" Langdon pressed. "You sent out my manuscript, didn't you?"

Faukman frowned, sensing Langdon was not happy about it. "The manuscript was clean, Robert, and I wanted to surprise you with some terrific blurbs."

A pause. "Did you send one to the curator of the Paris Louvre?"

"What do you think? Your manuscript referenced his Louvre collection several times, his books are in your bibliography, and the guy has some serious clout for foreign sales. Saunière was a no-brainer."

The silence on the other end lasted a long time. "When did you send it?"

"About a month ago. I also mentioned you would be in Paris soon and suggested you two chat. Did he ever call you to meet?" Faukman paused, rubbing his eyes. "Hold on, aren't you supposed to *be* in Paris this week?"

"I *am* in Paris."

Faukman sat upright. "You called me collect from *Paris?*"

"Take it out of my royalties, Jonas. Did you ever hear back from Saunière? Did he like the manuscript?"

"I don't know. I haven't yet heard from him."

"Well, don't hold your breath. I've got to run, but this explains a lot. Thanks."

"Robert—"

But Langdon was gone.

Faukman hung up the phone, shaking his head in disbelief. *Authors,* he thought. *Even the sane ones are nuts.*

INSIDE THE RANGE ROVER, Leigh Teabing let out a guffaw. "Robert, you're saying you wrote a manuscript that delves into a secret society, and your editor *sent* a copy to that secret society?"

Langdon slumped. "Evidently."

"A cruel coincidence, my friend."

Coincidence has nothing to do with it, Langdon knew. Asking Jacques Saunière to endorse a manuscript on goddess worship was as obvious as asking Tiger Woods to endorse a book on golf. Moreover, it was virtually guaranteed that any book on goddess worship would have to mention the Priory of Sion.

"Here's the million-dollar question," Teabing said, still chuckling. "Was your position on the Priory favorable or unfavorable?"

Langdon could hear Teabing's true meaning loud and clear. Many historians questioned why the Priory was still keeping the Sangreal documents hidden. Some felt the information should have been shared with the world long ago. "I took no position on the Priory's actions."

"You mean lack thereof."

Langdon shrugged. Teabing was apparently on the side of making the documents public. "I simply provided history on the brotherhood and described them as a modern goddess worship society, keepers of the Grail, and guardians of ancient documents."

Sophie looked at him. "Did you mention the keystone?"

Langdon winced. He had. Numerous times. "I talked about the supposed keystone as an example of the lengths to which the Priory would go to protect the Sangreal documents."

Sophie looked amazed. "I guess that explains *P.S. Find Robert Langdon*."

Langdon sensed it was actually something *else* in the manuscript that had piqued Saunière's interest, but that topic was something he would discuss with Sophie when they were alone.

"So," Sophie said, "you lied to Captain Fache."

"What?" Langdon demanded.

"You told him you had never corresponded with my grandfather."

"I didn't! My editor sent him a manuscript."

"Think about it, Robert. If Captain Fache didn't find the envelope in which your editor sent the manuscript, he would have to conclude that *you* sent it." She paused. "Or worse, that you hand-delivered it and lied about it."

WHEN THE RANGE ROVER arrived at Le Bourget Airfield, Rémy drove to a small hangar at the far end of the airstrip. As they approached, a tousled man in wrinkled khakis hurried from the hangar, waved, and slid open the enormous corrugated metal door to reveal a sleek white jet within.

Langdon stared at the glistening fuselage. "*That's* Elizabeth?"

Teabing grinned. "Beats the bloody Chunnel."

The man in khakis hurried toward them, squinting into the headlights. "Almost ready, sir," he called in a British accent. "My apologies for the delay, but you took me by surprise and—" He stopped short as the group unloaded. He looked at Sophie and Langdon, and then Teabing.

Teabing said, "My associates and I have urgent business in London. We've no time to waste. Please prepare to depart immediately." As he spoke, Teabing took the pistol out of the vehicle and handed it to Langdon.

The pilot's eyes bulged at the sight of the weapon. He walked over to Teabing and whispered, "Sir, my humble apologies, but my diplomatic flight allowance provides only for you and your manservant. I cannot take your guests."

"Richard," Teabing said, smiling warmly, "two thousand pounds sterling and that loaded gun say you *can* take my guests." He motioned to the Range Rover. "And the unfortunate fellow in the back."

THE HAWKER 731's twin Garrett TFE-731 engines thundered, powering the plane skyward with gut-wrenching force. Outside the window, Le Bourget Airfield dropped away with startling speed.

I'm fleeing the country, Sophie thought, her body forced back into the leather seat. Until this moment, she had believed her game of cat and mouse with Fache would be somehow justifiable to the Ministry of Defense. *I was attempting to protect an innocent man. I was trying to fulfill my grandfather's dying wishes.* That window of opportunity, Sophie knew, had just closed. She was leaving the country, without documentation, accompanying a wanted man, and transporting a bound hostage. If a "line of reason" had ever existed, she had just crossed it. *At almost the speed of sound.*

Sophie was seated with Langdon and Teabing near the front of the cabin—the *Fan Jet Executive Elite Design*, according to the gold medallion on the door. Their plush swivel chairs were bolted to tracks on the floor and could be repositioned and locked around a rectangular hardwood table. A mini-boardroom. The dignified surroundings, however, did little to camouflage the less than dignified state of affairs in the rear of the plane where, in a separate seating area near the rest room, Teabing's manservant Rémy sat with the pistol in hand, begrudgingly carrying out Teabing's orders to stand guard over the bloody monk who lay trussed at his feet like a piece of luggage.

"Before we turn our attention to the keystone," Teabing said, "I was wondering if you would permit me a few words." He sounded apprehensive, like a father about to give the birds-and-the-bees lecture to his children. "My friends, I realize

I am but a guest on this journey, and I am honored as such. And yet, as someone who has spent his life in search of the Grail, I feel it is my duty to warn you that you are about to step onto a path from which there is no return, regardless of the dangers involved." He turned to Sophie. "Miss Neveu, your grandfather gave you this cryptex in hopes you would keep the secret of the Holy Grail alive."

"Yes."

"Understandably, you feel obliged to follow the trail wherever it leads."

Sophie nodded, although she felt a second motivation still burning within her. *The truth about my family.* Despite Langdon's assurances that the keystone had nothing to do with her past, Sophie still sensed something deeply personal entwined within this mystery, as if this cryptex, forged by her grandfather's own hands, were trying to speak to her and offer some kind of resolution to the emptiness that had haunted her all these years.

"Your grandfather and three others died tonight," Teabing continued, "and they did so to keep this keystone away from the Church. Opus Dei came within inches tonight of possessing it. You understand, I hope, that this puts you in a position of exceptional responsibility. You have been handed a torch. A two-thousand-year-old flame that cannot be allowed to go out. This torch cannot fall into the wrong hands." He paused, glancing at the rosewood box. "I realize you have been given no choice in this matter, Miss Neveu, but considering what is at stake here, you must either fully embrace this responsibility . . . or you must pass that responsibility to someone else."

"My grandfather gave the cryptex to me. I'm sure he thought I could handle the responsibility."

Teabing looked encouraged but unconvinced. "Good. A strong will is necessary. And yet, I am curious if you understand that successfully unlocking the keystone will bring with it a far greater trial."

"How so?"

"My dear, imagine that you are suddenly holding a map that reveals the location of the Holy Grail. In that moment, you will be in possession of a truth capable of altering history forever. You will be the keeper of a truth that man has sought for centuries. You will be faced with the responsibility of revealing that truth to the world. The individual who does so will be revered by many and despised by many. The question is whether you will have the necessary strength to carry out that task."

Sophie paused. "I'm not sure that is *my* decision to make."

Teabing's eyebrows arched. "No? If not the possessor of the keystone, then who?"

"The brotherhood who has successfully protected the secret for so long."

"The Priory?" Teabing looked skeptical. "But how? The brotherhood was shattered tonight. *Decapitated,* as you so aptly put it. Whether they were infiltrated by some kind of eavesdropping or by a spy within their ranks, we will never know, but the fact remains that someone got to them and uncovered the identities of their four top members. I would not trust anyone who stepped forward from the brotherhood at this point."

"So what do you suggest?" Langdon asked.

"Robert, you know as well as I do that the Priory has not protected the truth all these years to have it gather dust until eternity. They have been waiting for the right moment in history to share their secret. A time when the world is ready to handle the truth."

"And you believe that moment has arrived?" Langdon asked.

"Absolutely. It could not be more obvious. All the historical signs are in place, and if the Priory did not intend to make their secret known very soon, why has the Church now attacked?"

Sophie argued, "The monk has not yet told us his purpose."

"The monk's purpose is the Church's purpose," Teabing replied, "to destroy the documents that reveal the great deception. The Church came closer tonight than they have ever come, and the Priory has put its trust in you, Miss Neveu. The task of saving the Holy Grail clearly includes carrying out the Priory's final wishes of sharing the truth with the world."

Langdon intervened. "Leigh, asking Sophie to make that decision is quite a load to drop on someone who only an hour ago learned the Sangreal documents exist."

Teabing sighed. "I apologize if I am pressing, Miss Neveu. Clearly I have always believed these documents should be made public, but in the end the decision belongs to you. I simply feel it is important that you begin to think about what happens should we succeed in opening the keystone."

"Gentlemen," Sophie said, her voice firm. "To quote your words, 'You do not find the Grail, the Grail finds you.' I am going to trust that the Grail has found me for a reason, and when the time comes, I will know what to do."

Both of them looked startled.

"So then," she said, motioning to the rosewood box. "Let's move on."

Chapter 50

*S*TANDING IN THE drawing room of Château Villette, Lieutenant Collet watched the dying fire and felt despondent. Captain Fache had arrived moments earlier and was now in the next room, yelling into the phone, trying to coordinate the failed attempt to locate the missing Range Rover.

It could be anywhere by now, Collet thought.

Having disobeyed Fache's direct orders and lost Langdon for a second time, Collet was grateful that PTS had located a bullet hole in the floor, which at least corroborated Collet's claims that a shot had been fired. Still, Fache's mood was sour, and Collet sensed there would be dire repercussions when the dust settled.

Unfortunately, the clues they were turning up here seemed to shed no light at all on what was going on or who was involved. The black Audi outside had been rented in a false name with false credit card numbers, and the prints in the car matched nothing in the Interpol database.

Another agent hurried into the living room, his eyes urgent. "Where's Captain Fache?"

Collet barely looked up from the burning embers. "He's on the phone."

"I'm off the phone," Fache snapped, stalking into the room. "What have you got?"

The second agent said, "Sir, Central just heard from André Vernet at the Depository Bank of Zurich. He wants to talk to you privately. He is changing his story."

"Oh?" Fache said.

Now Collet looked up.

"Vernet is admitting that Langdon and Neveu spent time inside his bank tonight."

"We figured that out," Fache said. "Why did Vernet lie about it?"

"He said he'll talk only to you, but he's agreed to cooperate fully."

"In exchange for what?"

"For our keeping his bank's name out of the news and also for helping him recover some stolen property. It sounds like Langdon and Neveu stole something from Saunière's account."

"What?" Collet blurted. "How?"

Fache never flinched, his eyes riveted on the second agent. "What did they steal?"

"Vernet didn't elaborate, but he sounds like he's willing to do anything to get it back."

Collet tried to imagine how this could happen. Maybe Langdon and Neveu had held a bank employee at gunpoint? Maybe they forced Vernet to open Saunière's account and facilitate an escape in the armored truck. As feasible as it was, Collet was having trouble believing Sophie Neveu could be involved in anything like that.

From the kitchen, another agent yelled to Fache. "Captain? I'm going through Mr. Teabing's speed dial numbers, and I'm on the phone with Le Bourget Airfield. I've got some bad news."

THIRTY SECONDS LATER, Fache was packing up and preparing to leave Château Villette. He had just learned that Teabing kept a private jet nearby at Le Bourget Airfield and that the plane had taken off about a half hour ago.

The Bourget representative on the phone had claimed not to know who was on the plane or where it was headed. The takeoff had been unscheduled, and no flight plan had been logged. Highly illegal, even for a small airfield. Fache was certain that by applying the right pressure, he could get the answers he was looking for.

"Lieutenant Collet," Fache barked, heading for the door. "I have no choice but to leave you in charge of the PTS investigation here. Try to do something right for a change."

A S THE HAWKER leveled off, with its nose aimed for England, Langdon carefully lifted the rosewood box from his lap, where he had been protecting it during takeoff. Now, as he set the box on the table, he could sense Sophie and Teabing leaning forward with anticipation.

Unlatching the lid and opening the box, Langdon turned his attention not to the lettered dials of the cryptex, but rather to the tiny hole on the underside of the box lid. Using the tip of a pen, he carefully removed the inlaid Rose on top and revealed the text beneath it. *Sub Rosa,* he mused, hoping a fresh look at the text would bring clarity. Focusing all his energies, Langdon studied the strange text.

After several seconds, he began to feel the initial frustration resurfacing. "Leigh, I just can't seem to place it."

FROM WHERE Sophie was seated across the table, she could not yet see the text, but Langdon's inability to immediately identify the language surprised her. *My grandfather spoke a language so obscure that even a symbologist can't identify it?* She quickly realized she should not find this surprising. This would not be the first secret Jacques Saunière had kept from his granddaughter.

OPPOSITE SOPHIE, Leigh Teabing felt ready to burst. Eager for his chance to see the text, he quivered with excitement, leaning in, trying to see around Langdon, who was still hunched over the box.

"I don't know," Langdon whispered intently. "My first guess is a Semitic, but now I'm not so sure. Most primary Semitics include *nekkudot*. This has none."

"Probably ancient," Teabing offered.

"Nekkudot?" Sophie inquired.

Teabing never took his eyes from the box. "Most modern Semitic alphabets have no vowels and use *nekkudot*—tiny dots and dashes written either below or within the consonants—to indicate what vowel sound accompanies them. Historically speaking, *nekkudot* are a relatively modern addition to language."

Langdon was still hovering over the script. "A Sephardic transliteration, perhaps . . . ?"

Teabing could bear it no longer. "Perhaps if I just . . ." Reaching over, he edged the box away from Langdon and pulled it toward himself. No doubt Langdon had a solid familiarity with the standard ancients—Greek, Latin, the Romances—but from the fleeting glance Teabing had of *this* language, he thought it looked more specialized, possibly a Rashi script or a STA"M with crowns.

Taking a deep breath, Teabing feasted his eyes upon the engraving. He said nothing for a very long time. With each passing second, Teabing felt his confidence deflating. "I'm astonished," he said. "This language looks like nothing I've ever seen!"

Langdon slumped.

"Might I see it?" Sophie asked.

Teabing pretended not to hear her. "Robert, you said earlier that you thought you'd *seen* something like this before?"

Langdon looked vexed. "I thought so. I'm not sure. The script looks familiar somehow."

"Leigh?" Sophie repeated, clearly not appreciating being left out of the discussion. "Might I have a look at the box my grandfather made?"

"Of course, dear," Teabing said, pushing it over to her. He hadn't meant to sound belittling, and yet Sophie Neveu was light-years out of her league. If a British Royal Historian and a Harvard symbologist could not even identify the language—

"Aah," Sophie said, seconds after examining the box. "I should have guessed."

Teabing and Langdon turned in unison, staring at her.

"Guessed *what?*" Teabing demanded.

Sophie shrugged. "Guessed that *this* would be the language my grandfather would have used."

"You're saying you can *read* this text?" Teabing exclaimed.

"Quite easily," Sophie chimed, obviously enjoying herself now. "My grandfather taught me this language when I was only six years old. I'm fluent." She leaned across the table and fixed Teabing with an admonishing glare. "And frankly, sir, considering your allegiance to the Crown, I'm a little surprised you didn't recognize it."

In a flash, Langdon knew.

No wonder the script looks so damned familiar!

Several years ago, Langdon had attended an event at Harvard's Fogg Museum. Harvard dropout Bill Gates had returned to his alma mater to lend to the museum one of his priceless acquisitions—eighteen sheets of paper he had recently purchased at auction from the Armand Hammer Estate.

His winning bid—a cool $30.8 million.

The author of the pages—Leonardo da Vinci.

The eighteen folios—now known as Leonardo's *Codex Leicester* after their famous owner, the Earl of Leicester—were all that remained of one of Leonardo's most fascinating notebooks: essays and drawings outlining Da Vinci's progressive theories on astronomy, geology, archaeology, and hydrology.

Langdon would never forget his reaction after waiting in line and finally viewing the priceless parchment. Utter letdown. The pages were unintelligible. Despite being beautifully preserved and written in an impeccably neat penmanship—crimson ink on cream paper—the codex looked like gibberish. At first Langdon thought he could not read them because Da Vinci wrote his notebooks in an archaic Italian. But after studying them more closely, he realized he could not identify a single Italian word, or even one letter.

"Try this, sir," whispered the female docent at the display case. She motioned to a hand mirror affixed to the display on a chain. Langdon picked it up and examined the text in the mirror's surface.

Instantly it was clear.

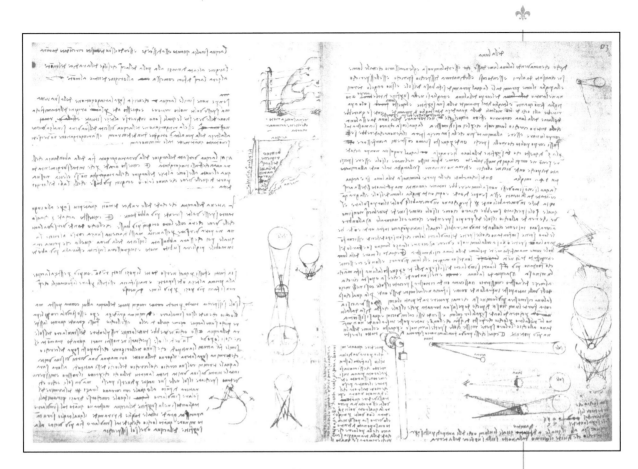

FROM *CODEX LEICESTER* BY LEONARDO DA VINCI

Langdon had been so eager to peruse some of the great thinker's ideas that he had forgotten one of the man's numerous artistic talents was an ability to write in a mirrored script that was virtually illegible to anyone other than himself. Historians still debated whether Da Vinci wrote this way simply to amuse himself or to keep people from peering over his shoulder and stealing his ideas, but the point was moot. Da Vinci did as he pleased.

SOPHIE SMILED INWARDLY to see that Robert understood her meaning. "I can read the first few words," she said. "It's English."

Teabing was still sputtering. "What's going on?"

"Reverse text," Langdon said. "We need a mirror."

"No we don't," Sophie said. "I bet this veneer is thin enough." She lifted the rosewood box up to a canister light on the wall and began examining the underside of the lid. Her grandfather couldn't actually write in reverse, so he always cheated by writing *normally* and then flipping the paper over and tracing the reversed impression. Sophie's guess was that he had wood-burned *normal* text into a block of wood and then run the back of the block through a sander until the wood was paper thin and the wood-burning could be seen *through* the wood. Then he'd simply flipped the piece over, and laid it in.

As Sophie moved the lid closer to the light, she saw she was right. The bright beam sifted through the thin layer of wood, and the script appeared in reverse on the underside of the lid.

Instantly legible.

"English," Teabing croaked, hanging his head in shame. "My native tongue."

AT THE REAR of the plane, Rémy Legaludec strained to hear beyond the rumbling engines, but the conversation up front was inaudible. Rémy did not like the way the night was progressing. Not at all. He looked down at the bound monk at his feet. The man lay perfectly still now, as if in a trance of acceptance, or perhaps, in silent prayer for deliverance.

FIFTEEN THOUSAND FEET in the air, Robert Langdon felt the physical world fade away as all of his thoughts converged on Saunière's mirror-image poem, which was illuminated through the lid of the box.

Sophie quickly found some paper and copied it down longhand. When she was done, the three of them took turns reading the text. It was like some kind of archaeological crossword . . . a riddle that promised to reveal how to open the cryptex. Langdon read the verse slowly.

An ancient word of wisdom frees this scroll . . . and helps us keep her scatter'd family whole . . . a headstone praised by templars is the key . . . and atbash will reveal the truth to thee.

Before Langdon could even ponder what ancient password the verse was trying to reveal, he felt something far more fundamental resonate within him—the meter of the poem. *Iambic pentameter.*

Langdon had come across this meter often over the years while researching secret societies across Europe, including just last year in the Vatican Secret Archives. For centuries, iambic pentameter had been a preferred poetic meter of outspoken literati across the globe, from the ancient Greek writer Archilochus to Shakespeare, Milton, Chaucer, and Voltaire—bold souls who chose to write their social commentaries in a meter that many of the day believed had mystical properties. The roots of iambic pentameter were deeply pagan.

Iambs. Two syllables with opposite emphasis. Stressed and unstressed. Yin yang. A balanced pair. Arranged in strings of five. Pentameter. Five for the pentacle of Venus and the sacred feminine.

"It's pentameter!" Teabing blurted, turning to Langdon. "And the verse is in English! *La lingua pura!*"

Langdon nodded. The Priory, like many European secret societies at odds with the Church, had considered English the only European *pure* language for centuries. Unlike French, Spanish, and Italian, which were rooted in Latin—*the tongue of the Vatican*—English was linguistically removed from Rome's propaganda machine, and

א	ALEPH
ב	BEYT
ג	GIMEL
ד	DALET
ה	HEY
ו	VAV
ז	ZAYIN
ח	HHET
ט	TET
י	YUD
כ,ך	KAPH
ל	LAMED
מ,ם	MEM
נ,ן	NUN
ס	SAMECH
ע	AYIN
פ,ף	PEY
צ,ץ	TSADEY
ק	QUPH
ר	RESH
ש,ש	SHIN,SIN
ת	TAV

therefore became a sacred, secret tongue for those brotherhoods educated enough to learn it.

"This poem," Teabing gushed, "references not only the Grail, but the Knights Templar and the scattered family of Mary Magdalene! What more could we ask for?"

"The password," Sophie said, looking again at the poem. "It sounds like we need some kind of ancient word of wisdom?"

"Abracadabra?" Teabing ventured, his eyes twinkling.

A word of five letters, Langdon thought, pondering the staggering number of ancient words that might be considered *words of wisdom*—selections from mystic chants, astrological prophecies, secret society inductions, Wicca incantations, Egyptian magic spells, pagan mantras—the list was endless.

"The password," Sophie said, "appears to have something to do with the Templars." She read the text aloud. "'A headstone praised by Templars is the key.'"

"Leigh," Langdon said, "you're the Templar specialist. Any ideas?"

Teabing was silent for several seconds and then sighed. "Well, a headstone is obviously a grave marker of some sort. It's possible the poem is referencing a gravestone the Templars praised at the tomb of Magdalene, but that doesn't help us much because we have no idea where her tomb is."

"The last line," Sophie said, "says that *Atbash* will reveal the truth. I've heard that word. Atbash."

"I'm not surprised," Langdon replied. "You probably heard it in Cryptology 101. The Atbash Cipher is one of the oldest codes known to man."

Of course! Sophie thought. *The famous Hebrew encoding system.*

The Atbash Cipher had indeed been part of Sophie's early cryptology training. The cipher dated back to 500 B.C. and was now used as a classroom example of a basic rotational substitution scheme. A common form of Jewish cryptogram, the Atbash Cipher was a simple substitution code based on the twenty-two-letter Hebrew alphabet. In Atbash, the first letter was substituted by the last letter, the second letter by the next to last letter, and so on.

"Atbash is sublimely appropriate," Teabing said. "Text encrypted with Atbash is found throughout the Kabbala, the Dead Sea Scrolls, and even the Old Testament. Jewish scholars and mystics are *still* finding hidden meanings using Atbash. The Priory certainly would include the Atbash Cipher as part of their teachings."

"The only problem," Langdon said, "is that we don't have anything on which to apply the cipher."

Teabing sighed. "There must be a code word on the headstone. We must find this headstone praised by Templars."

Sophie sensed from the grim look on Langdon's face that finding the Templar headstone would be no small feat.

Atbash is the key, Sophie thought. *But we don't have a door.*

It was three minutes later that Teabing heaved a frustrated sigh and shook his head. "My friends, I'm stymied. Let me ponder this while I get us some nibblies and check on Rémy and our guest." He stood up and headed for the back of the plane.

Sophie felt tired as she watched him go.

Outside the window, the blackness of the predawn was absolute. Sophie felt as if she were being hurtled through space with no idea where she would land. Having grown up solving her grandfather's riddles, she had the uneasy sense right now that this poem before them contained information they still had not seen.

There is more there, she told herself. *Ingeniously hidden . . . but present nonetheless.*

Also plaguing her thoughts was a fear that what they eventually found inside this cryptex would not be as simple as "a map to the Holy Grail." Despite Teabing's and Langdon's confidence that the truth lay just within the marble cylinder, Sophie had solved enough of her grandfather's treasure hunts to know that Jacques Saunière did not give up his secrets easily.

LE BOURGET AIRFIELD'S night-shift air traffic controller had been dozing before a blank radar screen when the captain of the Judicial Police practically broke down his door.

"Teabing's jet," Bezu Fache blared, marching into the small tower, "where did it go?"

The controller's initial response was a babbling, lame attempt to protect the privacy of their British client—one of the airfield's most respected customers. It failed miserably.

"Okay," Fache said, "I am placing you under arrest for permitting a private plane to take off without registering a flight plan." Fache motioned to another officer, who approached with handcuffs, and the traffic controller felt a surge of terror. He thought of the newspaper articles debating whether the nation's police captain was a hero or a menace. That question had just been answered.

"Wait!" the controller heard himself whimper at the sight of the handcuffs. "I can tell you this much. Sir Leigh Teabing makes frequent trips to London for medical treatments. He has a hangar at Biggin Hill Executive Airport in Kent. On the outskirts of London."

Fache waved off the man with the cuffs. "Is Biggin Hill his destination tonight?"

"I don't know," the controller said honestly. "The plane left on its usual tack, and his last radar contact suggested the United Kingdom. Biggin Hill is an extremely likely guess."

"Did he have others onboard?"

"I swear, sir, there is no way for me to know that. Our clients can drive directly to their hangars, and load as they please. Who is onboard is the responsibility of the customs officials at the receiving airport."

Fache checked his watch and gazed out at the scattering of jets parked in front of the terminal. "If they're going to Biggin Hill, how long until they land?"

The controller fumbled through his records. "It's a short flight. His plane could be on the ground by . . . around six-thirty. Fifteen minutes from now."

Fache frowned and turned to one of his men. "Get a transport up here. I'm going to London. And get me the Kent local police. Not British MI5. I want this quiet. Kent *local*. Tell them I want Teabing's plane to be permitted to land. Then I want it surrounded on the tarmac. Nobody deplanes until I get there."

"YOU'RE QUIET," Langdon said, gazing across the Hawker's cabin at Sophie.

"Just tired," she replied. "And the poem. I don't know."

Langdon was feeling the same way. The hum of the engines and the gentle rocking of the plane were hypnotic, and his head still throbbed where he'd been hit by the monk. Teabing was still in the back of the plane, and Langdon decided to take advantage of the moment alone with Sophie to tell her something that had been on his mind. "I think I know part of the reason why your grandfather conspired to put us together. I think there's something he wanted me to explain to you."

"The history of the Holy Grail and Mary Magdalene isn't enough?"

Langdon felt uncertain how to proceed. "The rift between you. The reason you haven't spoken to him in ten years. I think maybe he was hoping I could somehow make that right by explaining what drove you apart."

Sophie squirmed in her seat. "I haven't told you what drove us apart."

Langdon eyed her carefully. "You witnessed a sex rite. Didn't you?"

Sophie recoiled. "How do you know that?"

"Sophie, you told me you witnessed something that convinced you your grandfather was in a secret society. And whatever you saw upset you enough that you haven't spoken to him since. I know a fair amount about secret societies. It doesn't take the brains of Da Vinci to guess what you saw."

Sophie stared.

"Was it in the spring?" Langdon asked. "Sometime around the equinox? Mid-March?"

Sophie looked out the window. "I was on spring break from university. I came home a few days early."

"You want to tell me about it?"

"I'd rather not." She turned suddenly back to Langdon, her eyes welling with emotion. "I don't know what I saw."

"Were both men and women present?"

After a beat, she nodded.

"Dressed in white and black?"

She wiped her eyes and then nodded, seeming to open up a little. "The women were in white gossamer gowns . . . with golden shoes. They held golden orbs. The men wore black tunics and black shoes."

Langdon strained to hide his emotion, and yet he could not believe what he was hearing. Sophie Neveu had unwittingly witnessed a two-thousand-year-old sacred ceremony. "Masks?" he asked, keeping his voice calm. "Androgynous masks?"

"Yes. Everyone. Identical masks. White on the women. Black on the men."

Langdon had read descriptions of this ceremony and understood its mystic roots. "It's called Hieros Gamos," he said softly. "It dates back more than two thousand years. Egyptian priests and priestesses performed it regularly to celebrate the reproductive power of the female." He paused, leaning toward her. "And if you witnessed Hieros Gamos without being properly prepared to understand its meaning, I imagine it would be pretty shocking."

Sophie said nothing.

"Hieros Gamos is Greek," he continued. "It means *sacred marriage*."

"The ritual I saw was no marriage."

"Marriage as in *union,* Sophie."

"You mean as in sex."

"No."

"No?" she said, her olive eyes testing him.

Langdon backpedaled. "Well . . . yes, in a manner of speaking, but not as we understand it today." He explained that although what she saw probably *looked* like a sex ritual, Hieros Gamos had nothing to do with eroticism. It was a spiritual act. Historically, intercourse was the act through which male and female experienced God. The ancients believed that the male was spiritually incomplete until he had carnal knowledge of the sacred feminine. Physical union with the female remained the sole means through which man could become spiritually complete and ultimately achieve *gnosis*—knowledge of the divine. Since the days of Isis, sex rites had been considered man's only bridge from earth to heaven. "By communing with woman," Langdon said, "man could achieve a climactic instant when his mind went totally blank and he could see God."

THE GODDESS ISIS

Sophie looked skeptical. "Orgasm as prayer?"

Langdon gave a noncommittal shrug, although Sophie was essentially correct. Physiologically speaking, the male climax was accompanied by a split second entirely devoid of thought. A brief mental vacuum. A moment of clarity during which God could be glimpsed. Meditation gurus achieved similar states of thoughtlessness without sex and often described Nirvana as a never-ending spiritual orgasm.

"Sophie," Langdon said quietly, "it's important to remember that the ancients' view of sex was entirely opposite from ours today. Sex begot new life—the ultimate miracle—and miracles could be performed only by a god. The ability of the woman to produce life from her womb made her sacred. A god. Intercourse was the revered union of the two halves of the human spirit—male and female—through which the male could find spiritual wholeness and communion with God. What you saw was not about sex, it was about spirituality. The Hieros Gamos ritual is not a perversion. It's a deeply sacrosanct ceremony."

His words seemed to strike a nerve. Sophie had been remarkably poised all evening, but now, for the first time, Langdon saw the aura of composure beginning to crack. Tears materialized in her eyes again, and she dabbed them away with her sleeve.

He gave her a moment. Admittedly, the concept of sex as a pathway to God was mind-boggling at first. Langdon's Jewish students always looked flabbergasted when he first told them that the early Jewish tradition involved ritualistic sex. *In the Temple, no less.* Early Jews believed that the Holy of Holies in Solomon's Temple housed not only God but also His powerful female equal, Shekinah. Men seeking spiritual wholeness came to the Temple to visit priestesses—or *hierodules*—with whom they made love and experienced the divine through physical union. The Jewish tetragrammaton YHWH—the sacred name of God—in fact derived from Jehovah, an androgynous physical union between the masculine *Jah* and the pre-Hebraic name for Eve, *Havah.*

"For the early Church," Langdon explained in a soft voice, "mankind's use of sex to commune directly with God posed a serious threat to the Catholic power base. It left the Church out of the loop, undermining their self-proclaimed status as the *sole* conduit to God. For obvious reasons, they worked hard to demonize sex and recast it as a disgusting and sinful act. Other major religions did the same."

Sophie was silent, but Langdon sensed she was starting to understand her grandfather better. Ironically, Langdon had made this same point in a class lecture earlier this semester. "Is it surprising we feel conflicted about sex?" he asked his students. "Our ancient heritage and our very physiologies tell us sex is natural—a cherished route to spiritual fulfillment—and yet modern religion decries it as shameful, teaching us to fear our sexual desire as the hand of the devil."

Langdon decided not to shock his students with the fact that more than a dozen secret societies around the world—many of them quite influential—still practiced sex rites and kept the ancient traditions alive. Tom Cruise's character in the film *Eyes Wide Shut* discovered this the hard way when he sneaked into a private gathering of ultraelite Manhattanites only to find himself witnessing Hieros Gamos. Sadly, the filmmakers had gotten most of the specifics wrong, but the basic gist was there—a secret society communing to celebrate the magic of sexual union.

"Professor Langdon?" A male student in back raised his hand, sounding hopeful. "Are you saying that instead of going to chapel, we should have more sex?"

Langdon chuckled, not about to take the bait. From what he'd heard about Harvard parties, these kids were having more than enough sex. "Gentlemen," he said, knowing he was on tender ground, "might I offer a suggestion for all of you. Without being so bold as to condone premarital sex, and without being so naive as to think you're all chaste angels, I will give you this bit of advice about your sex lives."

All the men in the audience leaned forward, listening intently.

"The next time you find yourself with a woman, look in your heart and see if you cannot approach sex as a mystical, spiritual act. Challenge yourself to find that spark of divinity that man can only achieve through union with the sacred feminine."

The women smiled knowingly, nodding.

The men exchanged dubious giggles and off-color jokes.

Langdon sighed. College men were still boys.

SOPHIE'S FOREHEAD felt cold as she pressed it against the plane's window and stared blankly into the void, trying to process what Langdon had just told her. She felt a new regret well within her. *Ten years.* She pictured the stacks of unopened letters her grandfather had sent her. *I will tell Robert everything.* Without turning from the window, Sophie began to speak. Quietly. Fearfully.

As she began to recount what had happened that night, she felt herself drifting back . . . alighting in the woods outside her grandfather's Normandy château . . . searching the deserted house in confusion . . . hearing the voices below her . . . and then finding the hidden door. She inched down the stone staircase, one step at a time, into that basement grotto. She could taste the earthy air. Cool and light. It was March. In the shadows of her hiding place on the staircase, she watched as the strangers swayed and chanted by flickering orange candles.

I'm dreaming, Sophie told herself. *This is a dream. What else could this be?*

The women and men were staggered, black, white, black, white. The women's beautiful gossamer gowns billowed as they raised in their right hands golden orbs and called out in unison, *"I was with you in the beginning, in the dawn of all that is holy, I bore you from the womb before the start of day."*

The women lowered their orbs, and everyone rocked back and forth as if in a trance. They were revering something in the center of the circle.

What are they looking at?

The voices accelerated now. Louder. Faster.

"The woman whom you behold is love!" The women called, raising their orbs again. The men responded, *"She has her dwelling in eternity!"*

The chanting grew steady again. Accelerating. Thundering now. Faster. The participants stepped inward and knelt.

In that instant, Sophie could finally see what they were all watching.

On a low, ornate altar in the center of the circle lay a man. He was naked, positioned on his back, and wearing a black mask. Sophie instantly recognized his body and the birthmark on his shoulder. She almost cried out. *Grand-père!* This image alone would have shocked Sophie beyond belief, and yet there was more.

Straddling her grandfather was a naked woman wearing a white mask, her luxuriant silver hair flowing out behind it. Her body was plump, far from perfect, and she was gyrating in rhythm to the chanting—making love to Sophie's grandfather.

Sophie wanted to turn and run, but she couldn't. The stone walls of the grotto imprisoned her as the chanting rose to a fever pitch. The circle of participants seemed almost to be singing now, the noise rising in crescendo to a frenzy. With a sudden roar, the entire room seemed to erupt in climax. Sophie could not breathe. She suddenly realized she was quietly sobbing. She turned and staggered silently up the stairs, out of the house, and drove trembling back to Paris.

Chapter 95

THE CHARTERED turboprop was just passing over the twinkling lights of Monaco when Aringarosa hung up on Fache for the second time. He reached for the airsickness bag again but felt too drained even to be sick.

Just let it be over!

Fache's newest update seemed unfathomable, and yet almost nothing tonight made sense anymore. *What is going on?* Everything had spiraled wildly out of control. *What have I gotten Silas into? What have I gotten myself into!*

On shaky legs, Aringarosa walked to the cockpit. "I need to change destinations."

The pilot glanced over his shoulder and laughed. "You're joking, right?"

"No. I have to get to London immediately."

"Father, this is a charter flight, not a taxi."

"I will pay you extra, of course. How much? London is only one hour farther north and requires almost no change of direction, so—"

"It's not a question of money, Father, there are other issues."

"Ten thousand euro. Right now."

The pilot turned, his eyes wide with shock. "How much? What kind of priest carries that kind of cash?"

Aringarosa walked back to his black briefcase, opened it, and removed one of the bearer bonds. He handed it to the pilot.

"What is this?" the pilot demanded.

"A ten-thousand-euro bearer bond drawn on the Vatican Bank."

The pilot looked dubious.

"It's the same as cash."

"Only cash is cash," the pilot said, handing the bond back.

Aringarosa felt weak as he steadied himself against the cockpit door. "This is a matter of life or death. You must help me. I need to get to London."

The pilot eyed the bishop's gold ring. "Real diamonds?"

Aringarosa looked at the ring. "I could not possibly part with this."

The pilot shrugged, turning and focusing back out the windshield.

Aringarosa felt a deepening sadness. He looked at the ring. Everything it represented was about to be lost to the bishop anyway. After a long moment, he slid the ring from his finger and placed it gently on the instrument panel.

Aringarosa slunk out of the cockpit and sat back down. Fifteen seconds later, he could feel the pilot banking a few more degrees to the north.

Even so, Aringarosa's moment of glory was in shambles.

It had all begun as a holy cause. A brilliantly crafted scheme. Now, like a house of cards, it was collapsing in on itself . . . and the end was nowhere in sight.

Chapter 96

*L*ANGDON COULD see Sophie was still shaken from recounting her experience of Hieros Gamos. For his part, Langdon was amazed to have heard it. Not only had Sophie witnessed the full-blown ritual, but her own grandfather had been the celebrant . . . the Grand Master of the Priory of Sion. It was heady company. *Da Vinci, Botticelli, Isaac Newton, Victor Hugo, Jean Cocteau . . . Jacques Saunière.*

"I don't know what else I can tell you," Langdon said softly.

Sophie's eyes were a deep green now, tearful. "He raised me like his own daughter."

Langdon now recognized the emotion that had been growing in her eyes as they spoke. It was remorse. Distant and deep. Sophie Neveu had shunned her grandfather and was now seeing him in an entirely different light.

Outside, the dawn was coming fast, its crimson aura gathering off the starboard. The earth was still black beneath them.

"Victuals, my dears?" Teabing rejoined them with a flourish, presenting several cans of Coke and a box of old crackers. He apologized profusely for the limited fare as he doled out the goods. "Our friend the monk isn't talking yet," he chimed, "but give him time." He bit into a cracker and eyed the poem. "So, my lovely, any headway?" He looked at Sophie. "What is your grandfather trying to tell us here? Where the devil is this headstone? This headstone praised by Templars."

Sophie shook her head and remained silent.

While Teabing again dug into the verse, Langdon popped a Coke and turned to the window, his thoughts awash with images of secret rituals and unbroken codes. *A headstone praised by Templars is the key.* He took a long sip from the can. *A headstone praised by Templars.* The cola was warm.

The dissolving veil of night seemed to evaporate quickly, and as Langdon watched the transformation, he saw a shimmering ocean stretch out beneath them. *The English Channel*. It wouldn't be long now.

Langdon willed the light of day to bring with it a second kind of illumination, but the lighter it became outside, the further he felt from the truth. He heard the rhythms of iambic pentameter and chanting, Hieros Gamos and sacred rites, resonating with the rumble of the jet.

A headstone praised by Templars.

The plane was over land again when a flash of enlightenment struck him. Langdon set down his empty can of Coke hard. "You won't believe this," he said, turning to the others. "The Templar headstone—I figured it out."

Teabing's eyes turned to saucers. "You *know* where the headstone is?"

Langdon smiled. "Not *where* it is. *What* it is."

Sophie leaned in to hear.

"I think the headstone references a literal *stone head*," Langdon explained, savoring the familiar excitement of academic breakthrough. "Not a grave marker."

"A stone head?" Teabing demanded.

Sophie looked equally confused.

"Leigh," Langdon said, turning, "during the Inquisition, the Church accused the Knights Templar of all kinds of heresies, right?"

"Correct. They fabricated all kinds of charges. Sodomy, urination on the cross, devil worship, quite a list."

"And on that list was the worship of *false idols,* right? Specifically, the Church accused the Templars of secretly performing rituals in which they prayed to a carved stone head . . . the pagan god—"

"Baphomet!" Teabing blurted. "My heavens, Robert, you're right! A headstone praised by Templars!"

Langdon quickly explained to Sophie that Baphomet was a pagan fertility god associated with the creative force of reproduction. Baphomet's head was represented as that of a ram or goat, a common symbol of procreation and fecundity. The Templars honored Baphomet by encircling a stone replica of his head and chanting prayers.

"Baphomet," Teabing tittered. "The ceremony honored the creative magic of sexual union, but Pope Clement convinced everyone that Baphomet's head was in fact that of the devil. The Pope used the head of Baphomet as the linchpin in his case against the Templars."

Langdon concurred. The modern belief in a *horned* devil known as Satan could be traced back to Baphomet and the Church's attempts to recast the horned fertil-

BAPHOMET

ity god as a symbol of evil. The Church had obviously succeeded, although not entirely. Traditional American Thanksgiving tables still bore pagan, horned fertility symbols. The cornucopia or "horn of plenty" was a tribute to Baphomet's fertility and dated back to Zeus being suckled by a goat whose horn broke off and magically filled with fruit. Baphomet also appeared in group photographs when some joker raised two fingers behind a friend's head in the V-symbol of horns; certainly few of the pranksters realized their mocking gesture was in fact advertising their victim's robust sperm count.

"Yes, yes," Teabing was saying excitedly. "Baphomet *must* be what the poem is referring to. A headstone praised by Templars."

"Okay," Sophie said, "but if Baphomet is the headstone praised by Templars, then we have a new dilemma." She pointed to the dials on the cryptex. "Baphomet has eight letters. We only have room for five."

Teabing grinned broadly. "My dear, this is where the Atbash Cipher comes into play."

LANGDON WAS IMPRESSED. Teabing had just finished writing out the entire twenty-two-letter Hebrew alphabet—*alef-beit*—from memory. Granted, he'd used Roman equivalents rather than Hebrew characters, but even so, he was now reading through them with flawless pronunciation.

A B G D H V Z Ch T Y K L M N S O P Tz Q R Sh Th

"*Alef, Beit, Gimel, Dalet, Hei, Vav, Zayin, Chet, Tet, Yud, Kaf, Lamed, Mem, Nun, Samech, Ayin, Pei, Tzadik, Kuf, Reish, Shin, and Tav.*" Teabing dramatically mopped his brow and plowed on. "In formal Hebrew spelling, the vowel sounds are not written. Therefore, when we write the word *Baphomet* using the Hebrew alphabet, it will lose its three vowels in translation, leaving us—"

"Five letters," Sophie blurted.

Teabing nodded and began writing again. "Okay, here is the proper spelling of Baphomet in Hebrew letters. I'll sketch in the missing vowels for clarity's sake.

<u>B</u> a <u>P</u> o <u>M</u> e <u>Th</u>

"Remember, of course," he added, "that Hebrew is normally written in the opposite direction, but we can just as easily use Atbash this way. Next, all we have to do is create our substitution scheme by rewriting the entire alphabet in reverse order opposite the original alphabet."

"There's an easier way," Sophie said, taking the pen from Teabing. "It works for all reflectional substitution ciphers, including the Atbash. A little trick I learned at the Royal Holloway." Sophie wrote the first half of the alphabet from left to right, and then, beneath it, wrote the second half, right to left. "Cryptanalysts call it the fold-over. Half as complicated. Twice as clean."

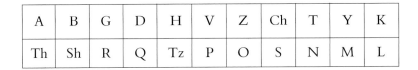

A	B	G	D	H	V	Z	Ch	T	Y	K
Th	Sh	R	Q	Tz	P	O	S	N	M	L

Teabing eyed her handiwork and chuckled. "Right you are. Glad to see those boys at the Holloway are doing their job."

Looking at Sophie's substitution matrix, Langdon felt a rising thrill that he imagined must have rivaled the thrill felt by early scholars when they first used the Atbash Cipher to decrypt the now-famous *Mystery of Sheshach*. For years, religious scholars had been baffled by biblical references to a city called *Sheshach*. The city did not appear on any map nor in any other documents, and yet it was mentioned repeatedly in the Book of Jeremiah—the king of Sheshach, the city of Sheshach, the people of Sheshach. Finally, a scholar applied the Atbash Cipher to the word, and his results were mind-numbing. The cipher revealed that Sheshach was in fact a *code word* for another very well-known city. The decryption process was simple.

Sheshach, in Hebrew, was spelled: Sh-Sh-K.

Sh-Sh-K, when placed in the substitution matrix, became B-B-L.

B-B-L, in Hebrew, spelled *Babel*.

The mysterious city of Sheshach was revealed as the city of Babel, and a frenzy of biblical examination ensued. Within weeks, several more Atbash code words were uncovered in the Old Testament, unveiling myriad hidden meanings that scholars had no idea were there.

"We're getting close," Langdon whispered, unable to control his excitement.

"Inches, Robert," Teabing said. He glanced over at Sophie and smiled. "You ready?"

She nodded.

"Okay, Baphomet in Hebrew without the vowels reads: *B-P-V-M-Th*. Now we simply apply your Atbash substitution matrix to translate the letters into our five-letter password."

Langdon's heart pounded. *B-P-V-M-Th*. The sun was pouring through the windows now. He looked at Sophie's substitution matrix and slowly began to make the conversion. *B is Sh . . . P is V . . .*

Teabing was grinning like a schoolboy at Christmas. "And the Atbash Cipher reveals . . ." He stopped short. "Good God!" His face went white.

Langdon's head snapped up.

"What's wrong?" Sophie demanded.

"You won't believe this." Teabing glanced at Sophie. "Especially you."

"What do you mean?" she said.

"This is . . . ingenious," he whispered. "Utterly ingenious!" Teabing wrote again on the paper. "Drumroll, please. Here is your password." He showed them what he had written.

Sh-V-P-Y-A

Sophie scowled. "What is it?"

Langdon didn't recognize it either.

Teabing's voice seemed to tremble with awe. "This, my friend, is actually an ancient word of wisdom."

Langdon read the letters again. *An ancient word of wisdom frees this scroll*. An instant later he got it. He had never seen this coming. "An ancient word of wisdom!"

Teabing was laughing. "Quite literally!"

Sophie looked at the word and then at the dial. Immediately she realized Langdon and Teabing had failed to see a serious glitch. "Hold on! This can't be the password," she argued. "The cryptex doesn't have an Sh on the dial. It uses a traditional Roman alphabet."

"*Read* the word," Langdon urged. "Keep in mind two things. In Hebrew, the symbol for the sound Sh can also be pronounced as S, depending on the accent. Just as the letter P can be pronounced F."

SVFYA? she thought, puzzled.

"Genius!" Teabing added. "The letter Vav is often a placeholder for the vowel sound O!"

Sophie again looked at the letters, attempting to sound them out.

"*S . . . o . . . f . . . y . . . a.*"

She heard the sound of her voice, and could not believe what she had just said. "Sophia? This spells Sophia?"

Langdon was nodding enthusiastically. "Yes! *Sophia* literally means *wisdom* in Greek. The root of your name, Sophie, is literally a 'word of wisdom.' "

Sophie suddenly missed her grandfather immensely. *He encrypted the Priory keystone with my name*. A knot caught in her throat. It all seemed so perfect. But as she turned her gaze to the five lettered dials on the cryptex, she realized a problem still existed. "But wait . . . the word Sophia has *six* letters."

Teabing's smile never faded. "Look at the poem again. Your grandfather wrote, 'An *ancient* word of wisdom.' "

"Yes?"

Teabing winked. "In ancient Greek, wisdom is spelled S-O-F-I-A."

*S*OPHIE FELT a wild excitement as she cradled the cryptex and began dialing in the letters. *An ancient word of wisdom frees this scroll.* Langdon and Teabing seemed to have stopped breathing as they looked on.

S . . . O . . . F . . .

"Carefully," Teabing urged. "Ever so carefully."

. . . I . . . A.

Sophie aligned the final dial. "Okay," she whispered, glancing up at the others. "I'm going to pull it apart."

"Remember the vinegar," Langdon whispered with fearful exhilaration. "Be careful."

Sophie knew that if this cryptex were like those she had opened in her youth, all she would need to do is grip the cylinder at both ends, just beyond the dials, and pull, applying slow, steady pressure in opposite directions. If the dials were properly aligned with the password, then one of the ends would slide off, much like a lens cap, and she could reach inside and remove the rolled papyrus document, which would be wrapped around the vial of vinegar. However, if the password they had entered were *incorrect,* Sophie's outward force on the ends would be transferred to a hinged lever inside, which would pivot downward into the cavity and apply pressure to the glass vial, eventually shattering it if she pulled too hard.

Pull gently, she told herself.

Teabing and Langdon both leaned in as Sophie wrapped her palms around the ends of the cylinder. In the excitement of deciphering the code word, Sophie had almost forgotten what they expected to find inside. *This is the Priory keystone.* According to Teabing, it contained a map to the Holy Grail, unveiling the tomb of Mary Magdalene and the Sangreal treasure . . . the ultimate treasure trove of secret truth.

Now gripping the stone tube, Sophie double-checked that all of the letters were properly aligned with the indicator. Then, slowly, she pulled. Nothing happened. She applied a little more force. Suddenly, the stone slid apart like a well-crafted telescope. The heavy end piece detached in her hand. Langdon and Teabing almost jumped to their feet. Sophie's heart rate climbed as she set the end cap on the table and tipped the cylinder to peer inside.

A scroll!

Peering down the hollow of the rolled paper, Sophie could see it had been wrapped around a cylindrical object—the vial of vinegar, she assumed. Strangely, though, the paper around the vinegar was not the customary delicate papyrus but rather, vellum. *That's odd,* she thought, *vinegar can't dissolve a lambskin vellum.* She looked again down the hollow of the scroll and realized the object in the center was not a vial of vinegar after all. It was something else entirely.

"What's wrong?" Teabing asked. "Pull out the scroll."

Frowning, Sophie grabbed the rolled vellum and the object around which it was wrapped, pulling them both out of the container.

"That's not papyrus," Teabing said. "It's too heavy."

"I know. It's padding."

"For what? The vial of vinegar?"

"No." Sophie unrolled the scroll and revealed what was wrapped inside. "For *this.*"

When Langdon saw the object inside the sheet of vellum, his heart sank.

"God help us," Teabing said, slumping. "Your grandfather was a pitiless architect."

Langdon stared in amazement. *I see Saunière has no intention of making this easy.*

On the table sat a second cryptex. Smaller. Made of black onyx. It had been nested within the first. Saunière's passion for dualism. *Two cryptexes.* Everything in pairs. *Double entendres. Male female. Black nested within white.* Langdon felt the web of symbolism stretching onward. *White gives birth to black.*

Every man sprang from woman.

White—female.

Black—male.

Reaching over, Langdon lifted the smaller cryptex. It looked identical to the first, except half the size and black. He heard the familiar gurgle. Apparently, the vial of vinegar they had heard earlier was inside this smaller cryptex.

"Well, Robert," Teabing said, sliding the page of vellum over to him. "You'll be pleased to hear that at least we're flying in the right direction."

Langdon examined the thick vellum sheet. Written in ornate penmanship was another four-line verse. Again, in iambic pentameter. The verse was cryptic, but

Langdon needed to read only as far as the first line to realize that Teabing's plan to come to Britain was going to pay off.

IN LONDON LIES A KNIGHT A POPE INTERRED.

The remainder of the poem clearly implied that the password for opening the second cryptex could be found by visiting this knight's tomb, somewhere in the city.

Langdon turned excitedly to Teabing. "Do you have any idea what knight this poem is referring to?"

Teabing grinned. "Not the foggiest. But I know in precisely which crypt we should look."

AT THAT MOMENT, fifteen miles ahead of them, six Kent police cars streaked down rain-soaked streets toward Biggin Hill Executive Airport.

LIEUTENANT COLLET helped himself to a Perrier from Teabing's refrigerator and strode back out through the drawing room. Rather than accompanying Fache to London where the action was, he was now baby-sitting the PTS team that had spread out through Château Villette.

So far, the evidence they had uncovered was unhelpful: a single bullet buried in the floor; a paper with several symbols scrawled on it along with the words *blade* and *chalice;* and a bloody spiked belt that PTS had told Collet was associated with the conservative Catholic group Opus Dei, which had caused a stir recently when a news program exposed their aggressive recruiting practices in Paris.

Collet sighed. *Good luck making sense of this unlikely mélange.*

Moving down a lavish hallway, Collet entered the vast ballroom study, where the chief PTS examiner was busy dusting for fingerprints. He was a corpulent man in suspenders.

"Anything?" Collet asked, entering.

The examiner shook his head. "Nothing new. Multiple sets matching those in the rest of the house."

"How about the prints on the *cilice* belt?"

"Interpol is still working. I uploaded everything we found."

Collet motioned to two sealed evidence bags on the desk. "And this?"

The man shrugged. "Force of habit. I bag anything peculiar."

Collet walked over. *Peculiar?*

"This Brit's a strange one," the examiner said. "Have a look at this." He sifted through the evidence bags and selected one, handing it to Collet.

The photo showed the main entrance of a Gothic cathedral—the traditional, recessed archway, narrowing through multiple, ribbed layers to a small doorway.

Collet studied the photo and turned. "This is peculiar?"

"Turn it over."

On the back, Collet found notations scrawled in English, describing a cathedral's long hollow nave as a secret pagan tribute to a woman's womb. This was strange. The notation describing the cathedral's *doorway,* however, was what startled him. "Hold on! He thinks a cathedral's entrance represents a woman's . . ."

The examiner nodded. "Complete with receding labial ridges and a nice little cinquefoil clitoris above the doorway." He sighed. "Kind of makes you want to go back to church."

GOTHIC CATHEDRAL ENTRANCE, NOTRE DAME, SEMUR-EN-AUXOIS, FRANCE

Collet picked up the second evidence bag. Through the plastic, he could see a large glossy photograph of what appeared to be an old document. The heading at the top read:

Les Dossiers Secrets—Number 4° lm¹ 249

"What's this?" Collet asked.

"No idea. He's got copies of it all over the place, so I bagged it."

Collet studied the document.

PRIEURÉ DE SION—LES NAUTONIERS/ GRAND MASTERS

JEAN DE GISORS	*1188–1220*
MARIE SAINT-CLAIR	*1220–1266*
GUILLAUME DE GISORS	*1266–1307*
ÉDOUARD DE BAR	*1307–1336*
JEANNE DE BAR	*1336–1351*
JEAN DE SAINT-CLAIR	*1351–1366*
BLANCHE D'ÉVREUX	*1366–1398*
NICOLAS FLAMEL	*1398–1418*
RENÉ D'ANJOU	*1418–1480*
IOLANDE DE BAR	*1480–1483*
SANDRO BOTTICELLI	*1483–1510*
LEONARDO DA VINCI	*1510–1519*
CONNÉTABLE DE BOURBON	*1519–1527*
FERDINAND DE GONZAGUE	*1527–1575*
LOUIS DE NEVERS	*1575–1595*
ROBERT FLUDD	*1595–1637*
J. VALENTIN ANDREA	*1637–1654*
ROBERT BOYLE	*1654–1691*
ISAAC NEWTON	*1691–1727*
CHARLES RADCLYFFE	*1727–1746*

CHARLES DE LORRAINE	*1746–1780*
MAXIMILIAN DE LORRAINE	*1780–1801*
CHARLES NODIER	*1801–1844*
VICTOR HUGO	*1844–1885*
CLAUDE DEBUSSY	*1885–1918*
JEAN COCTEAU	*1918–1963*

Prieuré de Sion? Collet wondered.

"Lieutenant?" Another agent stuck his head in. "The switchboard has an urgent call for Captain Fache, but they can't reach him. Will you take it?"

Collet returned to the kitchen and took the call.

It was André Vernet.

The banker's refined accent did little to mask the tension in his voice. "I thought Captain Fache said he would call me, but I have not yet heard from him."

"The captain is quite busy," Collet replied. "May I help you?"

"I was assured I would be kept abreast of your progress tonight."

For a moment, Collet thought he recognized the timbre of the man's voice, but he couldn't quite place it. "Monsieur Vernet, I am currently in charge of the Paris investigation. My name is Lieutenant Collet."

There was a long pause on the line. "Lieutenant, I have another call coming in. Please excuse me. I will call you later." He hung up.

For several seconds, Collet held the receiver. Then it dawned on him. *I knew I recognized that voice!* The revelation made him gasp.

The armored car driver.

With the fake Rolex.

Collet now understood why the banker had hung up so quickly. Vernet had remembered the name Lieutenant Collet—the officer he blatantly lied to earlier tonight.

Collet pondered the implications of this bizarre development. *Vernet is involved.* Instinctively, he knew he should call Fache. Emotionally, he knew this lucky break was going to be his moment to shine.

He immediately called Interpol and requested every shred of information they could find on the Depository Bank of Zurich and its president, André Vernet.

THE DA VINCI CODE

333

$\mathcal{S}$EAT BELTS, PLEASE," Teabing's pilot announced as the Hawker 731 descended into a gloomy morning drizzle. "We'll be landing in five minutes."

Teabing felt a joyous sense of homecoming when he saw the misty hills of Kent spreading wide beneath the descending plane. England was less than an hour from Paris, and yet a world away. This morning, the damp, spring green of his homeland looked particularly welcoming. *My time in France is over. I am returning to England victorious. The keystone has been found.* The question remained, of course, as to *where* the keystone would ultimately lead. *Somewhere in the United Kingdom.* Where exactly, Teabing had no idea, but he was already tasting the glory.

As Langdon and Sophie looked on, Teabing got up and went to the far side of the cabin, then slid aside a wall panel to reveal a discreetly hidden wall safe. He dialed in the combination, opened the safe, and extracted two passports. "Documentation for Rémy and myself." He then removed a thick stack of fifty-pound notes. "And documentation for you two."

Sophie looked leery. "A bribe?"

"Creative diplomacy. Executive airfields make certain allowances. A British customs official will greet us at my hangar and ask to board the plane. Rather than permitting him to come on, I'll tell him I'm traveling with a French celebrity who prefers that nobody knows she is in England—press considerations, you know—and I'll offer the official this generous tip as gratitude for his discretion."

Langdon looked amazed. "And the official will *accept?*"

"Not from *anyone,* they won't, but these people all know me. I'm not an arms dealer, for heaven's sake. I was knighted." Teabing smiled. "Membership has its privileges."

Rémy approached up the aisle now, the Heckler and Koch pistol cradled in his hand. "Sir, my agenda?"

Teabing glanced at his servant. "I'm going to have you stay onboard with our guest until we return. We can't very well drag him all over London with us."

Sophie looked wary. "Leigh, I was serious about the French police finding your plane before we return."

Teabing laughed. "Yes, imagine their surprise if they board and find Rémy."

Sophie looked surprised by his cavalier attitude. "Leigh, you transported a bound hostage across international borders. This is serious."

"So are my lawyers." He scowled toward the monk in the rear of the plane. "That animal broke into my home and almost killed me. That is a fact, and Rémy will corroborate."

"But you tied him up and flew him to London!" Langdon said.

Teabing held up his right hand and feigned a courtroom oath. "Your honor, forgive an eccentric old knight his foolish prejudice for the British court system. I realize I should have called the French authorities, but I'm a snob and do not trust those *laissez-faire* French to prosecute properly. This man almost murdered me. Yes, I made a rash decision forcing my manservant to help me bring him to England, but I was under great stress. Mea culpa. Mea culpa."

Langdon looked incredulous. "Coming from you, Leigh, that just might fly."

"Sir?" the pilot called back. "The tower just radioed. They've got some kind of maintenance problem out near your hangar, and they're asking me to bring the plane directly to the terminal instead."

Teabing had been flying to Biggin Hill for over a decade, and this was a first. "Did they mention what the problem is?"

"The controller was vague. Something about a gas leak at the pumping station? They asked me to park in front of the terminal and keep everyone onboard until further notice. Safety precaution. We're not supposed to deplane until we get the all-clear from airport authorities."

Teabing was skeptical. *Must be one hell of a gas leak.* The pumping station was a good half mile from his hangar.

Rémy also looked concerned. "Sir, this sounds highly irregular."

Teabing turned to Sophie and Langdon. "My friends, I have an unpleasant suspicion that we are about to be met by a welcoming committee."

Langdon gave a bleak sigh. "I guess Fache still thinks I'm his man."

"Either that," Sophie said, "or he is too deep into this to admit his error."

Teabing was not listening. Regardless of Fache's mind-set, action needed to be taken fast. *Don't lose sight of the ultimate goal. The Grail. We're so close.* Below them, the landing gear descended with a clunk.

"Leigh," Langdon said, sounding deeply remorseful, "I should turn myself in and sort this out legally. Leave you all out of it."

"Oh, heavens, Robert!" Teabing waved it off. "Do you really think they're going to let the rest of us go? I just transported you illegally. Miss Neveu assisted in your escape from the Louvre, and we have a man tied up in the back of the plane. Really now! We're all in this together."

"Maybe a different airport?" Sophie said.

Teabing shook his head. "If we pull up now, by the time we get clearance anywhere else, our welcoming party will include army tanks."

Sophie slumped.

Teabing sensed that if they were to have any chance of postponing confrontation with the British authorities long enough to find the Grail, bold action had to be taken. "Give me a minute," he said, hobbling toward the cockpit.

"What are you doing?" Langdon asked.

"Sales meeting," Teabing said, wondering how much it would cost him to persuade his pilot to perform one highly irregular maneuver.

Chapter 81

THE HAWKER is on final approach.

Simon Edwards—Executive Services Officer at Biggin Hill Airport—paced the control tower, squinting nervously at the rain-drenched runway. He never appreciated being awoken early on a Saturday morning, but it was particularly distasteful that he had been called in to oversee the arrest of one of his most lucrative clients. Sir Leigh Teabing paid Biggin Hill not only for a private hangar but a "per landing fee" for his frequent arrivals and departures. Usually, the airfield had advance warning of his schedule and was able to follow a strict protocol for his arrival. Teabing liked things just so. The custom-built Jaguar stretch limousine that he kept in his hangar was to be fully gassed, polished, and the day's *London Times* laid out on the back seat. A customs official was to be waiting for the plane at the hangar to expedite the mandatory documentation and luggage check. Occasionally, customs agents accepted large tips from Teabing in exchange for turning a blind eye to the transport of harmless organics—mostly luxury foods—French escargots, a particularly ripe unprocessed Roquefort, certain fruits. Many customs laws were absurd, anyway, and if Biggin Hill didn't accommodate its clients, certainly competing airfields would. Teabing was provided with what he wanted here at Biggin Hill, and the employees reaped the benefits.

Edwards's nerves felt frayed now as he watched the jet coming in. He wondered if Teabing's penchant for spreading the wealth had gotten him in trouble somehow; the French authorities seemed very intent on containing him. Edwards had not yet been told what the charges were, but they were obviously serious. At the French authorities' request, Kent police had ordered the Biggin Hill air traffic controller to radio the Hawker's pilot and order him directly to the terminal rather than to the client's hangar. The pilot had agreed, apparently believing the far-fetched story of a gas leak.

Though the British police did not generally carry weapons, the gravity of the situation had brought out an armed response team. Now, eight policemen with handguns stood just inside the terminal building, awaiting the moment when the plane's engines powered down. The instant this happened, a runway attendant would place safety wedges under the tires so the plane could no longer move. Then the police would step into view and hold the occupants at bay until the French police arrived to handle the situation.

The Hawker was low in the sky now, skimming the treetops to their right. Simon Edwards went downstairs to watch the landing from tarmac level. The Kent police were poised, just out of sight, and the maintenance man waited with his wedges. Out on the runway, the Hawker's nose tipped up, and the tires touched down in a puff of smoke. The plane settled in for deceleration, streaking from right to left in front of the terminal, its white hull glistening in the wet weather. But rather than braking and turning into the terminal, the jet coasted calmly past the access lane and continued on toward Teabing's hangar in the distance.

All the police spun and stared at Edwards. "I thought you said the pilot agreed to come to the terminal!"

Edwards was bewildered. "He *did!*"

Seconds later, Edwards found himself wedged in a police car racing across the tarmac toward the distant hangar. The convoy of police was still a good five hundred yards away as Teabing's Hawker taxied calmly into the private hangar and disappeared. When the cars finally arrived and skidded to a stop outside the gaping hangar door, the police poured out, guns drawn.

Edwards jumped out too.

The noise was deafening.

The Hawker's engines were still roaring as the jet finished its usual rotation inside the hangar, positioning itself nose-out in preparation for later departure. As the plane completed its 180-degree turn and rolled toward the front of the hangar, Edwards could see the pilot's face, which understandably looked surprised and fearful to see the barricade of police cars.

The pilot brought the plane to a final stop, and powered down the engines. The police streamed in, taking up positions around the jet. Edwards joined the Kent chief inspector, who moved warily toward the hatch. After several seconds, the fuselage door popped open.

Leigh Teabing appeared in the doorway as the plane's electronic stairs smoothly dropped down. As he gazed out at the sea of weapons aimed at him, he propped himself on his crutches and scratched his head. "Simon, did I win the policemen's lottery while I was away?" He sounded more bewildered than concerned.

Simon Edwards stepped forward, swallowing the frog in his throat. "Good morning, sir. I apologize for the confusion. We've had a gas leak and your pilot said he was coming to the terminal."

"Yes, yes, well, I told him to come here instead. I'm late for an appointment. I pay for this hangar, and this rubbish about avoiding a gas leak sounded overcautious."

"I'm afraid your arrival has taken us a bit off guard, sir."

"I know. I'm off my schedule, I am. Between you and me, the new medication gives me the tinkles. Thought I'd come over for a tune-up."

The policemen all exchanged looks. Edwards winced. "Very good, sir."

"Sir," the Kent chief inspector said, stepping forward. "I need to ask you to stay onboard for another half hour or so."

Teabing looked unamused as he hobbled down the stairs. "I'm afraid that is impossible. I have a medical appointment." He reached the tarmac. "I cannot afford to miss it."

The chief inspector repositioned himself to block Teabing's progress away from the plane. "I am here at the orders of the French Judicial Police. They claim you are transporting fugitives from the law on this plane."

Teabing stared at the chief inspector a long moment, and then burst out laughing. "Is this one of those hidden camera programs? Jolly good!"

The chief inspector never flinched. "This is serious, sir. The French police claim you also may have a hostage onboard."

Teabing's manservant Rémy appeared in the doorway at the top of the stairs. "I *feel* like a hostage working for Sir Leigh, but he assures me I am free to go." Rémy checked his watch. "Master, we really are running late." He nodded toward the Jaguar stretch limousine in the far corner of the hangar. The enormous automobile was ebony with smoked glass and whitewall tires. "I'll bring the car." Rémy started down the stairs.

"I'm afraid we cannot let you leave," the chief inspector said. "Please return to your aircraft. Both of you. Representatives from the French police will be landing shortly."

Teabing looked now toward Simon Edwards. "Simon, for heaven's sake, this is ridiculous! We don't have anyone else on board. Just the usual—Rémy, our pilot, and myself. Perhaps you could act as an intermediary? Go have a look onboard, and verify that the plane is empty."

Edwards knew he was trapped. "Yes, sir. I can have a look."

"The devil you will!" the Kent chief inspector declared, apparently knowing enough about executive airfields to suspect Simon Edwards might well lie about the plane's occupants in an effort to keep Teabing's business at Biggin Hill. "I will look myself."

Teabing shook his head. "No you won't, Inspector. This is private property and until you have a search warrant, you will stay off my plane. I am offering you a reasonable option here. Mr. Edwards can perform the inspection."

"No deal."

Teabing's demeanor turned frosty. "Inspector, I'm afraid I don't have time to indulge in your games. I'm late, and I'm leaving. If it is that important to you to stop me, you'll just have to shoot me." With that, Teabing and Rémy walked around the chief inspector and headed across the hangar toward the parked limousine.

THE KENT chief inspector felt only distaste for Leigh Teabing as the man hobbled around him in defiance. Men of privilege always felt like they were above the law.

They are not. The chief inspector turned and aimed at Teabing's back. "Stop! I will fire!"

"Go ahead," Teabing said without breaking stride or glancing back. "My lawyers will fricassee your testicles for breakfast. And if you dare board my plane without a warrant, your spleen will follow."

No stranger to power plays, the chief inspector was unimpressed. Technically, Teabing was correct and the police needed a warrant to board his jet, but because the flight had originated in France, and because the powerful Bezu Fache had given his authority, the Kent chief inspector felt certain his career would be far better served by finding out what it was on this plane that Teabing seemed so intent on hiding.

"Stop them," the inspector ordered. "I'm searching the plane."

His men raced over, guns leveled, and physically blocked Teabing and his servant from reaching the limousine.

Now Teabing turned. "Inspector, this is your last warning. Do not even think of boarding that plane. You will regret it."

Ignoring the threat, the chief inspector gripped his sidearm and marched up the plane's gangway. Arriving at the hatch, he peered inside. After a moment, he stepped into the cabin. *What the devil?*

With the exception of the frightened-looking pilot in the cockpit, the aircraft was empty. Entirely devoid of human life. Quickly checking the bathroom, the chairs, and the luggage areas, the inspector found no traces of anyone hiding . . . much less multiple individuals.

What the hell was Bezu Fache thinking? It seemed Leigh Teabing had been telling the truth.

The Kent chief inspector stood alone in the deserted cabin and swallowed hard. *Shit.* His face flushed, he stepped back onto the gangway, gazing across the hangar at Leigh Teabing and his servant, who were now under gunpoint near the limousine. "Let them go," the inspector ordered. "We received a bad tip."

Teabing's eyes were menacing even across the hangar. "You can expect a call from my lawyers. And for future reference, the French police cannot be trusted."

With that, Teabing's manservant opened the door at the rear of the stretch limousine and helped his crippled master into the back seat. Then the servant walked the length of the car, climbed in behind the wheel, and gunned the engine. Policemen scattered as the Jaguar peeled out of the hangar.

"WELL PLAYED, my good man," Teabing chimed from the rear seat as the limousine accelerated out of the airport. He turned his eyes now to the dimly lit front recesses of the spacious interior. "Everyone comfy?"

Langdon gave a weak nod. He and Sophie were still crouched on the floor beside the bound and gagged albino.

Moments earlier, as the Hawker taxied into the deserted hangar, Rémy had popped the hatch as the plane jolted to a stop halfway through its turn. With the police closing in fast, Langdon and Sophie dragged the monk down the gangway to ground level and out of sight behind the limousine. Then the jet engines had roared again, rotating the plane and completing its turn as the police cars came skidding into the hangar.

Now, as the limousine raced toward Kent, Langdon and Sophie clambered toward the rear of the limo's long interior, leaving the monk bound on the floor. They settled onto the long seat facing Teabing. The Brit gave them both a roguish smile and opened the cabinet on the limo's bar. "Could I offer you a drink? Some nibblies? Crisps? Nuts? Seltzer?"

Sophie and Langdon both shook their heads.

Teabing grinned and closed the bar. "So then, about this knight's tomb . . ."

LEET STREET?" Langdon asked, eyeing Teabing in the back of the limo. *There's a crypt on Fleet Street?* So far, Leigh was being playfully cagey about where he thought they would find the "knight's tomb," which, according to the poem, would provide the password for opening the smaller cryptex.

Teabing grinned and turned to Sophie. "Miss Neveu, give the Harvard boy one more shot at the verse, will you?"

Sophie fished in her pocket and pulled out the black cryptex, which was wrapped in the vellum. Everyone had decided to leave the rosewood box and larger cryptex behind in the plane's strongbox, carrying with them only what they needed, the far more portable and discreet black cryptex. Sophie unwrapped the vellum and handed the sheet to Langdon.

Although Langdon had read the poem several times onboard the jet, he had been

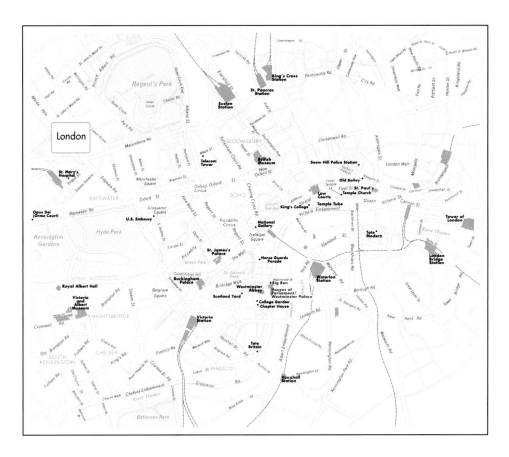

unable to extract any specific location. Now, as he read the words again, he processed them slowly and carefully, hoping the pentametric rhythms would reveal a clearer meaning now that he was on the ground.

> **In London lies a knight a Pope interred.**
> **His labor's fruit a Holy wrath incurred.**
> **You seek the orb that ought be on his tomb.**
> **It speaks of Rosy flesh and seeded womb.**

The language seemed simple enough. There was a knight buried in London. A knight who labored at something that angered the Church. A knight whose tomb was missing an orb that *should* be present. The poem's final reference—*Rosy flesh and seeded womb*—was a clear allusion to Mary Magdalene, the Rose who bore the seed of Jesus.

Despite the apparent straightforwardness of the verse, Langdon still had no idea *who* this knight was or where he was buried. Moreover, once they located the tomb, it sounded as if they would be searching for something that was absent. *The orb that ought be on his tomb?*

"No thoughts?" Teabing clucked in disappointment, although Langdon sensed the Royal Historian was enjoying being one up. "Miss Neveu?"

She shook her head.

"What would you two do without me?" Teabing said. "Very well, I will walk you through it. It's quite simple really. The first line is the key. Would you read it please?"

Langdon read aloud. "'In London lies a knight a Pope interred.'"

"Precisely. A knight a *Pope* interred." He eyed Langdon. "What does that mean to you?"

Langdon shrugged. "A knight buried by a Pope? A knight whose funeral was presided over by a Pope?"

Teabing laughed loudly. "Oh, that's rich. Always the optimist, Robert. Look at the second line. This knight obviously did something that incurred the Holy wrath of the Church. Think again. Consider the dynamic between the Church and the Knights Templar. A knight a Pope interred?"

"A knight a Pope *killed?*" Sophie asked.

Teabing smiled and patted her knee. "Well done, my dear. A knight a Pope *buried*. Or killed."

Langdon thought of the notorious Templar round-up in 1307—unlucky Friday the thirteenth—when Pope Clement killed and interred hundreds of Knights Templar. "But there must be endless graves of 'knights killed by Popes.' "

"Aha, not so!" Teabing said. "Many of them were burned at the stake and tossed unceremoniously into the Tiber River. But this poem refers to a *tomb*. A tomb in London. And there are few knights buried in London." He paused, eyeing Langdon as if waiting for light to dawn. Finally he huffed. "Robert, for heaven's sake! The church built in London by the Priory's military arm—the Knights Templar themselves!"

"The Temple Church?" Langdon drew a startled breath. "It has a crypt?"

"Ten of the most frightening tombs you will ever see."

Langdon had never actually visited the Temple Church, although he'd come across numerous references in his Priory research. Once the epicenter of all Templar/Priory activities in the United Kingdom, the Temple Church had been so named in honor of Solomon's Temple, from which the Knights Templar had extracted their own title, as well as the Sangreal documents that gave them all their influence in Rome. Tales abounded of knights performing strange, secretive rituals within the Temple Church's unusual sanctuary. "The Temple Church is on Fleet Street?"

"Actually, it's just off Fleet Street on Inner Temple Lane." Teabing looked mischievous. "I wanted to see you sweat a little more before I gave it away."

"Thanks."

"Neither of you has ever been there?"

Sophie and Langdon shook their heads.

"I'm not surprised," Teabing said. "The church is hidden now behind much larger buildings. Few people even know it's there. Eerie old place. The architecture is pagan to the core."

Sophie looked surprised. "Pagan?"

"Pantheonically pagan!" Teabing exclaimed. "The church is *round*. The Templars ignored the traditional Christian cruciform layout and built a perfectly circular church in honor of the sun." His eyebrows did a devilish dance. "A not-so-subtle howdy-do to the boys in Rome. They might as well have resurrected Stonehenge in downtown London."

Sophie eyed Teabing. "What about the rest of the poem?"

The historian's mirthful air faded. "I'm not sure. It's puzzling. We will need to examine each of the ten tombs carefully. With luck, one of them will have a conspicuously absent orb."

Langdon realized how close they really were. If the missing orb revealed the password, they would be able to open the second cryptex. He had a hard time imagining what they might find inside.

Langdon eyed the poem again. It was like some kind of primordial crossword puzzle. *A five-letter word that speaks of the Grail?* On the plane, they had already tried all the obvious passwords—GRAIL, GRAAL, GREAL, VENUS, MARIA, JESUS, SARAH—but the cylinder had not budged. *Far too obvious.* Apparently there existed some other five-letter reference to the Rose's seeded womb. The fact that the word was eluding a specialist like Leigh Teabing signified to Langdon that it was no ordinary Grail reference.

"Sir Leigh?" Rémy called over his shoulder. He was watching them in the rearview mirror through the open divider. "You said Fleet Street is near Blackfriars Bridge?"

"Yes, take Victoria Embankment."

"I'm sorry. I'm not sure where that is. We usually go only to the hospital."

Teabing rolled his eyes at Langdon and Sophie and grumbled, "I swear, sometimes it's like baby-sitting a child. One moment please. Help yourself to a drink and savory snacks." He left them, clambering awkwardly toward the open divider to talk to Rémy.

Sophie turned to Langdon now, her voice quiet. "Robert, nobody knows you and I are in England."

Langdon realized she was right. The Kent police would tell Fache the plane was empty, and Fache would have to assume they were still in France. *We are invisible.* Leigh's little stunt had just bought them a lot of time.

"Fache will not give up easily," Sophie said. "He has too much riding on this arrest now."

Langdon had been trying not to think about Fache. Sophie had promised she would do everything in her power to exonerate Langdon once this was over, but Langdon was starting to fear it might not matter. *Fache could easily be part of this plot.* Although Langdon could not imagine the Judicial Police tangled up in the Holy Grail, he sensed too much coincidence tonight to disregard Fache as a possible accomplice. *Fache is religious, and he is intent on pinning these murders on me.* Then again, Sophie had argued that Fache might simply be overzealous to make the arrest. After all, the evidence against Langdon was substantial. In addition to Langdon's name scrawled on the Louvre floor and in Saunière's date book, Langdon now appeared to have lied about his manuscript and then run away. *At Sophie's suggestion.*

"Robert, I'm sorry you're so deeply involved," Sophie said, placing her hand on his knee. "But I'm very glad you're here."

The comment sounded more pragmatic than romantic, and yet Langdon felt an unexpected flicker of attraction between them. He gave her a tired smile. "I'm a lot more fun when I've slept."

Sophie was silent for several seconds. "My grandfather asked me to trust you. I'm glad I listened to him for once."

"Your grandfather didn't even know me."

"Even so, I can't help but think you've done everything he would have wanted. You helped me find the keystone, explained the Sangreal, told me about the ritual in the basement." She paused. "Somehow I feel closer to my grandfather tonight than I have in years. I know he would be happy about that."

In the distance, now, the skyline of London began to materialize through the dawn drizzle. Once dominated by Big Ben and Tower Bridge, the horizon now bowed to the Millennium Eye—a colossal, ultramodern Ferris wheel that climbed five hundred feet and afforded breathtaking views of the city. Langdon had attempted to board it once, but the "viewing capsules" reminded him of sealed sarcophagi, and he opted to keep his feet on the ground and enjoy the view from the airy banks of the Thames.

Langdon felt a squeeze on his knee, pulling him back, and Sophie's green eyes were on him. He realized she had been speaking to him. "What do *you* think we should do with the Sangreal documents if we ever find them?" she whispered.

"What I think is immaterial," Langdon said. "Your grandfather gave the cryptex to you, and you should do with it what your instinct tells you he would want done."

"I'm asking for your opinion. You obviously wrote something in that manuscript that made my grandfather trust your judgment. He scheduled a private meeting with you. That's rare."

"Maybe he wanted to tell me I have it all wrong."

"Why would he tell me to find you unless he liked your ideas? In your manuscript, did you support the idea that the Sangreal documents should be revealed or stay buried?"

"Neither. I made no judgment either way. The manuscript deals with the symbology of the sacred feminine—tracing her iconography throughout history. I certainly didn't presume to know where the Grail is hidden or whether it should ever be revealed."

"And yet you're writing a book about it, so you obviously feel the information should be shared."

"There's an enormous difference between hypothetically discussing an alternate history of Christ, and . . ." He paused.

"And what?"

"And presenting to the world thousands of ancient documents as scientific evidence that the New Testament is false testimony."

"But you told me the New Testament is based on fabrications."

Langdon smiled. "Sophie, *every* faith in the world is based on fabrication. That is the definition of *faith*—acceptance of that which we imagine to be true, that which we cannot prove. Every religion describes God through metaphor, allegory, and exaggeration, from the early Egyptians through modern Sunday school. Metaphors are a way to help our minds process the unprocessible. The problems arise when we begin to believe literally in our own metaphors."

"So you are in favor of the Sangreal documents staying buried forever?"

"I'm a historian. I'm opposed to the destruction of documents, and I would love to see religious scholars have more information to ponder the exceptional life of Jesus Christ."

"You're arguing both sides of my question."

"Am I? The Bible represents a fundamental guidepost for millions of people on the planet, in much the same way the Koran, Torah, and Pali Canon offer guidance to people of other religions. If you and I could dig up documentation that contradicted the holy stories of Islamic belief, Judaic belief, Buddhist belief, pagan belief, should we do that? Should we wave a flag and tell the Buddhists that we have proof the Buddha did not come from a lotus blossom? Or that Jesus was not born of a *literal* virgin birth? Those who truly understand their faiths understand the stories are metaphorical."

Sophie looked skeptical. "My friends who are devout Christians definitely believe that Christ *literally* walked on water, *literally* turned water into wine, and was born of a *literal* virgin birth."

"My point exactly," Langdon said. "Religious allegory has become a part of the fabric of reality. And living in that reality helps millions of people cope and be better people."

"But it appears their reality is false."

Langdon chuckled. "No more false than that of a mathematical cryptographer who believes in the imaginary number '*i*' because it helps her break codes."

Sophie frowned. "That's not fair."

A moment passed.

"What was your question again?" Langdon asked.

"I can't remember."

He smiled. "Works every time."

LANGDON'S MICKEY MOUSE wristwatch read almost seven-thirty when he emerged from the Jaguar limousine onto Inner Temple Lane with Sophie and Teabing. The threesome wound through a maze of buildings to a small courtyard outside the Temple Church. The rough-hewn stone shimmered in the rain, and doves cooed in the architecture overhead.

London's ancient Temple Church was constructed entirely of Caen stone. A dramatic, circular edifice with a daunting facade, a central turret, and a protruding nave off one side, the church looked more like a military stronghold than a place of worship. Consecrated on the tenth of February in 1185 by Heraclius, Patriarch of Jerusalem, the Temple Church survived eight centuries of political turmoil, the Great Fire of London, and the First World War, only to be heavily damaged by Luftwaffe incendiary bombs in 1940. After the war, it was restored to its original, stark grandeur.

The simplicity of the circle, Langdon thought, admiring the building for the first time. The architecture was coarse and simple, more reminiscent of Rome's rugged Castel Sant'Angelo than the refined Pantheon. The boxy annex jutting out to the

TEMPLE CHURCH, LONDON

right was an unfortunate eyesore, although it did little to shroud the original pagan shape of the primary structure.

"It's early on a Saturday," Teabing said, hobbling toward the entrance, "so I'm assuming we won't have services to deal with."

The church's entryway was a recessed stone niche inside which stood a large wooden door. To the left of the door, looking entirely out of place, hung a bulletin board covered with concert schedules and religious service announcements.

Teabing frowned as he read the board. "They don't open to sightseers for another couple of hours." He moved to the door and tried it. The door didn't budge. Putting his ear to the wood, he listened. After a moment, he pulled back, a scheming look on his face as he pointed to the bulletin board. "Robert, check the service schedule, will you? Who is presiding this week?"

INSIDE THE CHURCH, an altar boy was almost finished vacuuming the communion kneelers when he heard a knocking on the sanctuary door. He ignored it. Father Harvey Knowles had his own keys and was not due for another couple of hours. The knocking was probably a curious tourist or indigent. The altar boy kept vacuuming, but the knocking continued. *Can't you read?* The sign on the door clearly stated that the church did not open until nine-thirty on Saturday. The altar boy remained with his chores.

Suddenly, the knocking turned to a forceful banging, as if someone were hitting the door with a metal rod. The young man switched off his vacuum cleaner and marched angrily toward the door. Unlatching it from within, he swung it open. Three people stood in the entryway. *Tourists,* he grumbled. "We open at nine-thirty."

The heavyset man, apparently the leader, stepped forward using metal crutches. "I am Sir Leigh Teabing," he said, his accent a highbrow, Saxonesque British. "As you are no doubt aware, I am escorting Mr. and Mrs. Christopher Wren the Fourth." He stepped aside, flourishing his arm toward the attractive couple behind them. The woman was soft-featured, with lush burgundy hair. The man was tall, dark-haired, and looked vaguely familiar.

The altar boy had no idea how to respond. Sir Christopher Wren was the Temple Church's most famous benefactor. He had made possible all the restorations following damage caused by the Great Fire. He had also been dead since the early eighteenth century. "Um . . . an honor to meet you?"

The man on crutches frowned. "Good thing you're not in sales, young man, you're not very convincing. Where is Father Knowles?"

"It's Saturday. He's not due in until later."

The crippled man's scowl deepened. "There's gratitude. He assured us he would be here, but it looks like we'll do it without him. It won't take long."

The altar boy remained blocking the doorway. "I'm sorry, *what* won't take long?"

The visitor's eyes sharpened now, and he leaned forward whispering as if to save everyone some embarrassment. "Young man, apparently you are new here. Every year Sir Christopher Wren's descendants bring a pinch of the old man's ashes to scatter in the Temple sanctuary. It is part of his last will and testament. Nobody is particularly happy about making the trip, but what can we do?"

The altar boy had been here a couple of years but had never heard of this custom. "It would be better if you waited until nine-thirty. The church isn't open yet, and I'm not finished hoovering."

The man on crutches glared angrily. "Young man, the only reason there's anything left of this building for you to hoover is on account of the gentleman in that woman's pocket."

"I'm sorry?"

"Mrs. Wren," the man on crutches said, "would you be so kind as to show this impertinent young man the reliquary of ashes?"

The woman hesitated a moment and then, as if awaking from a trance, reached in her sweater pocket and pulled out a small cylinder wrapped in protective fabric.

"There, you see?" the man on crutches snapped. "Now, you can either grant his dying wish and let us sprinkle his ashes in the sanctuary, or I tell Father Knowles how we've been treated."

The altar boy hesitated, well acquainted with Father Knowles's deep observance of church tradition . . . and, more important, with his foul temper when anything cast this time-honored shrine in anything but favorable light. Maybe Father Knowles had simply forgotten these family members were coming. If so, then there was far more risk in turning them away than in letting them in. *After all, they said it would only take a minute. What harm could it do?*

When the altar boy stepped aside to let the three people pass, he could have sworn Mr. and Mrs. Wren looked just as bewildered by all of this as he was. Uncertain, the boy returned to his chores, watching them out of the corner of his eye.

LANGDON HAD TO SMILE as the threesome moved deeper into the church. "Leigh," he whispered, "you lie entirely too well."

Teabing's eyes twinkled. "Oxford Theatre Club. They still talk of my Julius

Caesar. I'm certain nobody has ever performed the first scene of Act Three with more dedication."

Langdon glanced over. "I thought Caesar was *dead* in that scene."

Teabing smirked. "Yes, but my toga tore open when I fell, and I had to lie on stage for half an hour with my todger hanging out. Even so, I never moved a muscle. I was brilliant, I tell you."

Langdon cringed. *Sorry I missed it.*

As the group moved through the rectangular annex toward the archway leading into the main church, Langdon was surprised by the barren austerity. Although the altar layout resembled that of a linear Christian chapel, the furnishings were stark and cold, bearing none of the traditional ornamentation. "Bleak," he whispered.

Teabing chuckled. "Church of England. Anglicans drink their religion straight. Nothing to distract from their misery."

Sophie motioned through the vast opening that gave way to the circular section of the church. "It looks like a fortress in there," she whispered.

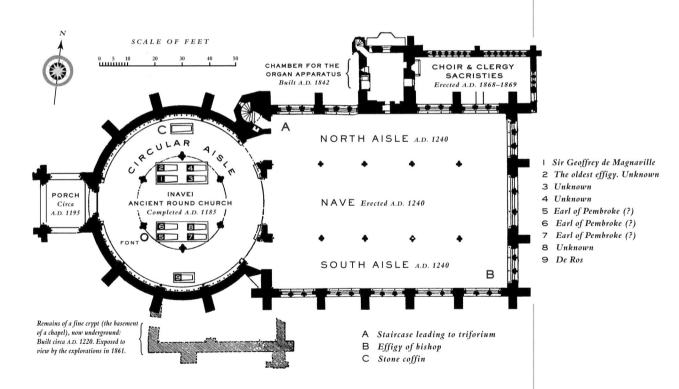

GROUND PLAN OF THE TEMPLE CHURCH

Langdon agreed. Even from here, the walls looked unusually robust.

"The Knights Templar were warriors," Teabing reminded, the sound of his aluminum crutches echoing in this reverberant space. "A religio-military society. Their churches were their strongholds and their banks."

"Banks?" Sophie asked, glancing at Leigh.

"Heavens, yes. The Templars *invented* the concept of modern banking. For European nobility, traveling with gold was perilous, so the Templars allowed nobles to deposit gold in their nearest Temple Church and then draw it from any *other* Temple Church across Europe. All they needed was proper documentation." He winked. "And a small commission. They were the original ATMs." Teabing pointed toward a stained-glass window where the breaking sun was refracting through a white-clad knight riding a rose-colored horse. "Alanus Marcel," Teabing said, "Master of the Temple in the early twelve hundreds. He and his successors actually held the Parliamentary chair of Primus Baro Angiae."

Langdon was surprised. "First Baron of the Realm?"

Teabing nodded. "The Master of the Temple, some claim, held more influence than the king himself." As they arrived outside the circular chamber, Teabing shot a glance over his shoulder at the altar boy, who was vacuuming in the distance. "You know," Teabing whispered to Sophie, "the Holy Grail is said to once have been stored in this church overnight while the Templars moved it from one hiding place to another. Can you imagine the four chests of Sangreal documents sitting right here with Mary Magdalene's sarcophagus? It gives me gooseflesh."

Langdon was feeling gooseflesh too as they stepped into the circular chamber. His eye traced the curvature of the chamber's pale stone perimeter, taking in the carvings of gargoyles, demons, monsters, and pained human faces, all staring inward. Beneath the carvings, a single stone pew curled around the entire circumference of the room.

"Theater in the round," Langdon whispered.

Teabing raised a crutch, pointing toward the far left of the room and then to the far right. Langdon had already seen them.

Ten stone knights.

Five on the left. Five on the right.

Lying supine on the floor, the carved, life-sized figures rested in peaceful poses. The knights were depicted wearing full armor, shields, and swords, and the tombs gave Langdon the uneasy sensation that someone had snuck in and poured plaster over the knights while they were sleeping. All of the figures were deeply weathered, and yet each was clearly unique—different armory pieces, distinct leg and arm positions, facial features, and markings on their shields.

KNIGHTS' EFFIGIES, TEMPLE CHURCH

In London lies a knight a Pope interred.
Langdon felt shaky as he inched deeper into the circular room.
This had to be the place.

*I*N A RUBBISH-STREWN alley very close to Temple Church, Rémy Legaludec pulled the Jaguar limousine to a stop behind a row of industrial waste bins. Killing the engine, he checked the area. Deserted. He got out of the car, walked toward the rear, and climbed back into the limousine's main cabin where the monk was.

Sensing Rémy's presence, the monk in the back emerged from a prayer-like trance, his red eyes looking more curious than fearful. All evening Rémy had been impressed with this trussed man's ability to stay calm. After some initial struggles in the Range Rover, the monk seemed to have accepted his plight and given over his fate to a higher power.

Loosening his bow tie, Rémy unbuttoned his high, starched, wing-tipped collar and felt as if he could breathe for the first time in years. He went to the limousine's wet bar, where he poured himself a Smirnoff vodka. He drank it in a single swallow and followed it with a second.

Soon I will be a man of leisure.

Searching the bar, Rémy found a standard service wine-opener and flicked open the sharp blade. The knife was usually employed to slice the lead foil from corks on fine bottles of wine, but it would serve a far more dramatic purpose this morning. Rémy turned and faced Silas, holding up the glimmering blade.

Now those red eyes flashed fear.

Rémy smiled and moved toward the back of the limousine. The monk recoiled, struggling against his bonds.

"Be still," Rémy whispered, raising the blade.

Silas could not believe that God had forsaken him. Even the physical pain of being bound Silas had turned into a spiritual exercise, asking the throb of his blood-starved muscles to remind him of the pain Christ endured. *I have been praying all night for liberation.* Now, as the knife descended, Silas clenched his eyes shut.

A slash of pain tore through his shoulder blades. He cried out, unable to believe he was going to die here in the back of this limousine, unable to defend himself. *I was doing God's work. The Teacher said he would protect me.*

Silas felt the biting warmth spreading across his back and shoulders and could picture his own blood, spilling out over his flesh. A piercing pain cut through his thighs now, and he felt the onset of that familiar undertow of disorientation—the body's defense mechanism against the pain.

As the biting heat tore through all of his muscles now, Silas clenched his eyes tighter, determined that the final image of his life would not be of his own killer. Instead he pictured a younger Bishop Aringarosa, standing before the small church in Spain . . . the church that he and Silas had built with their own hands. *The beginning of my life.*

Silas felt as if his body were on fire.

"Take a drink," the tuxedoed man whispered, his accent French. "It will help with your circulation."

Silas's eyes flew open in surprise. A blurry image was leaning over him, offering a glass of liquid. A mound of shredded duct tape lay on the floor beside the blood-less knife.

"Drink this," he repeated. "The pain you feel is the blood rushing into your muscles."

Silas felt the fiery throb transforming now to a prickling sting. The vodka tasted terrible, but he drank it, feeling grateful. Fate had dealt Silas a healthy share of bad luck tonight, but God had solved it all with one miraculous twist.

God has not forsaken me.

Silas knew what Bishop Aringarosa would call it.

Divine intervention.

"I had wanted to free you earlier," the servant apologized, "but it was impossible. With the police arriving at Château Villette, and then at Biggin Hill airport, this was the first possible moment. You understand, don't you, Silas?"

Silas recoiled, startled. "You know my name?"

The servant smiled.

Silas sat up now, rubbing his stiff muscles, his emotions a torrent of incredulity, appreciation, and confusion. "Are you . . . the Teacher?"

Rémy shook his head, laughing at the proposition. "I wish I had that kind of power. No, I am not the Teacher. Like you, I serve him. But the Teacher speaks highly of you. My name is Rémy."

Silas was amazed. "I don't understand. If you work for the Teacher, why did Langdon bring the keystone to *your* home?"

"Not my home. The home of the world's foremost Grail historian, Sir Leigh Teabing."

"But *you* live there. The odds . . ."

Rémy smiled, seeming to have no trouble with the apparent coincidence of Langdon's chosen refuge. "It was all utterly predictable. Robert Langdon was in possession of the keystone, and he needed help. What more logical place to run than to the home of Leigh Teabing? That I happen to live there is why the Teacher approached me in the first place." He paused. "How do you think the Teacher knows so much about the Grail?"

Now it dawned, and Silas was stunned. The Teacher had recruited a servant who had access to all of Sir Leigh Teabing's research. It was brilliant.

"There is much I have to tell you," Rémy said, handing Silas the loaded Heckler and Koch pistol. Then he reached through the open partition and retrieved a small, palm-sized revolver from the glove box. "But first, you and I have a job to do."

CAPTAIN FACHE descended from his transport plane at Biggin Hill and listened in disbelief to the Kent chief inspector's account of what had happened in Teabing's hangar.

"I searched the plane myself," the inspector insisted, "and there was no one inside." His tone turned haughty. "And I should add that if Sir Leigh Teabing presses charges against me, I will—"

"Did you interrogate the pilot?"

"Of course not. He is French, and our jurisdiction requires—"

"Take me to the plane."

Arriving at the hangar, Fache needed only sixty seconds to locate an anomalous smear of blood on the pavement near where the limousine had been parked. Fache walked up to the plane and rapped loudly on the fuselage.

"This is the captain of the French Judicial Police. Open the door!"

The terrified pilot opened the hatch and lowered the stairs.

Fache ascended. Three minutes later, with the help of his sidearm, he had a full confession, including a description of the bound albino monk. In addition, he learned that the pilot saw Langdon and Sophie leave something behind in Teabing's safe, a wooden box of some sort. Although the pilot denied knowing what was in the box, he admitted it had been the focus of Langdon's full attention during the flight to London.

"Open the safe," Fache demanded.

The pilot looked terrified. "I don't know the combination!"

"That's too bad. I was going to offer to let you keep your pilot's license."

The pilot wrung his hands. "I know some men in maintenance here. Maybe they could drill it?"

"You have half an hour."

The pilot leapt for his radio.

Fache strode to the back of the plane and poured himself a hard drink. It was early, but he had not yet slept, so this hardly counted as drinking before noon. Sitting in a plush bucket seat, he closed his eyes, trying to sort out what was going on. *The Kent police's blunder could cost me dearly.* Everyone was now on the lookout for a black Jaguar limousine.

Fache's phone rang, and he wished for a moment's peace. *"Allô?"*

"I'm en route to London." It was Bishop Aringarosa. "I'll be arriving in an hour."

Fache sat up. "I thought you were going to Paris."

"I am deeply concerned. I have changed my plans."

"You should not have."

"Do you have Silas?"

"No. His captors eluded the local police before I landed."

Aringarosa's anger rang sharply. "You assured me you would stop that plane!"

Fache lowered his voice. "Bishop, considering your situation, I recommend you not test my patience today. I will find Silas and the others as soon as possible. Where are you landing?"

"One moment." Aringarosa covered the receiver and then came back. "The pilot is trying to get clearance at Heathrow. I'm his only passenger, but our redirect was unscheduled."

"Tell him to come to Biggin Hill Executive Airport in Kent. I'll get him clearance. If I'm not here when you land, I'll have a car waiting for you."

"Thank you."

"As I expressed when we first spoke, Bishop, you would do well to remember that you are not the only man on the verge of losing everything."

Chapter 85

*Y*OU SEEK *the orb that ought be on his tomb.*

Each of the carved knights within the Temple Church lay on his back with his head resting on a rectangular stone pillow. Sophie felt a chill. The poem's reference to an "orb" conjured images of the night in her grandfather's basement.

Hieros Gamos. The orbs.

Sophie wondered if the ritual had been performed in this very sanctuary. The circular room seemed custom-built for such a pagan rite. A stone pew encircled a bare expanse of floor in the middle. *A theater in the round,* as Robert had called it. She imagined this chamber at night, filled with masked people, chanting by torchlight, all witnessing a "sacred communion" in the center of the room.

Forcing the image from her mind, she advanced with Langdon and Teabing toward the first group of knights. Despite Teabing's insistence that their investigation should be conducted meticulously, Sophie felt eager and pushed ahead of them, making a cursory walk-through of the five knights on the left.

Scrutinizing these first tombs, Sophie noted the similarities and differences between them. Every knight was on his back, but three of the knights had their legs extended straight out while two had their legs crossed. The oddity seemed to have no relevance to the missing orb. Examining their clothing, Sophie noted that two of the knights wore tunics over their armor, while the other three wore ankle-length robes. Again, utterly unhelpful. Sophie turned her attention to the only other obvious difference—their hand positions. Two knights clutched swords, two prayed, and one had his arms at his side. After a long moment looking at the hands, Sophie shrugged, having seen no hint anywhere of a conspicuously absent orb.

Feeling the weight of the cryptex in her sweater pocket, she glanced back at Langdon and Teabing. The men were moving slowly, still only at the third knight, apparently having no luck either. In no mood to wait, she turned away from them toward the second group of knights. As she crossed the open space, she quietly recited the poem she had read so many times now that it was committed to memory.

> **In London lies a knight a Pope interred.**
> **His labor's fruit a Holy wrath incurred.**
> **You seek the orb that ought be on his tomb.**
> **It speaks of Rosy flesh and seeded womb.**

When Sophie arrived at the second group of knights, she found that this second group was similar to the first. All lay with varied body positions, wearing armor and swords.

That was, all except the tenth and final tomb.

Hurrying over to it, she stared down.

No pillow. No armor. No tunic. No sword.

"Robert? Leigh?" she called, her voice echoing around the chamber. "There's something missing over here."

Both men looked up and immediately began to cross the room toward her.

"An orb?" Teabing called excitedly. His crutches clicked out a rapid staccato as he hurried across the room. "Are we missing an orb?"

"Not exactly," Sophie said, frowning at the tenth tomb. "We seem to be missing an entire knight."

Arriving beside her both men gazed down in confusion at the tenth tomb. Rather than a knight lying in the open air, this tomb was a sealed stone casket. The casket was trapezoidal, tapered at the feet, widening toward the top, with a peaked lid.

"Why isn't this knight shown?" Langdon asked.

"Fascinating," Teabing said, stroking his chin. "I had forgotten about this oddity. It's been years since I was here."

"This coffin," Sophie said, "looks like it was carved at the same time and by the same sculptor as the other nine tombs. So why is this knight in a casket rather than in the open?"

Teabing shook his head. "One of this church's mysteries. To the best of my knowledge, nobody has ever found any explanation for it."

"Hello?" the altar boy said, arriving with a perturbed look on his face. "Forgive me if this seems rude, but you told me you wanted to spread ashes, and yet you seem to be sightseeing."

Teabing scowled at the boy and turned to Langdon. "Mr. Wren, apparently your family's philanthropy does not buy you the time it used to, so perhaps we should take out the ashes and get on with it." Teabing turned to Sophie. "Mrs. Wren?"

Sophie played along, pulling the vellum-wrapped cryptex from her pocket.

"Now then," Teabing snapped at the boy, "if you would give us some privacy?"

The altar boy did not move. He was eyeing Langdon closely now. "You look familiar."

Teabing huffed. "Perhaps that is because Mr. Wren comes here every year!"

Or perhaps, Sophie now feared, *because he saw Langdon on television at the Vatican last year.*

"I have never met Mr. Wren," the altar boy declared.

"You're mistaken," Langdon said politely. "I believe you and I met in passing last year. Father Knowles failed to formally introduce us, but I recognized your face as we came in. Now, I realize this is an intrusion, but if you could afford me a few more minutes, I have traveled a great distance to scatter ashes amongst these tombs." Langdon spoke his lines with Teabing-esque believability.

The altar boy's expression turned even more skeptical. "These are not *tombs*."

"I'm sorry?" Langdon said.

"Of course they are tombs," Teabing declared. "What are you talking about?"

The altar boy shook his head. "Tombs contain bodies. These are effigies. Stone tributes to real men. There are no bodies beneath these figures."

"This is a crypt!" Teabing said.

"Only in outdated history books. This was believed to be a crypt but was revealed as nothing of the sort during the 1950 renovation." He turned back to Langdon. "And I imagine Mr. Wren would *know* that. Considering it was his family that uncovered that fact."

An uneasy silence fell.

It was broken by the sound of a door slamming out in the annex.

"That must be Father Knowles," Teabing said. "Perhaps you should go see?"

The altar boy looked doubtful but stalked back toward the annex, leaving Langdon, Sophie, and Teabing to eye one another gloomily.

"Leigh," Langdon whispered. "No bodies? What is he talking about?"

Teabing looked distraught. "I don't know. I always thought . . . certainly, this *must* be the place. I can't imagine he knows what he is talking about. It makes no sense!"

"Can I see the poem again?" Langdon said.

Sophie pulled the cryptex from her pocket and carefully handed it to him.

Langdon unwrapped the vellum, holding the cryptex in his hand while he examined the poem. "Yes, the poem definitely references a *tomb*. Not an effigy."

"Could the poem be wrong?" Teabing asked. "Could Jacques Saunière have made the same mistake I just did?"

Langdon considered it and shook his head. "Leigh, you said it yourself. This church was built by Templars, the military arm of the Priory. Something tells me the Grand Master of the Priory would have a pretty good idea if there were knights buried here."

Teabing looked flabbergasted. "But this place is perfect." He wheeled back toward the knights. "We must be missing something!"

Entering the annex, the altar boy was surprised to find it deserted. "Father Knowles?" *I know I heard the door,* he thought, moving forward until he could see the entryway.

A thin man in a tuxedo stood near the doorway, scratching his head and looking lost. The altar boy gave an irritated huff, realizing he had forgotten to relock the door when he let the others in. Now some pathetic sod had wandered in off the street, looking for directions to some wedding from the looks of it. "I'm sorry," he called out, passing a large pillar, "we're closed."

A flurry of cloth ruffled behind him, and before the altar boy could turn, his head snapped backward, a powerful hand clamping hard over his mouth from behind, muffling his scream. The hand over the boy's mouth was snow-white, and he smelled alcohol.

The prim man in the tuxedo calmly produced a very small revolver, which he aimed directly at the boy's forehead.

The altar boy felt his groin grow hot and realized he had wet himself.

"Listen carefully," the tuxedoed man whispered. "You will exit this church silently, and you will run. You will not stop. Is that clear?"

The boy nodded as best he could with the hand over his mouth.

"If you call the police . . ." The tuxedoed man pressed the gun to his skin. "I will find you."

The next thing the boy knew, he was sprinting across the outside courtyard with no plans of stopping until his legs gave out.

*L*IKE A GHOST, Silas drifted silently behind his target. Sophie Neveu sensed him too late. Before she could turn, Silas pressed the gun barrel into her spine and wrapped a powerful arm across her chest, pulling her back against his hulking body. She yelled in surprise. Teabing and Langdon both turned now, their expressions astonished and fearful.

"What . . . ?" Teabing choked out. "What did you do to Rémy!"

"Your only concern," Silas said calmly, "is that I leave here with the keystone." This recovery mission, as Rémy had described it, was to be clean and simple: *Enter the church, take the keystone, and walk out; no killing, no struggle.*

Holding Sophie firm, Silas dropped his hand from her chest, down to her waist, slipping it inside her deep sweater pockets, searching. He could smell the soft fragrance of her hair through his own alcohol-laced breath. "Where is it?" he whispered. *The keystone was in her sweater pocket earlier. So where is it now?*

"It's over here," Langdon's deep voice resonated from across the room.

Silas turned to see Langdon holding the black cryptex before him, waving it back and forth like a matador tempting a dumb animal.

"Set it down," Silas demanded.

"Let Sophie and Leigh leave the church," Langdon replied. "You and I can settle this."

Silas pushed Sophie away from him and aimed the gun at Langdon, moving toward him.

"Not a step closer," Langdon said. "Not until they leave the building."

"You are in no position to make demands."

"I disagree." Langdon raised the cryptex high over his head. "I will not hesitate to smash this on the floor and break the vial inside."

Although Silas sneered outwardly at the threat, he felt a flash of fear. This was unexpected. He aimed the gun at Langdon's head and kept his voice as steady as his hand. "You would never break the keystone. You want to find the Grail as much as I do."

"You're wrong. You want it much more. You've proven you're willing to kill for it."

Forty feet away, peering out from the annex pews near the archway, Rémy Legaludec felt a rising alarm. The maneuver had not gone as planned, and even from here, he could see Silas was uncertain how to handle the situation. At the Teacher's orders, Rémy had forbidden Silas to fire his gun.

"Let them go," Langdon again demanded, holding the cryptex high over his head and staring into Silas's gun.

The monk's red eyes filled with anger and frustration, and Rémy tightened with fear that Silas might actually shoot Langdon while he was holding the cryptex. *The cryptex cannot fall!*

The cryptex was to be Rémy's ticket to freedom and wealth. A little over a year ago, he was simply a fifty-five-year-old manservant living within the walls of Château Villette, catering to the whims of the insufferable cripple Sir Leigh

Teabing. Then he was approached with an extraordinary proposition. Rémy's association with Sir Leigh Teabing—the preeminent Grail historian on earth—was going to bring Rémy everything he had ever dreamed of in life. Since then, every moment he had spent inside Château Villette had been leading him to this very instant.

I am so close, Rémy told himself, gazing into the sanctuary of the Temple Church and the keystone in Robert Langdon's hand. If Langdon dropped it, all would be lost.

Am I willing to show my face? It was something the Teacher had strictly forbidden. Rémy was the only one who knew the Teacher's identity.

"Are you certain you want *Silas* to carry out this task?" Rémy had asked the Teacher less than half an hour ago, upon getting orders to steal the keystone. "I myself am capable."

The Teacher was resolute. "Silas served us well with the four Priory members. He will recover the keystone. *You* must remain anonymous. If others see you, they will need to be eliminated, and there has been enough killing already. Do not reveal your face."

My face will change, Rémy thought. *With what you've promised to pay me, I will become an entirely new man.* Surgery could even change his fingerprints, the Teacher had told him. Soon he would be free—another unrecognizable, beautiful face soaking up the sun on the beach. "Understood," Rémy said. "I will assist Silas from the shadows."

"For your own knowledge, Rémy," the Teacher had told him, "the tomb in question is not in the Temple Church. So have no fear. They are looking in the wrong place."

Rémy was stunned. "And you know where the tomb is?"

"Of course. Later, I will tell you. For the moment, you must act quickly. If the others figure out the true location of the tomb and leave the church before you take the cryptex, we could lose the Grail forever."

Rémy didn't give a damn about the Grail, except that the Teacher refused to pay him until it was found. Rémy felt giddy every time he thought of the money he soon would have. *One third of twenty million euro. Plenty to disappear forever.* Rémy had pictured the beach towns on the Côte d'Azur, where he planned to live out his days basking in the sun and letting others serve him for a change.

Now, however, here in the Temple Church, with Langdon threatening to break the keystone, Rémy's future was at risk. Unable to bear the thought of coming this close only to lose it all, Rémy made the decision to take bold action. The gun in his hand was a concealable, small-caliber, J-frame Medusa, but it would be plenty deadly at close range.

Stepping from the shadows, Rémy marched into the circular chamber and aimed the gun directly at Teabing's head. "Old man, I've been waiting a long time to do this."

SIR LEIGH TEABING's heart practically stalled to see Rémy aiming a gun at him. *What is he doing!* Teabing recognized the tiny Medusa revolver as his own, the one he kept locked in the limousine glove box for safety.

"Rémy?" Teabing sputtered in shock. "What is going on?"

Langdon and Sophie looked equally dumbstruck.

Rémy circled behind Teabing and rammed the pistol barrel into his back, high and on the left, directly behind his heart.

Teabing felt his muscles seize with terror. "Rémy, I don't—"

"I'll make it simple," Rémy snapped, eyeing Langdon over Teabing's shoulder. "Set down the keystone, or I pull the trigger."

Langdon seemed momentarily paralyzed. "The keystone is worthless to you," he stammered. "You cannot possibly open it."

"Arrogant fools," Rémy sneered. "Have you not noticed that I have been listening tonight as you discussed these poems? Everything I heard, I have shared with others. Others who know more than you. You are not even looking in the right place. The tomb you seek is in another location entirely!"

Teabing felt panicked. *What is he saying!*

"Why do you want the Grail?" Langdon demanded. "To destroy it? Before the End of Days?"

Rémy called to the monk. "Silas, take the keystone from Mr. Langdon."

As the monk advanced, Langdon stepped back, raising the keystone high, looking fully prepared to hurl it at the floor.

"I would rather break it," Langdon said, "than see it in the wrong hands."

Teabing now felt a wave of horror. He could see his life's work evaporating before his eyes. All his dreams about to be shattered.

"Robert, no!" Teabing exclaimed. "Don't! That's the Grail you're holding! Rémy would *never* shoot me. We've known each other for ten—"

Rémy aimed at the ceiling and fired the Medusa. The blast was enormous for such a small weapon, the gunshot echoing like thunder inside the stone chamber.

Everyone froze.

"I am not playing games," Rémy said. "The next one is in his back. Hand the keystone to Silas."

Langdon reluctantly held out the cryptex. Silas stepped forward and took it, his red eyes gleaming with the self-satisfaction of vengeance. Slipping the keystone in the pocket of his robe, Silas backed off, still holding Langdon and Sophie at gunpoint.

Teabing felt Rémy's arm clamp hard around his neck as the servant began backing out of the building, dragging Teabing with him, the gun still pressed in his back.

"Let him go," Langdon demanded.

"We're taking Mr. Teabing for a drive," Rémy said, still backing up. "If you call the police, he will die. If you do anything to interfere, he will die. Is that clear?"

"Take me," Langdon demanded, his voice cracking with emotion. "Let Leigh go."

Rémy laughed. "I don't think so. He and I have such a nice history. Besides, he still might prove useful."

Silas was backing up now, keeping Langdon and Sophie at gunpoint as Rémy pulled Leigh toward the exit, his crutches dragging behind him.

Sophie's voice was unwavering. "Who are you working for?"

The question brought a smirk to the departing Rémy's face. "You would be surprised, Mademoiselle Neveu."

THE FIREPLACE in Château Villette's drawing room was cold, but Collet paced before it nonetheless as he read the faxes from Interpol.

Not at all what he expected.

André Vernet, according to official records, was a model citizen. No police record—not even a parking ticket. Educated at prep school and the Sorbonne, he had a *cum laude* degree in international finance. Interpol said Vernet's name appeared in the newspapers from time to time, but always in a positive light.

Apparently the man had helped design the security parameters that kept the Depository Bank of Zurich a leader in the ultramodern world of electronic security. Vernet's credit card records showed a penchant for art books, expensive wine, and classical CD's—mostly Brahms—which he apparently enjoyed on an exceptionally high-end stereo system he had purchased several years ago.

Zero, Collet sighed.

The only red flag tonight from Interpol had been a set of fingerprints that apparently belonged to Teabing's servant. The chief PTS examiner was reading the report in a comfortable chair across the room.

Collet looked over. "Anything?"

The examiner shrugged. "Prints belong to Rémy Legaludec. Wanted for petty crime. Nothing serious. Looks like he got kicked out of university for rewiring phone jacks to get free service . . . later did some petty theft. Breaking and entering. Skipped out on a hospital bill once for an emergency tracheotomy." He glanced up, chuckling. "Peanut allergy."

Collet nodded, recalling a police investigation into a restaurant that had failed to notate on its menu that the chili recipe contained peanut oil. An unsuspecting patron had died of anaphylactic shock at the table after a single bite.

"Legaludec is probably a live-in here to avoid getting picked up." The examiner looked amused. "His lucky night."

Collet sighed. "All right, you better forward this info to Captain Fache."

The examiner headed off just as another PTS agent burst into the living room. "Lieutenant! We found something in the barn."

THE BARN AT CHÂTEAU VILLETTE

From the anxious look on the agent's face, Collet could only guess. "A body."

"No, sir. Something more . . ." He hesitated. "Unexpected."

Rubbing his eyes, Collet followed the agent out to the barn. As they entered the musty, cavernous space, the agent motioned toward the center of the room, where a wooden ladder now ascended high into the rafters, propped against the ledge of a hayloft suspended high above them.

"That ladder wasn't there earlier," Collet said.

"No, sir. I set that up. We were dusting for prints near the Rolls when I saw the ladder lying on the floor. I wouldn't have given it a second thought except the rungs were worn and muddy. This ladder gets regular use. The height of the hayloft matched the ladder, so I raised it and climbed up to have a look."

Collet's eyes climbed the ladder's steep incline to the soaring hayloft. *Someone goes up there regularly?* From down here, the loft appeared to be a deserted platform, and yet admittedly most of it was invisible from this line of sight.

A senior PTS agent appeared at the top of the ladder, looking down. "You'll definitely want to see this, Lieutenant," he said, waving Collet up with a latex-gloved hand.

Nodding tiredly, Collet walked over to the base of the old ladder and grasped the bottom rungs. The ladder was an antique tapered design and narrowed as Collet ascended. As he neared the top, Collet almost lost his footing on a thin rung. The barn below him spun. Alert now, he moved on, finally reaching the top. The agent above him reached out, offering his wrist. Collet grabbed it and made the awkward transition onto the platform.

"It's over there," the PTS agent said, pointing deep into the immaculately clean loft. "Only one set of prints up here. We'll have an ID shortly."

Collet squinted through the dim light toward the far wall. *What the hell?* Nestled against the far wall sat an elaborate computer workstation—two tower CPUs, a flat-screen video monitor with speakers, an array of hard drives, and a multichannel audio console that appeared to have its own filtered power supply.

Why in the world would anyone work all the way up here? Collet moved toward the gear. "Have you examined the system?"

"It's a listening post."

Collet spun. "Surveillance?"

The agent nodded. "Very advanced surveillance." He motioned to a long project table strewn with electronic parts, manuals, tools, wires, soldering irons, and other electronic components. "Someone clearly knows what he's doing. A lot of this gear is as sophisticated as our own equipment. Miniature microphones, photoelectric recharging cells, high-capacity RAM chips. He's even got some of those new nano drives."

Collet was impressed.

"Here's a complete system," the agent said, handing Collet an assembly not much larger than a pocket calculator. Dangling off the contraption was a foot-long wire with a stamp-sized piece of wafer-thin foil stuck on the end. "The base is a high-capacity hard disk audio recording system with rechargeable battery. That strip of foil at the end of the wire is a combination microphone and photoelectric recharging cell."

Collet knew them well. These foil-like, photocell microphones had been an enormous breakthrough a few years back. Now, a hard disk recorder could be affixed behind a lamp, for example, with its foil microphone molded into the contour of the base and dyed to match. As long as the microphone was positioned such that it received a few hours of sunlight per day, the photo cells would keep recharging the system. Bugs like this one could listen indefinitely.

"Reception method?" Collet asked.

The agent signaled to an insulated wire that ran out of the back of the computer, up the wall, through a hole in the barn roof. "Simple radio wave. Small antenna on the roof."

Collet knew these recording systems were generally placed in offices, were voice-activated to save hard disk space, and recorded snippets of conversation during the day, transmitting compressed audio files at night to avoid detection. After transmitting, the hard drive erased itself and prepared to do it all over again the next day.

Collet's gaze moved now to a shelf on which were stacked several hundred audio cassettes, all labeled with dates and numbers. *Someone has been very busy*. He turned back to the agent. "Do you have any idea what target is being bugged?"

"Well, Lieutenant," the agent said, walking to the computer and launching a piece of software. "It's the strangest thing. . . ."

Chapter 88

ANGDON FELT utterly spent as he and Sophie hurdled a turnstile at the Temple tube station and dashed deep into the grimy labyrinth of tunnels and platforms. The guilt ripped through him.

I involved Leigh, and now he's in enormous danger.

Rémy's involvement had been a shock, and yet it made sense. Whoever was pursuing the Grail had recruited someone on the inside. *They went to Teabing's for the same reason I did.* Throughout history, those who held knowledge of the Grail had always been magnets for thieves and scholars alike. The fact that Teabing had been a target all along should have made Langdon feel less guilty about involving him. It did not. *We need to find Leigh and help him. Immediately.*

Langdon followed Sophie to the westbound District and Circle Line platform, where she hurried to a pay phone to call the police, despite Rémy's warning to the contrary. Langdon sat on a grungy bench nearby, feeling remorseful.

"The best way to help Leigh," Sophie reiterated as she dialed, "is to involve the London authorities immediately. Trust me."

Langdon had not initially agreed with this idea, but as they had hatched their plan, Sophie's logic began to make sense. Teabing was safe at the moment. Even if Rémy and the others knew where the knight's tomb was located, they still might need Teabing's help deciphering the orb reference. What worried Langdon was what would happen *after* the Grail map had been found. *Leigh will become a huge liability.*

If Langdon were to have any chance of helping Leigh, or of ever seeing the keystone again, it was essential that he find the tomb first. *Unfortunately, Rémy has a big head start.*

Slowing Rémy down had become Sophie's task.

Finding the right tomb had become Langdon's.

Sophie would make Rémy and Silas fugitives of the London police, forcing them into hiding or, better yet, catching them. Langdon's plan was less certain—to take the tube to nearby King's College, which was renowned for its electronic theological database. *The ultimate research tool,* Langdon had heard. *Instant answers to any religious historical question.* He wondered what the database would have to say about "a knight a Pope interred."

He stood up and paced, wishing the train would hurry.

AT THE PAY PHONE, Sophie's call finally connected to the London police.

"Snow Hill Division," the dispatcher said. "How may I direct your call?"

"I'm reporting a kidnapping." Sophie knew to be concise.

"Name please?"

Sophie paused. "Agent Sophie Neveu with the French Judicial Police."

The title had the desired effect. "Right away, ma'am. Let me get a detective on the line for you."

As the call went through, Sophie began wondering if the police would even believe her description of Teabing's captors. *A man in a tuxedo.* How much easier to identify could a suspect be? Even if Rémy changed clothes, he was partnered with an albino monk. *Impossible to miss.* Moreover, they had a hostage and could not take public transportation. She wondered how many Jaguar stretch limos there could be in London.

Sophie's connection to the detective seemed to be taking forever. *Come on!* She could hear the line clicking and buzzing, as if she was being transferred.

Fifteen seconds passed.

Finally a man came on the line. "Agent Neveu?"

Stunned, Sophie registered the gruff tone immediately.

"Agent Neveu," Bezu Fache demanded. "Where the hell are you?"

Sophie was speechless. Captain Fache had apparently requested the London police dispatcher alert him if Sophie called in.

"Listen," Fache said, speaking to her in terse French. "I made a terrible mistake tonight. Robert Langdon is innocent. All charges against him have been dropped. Even so, both of you are in danger. You need to come in."

Sophie's jaw fell slack. She had no idea how to respond. Fache was not a man who apologized for anything.

"You did not tell me," Fache continued, "that Jacques Saunière was your grandfather. I fully intend to overlook your insubordination last night on account of the emotional stress you must be under. At the moment, however, you and Langdon need to go to the nearest London police headquarters for refuge."

He knows I'm in London? What else does Fache know? Sophie heard what sounded like drilling or machinery in the background. She also heard an odd clicking on the line. "Are you tracing this call, Captain?"

Fache's voice was firm now. "You and I need to cooperate, Agent Neveu. We both have a lot to lose here. This is damage control. I made errors in judgment last night, and if those errors result in the deaths of an American professor and a DCPJ cryptologist, my career will be over. I've been trying to pull you back into safety for the last several hours."

A warm wind was now pushing through the station as a train approached with a low rumble. Sophie had every intention of being on it. Langdon apparently had the same idea; he was gathering himself together and moving toward her now.

"The man you want is Rémy Legaludec," Sophie said. "He is Teabing's servant. He just kidnapped Teabing inside the Temple Church and—"

"Agent Neveu!" Fache bellowed as the train thundered into the station. "This is not something to discuss on an open line. You and Langdon will come in now. For your own well-being! That is a direct order!"

Sophie hung up and dashed with Langdon onto the train.

THE IMMACULATE CABIN of Teabing's Hawker was now covered with steel shavings and smelled of compressed air and propane. Bezu Fache had sent everyone away and sat alone with his drink and the heavy wooden box found in Teabing's safe.

Running his finger across the inlaid Rose, he lifted the ornate lid. Inside he found a stone cylinder with lettered dials. The five dials were arranged to spell

SOFIA. Fache stared at the word a long moment and then lifted the cylinder from its padded resting place and examined every inch. Then, pulling slowly on the ends, Fache slid off one of the end caps. The cylinder was empty.

Fache set it back in the box and gazed absently out the jet's window at the hangar, pondering his brief conversation with Sophie, as well as the information he'd received from PTS in Château Villette. The sound of his phone shook him from his daydream.

It was the DCPJ switchboard. The dispatcher was apologetic. The president of the Depository Bank of Zurich had been calling repeatedly, and although he had been told several times that the captain was in London on business, he just kept calling. Begrudgingly Fache told the operator to forward the call.

"Monsieur Vernet," Fache said, before the man could even speak, "I am sorry I did not call you earlier. I have been busy. As promised, the name of your bank has not appeared in the media. So what precisely is your concern?"

Vernet's voice was anxious as he told Fache how Langdon and Sophie had extracted a small wooden box from the bank and then persuaded Vernet to help them escape. "Then when I heard on the radio that they were criminals," Vernet said, "I pulled over and demanded the box back, but they attacked me and stole the truck."

"You are concerned for a wooden box," Fache said, eyeing the Rose inlay on the cover and again gently opening the lid to reveal the white cylinder. "Can you tell me what was in the box?"

"The contents are immaterial," Vernet fired back. "I am concerned with the reputation of my bank. We have never had a robbery. *Ever.* It will ruin us if I cannot recover this property on behalf of my client."

"You said Agent Neveu and Robert Langdon had a password and a key. What makes you say they stole the box?"

"They *murdered* people tonight. Including Sophie Neveu's grandfather. The key and password were obviously ill-gotten."

"Mr. Vernet, my men have done some checking into your background and your interests. You are obviously a man of great culture and refinement. I would imagine you are a man of honor, as well. As am I. That said, I give you my word as commanding officer of the *Police Judiciaire* that your box, along with your bank's reputation, are in the safest of hands."

HIGH IN THE HAYLOFT at Château Villette, Collet stared at the computer monitor in amazement. "This system is eavesdropping on *all* these locations?"

"Yes," the agent said. "It looks like data has been collected for over a year now."

Collet read the list again, speechless.

COLBERT SOSTAQUE—Chairman of the Conseil Constitutionnel

JEAN CHAFFÉE—Curator, Musée du Jeu de Paume

ÉDOUARD DESROCHERS—Senior Archivist, Mitterrand Library

JACQUES SAUNIÈRE—Curator, Musée du Louvre

MICHEL BRETON—Head of DAS (French Intelligence)

The agent pointed to the screen. "Number four is of obvious concern."

Collet nodded blankly. He had noticed it immediately. *Jacques Saunière was being bugged.* He looked at the rest of the list again. *How could anyone possibly manage to bug these prominent people?* "Have you heard any of the audio files?"

"A few. Here's one of the most recent." The agent clicked a few computer keys. The speakers crackled to life. *"Capitaine, un agent du Département de Cryptographie est arrivé."*

Collet could not believe his ears. "That's me! That's my voice!" He recalled sitting at Saunière's desk and radioing Fache in the Grand Gallery to alert him of Sophie Neveu's arrival.

The agent nodded. "A lot of our Louvre investigation tonight would have been audible if someone had been interested."

"Have you sent anyone in to sweep for the bug?"

"No need. I know exactly where it is." The agent went to a pile of old notes and blueprints on the worktable. He selected a page and handed it to Collet. "Look familiar?"

Collet was amazed. He was holding a photocopy of an ancient schematic diagram, which depicted a rudimentary machine. He was unable to read the handwritten Italian labels, and yet he knew what he was looking at. A model for a fully articulated medieval French knight.

The knight sitting on Saunière's desk!

Collet's eyes moved to the margins, where someone had scribbled notes on the photocopy in red felt-tipped marker. The notes were in French and appeared to be ideas outlining how best to insert a listening device into the knight.

ILAS SAT in the passenger seat of the parked Jaguar limousine near the Temple Church. His hands felt damp on the keystone as he waited for Rémy to finish tying and gagging Teabing in back with the rope they had found in the trunk.

Finally, Rémy climbed out of the rear of the limo, walked around, and slid into the driver's seat beside Silas.

"Secure?" Silas asked.

Rémy chuckled, shaking off the rain and glancing over his shoulder through the open partition at the crumpled form of Leigh Teabing, who was barely visible in the shadows in the rear. "He's not going anywhere."

Silas could hear Teabing's muffled cries and realized Rémy had used some of the old duct tape to gag him.

"*Ferme ta gueule!*" Rémy shouted over his shoulder at Teabing. Reaching to a control panel on the elaborate dash, Rémy pressed a button. An opaque partition raised behind them, sealing off the back. Teabing disappeared, and his voice was silenced. Rémy glanced at Silas. "I've been listening to his miserable whimpering long enough."

MINUTES LATER, as the Jaguar stretch limo powered through the streets, Silas's cell phone rang. *The Teacher.* He answered excitedly. "Hello?"

"Silas," the Teacher's familiar French accent said, "I am relieved to hear your voice. This means you are safe."

Silas was equally comforted to hear the Teacher. It had been hours, and the operation had veered wildly off course. Now, at last, it seemed to be back on track. "I have the keystone."

"This is superb news," the Teacher told him. "Is Rémy with you?"

Silas was surprised to hear the Teacher use Rémy's name. "Yes. Rémy freed me."

"As I ordered him to do. I am only sorry you had to endure captivity for so long."

"Physical discomfort has no meaning. The important thing is that the keystone is ours."

"Yes. I need it delivered to me at once. Time is of the essence."

Silas was eager to meet the Teacher face-to-face at last. "Yes, sir, I would be honored."

"Silas, I would like *Rémy* to bring it to me."

Rémy? Silas was crestfallen. After everything Silas had done for the Teacher, he had believed *he* would be the one to hand over the prize. *The Teacher favors Rémy?*

"I sense your disappointment," the Teacher said, "which tells me you do not understand my meaning." He lowered his voice to a whisper. "You must believe that I would much prefer to receive the keystone from *you*—a man of God rather than a criminal—but Rémy must be dealt with. He disobeyed my orders and made a grave mistake that has put our entire mission at risk."

Silas felt a chill and glanced over at Rémy. Kidnapping Teabing had not been part of the plan, and deciding what to do with him posed a new problem.

"You and I are men of God," the Teacher whispered. "We cannot be deterred from our goal." There was an ominous pause on the line. "For this reason alone, I will ask Rémy to bring me the keystone. Do you understand?"

Silas sensed anger in the Teacher's voice and was surprised the man was not more understanding. *Showing his face could not be avoided*, Silas thought. *Rémy did what he had to do. He saved the keystone.* "I understand," Silas managed.

"Good. For your own safety, you need to get off the street immediately. The police will be looking for the limousine soon, and I do not want you caught. Opus Dei has a residence in London, no?"

"Of course."

"And you are welcome there?"

"As a brother."

"Then go there and stay out of sight. I will call you the moment I am in possession of the keystone and have attended to my current problem."

"You are in London?"

"Do as I say, and everything will be fine."

"Yes, sir."

The Teacher heaved a sigh, as if what he now had to do was profoundly regrettable. "It's time I speak to Rémy."

Silas handed Rémy the phone, sensing it might be the last call Rémy Legaludec ever took.

AS RÉMY took the phone, he knew this poor, twisted monk had no idea what fate awaited him now that he had served his purpose.

The Teacher used you, Silas.

And your bishop is a pawn.

Rémy still marveled at the Teacher's powers of persuasion. Bishop Aringarosa had trusted everything. He had been blinded by his own desperation. *Aringarosa was far too eager to believe.* Although Rémy did not particularly like the Teacher, he felt pride at having gained the man's trust and helped him so substantially. *I have earned my payday.*

"Listen carefully," the Teacher said. "Take Silas to the Opus Dei residence hall and drop him off a few streets away. Then drive to St. James's Park. It is adjacent to Parliament and Big Ben. You can park the limousine on Horse Guards Parade. We'll talk there."

With that, the connection went dead.

ING'S COLLEGE, established by King George IV in 1829, houses its Department of Theology and Religious Studies adjacent to Parliament on property granted by the Crown. King's College Religion Department boasts not only 150 years' experience in teaching and research, but the 1982 establishment of the Research Institute in Systematic Theology, which possesses one of the most complete and electronically advanced religious research libraries in the world.

Langdon still felt shaky as he and Sophie came in from the rain and entered the library. The primary research room was as Teabing had described it—a dramatic octagonal chamber dominated by an enormous round table around which King Arthur and his knights might have been comfortable were it not for the presence of twelve flat-screen computer workstations. On the far side of the room, a reference librarian was just pouring a pot of tea and settling in for her day of work.

"Lovely morning," she said in a cheerful British accent, leaving the tea and walking over. "May I help you?"

"Thank you, yes," Langdon replied. "My name is—"

"Robert Langdon." She gave a pleasant smile. "I know who you are."

For an instant, he feared Fache had put him on English television as well, but the librarian's smile suggested otherwise. Langdon still had not gotten used to these moments of unexpected celebrity. Then again, if anyone on earth were going to recognize his face, it would be a librarian in a Religious Studies reference facility.

"Pamela Gettum," the librarian said, offering her hand. She had a genial, erudite face and a pleasingly fluid voice. The horn-rimmed glasses hanging around her neck were thick.

"A pleasure," Langdon said. "This is my friend Sophie Neveu."

The two women greeted one another, and Gettum turned immediately back to Langdon. "I didn't know you were coming."

KING'S COLLEGE, LONDON

"Neither did we. If it's not too much trouble, we could really use your help finding some information."

Gettum shifted, looking uncertain. "Normally our services are by petition and appointment only, unless of course you're the guest of someone at the college?"

Langdon shook his head. "I'm afraid we've come unannounced. A friend of mine speaks very highly of you. Sir Leigh Teabing?" Langdon felt a pang of gloom as he said the name. "The British Royal Historian."

Gettum brightened now, laughing. "Heavens, yes. What a character. Fanatical! Every time he comes in, it's always the same search strings. Grail. Grail. Grail. I swear that man will die before he gives up on that quest." She winked. "Time and money afford one such lovely luxuries, wouldn't you say? A regular Don Quixote, that one."

"Is there any chance you can help us?" Sophie asked. "It's quite important."

Gettum glanced around the deserted library and then winked at them both. "Well, I can't very well claim I'm too busy, now can I? As long as you sign in, I can't imagine anyone being too upset. What did you have in mind?"

"We're trying to find a tomb in London."

Gettum looked dubious. "We've got about twenty thousand of them. Can you be a little more specific?"

"It's the tomb of a *knight*. We don't have a name."

"A knight. That tightens the net substantially. Much less common."

"We don't have much information about the knight we're looking for," Sophie said, "but this is what we know." She produced a slip of paper on which she had written only the first two lines of the poem.

Hesitant to show the entire poem to an outsider, Langdon and Sophie had decided to share just the first two lines, those that identified the knight. *Compartmentalized cryptography,* Sophie had called it. When an intelligence agency intercepted a code containing sensitive data, cryptographers each worked on a discrete section of the code. This way, when they broke it, no single cryptographer possessed the entire deciphered message.

In this case, the precaution was probably excessive; even if this librarian saw the entire poem, identified the knight's tomb, and knew what orb was missing, the information was useless without the cryptex.

GETTUM SENSED an urgency in the eyes of this famed American scholar, almost as if his finding this tomb quickly were a matter of critical importance. The green-eyed woman accompanying him also seemed anxious.

Puzzled, Gettum put on her glasses and examined the paper they had just handed her.

In London lies a knight a Pope interred.
His labor's fruit a Holy wrath incurred.

She glanced at her guests. "What is this? Some kind of Harvard scavenger hunt?"

Langdon's laugh sounded forced. "Yeah, something like that."

Gettum paused, feeling she was not getting the whole story. Nonetheless, she felt intrigued and found herself pondering the verse carefully. "According to this rhyme, a knight did something that incurred displeasure with God, and yet a Pope was kind enough to bury him in London."

Langdon nodded. "Does it ring any bells?"

Gettum moved toward one of the workstations. "Not offhand, but let's see what we can pull up in the database."

Over the past two decades, King's College Research Institute in Systematic Theology had used optical character recognition software in unison with linguistic translation devices to digitize and catalog an enormous collection of texts—encyclopedias of religion, religious biographies, sacred scriptures in dozens of languages, histories, Vatican letters, diaries of clerics, anything at all that qualified as writings on human spirituality. Because the massive collection was now in the form of bits and bytes rather than physical pages, the data was infinitely more accessible.

Settling into one of the workstations, Gettum eyed the slip of paper and began typing. "To begin, we'll run a straight Boolean with a few obvious keywords and see what happens."

"Thank you."

Gettum typed in a few words:

```
London, Knight, Pope
```

As she clicked the SEARCH button, she could feel the hum of the massive mainframe downstairs scanning data at a rate of 500 MB/sec. "I'm asking the system to show us any documents whose complete text contains all three of these keywords. We'll get more hits than we want, but it's a good place to start."

The screen was already showing the first of the hits now.

```
Painting the Pope. The Collected Portraits of
Sir Joshua Reynolds. London University Press.
```

Gettum shook her head. "Obviously not what you're looking for."

She scrolled to the next hit.

The London Writings of Alexander Pope
by G. Wilson Knight.

Again she shook her head.

As the system churned on, the hits came up more quickly than usual. Dozens of texts appeared, many of them referencing the eighteenth-century British writer Alexander Pope, whose counterreligious, mock-epic poetry apparently contained plenty of references to knights and London.

Gettum shot a quick glance to the numeric field at the bottom of the screen. This computer, by calculating the current number of hits and multiplying by the percentage of the database left to search, provided a rough guess of how much information would be found. This particular search looked like it was going to return an obscenely large amount of data.

Estimated number of total hits: 2,692

"We need to refine the parameters further," Gettum said, stopping the search. "Is this all the information you have regarding the tomb? There's nothing else to go on?"

Langdon glanced at Sophie Neveu, looking uncertain.

This is no scavenger hunt, Gettum sensed. She had heard the whisperings of Robert Langdon's experience in Rome last year. This American had been granted access to the most secure library on earth—the Vatican Secret Archives. She wondered what kinds of secrets Langdon might have learned inside and if his current desperate hunt for a mysterious London tomb might relate to information he had gained within the Vatican. Gettum had been a librarian long enough to know the most common reason people came to London to look for knights. *The Grail.*

Gettum smiled and adjusted her glasses. "You are friends with Leigh Teabing, you are in England, and you are looking for a knight." She folded her hands. "I can only assume you are on a Grail quest."

Langdon and Sophie exchanged startled looks.

Gettum laughed. "My friends, this library is a base camp for Grail seekers. Leigh Teabing among them. I wish I had a shilling for every time I'd run searches for the Rose, Mary Magdalene, Sangreal, Merovingian, Priory of Sion, et cetera, et cetera. Everyone loves a conspiracy." She took off her glasses and eyed them. "I need more information."

In the silence, Gettum sensed her guests' desire for discretion was quickly being outweighed by their eagerness for a fast result.

"Here," Sophie Neveu blurted. "This is everything we know." Borrowing a pen from Langdon, she wrote two more lines on the slip of paper and handed it to Gettum.

> You seek the orb that ought be on his tomb.
> It speaks of Rosy flesh and seeded womb.

Gettum gave an inward smile. *The Grail indeed,* she thought, noting the references to the Rose and her seeded womb. "I can help you," she said, looking up from the slip of paper. "Might I ask where this verse came from? And why you are seeking an orb?"

"You might ask," Langdon said, with a friendly smile, "but it's a long story and we have very little time."

"Sounds like a polite way of saying 'mind your own business.' "

"We would be forever in your debt, Pamela," Langdon said, "if you could find out who this knight is and where he is buried."

"Very well," Gettum said, typing again. "I'll play along. If this is a Grail-related issue, we should cross-reference against Grail keywords. I'll add a proximity parameter and remove the title weighting. That will limit our hits only to those instances of textual keywords that occur *near* a Grail-related word."

Search for:
KNIGHT LONDON, POPE, TOMB

Within 100 word proximity of:
GRAIL, ROSE, SANGREAL, CHALICE

"How long will this take?" Sophie asked.

"A few hundred terabytes with multiple cross-referencing fields?" Gettum's eyes glimmered as she clicked the SEARCH key. "A mere fifteen minutes."

Langdon and Sophie said nothing, but Gettum sensed this sounded like an eternity to them.

"Tea?" Gettum asked, standing and walking toward the pot she had made earlier. "Leigh always loves my tea."

Chapter 95

L ONDON'S OPUS Dei Centre is a modest brick building at 5 Orme Court, overlooking the North Walk at Kensington Gardens. Silas had never been here, but he felt a rising sense of refuge and asylum as he approached the building on foot. Despite the rain, Rémy had dropped him off a short distance away in order to keep the limousine off the main streets. Silas didn't mind the walk. The rain was cleansing.

At Rémy's suggestion, Silas had wiped down his gun and disposed of it through a sewer grate. He was glad to get rid of it. He felt lighter. His legs still ached from being bound all that time, but Silas had endured far greater pain. He wondered, though, about Teabing, whom Rémy had left bound in the back of the limousine. The Briton certainly had to be feeling the pain by now.

"What will you do with him?" Silas had asked Rémy as they drove over here.

Rémy had shrugged. "That is a decision for the Teacher." There was an odd finality in his tone.

Now, as Silas approached the Opus Dei building, the rain began to fall harder, soaking his heavy robe, stinging the wounds of the day before. He was ready to leave behind the sins of the last twenty-four hours and purge his soul. His work was done.

Moving across a small courtyard to the front door, Silas was not surprised to find the door unlocked. He opened it and stepped into the minimalist foyer. A muted electronic chime sounded upstairs as Silas stepped onto the carpet. The bell was a common feature in these halls where the residents spent most of the day in their rooms in prayer. Silas could hear movement above on the creaky wood floors.

A man in a cloak came downstairs. "May I help you?" He had kind eyes that seemed not even to register Silas's startling physical appearance.

"Thank you. My name is Silas. I am an Opus Dei numerary."

"American?"

Silas nodded. "I am in town only for the day. Might I rest here?"

"You need not even ask. There are two empty rooms on the third floor. Shall I bring you some tea and bread?"

"Thank you." Silas was famished.

Silas went upstairs to a modest room with a window, where he took off his wet robe and knelt down to pray in his undergarments. He heard his host come up and lay a tray outside his door. Silas finished his prayers, ate his food, and lay down to sleep.

THREE STORIES BELOW, a phone was ringing. The Opus Dei numerary who had welcomed Silas answered the line.

"This is the London police," the caller said. "We are trying to find an albino monk. We've had a tip-off that he might be there. Have you seen him?"

The numerary was startled. "Yes, he is here. Is something wrong?"

"He is there *now?*"

"Yes, upstairs praying. What is going on?"

"Leave him precisely where he is," the officer commanded. "Don't say a word to anyone. I'm sending officers over right away."

S
T. JAMES'S PARK is a sea of green in the middle of London, a public park bordering the palaces of Westminster, Buckingham, and St. James's. Once enclosed by King Henry VIII and stocked with deer for the hunt, St. James's Park is now open to the public. On sunny afternoons, Londoners picnic beneath the willows and feed the pond's resident pelicans, whose ancestors were a gift to Charles II from the Russian ambassador.

ST. JAMES'S PARK, LONDON

The Teacher saw no pelicans today. The stormy weather had brought instead seagulls from the ocean. The lawns were covered with them—hundreds of white bodies all facing the same direction, patiently riding out the damp wind. Despite the morning fog, the park afforded splendid views of the Houses of Parliament and Big Ben. Gazing across the sloping lawns, past the duck pond and the delicate silhouettes of the weeping willows, the Teacher could see the spires of the building that housed the knight's tomb—the real reason he had told Rémy to come to this spot.

As the Teacher approached the front passenger door of the parked limousine, Rémy leaned across and opened the door. The Teacher paused outside, taking a pull from the flask of cognac he was carrying. Then, dabbing his mouth, he slid in beside Rémy and closed the door.

Rémy held up the keystone like a trophy. "It was almost lost."

"You have done well," the Teacher said.

"*We* have done well," Rémy replied, laying the keystone in the Teacher's eager hands.

The Teacher admired it a long moment, smiling. "And the gun? You wiped it down?"

"Back in the glove box where I found it."

"Excellent." The Teacher took another drink of cognac and handed the flask to Rémy. "Let's toast our success. The end is near."

RÉMY ACCEPTED the bottle gratefully. The cognac tasted salty, but Rémy didn't care. He and the Teacher were truly partners now. He could feel himself ascending to a higher station in life. *I will never be a servant again.* As Rémy gazed down the embankment at the duck pond below, Château Villette seemed miles away.

Taking another swig from the flask, Rémy could feel the cognac warming his blood. The warmth in Rémy's throat, however, mutated quickly to an uncomfortable heat. Loosening his bow tie, Rémy tasted an unpleasant grittiness and handed the flask back to the Teacher. "I've probably had enough," he managed, weakly.

Taking the flask, the Teacher said, "Rémy, as you are aware, you are the only one who knows my face. I placed enormous trust in you."

"Yes," he said, feeling feverish as he loosened his tie further. "And your identity shall go with me to the grave."

The Teacher was silent a long moment. "I believe you." Pocketing the flask and the keystone, the Teacher reached for the glove box and pulled out the tiny Medusa revolver. For an instant, Rémy felt a surge of fear, but the Teacher simply slipped it in his trousers pocket.

What is he doing? Rémy felt himself sweating suddenly.

"I know I promised you freedom," the Teacher said, his voice now sounding regretful. "But considering your circumstances, this is the best I can do."

The swelling in Rémy's throat came on like an earthquake, and he lurched against the steering column, grabbing his throat and tasting vomit in his narrowing trachea. He let out a muted croak of a scream, not even loud enough to be heard outside the car. The saltiness in the cognac now registered.

I'm being murdered!

Incredulous, Rémy turned to see the Teacher sitting calmly beside him, staring straight ahead out the windshield. Rémy's eyesight blurred, and he gasped for breath. *I made everything possible for him! How could he do this!* Whether the Teacher had intended to kill Rémy all along or whether it had been Rémy's actions in the Temple Church that had made the Teacher lose faith, Rémy would never know. Terror and rage coursed through him now. Rémy tried to lunge for the Teacher, but his stiffening body could barely move. *I trusted you with everything!*

Rémy tried to lift his clenched fists to blow the horn, but instead he slipped sideways, rolling onto the seat, lying on his side beside the Teacher, clutching at his throat. The rain fell harder now. Rémy could no longer see, but he could sense his oxygen-deprived brain straining to cling to his last faint shreds of lucidity. As his world slowly went black, Rémy Legaludec could have sworn he heard the sounds of the soft Riviera surf.

THE TEACHER stepped from the limousine, pleased to see that nobody was looking in his direction. *I had no choice,* he told himself, surprised how little remorse he felt for what he had just done. *Rémy sealed his own fate.* The Teacher had feared all along that Rémy might need to be eliminated when the mission was complete, but by brazenly showing himself in the Temple Church, Rémy had accelerated the necessity dramatically. Robert Langdon's unexpected visit to Château Villette had brought the Teacher both a fortuitous windfall and an intricate dilemma. Langdon had delivered the keystone directly to the heart of the operation, which was a pleasant surprise, and yet he had brought the police on his tail. Rémy's prints were all over Château Villette, as well as in the barn's listening post, where Rémy had carried out the surveillance. The Teacher was grateful he had taken so much care in preventing any ties between Rémy's activities and his own. Nobody could implicate the Teacher unless Rémy talked, and that was no longer a concern.

One more loose end to tie up here, the Teacher thought, moving now toward the rear door of the limousine. *The police will have no idea what happened . . . and no living witness left to tell them.* Glancing around to ensure nobody was watching, he pulled open the door and climbed into the spacious rear compartment.

MINUTES LATER, the Teacher was crossing St. James's Park. *Only two people now remain. Langdon and Neveu.* They were more complicated. But manageable. At the moment, however, the Teacher had the cryptex to attend to.

Gazing triumphantly across the park, he could see his destination. *In London lies a knight a Pope interred.* As soon as the Teacher had heard the poem, he had known the answer. Even so, that the others had not figured it out was not surprising. *I have an unfair advantage.* Having listened to Saunière's conversations for months now, the Teacher had heard the Grand Master mention this famous knight on occasion, expressing esteem almost matching that he held for Da Vinci. The poem's reference to the knight was brutally simple once one saw it—a credit to Saunière's wit—and yet how this tomb would reveal the final password was still a mystery.

You seek the orb that ought be on his tomb.

The Teacher vaguely recalled photos of the famous tomb and, in particular, its most distinguishing feature. *A magnificent orb.* The huge sphere mounted atop the tomb was almost as large as the tomb itself. The presence of the orb seemed both encouraging and troubling to the Teacher. On one hand, it felt like a signpost, and yet, according to the poem, the missing piece of the puzzle was an orb that *ought* to be on his tomb . . . not one that was already there. He was counting on his closer inspection of the tomb to unveil the answer.

The rain was getting heavier now, and he tucked the cryptex deep in his right-hand pocket to protect it from the dampness. He kept the tiny Medusa revolver in his left, out of sight. Within minutes, he was stepping into the quiet sanctuary of London's grandest nine-hundred-year-old building.

JUST AS THE Teacher was stepping out of the rain, Bishop Aringarosa was stepping into it. On the rainy tarmac at Biggin Hill Executive Airport, Aringarosa emerged from his cramped plane, bundling his cassock against the cold damp. He had hoped to be greeted by Captain Fache. Instead a young British police officer approached with an umbrella.

"Bishop Aringarosa? Captain Fache had to leave. He asked me to look after you. He suggested I take you to Scotland Yard. He thought it would be safest."

Safest? Aringarosa looked down at the heavy briefcase of Vatican bonds clutched in his hand. He had almost forgotten. "Yes, thank you."

Aringarosa climbed into the police car, wondering where Silas could be. Minutes later, the police scanner crackled with the answer.

5 Orme Court.

Aringarosa recognized the address instantly.

The Opus Dei Centre in London.

He spun to the driver. "Take me there at once!"

*L*ANGDON'S EYES had not left the computer screen since the search began.

Five minutes. Only two hits. Both irrelevant.

He was starting to get worried.

Pamela Gettum was in the adjoining room, preparing hot drinks. Langdon and Sophie had inquired unwisely if there might be some *coffee* brewing alongside the tea Gettum had offered, and from the sound of the microwave beeps in the next room, Langdon suspected their request was about to be rewarded with instant Nescafé.

Finally, the computer pinged happily.

"Sounds like you got another," Gettum called from the next room. "What's the title?"

Langdon eyed the screen.

> Grail Allegory in Medieval Literature:
> A Treatise on *Sir Gawain and the Green Knight.*

"Allegory of the Green Knight," he called back.

"No good," Gettum said. "Not many mythological green giants buried in London."

Langdon and Sophie sat patiently in front of the screen and waited through two more dubious returns. When the computer pinged again, though, the offering was unexpected.

> DIE OPERN VON RICHARD WAGNER

"The operas of Wagner?" Sophie asked.

Gettum peeked back in the doorway, holding a packet of instant coffee. "That seems like a strange match. Was Wagner a knight?"

"No," Langdon said, feeling a sudden intrigue. "But he was a well-known Freemason." *Along with Mozart, Beethoven, Shakespeare, Gershwin, Houdini, and Disney.* Volumes had been written about the ties between the Masons and the Knights Templar, the Priory of Sion, and the Holy Grail. "I want to look at this one. How do I see the full text?"

"You don't want the full text," Gettum called. "Click on the hypertext title. The computer will display your keyword hits along with mono prelogs and triple post-logs for context."

Langdon had no idea what she had just said, but he clicked anyway.

A new window popped up.

```
. . . mythological knight named Parsifal who . . .
. . . metaphorical Grail quest that arguably . . .
   . . . the London Philharmonic in 1855 . . .
Rebecca Pope's opera anthology "Diva's . . .
. . . Wagner's tomb in Bayreuth, Germany . . .
```

"Wrong Pope," Langdon said, disappointed. Even so, he was amazed by the system's ease of use. The keywords with context were enough to remind him that Wagner's opera *Parsifal* was a tribute to Mary Magdalene and the bloodline of Jesus Christ, told through the story of a young knight on a quest for truth.

"Just be patient," Gettum urged. "It's a numbers game. Let the machine run."

Over the next few minutes, the computer returned several more Grail references, including a text about *troubadours*—France's famous wandering minstrels. Langdon knew it was no coincidence that the word *minstrel* and *minister* shared an etymological root. The troubadours were the traveling servants or "ministers" of the Church of Mary Magdalene, using

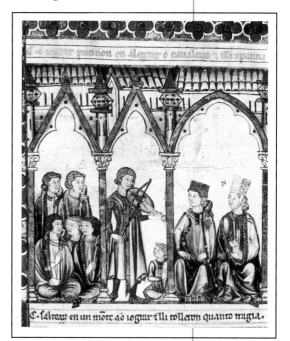

TROUBADOURS
(SPANISH SCHOOL, 13TH CENTURY)

music to disseminate the story of the sacred feminine among the common folk. To this day, the troubadours sang songs extolling the virtues of "our Lady"—a mysterious and beautiful woman to whom they pledged themselves forever.

Eagerly, he checked the hypertext but found nothing.

The computer pinged again.

KNIGHTS, KNAVES, POPES AND PENTACLES:
THE HISTORY OF THE HOLY GRAIL THROUGH TAROT

"Not surprising," Langdon said to Sophie. "Some of our keywords have the same names as individual cards." He reached for the mouse to click on a hyperlink. "I'm not sure if your grandfather ever mentioned it when you played Tarot with him, Sophie, but this game is a 'flash-card catechism' into the story of the Lost Bride and her subjugation by the evil Church."

Sophie eyed him, looking incredulous. "I had no idea."

"That's the point. By teaching through a metaphorical game, the followers of the Grail disguised their message from the watchful eye of the Church." Langdon often wondered how many modern card players had any clue that their four suits—spades, hearts, clubs, diamonds—were Grail-related symbols that came directly from Tarot's four suits of swords, cups, scepters, and pentacles.

Spades were Swords—The blade. Male.

Hearts were Cups—The chalice. Feminine.

Clubs were Scepters—The Royal Line. The flowering staff.

Diamonds were Pentacles—The goddess. The sacred feminine.

FOUR MINUTES LATER, as Langdon began feeling fearful they would not find what they had come for, the computer produced another hit.

The Gravity of Genius:
Biography of a Modern Knight.

"*Gravity of Genius?*" Langdon called out to Gettum. "Bio of a modern knight?"

Gettum stuck her head around the corner. "How modern? Please don't tell me it's your Sir Rudy Giuliani. Personally, I found that one a bit off the mark."

Langdon had his own qualms about the newly knighted Sir Mick Jagger, but this hardly seemed the moment to debate the politics of modern British knighthood. "Let's have a look." Langdon summoned up the hypertext keywords.

```
      . . . honorable knight, Sir Isaac Newton . . .
             . . . in London in 1727 and . . .
          . . . his tomb in Westminster Abbey . . .
      . . . Alexander Pope, friend and colleague . . .
```

"I guess 'modern' is a relative term," Sophie called to Gettum. "It's an old book. About Sir Isaac Newton."

Gettum shook her head in the doorway. "No good. Newton was buried in Westminster Abbey, the seat of English Protestantism. There's no way a Catholic Pope was present. Cream and sugar?"

Sophie nodded.

Gettum waited. "Robert?"

Langdon's heart was hammering. He pulled his eyes from the screen and stood up. "Sir Isaac Newton is our knight."

Sophie remained seated. "What are you talking about?"

"Newton is buried in London," Langdon said. "His labors produced new sciences that incurred the wrath of the Church. And he was a Grand Master of the Priory of Sion. What more could we want?"

"What more?" Sophie pointed to the poem. "How about a knight a Pope interred? You heard Ms. Gettum. Newton was not buried by a Catholic Pope."

Langdon reached for the mouse. "Who said anything about a *Catholic* Pope?" He clicked on the "Pope" hyperlink, and the complete sentence appeared.

```
Sir Isaac Newton's burial, attended by kings and nobles,
        was presided over by Alexander Pope,
    friend and colleague, who gave a stirring eulogy
          before sprinkling dirt on the tomb.
```

Langdon looked at Sophie. "We had the correct Pope on our second hit. Alexander." He paused. "A. Pope."

In London lies a knight A. Pope interred.

Sophie stood up, looking stunned.

Jacques Saunière, the master of double entendres, had proven once again that he was a frighteningly clever man.

ILAS AWOKE with a start.

He had no idea what had awoken him or how long he had been asleep. *Was I dreaming?* Sitting up now on his straw mat, he listened to the quiet breathing of the Opus Dei residence hall, the stillness textured only by the soft murmurs of someone praying aloud in a room below him. These were familiar sounds and should have comforted him.

And yet he felt a sudden and unexpected wariness.

Standing, wearing only his undergarments, Silas walked to the window. *Was I followed?* The courtyard below was deserted, exactly as he had seen it when he entered. He listened. Silence. *So why am I uneasy?* Long ago Silas had learned to trust his intuition. Intuition had kept him alive as a child on the streets of Marseilles long before prison . . . long before he was born again by the hand of Bishop Aringarosa. Peering out the window, he now saw the faint outline of a car through the hedge. On the car's roof was a police siren. A floorboard creaked in the hallway. A door latch moved.

Silas reacted on instinct, surging across the room and sliding to a stop just behind the door as it crashed open. The first police officer stormed through, swinging his gun left then right at what appeared an empty room. Before he realized where Silas was, Silas had thrown his shoulder into the door, crushing a second officer as he came through. As the first officer wheeled to shoot, Silas dove for his legs. The gun went off, the bullet sailing above Silas's head, just as he connected with the officer's shins, driving his legs out from under him, and sending the man down, his head hitting the floor. The second officer staggered to his feet in the doorway, and Silas drove a knee into his groin, then went clambering over the writhing body into the hall.

Almost naked, Silas hurled his pale body down the staircase. He knew he had been betrayed, but by whom? When he reached the foyer, more officers were surging through the front door. Silas turned the other way and dashed deeper into the residence hall. *The women's entrance. Every Opus Dei building has one.* Winding down narrow hallways, Silas snaked through a kitchen, past terrified workers, who left to avoid the naked albino as he knocked over bowls and silverware, bursting into a dark hallway near the boiler room. He now saw the door he sought, an exit light gleaming at the end.

Running full speed through the door out into the rain, Silas leapt off the low landing, not seeing the officer coming the other way until it was too late. The two men collided, Silas's broad, naked shoulder grinding into the man's sternum with crushing force. He drove the officer backward onto the pavement, landing hard on top of him. The officer's gun clattered away. Silas could hear men running down the hall shouting. Rolling, he grabbed the loose gun just as the officers emerged. A shot rang out on the stairs, and Silas felt a searing pain below his ribs. Filled with rage, he opened fire at all three officers, their blood spraying.

A dark shadow loomed behind, coming out of nowhere. The angry hands that grabbed at his bare shoulders felt as if they were infused with the power of the devil himself. The man roared in his ear. *SILAS, NO!*

Silas spun and fired. Their eyes met. Silas was already screaming in horror as Bishop Aringarosa fell.

ORE THAN three thousand people are entombed or enshrined within Westminster Abbey. The colossal stone interior burgeons with the remains of kings, statesmen, scientists, poets, and musicians. Their tombs, packed into every last niche and alcove, range in grandeur from the most regal of mausoleums—that of Queen Elizabeth I, whose canopied sarcophagus inhabits its own private, apsidal chapel—

WESTMINSTER ABBEY, LONDON

down to the most modest etched floor tiles whose inscriptions have worn away with centuries of foot traffic, leaving it to one's imagination whose relics might lie below the tile in the undercroft.

Designed in the style of the great cathedrals of Amiens, Chartres, and Canterbury, Westminster Abbey is considered neither cathedral nor parish church. It bears the classification of *royal peculiar,* subject only to the Sovereign. Since hosting the coronation of William the Conqueror on Christmas Day in 1066, the dazzling sanctuary has witnessed an endless procession of royal ceremonies and affairs of state—from the canonization of Edward the Confessor, to the marriage of

Prince Andrew and Sarah Ferguson, to the funerals of Henry V, Queen Elizabeth I, and Diana, Princess of Wales.

Even so, Robert Langdon currently felt no interest in any of the abbey's ancient history, save one event—the funeral of the British knight Sir Isaac Newton.

In London lies a knight a Pope interred.

Hurrying through the grand portico on the north transept, Langdon and Sophie were met by guards who politely ushered them through the abbey's newest addition—a large walk-through metal detector—now present in most historic buildings in London. They both passed through without setting off the alarm and continued to the abbey entrance.

Stepping across the threshold into Westminster Abbey, Langdon felt the outside world evaporate with a sudden hush. No rumble of traffic. No hiss of rain. Just a deafening silence, which seemed to reverberate back and forth as if the building were whispering to itself.

Langdon's and Sophie's eyes, like those of almost every visitor, shifted immediately skyward, where the abbey's great abyss seemed to explode overhead. Gray stone columns ascended like redwoods into the shadows, arching gracefully over

VAULTED CEILING, WESTMINSTER ABBEY

dizzying expanses, and then shooting back down to the stone floor. Before them, the wide alley of the north transept stretched out like a deep canyon, flanked by sheer cliffs of stained glass. On sunny days, the abbey floor was a prismatic patchwork of light. Today, the rain and darkness gave this massive hollow a wraithlike aura . . . more like that of the crypt it truly was.

"It's practically empty," Sophie whispered.

Langdon felt disappointed. He had hoped for a lot more people. *A more public place.* Their earlier experience in the deserted Temple Church was not one Langdon wanted to repeat. He had been anticipating a certain feeling of security in the popular tourist destination, but Langdon's recollections of bustling throngs in a well-lit abbey had been formed during the peak summer tourist season. Today was a rainy April morning. Rather than crowds and shimmering stained glass, all Langdon saw was acres of desolate floor and shadowy, empty alcoves.

"We passed through metal detectors," Sophie reminded, apparently sensing Langdon's apprehension. "If anyone is in here, they can't be armed."

Langdon nodded but still felt circumspect. He had wanted to bring the London police with them, but Sophie's fears of who might be involved put a damper on any contact with the authorities. *We need to recover the cryptex,* Sophie had insisted. *It is the key to everything.*

She was right, of course.

The key to getting Leigh back alive.

The key to finding the Holy Grail.

The key to learning who is behind this.

Unfortunately, their only chance to recover the keystone seemed to be here and now . . . at the tomb of Isaac Newton. Whoever held the cryptex would have to pay a visit to the tomb to decipher the final clue, and if they had not already come and gone, Sophie and Langdon intended to intercept them.

Striding toward the left wall to get out of the open, they moved into an obscure side aisle behind a row of pilasters. Langdon couldn't shake the image of Leigh Teabing being held captive, probably tied up in the back of his own limousine. Whoever had ordered the top Priory members killed would not hesitate to eliminate others who stood in the way. It seemed a cruel irony that Teabing—a modern British knight—was a hostage in the search for his own countryman, Sir Isaac Newton.

"Which way is it?" Sophie asked, looking around.

The tomb. Langdon had no idea. "We should find a docent and ask."

Langdon knew better than to wander aimlessly in here. Westminster Abbey was a tangled warren of mausoleums, perimeter chambers, and walk-in burial niches.

Like the Louvre's Grand Gallery, it had a lone point of entry—the door through which they had just passed—easy to find your way in, but impossible to find your way out. *A literal tourist trap,* one of Langdon's befuddled colleagues had called it. Keeping architectural tradition, the abbey was laid out in the shape of a giant crucifix. Unlike most churches, however, it had its entrance on the *side,* rather than the standard rear of the church via the narthex at the bottom of the nave. Moreover, the abbey had a series of sprawling cloisters attached. One false step through the wrong archway, and a visitor was lost in a labyrinth of outdoor passageways surrounded by high walls.

"Docents wear crimson robes," Langdon said, approaching the center of the church. Peering obliquely across the towering gilded altar to the far end of the south transept, Langdon saw several people crawling on their hands and knees. This prostrate pilgrimage was a common occurrence in Poets' Corner, although it was far less holy than it appeared. *Tourists doing grave rubbings.*

"I don't see any docents," Sophie said. "Maybe we can find the tomb on our own?"

POETS' CORNER, WESTMINSTER ABBEY

Without a word, Langdon led her another few steps to the center of the abbey and pointed to the right.

Sophie drew a startled breath as she looked down the length of the abbey's nave, the full magnitude of the building now visible. "Aah," she said. "Let's find a docent."

AT THAT MOMENT, a hundred yards down the nave, out of sight behind the choir screen, the stately tomb of Sir Isaac Newton had a lone visitor. The Teacher had been scrutinizing the monument for ten minutes now.

Newton's tomb consisted of a massive black-marble sarcophagus on which reclined the sculpted form of Sir Isaac Newton, wearing classical costume, and leaning proudly against a stack of his own books—*Divinity, Chronology, Opticks,* and *Philosophiae Naturalis Principia Mathematica.* At Newton's feet stood two winged boys holding a scroll. Behind Newton's recumbent body rose an austere pyramid. Although the pyramid itself seemed an oddity, it was the giant shape mounted halfway *up* the pyramid that most intrigued the Teacher.

An orb.

The Teacher pondered Saunière's beguiling riddle. *You seek the orb that ought be on his tomb.* The massive orb protruding from the face of the pyramid was carved in basso-relievo and depicted all kinds of heavenly bodies—constellations, signs of the zodiac, comets, stars, and planets. Above it, the image of the Goddess of Astronomy beneath a field of stars.

Countless orbs.

The Teacher had been convinced that once he found the tomb, discerning the missing orb would be easy. Now he was not so sure. He was gazing at a complicated map of the heavens. Was there a missing planet? Had some astronomical orb been omitted from a constellation? He had no idea. Even so, the Teacher could not help but suspect that the solution would be ingeniously clean and simple—"a knight a pope interred." *What orb am I looking for?* Certainly, an advanced knowledge of astrophysics was not a prerequisite for finding the Holy Grail, was it?

It speaks of Rosy flesh and seeded womb.

The Teacher's concentration was broken by several approaching tourists. He slipped the cryptex back in his pocket and watched warily as the visitors went to a nearby table, left a donation in the cup, and restocked on the complimentary grave-rubbing supplies set out by the abbey. Armed with fresh charcoal pencils and large sheets of heavy paper, they headed off toward the front of the abbey, probably to

SIR ISAAC NEWTON MONUMENT

the popular Poets' Corner to pay their respects to Chaucer, Tennyson, and Dickens by rubbing furiously on their graves.

Alone again, he stepped closer to the tomb, scanning it from bottom to top. He began with the clawed feet beneath the sarcophagus, moved upward past Newton, past his books on science, past the two boys with their mathematical scroll, up the face of the pyramid to the giant orb with its constellations, and finally up to the niche's star-filled canopy.

What orb ought to be here . . . and yet is missing? He touched the cryptex in his pocket as if he could somehow divine the answer from Saunière's crafted marble. *Only five letters separate me from the Grail.*

Pacing now near the corner of the choir screen, he took a deep breath and glanced up the long nave toward the main altar in the distance. His gaze dropped from the gilded altar down to the bright crimson robe of an abbey docent who was being waved over by two very familiar individuals.

Langdon and Neveu.

Calmly, the Teacher moved two steps back behind the choir screen. *That was fast.* He had anticipated Langdon and Sophie would eventually decipher the poem's meaning and come to Newton's tomb, but this was sooner than he had imagined. Taking a deep breath, the Teacher considered his options. He had grown accustomed to dealing with surprises.

I am holding the cryptex.

Reaching down to his pocket, he touched the second object that gave him his confidence: the Medusa revolver. As expected, the abbey's metal detectors had blared as the Teacher passed through with the concealed gun. Also as expected, the guards had backed off at once when the Teacher glared indignantly and flashed his identification card. Official rank always commanded the proper respect.

Although initially the Teacher had hoped to solve the cryptex alone and avoid any further complications, he now sensed that the arrival of Langdon and Neveu was actually a welcome development. Considering the lack of success he was having with the "orb" reference, he might be able to use their expertise. After all, if Langdon had deciphered the poem to find the tomb, there was a reasonable chance he also knew something about the orb. And if Langdon knew the password, then it was just a matter of applying the right pressure.

Not here, of course.

Somewhere private.

The Teacher recalled a small announcement sign he had seen on his way into the abbey. Immediately he knew the perfect place to lure them.

The only question now . . . what to use as bait.

*L*ANGDON AND SOPHIE moved slowly down the north aisle, keeping to the shadows behind the ample pillars that separated it from the open nave. Despite having traveled more than halfway down the nave, they still had no clear view of Newton's tomb. The sarcophagus was recessed in a niche, obscured from this oblique angle.

"At least there's nobody over there," Sophie whispered.

Langdon nodded, relieved. The entire section of the nave near Newton's tomb was deserted. "I'll go over," he whispered. "You should stay hidden just in case someone—"

Sophie had already stepped from the shadows and was headed across the open floor.

"—is watching," Langdon sighed, hurrying to join her.

Crossing the massive nave on a diagonal, Langdon and Sophie remained silent as the elaborate sepulchre revealed itself in tantalizing increments . . . a black-marble sarcophagus . . . a reclining statue of Newton . . . two winged boys . . . a huge pyramid . . . and . . . *an enormous orb*.

"Did you know about that?" Sophie said, sounding startled.

Langdon shook his head, also surprised.

"Those look like constellations carved on it," Sophie said.

As they approached the niche, Langdon felt a slow sinking sensation. Newton's tomb was *covered* with orbs—stars, comets, planets. *You seek the orb that ought be on his tomb?* It could turn out to be like trying to find a missing blade of grass on a golf course.

"Astronomical bodies," Sophie said, looking concerned. "And a lot of them."

Langdon frowned. The only link between the planets and the Grail that Langdon could imagine was the pentacle of Venus, and he had already tried the password "Venus" en route to the Temple Church.

Sophie moved directly to the sarcophagus, but Langdon hung back a few feet, keeping an eye on the abbey around them.

"Divinity," Sophie said, tilting her head and reading the titles of the books on which Newton was leaning. *"Chronology. Opticks. Philosophiae Naturalis Principia Mathematica?"* She turned to him. "Ring any bells?"

Langdon stepped closer, considering it. *"Principia Mathematica,* as I remember, has something to do with the gravitation pull of planets . . . which admittedly are orbs, but it seems a little far-fetched."

"How about the signs of the zodiac?" Sophie asked, pointing to the constellations on the orb. "You were talking about Pisces and Aquarius earlier, weren't you?"

The End of Days, Langdon thought. "The end of Pisces and the beginning of Aquarius was allegedly the historical marker at which the Priory planned to release the Sangreal documents to the world." *But the millennium came and went without incident, leaving historians uncertain when the truth was coming.*

"It seems possible," Sophie said, "that the Priory's plans to reveal the truth might be related to the last line of the poem."

It speaks of Rosy flesh and seeded womb. Langdon felt a shiver of potential. He had not considered the line that way before.

"You told me earlier," she said, "that the timing of the Priory's plans to unveil the truth about 'the Rose' and her fertile womb was linked directly to the position of planets—orbs."

Langdon nodded, feeling the first faint wisps of possibility materializing. Even so, his intuition told him astronomy was not the key. The Grand Master's previous solutions had all possessed an eloquent, symbolic significance—the *Mona Lisa, Madonna of the Rocks,* SOFIA. This eloquence was definitely lacking in the concept of planetary orbs and the zodiac. Thus far, Jacques Saunière had proven himself a meticulous code writer, and Langdon had to believe that his final password—those five letters that unlocked the Priory's ultimate secret—would prove to be not only symbolically fitting but also crystal clear. If this solution were anything like the others, it would be painfully obvious once it dawned.

"Look!" Sophie gasped, jarring his thoughts as she grabbed his arm. From the fear in her touch Langdon sensed someone must be approaching, but when he turned to her, she was staring aghast at the top of the black marble sarcophagus. "Someone was here," she whispered, pointing to a spot on the sarcophagus near Newton's outstretched right foot.

Langdon did not understand her concern. A careless tourist had left a charcoal, grave-rubbing pencil on the sarcophagus lid near Newton's foot. *It's nothing.* Langdon reached out to pick it up, but as he leaned toward the sarcophagus, the light shifted on the polished black-marble slab, and Langdon froze. Suddenly, he saw why Sophie was afraid.

Scrawled on the sarcophagus lid, at Newton's feet, shimmered a barely visible charcoal-pencil message:

I have Teabing.
Go through Chapter House,
out south exit, to public garden.

Langdon read the words twice, his heart pounding wildly.

Sophie turned and scanned the nave.

Despite the pall of trepidation that settled over him upon seeing the words, Langdon told himself this was good news. *Leigh is still alive.* There was another implication here too. "They don't know the password either," he whispered.

Sophie nodded. Otherwise why make their presence known?

"They may want to trade Leigh for the password."

"Or it's a trap."

Langdon shook his head. "I don't think so. The garden is *outside* the abbey walls. A very public place." Langdon had once visited the abbey's famous College Garden—a small fruit orchard and herb garden—left over from the days when monks grew natural pharmacological remedies here. Boasting the oldest living fruit trees in Great Britain, College Garden was a popular spot for tourists to visit without having to enter the abbey. "I think sending us outside is a show of faith. So we feel safe."

Sophie looked dubious. "You mean outside, where there are no metal detectors?"

Langdon scowled. She had a point.

Gazing back at the orb-filled tomb, Langdon wished he had some idea about the cryptex password . . . something with which to negotiate. *I got Leigh involved in this, and I'll do whatever it takes if there is a chance to help him.*

"The note says to go through the Chapter House to the south exit," Sophie said. "Maybe from the exit we would have a view of the garden? That way we could assess the situation before we walked out there and exposed ourselves to any danger?"

The idea was a good one. Langdon vaguely recalled the Chapter House as a huge octagonal hall where the original British Parliament convened in the days before the modern Parliament building existed. It had been years since he had been there, but he remembered it being out through the cloister somewhere. Taking several steps back from the tomb, Langdon peered around the choir screen to his right, across the nave to the side opposite that which they had descended.

A gaping vaulted passageway stood nearby, with a large sign.

THIS WAY TO:

CLOISTERS
DEANERY
COLLEGE HALL
MUSEUM
PYX CHAMBER
ST. FAITH'S CHAPEL
CHAPTER HOUSE

Langdon and Sophie were jogging as they passed beneath the sign, moving too quickly to notice the small announcement apologizing that certain areas were closed for renovations.

They emerged immediately into a high-walled, open-roof courtyard through which morning rain was falling. Above them, the wind howled across the opening with a low drone, like someone blowing over the mouth of a bottle. Entering the narrow, low-hanging walkways that bordered the courtyard perimeter, Langdon felt the familiar uneasiness he always felt in enclosed spaces. These walkways were called *cloisters,* and Langdon noted with uneasiness that these particular *cloisters* lived up to their Latin ties to the word *claustrophobic*.

Focusing his mind straight ahead toward the end of the tunnel, Langdon followed the signs for the Chapter House. The rain was spitting now, and the walkway was cold and damp with gusts of rain that blew through the lone pillared wall that was the cloister's only source of light. Another couple scurried past them the other way, hurrying to get out of the worsening weather. The cloisters looked deserted now, admittedly the abbey's least enticing section in the wind and rain.

Forty yards down the east cloister, an archway materialized on their left, giving way to another hallway. Although this was the entrance they were looking for, the opening was cordoned off by a swag and an official-looking sign.

CLOSED FOR RENOVATION

PYX CHAMBER
ST. FAITH'S CHAPEL
CHAPTER HOUSE

The long, deserted corridor beyond the swag was littered with scaffolding and drop cloths. Immediately beyond the swag, Langdon could see the entrances to the Pyx Chamber and St. Faith's Chapel on the right and left. The entrance to the Chapter House, however, was much farther away, at the far end of the long hallway. Even from here, Langdon could see that its heavy wooden door was wide open, and the spacious octagonal interior was bathed in a grayish natural light from the room's enormous windows that looked out on College Garden. *Go through Chapter House, out south exit, to public garden.*

"We just left the east cloister," Langdon said, "so the south exit to the garden must be through there and to the right."

Sophie was already stepping over the swag and moving forward.

As they hurried down the dark corridor, the sounds of the wind and rain from the open cloister faded behind them. The Chapter House was a kind of satellite structure—a freestanding annex at the end of the long hallway to ensure the privacy of the Parliament proceedings housed there.

"It looks huge," Sophie whispered as they approached.

Langdon had forgotten just how large this room was. Even from out-

CHAPTER HOUSE,
WESTMINSTER ABBEY

side the entrance, he could gaze across the vast expanse of floor to the breathtaking windows on the far side of the octagon, which rose five stories to a vaulted ceiling. They would certainly have a clear view of the garden from in here.

Crossing the threshold, both Langdon and Sophie found themselves having to squint. After the gloomy cloisters, the Chapter House felt like a solarium. They were a good ten feet into the room, searching the south wall, when they realized the door they had been promised was not there.

They were standing in an enormous dead end.

The creaking of a heavy door behind them made them turn, just as the door closed with a resounding thud and the latch fell into place. The lone man who had been standing behind the door looked calm as he aimed a small revolver at them. He was portly and was propped on a pair of aluminum crutches.

For a moment Langdon thought he must be dreaming.

It was Leigh Teabing.

*S*IR LEIGH TEABING felt rueful as he gazed out over the barrel of his Medusa revolver at Robert Langdon and Sophie Neveu. "My friends," he said, "since the moment you walked into my home last night, I have done everything in my power to keep you out of harm's way. But your persistence has now put me in a difficult position."

He could see the expressions of shock and betrayal on Sophie's and Langdon's faces, and yet he was confident that soon they would both understand the chain of events that had guided the three of them to this unlikely crossroads.

There is so much I have to tell you both . . . so much you do not yet understand.

"Please believe," Teabing said, "I never had any intention of your being involved. You came to my home. *You* came searching for *me*."

"Leigh?" Langdon finally managed. "What the hell are you doing? We thought you were in trouble. We came here to help you!"

"As I trusted you would," he said. "We have much to discuss."

Langdon and Sophie seemed unable to tear their stunned gazes from the revolver aimed at them.

"It is simply to ensure your full attention," Teabing said. "If I had wanted to harm you, you would be dead by now. When you walked into my home last night, I risked everything to spare your lives. I am a man of honor, and I vowed in my deepest conscience only to sacrifice those who had betrayed the Sangreal."

"What are you talking about?" Langdon said. "Betrayed the Sangreal?"

"I discovered a terrible truth," Teabing said, sighing. "I learned *why* the Sangreal documents were never revealed to the world. I learned that the Priory had decided not to release the truth after all. That's why the millennium passed without any revelation, why nothing happened as we entered the End of Days."

Langdon drew a breath, about to protest.

"The Priory," Teabing continued, "was given a sacred charge to share the truth. To release the Sangreal documents when the End of Days arrived. For centuries, men like Da Vinci, Botticelli, and Newton risked everything to protect the documents and carry out that charge. And now, at the ultimate moment of truth, Jacques Saunière changed his mind. The man honored with the greatest responsibility in Christian history eschewed his duty. He decided the time was not right." Teabing turned to Sophie. "He failed the Grail. He failed the Priory. And he failed the memory of all the generations that had worked to make that moment possible."

"You?" Sophie declared, glancing up now, her green eyes boring into him with rage and realization. "*You* are the one responsible for my grandfather's murder?"

Teabing scoffed. "Your grandfather and his *sénéchaux* were traitors to the Grail."

Sophie felt a fury rising from deep within. *He's lying!*

Teabing's voice was relentless. "Your grandfather sold out to the Church. It is obvious they pressured him to keep the truth quiet."

Sophie shook her head. "The Church had no influence on my grandfather!"

Teabing laughed coldly. "My dear, the Church has two thousand years of experience pressuring those who threaten to unveil its lies. Since the days of Constantine, the Church has successfully hidden the truth about Mary Magdalene and Jesus. We should not be surprised that *now,* once again, they have found a way to keep the world in the dark. The Church may no longer employ crusaders to slaughter nonbelievers, but their influence is no less persuasive. No less insidious." He paused, as if to punctuate his next point. "Miss Neveu, for some time now your grandfather has wanted to tell you the truth about your family."

Sophie was stunned. "How could you know that?"

"My methods are immaterial. The important thing for you to grasp right now is this." He took a deep breath. "The deaths of your mother, father, grandmother, and brother were *not* accidental."

The words sent Sophie's emotions reeling. She opened her mouth to speak but was unable.

Langdon shook his head. "What are you saying?"

"Robert, it explains everything. All the pieces fit. History repeats itself. The Church has a precedent of murder when it comes to silencing the Sangreal. With the End of Days imminent, killing the Grand Master's loved ones sent a very clear message. Be quiet, or you and Sophie are next."

"It was a car accident," Sophie stammered, feeling the childhood pain welling inside her. "An *accident!*"

"Bedtime stories to protect your innocence," Teabing said. "Consider that only two family members went untouched—the Priory's Grand Master and his lone granddaughter—the perfect pair to provide the Church with control over the brotherhood. I can only imagine the terror the Church wielded over your grandfather these past years, threatening to kill *you* if he dared release the Sangreal secret, threatening to finish the job they started unless Saunière influenced the Priory to reconsider its ancient vow."

"Leigh," Langdon argued, now visibly riled, "certainly you have no proof that the Church had anything to do with those deaths, or that it influenced the Priory's decision to remain silent."

"Proof?" Teabing fired back. "You want proof the Priory was influenced? The new millennium has arrived, and yet the world remains ignorant! Is that not proof enough?"

In the echoes of Teabing's words, Sophie heard another voice speaking. *Sophie, I must tell you the truth about your family*. She realized she was trembling. Could *this* possibly be that truth her grandfather had wanted to tell her? That her family had been *murdered?* What did she truly know about the crash that took her family? Only sketchy details. Even the stories in the newspaper had been vague. An accident? Bedtime stories? Sophie flashed suddenly on her grandfather's overprotectiveness, how he never liked to leave her alone when she was young. Even when Sophie was grown and away at university, she had the sense her grandfather was watching over. She wondered if there had been Priory members in the shadows throughout her entire life, looking after her.

"You suspected he was being manipulated," Langdon said, glaring with disbelief at Teabing. "So you *murdered* him?"

"I did not pull the trigger," Teabing said. "Saunière was dead years ago, when the Church stole his family from him. He was compromised. Now he is free of that pain, released from the shame caused by his inability to carry out his sacred duty. Consider the alternative. Something had to be done. Shall the world be ignorant forever? Shall the Church be allowed to cement its lies into our history books for all eternity? Shall the Church be permitted to influence indefinitely with murder and extortion? No, something needed to be done! And now we are poised to carry out Saunière's legacy and right a terrible wrong." He paused. "The three of us. Together."

Sophie felt only incredulity. "How could you *possibly* believe that we would help you?"

"Because, my dear, *you* are the reason the Priory failed to release the documents. Your grandfather's love for you prevented him from challenging the Church. His fear of reprisal against his only remaining family crippled him. He never had a chance to explain the truth because you rejected him, tying his hands, making him wait. Now you owe the world the truth. You owe it to the memory of your grandfather."

ROBERT LANGDON had given up trying to get his bearings. Despite the torrent of questions running through his mind, he knew only one thing mattered now—getting Sophie out of here alive. All the guilt Langdon had mistakenly felt earlier for involving Teabing had now been transferred to Sophie.

I took her to Château Villette. I am responsible.

Langdon could not fathom that Leigh Teabing would be capable of killing them in cold blood here in the Chapter House, and yet Teabing certainly had been involved in killing others during his misguided quest. Langdon had the uneasy feeling that gunshots in this secluded, thick-walled chamber would go unheard, especially in this rain. *And Leigh just admitted his guilt to us.*

Langdon glanced at Sophie, who looked shaken. *The Church murdered Sophie's family to silence the Priory?* Langdon felt certain the modern Church did not murder people. There had to be some other explanation.

"Let Sophie leave," Langdon declared, staring at Leigh. "You and I should discuss this alone."

Teabing gave an unnatural laugh. "I'm afraid that is one show of faith I cannot afford. I can, however, offer you *this*." He propped himself fully on his crutches, gracelessly keeping the gun aimed at Sophie, and removed the keystone from his pocket. He swayed a bit as he held it out for Langdon. "A token of trust, Robert."

Robert felt wary and didn't move. *Leigh is giving the keystone back to us?*

"Take it," Teabing said, thrusting it awkwardly toward Langdon.

Langdon could imagine only one reason Teabing would give it back. "You opened it already. You removed the map."

Teabing was shaking his head. "Robert, if I had solved the keystone, I would have disappeared to find the Grail myself and kept you uninvolved. No, I do not know the answer. And I can admit that freely. A true knight learns humility in the face of the Grail. He learns to obey the signs placed before him. When I saw you enter the abbey, I understood. You were here for a reason. To help. I am not looking for singular glory here. I serve a far greater master than my own pride. The Truth. Mankind deserves to know that truth. The Grail found us all, and now she is begging to be revealed. We must work together."

Despite Teabing's pleas for cooperation and trust, his gun remained trained on Sophie as Langdon stepped forward and accepted the cold marble cylinder. The vinegar inside gurgled as Langdon grasped it and stepped backward. The dials were still in random order, and the cryptex remained locked.

Langdon eyed Teabing. "How do you know I won't smash it right now?"

Teabing's laugh was an eerie chortle. "I should have realized your threat to break it in the Temple Church was an empty one. Robert Langdon would never break the keystone. You are an historian, Robert. You are holding the key to two thousand years of history—the lost key to the Sangreal. You can feel the souls of all the knights burned at the stake to protect her secret. Would you have them die in vain? No, you will vindicate them. You will join the ranks of the great men you admire—Da Vinci, Botticelli, Newton—each of whom would have been honored to be in your shoes right now. The contents of the keystone are crying out to us. Longing to be set free. The time has come. Destiny has led us to this moment."

"I cannot help you, Leigh. I have no idea how to open this. I only saw Newton's tomb for a moment. And even if I knew the password . . ." Langdon paused, realizing he had said too much.

"You would not tell me?" Teabing sighed. "I am disappointed and surprised, Robert, that you do not appreciate the extent to which you are in my debt. My task would have been far simpler had Rémy and I eliminated you both when you walked into Château Villette. Instead I risked everything to take the nobler course."

"This is *noble?*" Langdon demanded, eyeing the gun.

"Saunière's fault," Teabing said. "He and his *sénéchaux* lied to Silas. Otherwise, I would have obtained the keystone without complication. How was I to imagine the Grand Master would go to such ends to deceive me and bequeath the keystone to an estranged granddaughter?" Teabing looked at Sophie with disdain. "Someone so unqualified to hold this knowledge that she required a symbologist baby-sitter." Teabing glanced back at Langdon. "Fortunately, Robert, your involvement turned out to be my saving grace. Rather than the keystone remaining locked in the Depository Bank forever, you extracted it and walked into my home."

Where else would I run? Langdon thought. *The community of Grail historians is small, and Teabing and I have a history together.*

Teabing now looked smug. "When I learned Saunière left you a dying message, I had a pretty good idea you were holding valuable Priory information. Whether it was the keystone itself, or information on where to find it, I was not sure. But with the police on your heels, I had a sneaking suspicion you might arrive on my doorstep."

Langdon glared. "And if we had not?"

"I was formulating a plan to extend you a helping hand. One way or another, the keystone was coming to Château Villette. The fact that you delivered it into my waiting hands only serves as proof that my cause is just."

"What!" Langdon was appalled.

"Silas was supposed to break in and steal the keystone from you in Château Villette—thus removing you from the equation without hurting you, and exonerating me from any suspicion of complicity. However, when I saw the intricacy of Saunière's codes, I decided to include you both in my quest a bit longer. I could have Silas steal the keystone later, once I knew enough to carry on alone."

"The Temple Church," Sophie said, her tone awash with betrayal.

LIGHT BEGINS TO DAWN, Teabing thought. The Temple Church was the perfect location to steal the keystone from Robert and Sophie, and its apparent relevance to the poem made it a plausible decoy. Rémy's orders had been clear—stay out of sight while Silas recovers the keystone. Unfortunately, Langdon's threat to smash the keystone on the chapel floor had caused Rémy to panic. *If only Rémy had not revealed himself,* Teabing thought ruefully, recalling his own mock kidnapping. *Rémy was the sole link to me, and he showed his face!*

Fortunately, Silas remained unaware of Teabing's true identity and was easily fooled into taking him from the church and then watching naively as Rémy pretended to tie their hostage in the back of the limousine. With the soundproof divider raised, Teabing was able to phone Silas in the front seat, use the fake French accent of the Teacher, and direct Silas to go straight to Opus Dei. A simple anonymous tip to the police was all it would take to remove Silas from the picture.

One loose end tied up.

The other loose end was harder. *Rémy.*

Teabing struggled deeply with the decision, but in the end Rémy had proven himself a liability. *Every Grail quest requires sacrifice.* The cleanest solution had been staring Teabing in the face from the limousine's wet bar—a flask, some cognac, and a can of peanuts. The powder at the bottom of the can would be more than enough to trigger Rémy's deadly allergy. When Rémy parked the limo on Horse Guards Parade, Teabing climbed out of the back, walked to the side passenger door, and sat in the front next to Rémy. Minutes later, Teabing got out of the car, climbed into the rear again, cleaned up the evidence, and finally emerged to carry out the final phase of his mission.

Westminster Abbey had been a short walk, and although Teabing's leg braces, crutches, and gun had set off the metal detector, the rent-a-cops never knew what to do. *Do we ask him to remove his braces and crawl through? Do we frisk his deformed body?* Teabing presented the flustered guards a far easier solution—an embossed card identifying him as Knight of the Realm. The poor fellows practically tripped over one another ushering him in.

Now, eyeing the bewildered Langdon and Neveu, Teabing resisted the urge to reveal how he had brilliantly implicated Opus Dei in the plot that would soon bring about the demise of the entire Church. That would have to wait. Right now there was work to do.

"*Mes amis,*" Teabing declared in flawless French, "*vous ne trouvez pas le Saint-Graal, c'est le Saint-Graal qui vous trouve.*" He smiled. "Our paths together could not be more clear. The Grail has found us."

Silence.

He spoke to them in a whisper now. "Listen. Can you hear it? The Grail is speaking to us across the centuries. She is begging to be saved from the Priory's folly. I implore you both to recognize this opportunity. There could not possibly be three more capable people assembled at this moment to break the final code and open the cryptex." Teabing paused, his eyes alight. "We need to swear an oath together. A pledge of faith to one another. A knight's allegiance to uncover the truth and make it known."

Sophie stared deep into Teabing's eyes and spoke in a steely tone. "I will never swear an oath with my grandfather's murderer. Except an oath that I will see you go to prison."

Teabing's heart turned grave, then resolute. "I am sorry you feel that way, mademoiselle." He turned and aimed the gun at Langdon. "And you, Robert? Are you with me, or against me?"

Chapter 100

BISHOP MANUEL ARINGAROSA'S body had endured many kinds of pain, and yet the searing heat of the bullet wound in his chest felt profoundly foreign to him. Deep and grave. Not a wound of the flesh . . . but closer to the soul.

He opened his eyes, trying to see, but the rain on his face blurred his vision. *Where am I?* He could feel powerful arms holding him, carrying his limp body like a rag doll, his black cassock flapping.

Lifting a weary arm, he mopped his eyes and saw the man holding him was Silas. The great albino was struggling down a misty sidewalk, shouting for a hospital, his voice a heartrending wail of agony. His red eyes were focused dead ahead, tears streaming down his pale, blood-spattered face.

"My son," Aringarosa whispered, "you're hurt."

Silas glanced down, his visage contorted in anguish. "I am so very sorry, Father." He seemed almost too pained to speak.

"No, Silas," Aringarosa replied. "It is I who am sorry. This is my fault." *The Teacher promised me there would be no killing, and I told you to obey him fully.* "I was too eager. Too fearful. You and I were deceived." *The Teacher was never going to deliver us the Holy Grail.*

Cradled in the arms of the man he had taken in all those years ago, Bishop Aringarosa felt himself reel back in time. To Spain. To his modest beginnings, building a small Catholic church in Oviedo with Silas. And later, to New York

City, where he had proclaimed the glory of God with the towering Opus Dei Center on Lexington Avenue.

Five months ago, Aringarosa had received devastating news. His life's work was in jeopardy. He recalled, with vivid detail, the meeting inside Castel Gandolfo that had changed his life . . . the news that had set this entire calamity into motion.

Aringarosa had entered Gandolfo's Astronomy Library with his head held high, fully expecting to be lauded by throngs of welcoming hands, all eager to pat him on the back for his superior work representing Catholicism in America.

But only three people were present.

The Vatican secretarius. Obese. Dour.

Two high-ranking Italian cardinals. Sanctimonious. Smug.

"Secretarius?" Aringarosa said, puzzled.

The rotund overseer of legal affairs shook Aringarosa's hand and motioned to the chair opposite him. "Please, make yourself comfortable."

Aringarosa sat, sensing something was wrong.

"I am not skilled in small talk, Bishop," the secretarius said, "so let me be direct about the reason for your visit."

"Please. Speak openly." Aringarosa glanced at the two cardinals, who seemed to be measuring him with self-righteous anticipation.

"As you are well aware," the secretarius said, "His Holiness and others in Rome have been concerned lately with the political fallout from Opus Dei's more controversial practices."

Aringarosa felt himself bristle instantly. He already had been through this on numerous occasions with the new pontiff, who, to Aringarosa's great dismay, had turned out to be a distressingly fervent voice for liberal change in the Church.

"I want to assure you," the secretarius added quickly, "that His Holiness does not seek to change anything about the way you run your ministry."

I should hope not! "Then why am I here?"

The enormous man sighed. "Bishop, I am not sure how to say this delicately, so I will state it directly. Two days ago, the Secretariat Council voted unanimously to revoke the Vatican's sanction of Opus Dei."

Aringarosa was certain he had heard incorrectly. "I beg your pardon?"

"Plainly stated, six months from today, Opus Dei will no longer be considered a prelature of the Vatican. You will be a church unto yourself. The Holy See will be disassociating itself from you. His Holiness agrees and we are already drawing up the legal papers."

"But . . . that is impossible!"

"On the contrary, it is quite possible. And necessary. His Holiness has become uneasy with your aggressive recruiting policies and your practices of corporal mortification." He paused. "Also your policies regarding women. Quite frankly, Opus Dei has become a liability and an embarrassment."

Bishop Aringarosa was stupefied. "An *embarrassment?*"

"Certainly you cannot be surprised it has come to this."

"Opus Dei is the only Catholic organization whose numbers are growing! We now have over eleven hundred priests!"

"True. A troubling issue for us all."

Aringarosa shot to his feet. "Ask His Holiness if Opus Dei was an embarrassment in 1982 when we helped the Vatican Bank!"

"The Vatican will always be grateful for that," the secretarius said, his tone appeasing, "and yet there are those who still believe your financial munificence in 1982 is the only reason you were granted prelature status in the first place."

"That is not true!" The insinuation offended Aringarosa deeply.

"Whatever the case, we plan to act in good faith. We are drawing up severance terms that will include a reimbursement of those monies. It will be paid in five installments."

"You are buying me off?" Aringarosa demanded. "Paying me to go quietly? When Opus Dei is the only remaining voice of reason!"

One of the cardinals glanced up. "I'm sorry, did you say *reason?*"

Aringarosa leaned across the table, sharpening his tone to a point. "Do you really wonder why Catholics are leaving the Church? Look around you, Cardinal. People have lost respect. The rigors of faith are gone. The doctrine has become a buffet line. Abstinence, confession, communion, baptism, mass—take your pick—choose whatever combination pleases you and ignore the rest. What kind of spiritual guidance is the Church offering?"

"Third-century laws," the second cardinal said, "cannot be applied to the modern followers of Christ. The rules are not workable in today's society."

"Well, they seem to be working for Opus Dei!"

"Bishop Aringarosa," the secretarius said, his voice conclusive. "Out of respect for your organization's relationship with the previous Pope, His Holiness will be giving Opus Dei six months to *voluntarily* break away from the Vatican. I suggest you cite your differences of opinion with the Holy See and establish yourself as your own Christian organization."

"I refuse!" Aringarosa declared. "And I'll tell him that in person!"

"I'm afraid His Holiness no longer cares to meet with you."

Aringarosa stood up. "He would not *dare* abolish a personal prelature established by a previous Pope!"

"I'm sorry." The secretarius's eyes did not flinch. "The Lord giveth and the Lord taketh away."

Aringarosa had staggered from that meeting in bewilderment and panic. Returning to New York, he stared out at the skyline in disillusionment for days, overwhelmed with sadness for the future of Christianity.

It was several weeks later that he received the phone call that changed all that. The caller sounded French and identified himself as *the Teacher*—a title common in the prelature. He said he knew of the Vatican's plans to pull support from Opus Dei.

How could he know that? Aringarosa wondered. He had hoped only a handful of Vatican power brokers knew of Opus Dei's impending annulment. Apparently the word was out. When it came to containing gossip, no walls in the world were as porous as those surrounding Vatican City.

"I have ears everywhere, Bishop," the Teacher whispered, "and with these ears I have gained certain knowledge. With your help, I can uncover the hiding place of a sacred relic that will bring you enormous power . . . enough power to make the Vatican bow before you. Enough power to save the Faith." He paused. "Not just for Opus Dei. But for all of us."

The Lord taketh away . . . and the Lord giveth. Aringarosa felt a glorious ray of hope. "Tell me your plan."

BISHOP ARINGAROSA was unconscious when the doors of St. Mary's Hospital hissed open. Silas lurched into the entryway delirious with exhaustion. Dropping to his knees on the tile floor, he cried out for help. Everyone in the reception area gaped in wonderment at the half-naked albino offering forth a bleeding clergyman.

The doctor who helped Silas heave the delirious bishop onto a gurney looked gloomy as he felt Aringarosa's pulse. "He's lost a lot of blood. I am not hopeful."

Aringarosa's eyes flickered, and he returned for a moment, his gaze locating Silas. "My child . . ."

Silas's soul thundered with remorse and rage. "Father, if it takes my lifetime, I will find the one who deceived us, and I will kill him."

Aringarosa shook his head, looking sad as they prepared to wheel him away. "Silas . . . if you have learned nothing from me, please . . . learn this." He took Silas's hand and gave it a firm squeeze. "Forgiveness is God's greatest gift."

"But Father . . ."

Aringarosa closed his eyes. "Silas, you must pray."

ROBERT LANGDON stood beneath the lofty cupola of the deserted Chapter House and stared into the barrel of Leigh Teabing's gun.

Robert, are you with me, or against me? The Royal Historian's words echoed in the silence of Langdon's mind.

There was no viable response, Langdon knew. Answer *yes,* and he would be selling out Sophie. Answer *no,* and Teabing would have no choice but to kill them both.

Langdon's years in the classroom had not imbued him with any skills relevant to handling confrontations at gunpoint, but the classroom *had* taught him something about answering paradoxical questions. *When a question has no correct answer, there is only one honest response.*

The gray area between yes and no.

Silence.

Staring at the cryptex in his hands, Langdon chose simply to walk away.

Without ever lifting his eyes, he stepped backward, out into the room's vast empty spaces. *Neutral ground.* He hoped his focus on the cryptex signaled Teabing that collaboration might be an option, and that his silence signaled Sophie he had not abandoned her.

All the while buying time to think.

The act of thinking, Langdon suspected, was exactly what Teabing wanted him to do. *That's why he handed me the cryptex. So I could feel the weight of my decision.* The British historian hoped the touch of the Grand Master's cryptex would make Langdon fully grasp the magnitude of its contents, coaxing his academic curiosity to overwhelm all else, forcing him to realize that failure to unlock the keystone would mean the loss of history itself.

With Sophie at gunpoint across the room, Langdon feared that discovering the cryptex's elusive password would be his only remaining hope of bartering her

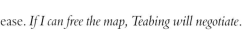

release. *If I can free the map, Teabing will negotiate.* Forcing his mind to this critical task, Langdon moved slowly toward the far windows . . . allowing his mind to fill with the numerous astronomical images on Newton's tomb.

> **You seek the orb that ought be on his tomb.**
> **It speaks of Rosy flesh and seeded womb.**

Turning his back to the others, he walked toward the towering windows, searching for any inspiration in their stained-glass mosaics. There was none.

Place yourself in Saunière's mind, he urged, gazing outward now into College Garden. *What would he believe is the orb that ought be on Newton's tomb?* Images of stars, comets, and planets twinkled in the falling rain, but Langdon ignored them. Saunière was not a man of science. He was a man of humanity, of art, of history. *The sacred feminine . . . the chalice . . . the Rose . . . the banished Mary Magdalene . . . the decline of the goddess . . . the Holy Grail.*

Legend had always portrayed the Grail as a cruel mistress, dancing in the shadows just out of sight, whispering in your ear, luring you one more step and then evaporating into the mist.

Gazing out at the rustling trees of College Garden, Langdon sensed her playful presence. The signs were everywhere. Like a taunting silhouette emerging from the fog, the branches of Britain's oldest apple tree burgeoned with five-petaled blossoms, all glistening like Venus. The goddess was in the garden now. She was dancing in the rain, singing songs of the ages, peeking out from behind the bud-filled branches as if to remind Langdon that the fruit of knowledge was growing just beyond his reach.

FIVE-PETAL APPLE BLOSSOM

ACROSS THE ROOM, Sir Leigh Teabing watched with confidence as Langdon gazed out the window as if under a spell.

Exactly as I hoped, Teabing thought. *He will come around.*

For some time now, Teabing had suspected Langdon might hold the key to the Grail. It was no coincidence that Teabing launched his plan into action on the same night Langdon was scheduled to meet Jacques Saunière. Listening in on the curator, Teabing was certain the man's eagerness to meet privately with Langdon could mean only one thing. *Langdon's mysterious manuscript has touched a nerve with the Priory. Langdon has stumbled onto a truth, and Saunière fears its release.* Teabing felt certain the Grand Master was summoning Langdon to silence him.

The Truth has been silenced long enough!

Teabing knew he had to act quickly. Silas's attack would accomplish two goals. It would prevent Saunière from persuading Langdon to keep quiet, and it would ensure that once the keystone was in Teabing's hands, Langdon would be in Paris for recruitment should Teabing need him.

Arranging the fatal meeting between Saunière and Silas had been almost too easy. *I had inside information about Saunière's deepest fears.* Yesterday afternoon, Silas had phoned the curator and posed as a distraught priest. "Monsieur Saunière, forgive me, I must speak to you at once. I should never breach the sanctity of the confessional, but in this case, I feel I must. I just took confession from a man who claimed to have murdered members of your family."

Saunière's response was startled but wary. "My family died in an accident. The police report was conclusive."

"Yes, a *car* accident," Silas said, baiting the hook. "The man I spoke to said he forced their car off the road into a river."

Saunière fell silent.

"Monsieur Saunière, I would never have phoned you directly except this man made a comment which makes me now fear for *your* safety." He paused. "The man also mentioned your granddaughter, Sophie."

The mention of Sophie's name had been the catalyst. The curator leapt into action. He ordered Silas to come see him immediately in the safest location Saunière knew—his Louvre office. Then he phoned Sophie to warn her she might be in danger. Drinks with Robert Langdon were instantly abandoned.

Now, with Langdon separated from Sophie on the far side of the room, Teabing sensed he had successfully alienated the two companions from one another. Sophie Neveu remained defiant, but Langdon clearly saw the larger picture. He was trying to figure out the password. *He understands the importance of finding the Grail and releasing her from bondage.*

"He won't open it for you," Sophie said coldly. "Even if he can."

Teabing was glancing at Langdon as he held the gun on Sophie. He was fairly certain now he was going to have to use the weapon. Although the idea troubled him, he knew he would not hesitate if it came to that. *I have given her every opportunity to do the right thing. The Grail is bigger than any one of us.*

At that moment, Langdon turned from the window. "The tomb . . ." he said suddenly, facing them with a faint glimmer of hope in his eyes. "I know where to look on Newton's tomb. Yes, I think I can find the password!"

Teabing's heart soared. "Where, Robert? Tell me!"

Sophie sounded horrified. "Robert, no! You're not going to help him, *are* you?"

Langdon approached with a resolute stride, holding the cryptex before him. "No," he said, his eyes hardening as he turned to Leigh. "Not until he lets you go."

Teabing's optimism darkened. "We are so close, Robert. Don't you dare start playing games with me!"

"No games," Langdon said. "Let her go. Then I'll take you to Newton's tomb. We'll open the cryptex together."

"I'm not going anywhere," Sophie declared, her eyes narrowing with rage. "That cryptex was given to me by my grandfather. It is not *yours* to open."

Langdon wheeled, looking fearful. "Sophie, please! You're in danger. I'm trying to help you!"

"How? By unveiling the secret my grandfather died trying to protect? He trusted you, Robert. *I* trusted you!"

Langdon's blue eyes showed panic now, and Teabing could not help but smile to see the two of them working against one another. Langdon's attempts to be gallant were more pathetic than anything. *On the verge of unveiling one of history's greatest secrets, and he troubles himself with a woman who has proven herself unworthy of the quest.*

"Sophie," Langdon pleaded. "Please . . . you must leave."

She shook her head. "Not unless you either hand me the cryptex or smash it on the floor."

"What?" Langdon gasped.

"Robert, my grandfather would prefer his secret lost forever than see it in the hands of his murderer." Sophie's eyes looked as if they would well with tears, but they did not. She stared directly back at Teabing. "Shoot me if you have to. I am not leaving my grandfather's legacy in your hands."

Very well. Teabing aimed the weapon.

"No!" Langdon shouted, raising his arm and suspending the cryptex precariously over the hard stone floor. "Leigh, if you even think about it, I will drop this."

Teabing laughed. "That bluff worked on Rémy. Not on me. I know you better than that."

"Do you, Leigh?"

Yes I do. Your poker face needs work, my friend. It took me several seconds, but I can see now that you are lying. You have no idea where on Newton's tomb the answer lies. "Truly, Robert? You know where on the tomb to look?"

"I do."

The falter in Langdon's eyes was fleeting but Leigh caught it. There was a lie there. A desperate, pathetic ploy to save Sophie. Teabing felt a profound disappointment in Robert Langdon.

I am a lone knight, surrounded by unworthy souls. And I will have to decipher the keystone on my own.

Langdon and Neveu were nothing but a threat to Teabing now . . . and to the Grail. As painful as the solution was going to be, he knew he could carry it out with a clean conscience. The only challenge would be to persuade Langdon to set down the keystone so Teabing could safely end this charade.

"A show of faith," Teabing said, lowering the gun from Sophie. "Set down the keystone, and we'll talk."

LANGDON KNEW his lie had failed.

He could see the dark resolve in Teabing's face and knew the moment was upon them. *When I set this down, he will kill us both.* Even without looking at Sophie, he could hear her heart beseeching him in silent desperation. *Robert, this man is not worthy of the Grail. Please do not place it in his hands. No matter what the cost.*

Langdon had already made his decision several minutes ago, while standing alone at the window overlooking College Garden.

Protect Sophie.

Protect the Grail.

Langdon had almost shouted out in desperation. *But I cannot see how!*

The stark moments of disillusionment had brought with them a clarity unlike any he had ever felt. *The Truth is right before your eyes, Robert.* He knew not from where the epiphany came. *The Grail is not mocking you, she is calling out to a worthy soul.*

Now, bowing down like a subject several yards in front of Leigh Teabing, Langdon lowered the cryptex to within inches of the stone floor.

"Yes, Robert," Teabing whispered, aiming the gun at him. "Set it down."

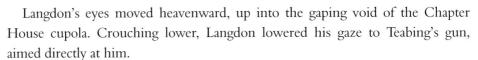

Langdon's eyes moved heavenward, up into the gaping void of the Chapter House cupola. Crouching lower, Langdon lowered his gaze to Teabing's gun, aimed directly at him.

"I'm sorry, Leigh."

In one fluid motion, Langdon leapt up, swinging his arm skyward, launching the cryptex straight up toward the dome above.

LEIGH TEABING did not feel his finger pull the trigger, but the Medusa discharged with a thundering crash. Langdon's crouched form was now vertical, almost airborne, and the bullet exploded in the floor near Langdon's feet. Half of Teabing's brain attempted to adjust his aim and fire again in rage, but the more powerful half dragged his eyes upward into the cupola.

The keystone!

Time seemed to freeze, morphing into a slow-motion dream as Teabing's entire world became the airborne keystone. He watched it rise to the apex of its climb . . . hovering for a moment in the void . . . and then tumbling downward, end over end, back toward the stone floor.

All of Teabing's hopes and dreams were plummeting toward earth. *It cannot strike the floor! I can reach it!* Teabing's body reacted on instinct. He released the gun and heaved himself forward, dropping his crutches as he reached out with his soft, manicured hands. Stretching his arms and fingers, he snatched the keystone from midair.

Falling forward with the keystone victoriously clutched in his hand, Teabing knew he was falling too fast. With nothing to break his fall, his outstretched arms hit first, and the cryptex collided hard with the floor.

There was a sickening crunch of glass within.

For a full second, Teabing did not breathe. Lying there outstretched on the cold floor, staring the length of his outstretched arms at the marble cylinder in his bare palms, he implored the glass vial inside to hold. Then the acrid tang of vinegar cut the air, and Teabing felt the cool liquid flowing out through the dials onto his palm.

Wild panic gripped him. *NO!* The vinegar was streaming now, and Teabing pictured the papyrus dissolving within. *Robert, you fool! The secret is lost!*

Teabing felt himself sobbing uncontrollably. *The Grail is gone. Everything destroyed.* Shuddering in disbelief over Langdon's actions, Teabing tried to force the cylinder apart, longing to catch a fleeting glimpse of history before it dissolved forever. To his shock, as he pulled the ends of the keystone, the cylinder separated.

He gasped and peered inside. It was empty except for shards of wet glass. No dissolving papyrus. Teabing rolled over and looked up at Langdon. Sophie stood beside him, aiming the gun down at Teabing.

Bewildered, Teabing looked back at the keystone and saw it. The dials were no longer at random. They spelled a five-letter word: APPLE.

"THE ORB from which Eve partook," Langdon said coolly, "incurring the Holy wrath of God. Original sin. The symbol of the fall of the sacred feminine."

Teabing felt the truth come crashing down on him in excruciating austerity. The orb that ought be on Newton's tomb could be none other than the Rosy apple that fell from heaven, struck Newton on the head, and inspired his life's work. *His labor's fruit! The Rosy flesh with a seeded womb!*

"Robert," Teabing stammered, overwhelmed. "You opened it. Where . . . is the map?"

Without blinking, Langdon reached into the breast pocket of his tweed coat and carefully extracted a delicate rolled papyrus. Only a few yards from where Teabing lay, Langdon unrolled the scroll and looked at it. After a long moment, a knowing smile crossed Langdon's face.

He knows! Teabing's heart craved that knowledge. His life's dream was right in front of him. "Tell me!" Teabing demanded. "Please! Oh God, please! It's not too late!"

As the sound of heavy footsteps thundered down the hall toward the Chapter House, Langdon quietly rolled the papyrus and slipped it back in his pocket.

"No!" Teabing cried out, trying in vain to stand.

When the doors burst open, Bezu Fache entered like a bull into a ring, his feral eyes scanning, finding his target—Leigh Teabing—helpless on the floor. Exhaling in relief, Fache holstered his Manurhin sidearm and turned to Sophie. "Agent Neveu, I am relieved you and Mr. Langdon are safe. You should have come in when I asked."

The British police entered on Fache's heels, seizing the anguished prisoner and placing him in handcuffs.

Sophie seemed stunned to see Fache. "How did you find us?"

Fache pointed to Teabing. "He made the mistake of showing his ID when he entered the abbey. The guards heard a police broadcast about our search for him."

"It's in Langdon's pocket!" Teabing was screaming like a madman. "The map to the Holy Grail!"

As they hoisted Teabing and carried him out, he threw back his head and howled. "Robert! Tell me where it's hidden!"

As Teabing passed, Langdon looked him in the eye. "Only the worthy find the Grail, Leigh. You taught me that."

Chapter 102

*T*HE MIST had settled low on Kensington Gardens as Silas limped into a quiet hollow out of sight. Kneeling on the wet grass, he could feel a warm stream of blood flowing from the bullet wound below his ribs. Still, he stared straight ahead.

The fog made it look like heaven here.

Raising his bloody hands to pray, he watched the raindrops caress his fingers, turning them white again. As the droplets fell harder across his back and shoulders, he could feel his body disappearing bit by bit into the mist.

I am a ghost.

A breeze rustled past him, carrying the damp, earthy scent of new life. With every living cell in his broken body, Silas prayed. He prayed for forgiveness. He prayed for mercy. And, above all, he prayed for his mentor . . . Bishop Aringarosa . . . that the Lord would not take him before his time. *He has so much work left to do.*

The fog was swirling around him now, and Silas felt so light that he was sure the wisps would carry him away. Closing his eyes, he said a final prayer.

From somewhere in the mist, the voice of Manuel Aringarosa whispered to him.

Our Lord is a good and merciful God.

Silas's pain at last began to fade, and he knew the bishop was right.

Chapter 105

IT WAS LATE afternoon when the London sun broke through and the city began to dry. Bezu Fache felt weary as he emerged from the interrogation room and hailed a cab. Sir Leigh Teabing had vociferously proclaimed his innocence, and yet from his incoherent rantings about the Holy Grail, secret documents, and mysterious brotherhoods, Fache suspected the wily historian was setting the stage for his lawyers to plead an insanity defense.

Sure, Fache thought. *Insane.* Teabing had displayed ingenious precision in formulating a plan that protected his innocence at every turn. He had exploited both the Vatican and Opus Dei, two groups that turned out to be completely innocent. His dirty work had been carried out unknowingly by a fanatical monk and a desperate bishop. More clever still, Teabing had situated his electronic listening post in the *one* place a man with polio could not possibly reach. The actual surveillance had been carried out by his manservant, Rémy—the lone person privy to Teabing's true identity—now conveniently dead of an allergic reaction.

Hardly the handiwork of someone lacking mental faculties, Fache thought.

The information coming from Collet out of Château Villette suggested that Teabing's cunning ran so deep that Fache himself might even learn from it. To successfully hide bugs in some of Paris's most powerful offices, the British historian had turned to the Greeks. *Trojan horses.* Some of Teabing's intended targets received lavish gifts of artwork, others unwittingly bid at auctions in which Teabing had placed specific lots. In Saunière's case, the curator had received a dinner invitation to Château Villette to discuss the possibility of Teabing's funding a new Da Vinci Wing at the Louvre. Saunière's invitation had contained an innocuous postscript expressing fascination with a robotic knight that Saunière was rumored to have built. *Bring him to dinner,* Teabing had suggested. Saunière apparently had done just that and left the knight unattended long enough for Rémy Legaludec to make one inconspicuous addition.

Now, sitting in the back of the cab, Fache closed his eyes. *One more thing to attend to before I return to Paris.*

THE ST. MARY'S Hospital recovery room was sunny.

"You've impressed us all," the nurse said, smiling down at him. "Nothing short of miraculous."

Bishop Aringarosa gave a weak smile. "I have always been blessed."

The nurse finished puttering, leaving the bishop alone. The sunlight felt welcome and warm on his face. Last night had been the darkest night of his life.

Despondently, he thought of Silas, whose body had been found in the park.

Please forgive me, my son.

Aringarosa had longed for Silas to be part of his glorious plan. Last night, however, Aringarosa had received a call from Bezu Fache, questioning the bishop about his apparent connection to a nun who had been murdered in Saint-Sulpice. Aringarosa realized the evening had taken a horrifying turn. News of the four additional murders transformed his horror to anguish. *Silas, what have you done!* Unable to reach the Teacher, the bishop knew he had been cut loose. *Used.* The only way to stop the horrific chain of events he had helped put in motion was to confess everything to Fache, and from that moment on, Aringarosa and Fache had been racing to catch up with Silas before the Teacher persuaded him to kill again.

Feeling bone weary, Aringarosa closed his eyes and listened to the television coverage of the arrest of a prominent British knight, Sir Leigh Teabing. *The Teacher laid bare for all to see.* Teabing had caught wind of the Vatican's plans to disassociate itself from Opus Dei. He had chosen Aringarosa as the perfect pawn in his plan. *After all, who more likely to leap blindly after the Holy Grail than a man like myself with everything to lose? The Grail would have brought enormous power to anyone who possessed it.*

Leigh Teabing had protected his identity shrewdly—feigning a French accent and a pious heart, and demanding as payment the one thing he did not need—money. Aringarosa had been far too eager to be suspicious. The price tag of twenty million euro was paltry when compared with the prize of obtaining the Grail, and with the Vatican's separation payment to Opus Dei, the finances had worked nicely. *The blind see what they want to see.* Teabing's ultimate insult, of course, had been to demand payment in Vatican bonds, such that if anything went wrong, the investigation would lead to Rome.

"I am glad to see you're well, My Lord."

Aringarosa recognized the gruff voice in the doorway, but the face was unexpected—stern, powerful features, slicked-back hair, and a broad neck that strained against his dark suit. "Captain Fache?" Aringarosa asked. The compassion and concern the captain had shown for Aringarosa's plight last night had conjured images of a far gentler physique.

The captain approached the bed and hoisted a familiar, heavy black briefcase onto a chair. "I believe this belongs to you."

Aringarosa looked at the briefcase filled with bonds and immediately looked away, feeling only shame. "Yes . . . thank you." He paused while working his fingers across the seam of his bedsheet, then continued. "Captain, I have been giving this deep thought, and I need to ask a favor of you."

"Of course."

"The families of those in Paris who Silas . . ." He paused, swallowing the emotion. "I realize no sum could possibly serve as sufficient restitution, and yet, if you could be kind enough to divide the contents of this briefcase among them . . . the families of the deceased."

Fache's dark eyes studied him a long moment. "A virtuous gesture, My Lord. I will see to it your wishes are carried out."

A heavy silence fell between them.

On the television, a lean French police officer was giving a press conference in front of a sprawling mansion. Fache saw who it was and turned his attention to the screen.

"Lieutenant Collet," a BBC reporter said, her voice accusing. "Last night, your captain publicly charged two innocent people with murder. Will Robert Langdon and Sophie Neveu be seeking accountability from your department? Will this cost Captain Fache his job?"

Lieutenant Collet's smile was tired but calm. "It is my experience that Captain Bezu Fache seldom makes mistakes. I have not yet spoken to him on this matter, but knowing how he operates, I suspect his public manhunt for Agent Neveu and Mr. Langdon was part of a ruse to lure out the real killer."

The reporters exchanged surprised looks.

Collet continued. "Whether or not Mr. Langdon and Agent Neveu were willing participants in the sting, I do not know. Captain Fache tends to keep his more creative methods to himself. All I can confirm at this point is that the captain has successfully arrested the man responsible, and that Mr. Langdon and Agent Neveu are both innocent and safe."

Fache had a faint smile on his lips as he turned back to Aringarosa. "A good man, that Collet."

Several moments passed. Finally, Fache ran his hand over his forehead, slicking back his hair as he gazed down at Aringarosa. "My Lord, before I return to Paris, there is one final matter I'd like to discuss—your impromptu flight to London. You bribed a pilot to change course. In doing so, you broke a number of international laws."

Aringarosa slumped. "I was desperate."

"Yes. As was the pilot when my men interrogated him." Fache reached in his pocket and produced a purple amethyst ring with a familiar hand-tooled mitre-crozier appliqué.

Aringarosa felt tears welling as he accepted the ring and slipped it back on his finger. "You've been so kind." He held out his hand and clasped Fache's. "Thank you."

Fache waved off the gesture, walking to the window and gazing out at the city, his thoughts obviously far away. When he turned, there was an uncertainty about him. "My Lord, where do you go from here?"

Aringarosa had been asked the exact same question as he left Castel Gandolfo the night before. "I suspect my path is as uncertain as yours."

"Yes." Fache paused. "I suspect I will be retiring early."

Aringarosa smiled. "A little faith can do wonders, Captain. A little faith."

OSSLYN CHAPEL—often called the Cathedral of Codes—stands seven miles south of Edinburgh, Scotland, on the site of an ancient Mithraic temple. Built by the Knights Templar in 1446, the chapel is engraved with a mind-boggling array of symbols from the Jewish, Christian, Egyptian, Masonic, and pagan traditions.

ROSSLYN CHAPEL

The chapel's geographic coordinates fall precisely on the north-south meridian that runs through Glastonbury. This longitudinal Rose Line is the traditional marker of King Arthur's Isle of Avalon and is considered the central pillar of Britain's sacred geometry. It is from this hallowed Rose Line that Rosslyn—originally spelled Roslin—takes its name.

Rosslyn's rugged spires were casting long evening shadows as Robert Langdon and Sophie Neveu pulled their rental car into the grassy parking area at the foot of the bluff on which the chapel stood. Their short flight from London to Edinburgh had been restful, although neither of them had slept for the anticipation of what lay ahead. Gazing up at the stark edifice framed against a cloud-swept sky, Langdon felt like Alice falling headlong into the rabbit hole. *This must be a dream*. And yet he knew the text of Saunière's final message could not have been more specific.

The Holy Grail 'neath ancient Roslin waits.

Langdon had fantasized that Saunière's "Grail map" would be a diagram—a drawing with an X-marks-the-spot—and yet the Priory's final secret had been unveiled in the same way Saunière had spoken to them from the beginning. *Simple verse.* Four explicit lines that pointed without a doubt to this very spot. In addition to identifying Rosslyn by name, the verse made reference to several of the chapel's renowned architectural features.

Despite the clarity of Saunière's final revelation, Langdon had been left feeling more off balance than enlightened. To him, Rosslyn Chapel seemed far too obvious a location. For centuries, this stone chapel had echoed with whispers of the Holy Grail's presence. The whispers had turned to shouts in recent decades when ground-penetrating radar revealed the presence of an astonishing structure *beneath* the chapel—a massive subterranean chamber. Not only did this deep vault dwarf the chapel atop it, but it appeared to have no entrance or exit. Archaeologists petitioned to begin blasting through the bedrock to reach the mysterious chamber, but the Rosslyn Trust expressly forbade any excavation of the sacred site. Of course, this only fueled the fires of speculation. What was the Rosslyn Trust trying to hide?

Rosslyn had now become a pilgrimage site for mystery seekers. Some claimed they were drawn here by the powerful magnetic field that emanated inexplicably from these coordinates, some claimed they came to search the hillside for a hidden entrance to the vault, but most admitted they had come simply to wander the grounds and absorb the lore of the Holy Grail.

Although Langdon had never been to Rosslyn before now, he always chuckled when he heard the chapel described as the current home of the Holy Grail. Admittedly, Rosslyn *once* might have been home to the Grail, long ago . . . but certainly no longer. Far too much attention had been drawn to Rosslyn in past decades, and sooner or later someone would find a way to break into the vault.

True Grail academics agreed that Rosslyn was a decoy—one of the devious dead ends the Priory crafted so convincingly. Tonight, however, with the Priory's keystone offering a verse that pointed directly to this spot, Langdon no longer felt so smug. A perplexing question had been running through his mind all day:

Why would Saunière go to such effort to guide us to so obvious a location?

There seemed only one logical answer.

There is something about Rosslyn we have yet to understand.

"Robert?" Sophie was standing outside the car, looking back at him. "Are you coming?" She was holding the rosewood box, which Captain Fache had returned to them. Inside, both cryptexes had been reassembled and nested as they had been found. The papyrus verse was locked safely at its core—minus the shattered vial of vinegar.

Making their way up the long gravel path, Langdon and Sophie passed the famous west wall of the chapel. Casual visitors assumed this oddly protruding wall was a section of the chapel that had not been finished. The truth, Langdon recalled, was far more intriguing.

The west wall of Solomon's Temple.

The Knights Templar had designed Rosslyn Chapel as an exact architectural blueprint of Solomon's Temple in Jerusalem—complete with a west wall, a narrow rectangular sanctuary, and a subterranean vault like the Holy of Holies, in which the original nine knights had first unearthed their priceless treasure. Langdon had to admit, there existed an intriguing symmetry in the idea of the Templars building a modern Grail repository that echoed the Grail's original hiding place.

Rosslyn Chapel's entrance was more modest than Langdon expected. The small wooden door had two iron hinges and a simple, oak sign.

ROSLIN

This ancient spelling, Langdon explained to Sophie, derived from the Rose Line meridian on which the chapel sat; or, as Grail academics preferred to believe, from the "Line of Rose"—the ancestral lineage of Mary Magdalene.

The chapel would be closing soon, and as Langdon pulled open the door, a warm puff of air escaped, as if the ancient edifice were heaving a weary sigh at the end of a long day. Her entry arches burgeoned with carved cinquefoils.

Roses. The womb of the goddess.

Entering with Sophie, Langdon felt his eyes reaching across the famous sanctuary and taking it all in. Although he had read accounts of Rosslyn's arrestingly intricate stonework, seeing it in person was an overwhelming encounter.

Symbology heaven, one of Langdon's colleagues had called it.

Every surface in the chapel had been carved with symbols—Christian cruciforms, Jewish stars, Masonic seals, Templar crosses, cornucopias, pyramids, astrological signs, plants, vegetables, pentacles, and roses. The Knights Templar had been master stonemasons, erecting Templar churches all over Europe, but Rosslyn was considered their most sublime labor of love and veneration. The master masons had left no stone uncarved. Rosslyn Chapel was a shrine to all faiths . . . to all traditions . . . and, above all, to nature and the goddess.

The sanctuary was empty except for a handful of visitors listening to a young man giving the day's last tour. He was leading them in a single-file line along a well-known route on the floor—an invisible pathway linking six key architectural points within the sanctuary. Generations of visitors had walked these straight lines, connecting the points, and their countless footsteps had engraved an enormous symbol on the floor.

The Star of David, Langdon thought. *No coincidence there.* Also known as Solomon's Seal, this hexagram had once been the secret symbol of the stargazing priests and was later adopted by the Israelite kings—David and Solomon.

The docent had seen Langdon and Sophie enter, and although it was closing time, offered a pleasant smile and motioned for them to feel free to look around.

Langdon nodded his thanks and began to move deeper into the sanctuary. Sophie, however, stood riveted in the entryway, a puzzled look on her face.

"What is it?" Langdon asked.

Sophie stared out at the chapel. "I think . . . I've been here."

Langdon was surprised. "But you said you hadn't even *heard* of Rosslyn."

"I hadn't . . ." She scanned the sanctuary, looking uncertain. "My grandfather must have brought me here when I was very young. I don't know. It feels familiar." As her eyes scanned the room, she began nodding with more certainty. "Yes." She pointed to the front of the sanctuary. "Those two pillars . . . I've seen them."

Langdon looked at the pair of intricately sculpted columns at the far end of the sanctuary. Their white lacework carvings seemed to smolder with a ruddy glow as the last of the day's sunlight streamed in through the west window. The pillars—positioned where the altar would normally stand—were an oddly matched pair. The pillar on the left was carved with simple, vertical lines, while the pillar on the right was embellished with an ornate, flowering spiral.

Sophie was already moving toward them. Langdon hurried after her, and as they reached the pillars, Sophie was nodding with incredulity. "Yes, I'm positive I have seen these!"

"I don't doubt you've seen them," Langdon said, "but it wasn't necessarily *here*."

She turned. "What do you mean?"

"These two pillars are the most duplicated architectural structures in history. Replicas exist all over the world."

"Replicas of Rosslyn?" She looked skeptical.

"No. Of the pillars. Do you remember earlier that I mentioned Rosslyn *itself* is a copy of Solomon's Temple? Those two pillars are exact replicas of the two pillars that stood at the head of Solomon's Temple." Langdon pointed to the pillar on

PILLARS OF ROSSLYN CHAPEL (BOAZ AND JACHIN)

the left. "That's called *Boaz*—or the Mason's Pillar. The other is called *Jachin*—or the Apprentice Pillar." He paused. "In fact, virtually every Masonic temple in the world has two pillars like these."

Langdon had already explained to her about the Templars' powerful historic ties to the modern Masonic secret societies, whose primary degrees—Apprentice Freemason, Fellowcraft Freemason, and Master Mason—harked back to early Templar days. Sophie's grandfather's final verse made direct reference to the Master Masons who adorned Rosslyn with their carved artistic offerings. It also noted Rosslyn's central ceiling, which was covered with carvings of stars and planets.

"I've never been in a Masonic temple," Sophie said, still eyeing the pillars. "I am almost positive I saw these *here*." She turned back into the chapel, as if looking for something else to jog her memory.

The rest of the visitors were now leaving, and the young docent made his way across the chapel to them with a pleasant smile. He was a handsome young man in his late twenties, with a Scottish brogue and strawberry blond hair. "I'm about to close up for the day. May I help you find anything?"

How about the Holy Grail? Langdon wanted to say.

"The code," Sophie blurted, in sudden revelation. "There's a code here!"

The docent looked pleased by her enthusiasm. "Yes there is, ma'am."

"It's on the ceiling," she said, turning to the right-hand wall. "Somewhere over . . . there."

He smiled. "Not your first visit to Rosslyn, I see."

The code, Langdon thought. He had forgotten that little bit of lore. Among Rosslyn's numerous mysteries was a vaulted archway from which hundreds of stone blocks protruded, jutting down to form a bizarre multifaceted surface. Each block was carved with a symbol, seemingly at random, creating a cipher of unfathomable proportion. Some people believed the code revealed the entrance to the vault beneath the chapel. Others believed it told the true Grail legend. Not that it mattered—cryptographers had been trying for centuries to decipher its meaning. To this day the Rosslyn Trust offered a generous reward to anyone who could unveil the secret meaning, but the code remained a mystery.

"I'd be happy to show . . ."

ENCODED CEILING, ROSSLYN CHAPEL

THE DOCENT'S VOICE trailed off.

My first code, Sophie thought, moving alone, in a trance, toward the encoded archway. Having handed the rosewood box to Langdon, she could feel herself momentarily forgetting all about the Holy Grail, the Priory of Sion, and all the mysteries of the past day. When she arrived beneath the encoded ceiling and saw the symbols above her, the memories came flooding back. She was recalling her first visit here, and strangely, the memories conjured an unexpected sadness.

She was a little girl . . . a year or so after her family's death. Her grandfather had brought her to Scotland on a short vacation. They had come to see Rosslyn Chapel before going back to Paris. It was late evening, and the chapel was closed. But they were still inside.

"Can we go home, *Grand-père?*" Sophie begged, feeling tired.

"Soon, dear, very soon." His voice was melancholy. "I have one last thing I need to do here. How about if you wait in the car?"

"You're doing another big-person thing?"

He nodded. "I'll be fast. I promise."

"Can I do the archway code again? That was fun."

"I don't know. I have to step outside. You won't be frightened in here alone?"

"Of course not!" she said with a huff. "It's not even dark yet!"

He smiled. "Very well then." He led her over to the elaborate archway he had shown her earlier.

Sophie immediately plopped down on the stone floor, lying on her back and staring up at the collage of puzzle pieces overhead. "I'm going to break this code before you get back!"

"It's a race then." He bent over, kissed her forehead, and walked to the nearby side door. "I'll be right outside. I'll leave the door open. If you need me, just call." He exited into the soft evening light.

Sophie lay there on the floor, gazing up at the code. Her eyes felt sleepy. After a few minutes, the symbols got fuzzy. And then they disappeared.

When Sophie awoke, the floor felt cold.

"Grand-père?"

There was no answer. Standing up, she brushed herself off. The side door was still open. The evening was getting darker. She walked outside and could see her grandfather standing on the porch of a nearby stone house directly behind the church. Her grandfather was talking quietly to a person barely visible inside the screened door.

"Grand-père?" she called.

Her grandfather turned and waved, motioning for her to wait just a moment.

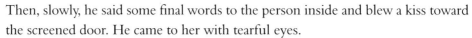

Then, slowly, he said some final words to the person inside and blew a kiss toward the screened door. He came to her with tearful eyes.

"Why are you crying, *Grand-père?*"

He picked her up and held her close. "Oh, Sophie, you and I have said good-bye to a lot of people this year. It's hard."

Sophie thought of the accident, of saying good-bye to her mother and father, her grandmother and baby brother. "Were you saying good-bye to *another* person?"

"To a dear friend whom I love very much," he replied, his voice heavy with emotion. "And I fear I will not see her again for a very long time."

STANDING with the docent, Langdon had been scanning the chapel walls and feeling a rising wariness that a dead end might be looming. Sophie had wandered off to look at the code and left Langdon holding the rosewood box, which contained a Grail map that now appeared to be no help at all. Although Saunière's poem clearly indicated Rosslyn, Langdon was not sure what to do now that they had arrived. The poem made reference to a "blade and chalice," which Langdon saw nowhere.

The Holy Grail 'neath ancient Roslin waits.
The blade and chalice guarding o'er Her gates.

Again Langdon sensed there remained some facet of this mystery yet to reveal itself.

"I hate to pry," the docent said, eyeing the rosewood box in Langdon's hands. "But this box . . . might I ask where you got it?"

Langdon gave a weary laugh. "That's an exceptionally long story."

The young man hesitated, his eyes on the box again. "It's the strangest thing— my grandmother has a box *exactly* like that—a jewelry box. Identical polished rosewood, same inlaid rose, even the hinges look the same."

Langdon knew the young man must be mistaken. If ever a box had been one of a kind, it was *this* one—the box custom-made for the Priory keystone. "The two boxes may be similar but—"

The side door closed loudly, drawing both of their gazes. Sophie had exited without a word and was now wandering down the bluff toward a fieldstone house nearby. Langdon stared after her. *Where is she going?* She had been acting strangely ever since they entered the building. He turned to the docent. "Do you know what that house is?"

He nodded, also looking puzzled that Sophie was going down there. "That's the chapel rectory. The chapel curator lives there. She also happens to be the head of the Rosslyn Trust." He paused. "And my grandmother."

"Your grandmother heads the Rosslyn Trust?"

INTERIOR, ROSSLYN CHAPEL

The young man nodded. "I live with her in the rectory and help keep up the chapel and give tours." He shrugged. "I've lived here my whole life. My grandmother raised me in that house."

Concerned for Sophie, Langdon moved across the chapel toward the door to call out to her. He was only halfway there when he stopped short. Something the young man said just registered.

My grandmother raised me.

Langdon looked out at Sophie on the bluff, then down at the rosewood box in his hand. *Impossible.* Slowly, Langdon turned back to the young man. "You said your grandmother has a box like this one?"

"Almost identical."

"Where did she get it?"

"My grandfather made it for her. He died when I was a baby, but my grandmother still talks about him. She says he was a genius with his hands. He made all kinds of things."

Langdon glimpsed an unimaginable web of connections emerging. "You said your grandmother raised you. Do you mind my asking what happened to your parents?"

The young man looked surprised. "They died when I was young." He paused. "The same day as my grandfather."

Langdon's heart pounded. "In a car accident?"

The docent recoiled, a look of bewilderment in his olive-green eyes. "Yes. In a car accident. My entire family died that day. I lost my grandfather, my parents, and . . ." He hesitated, glancing down at the floor.

"And your sister," Langdon said.

Out on the bluff, the fieldstone house was exactly as Sophie remembered it. Night was falling now, and the house exuded a warm and inviting aura. The smell of bread wafted through the opened screened door, and a golden light shone in the windows. As Sophie approached, she could hear the quiet sounds of sobbing from within.

Through the screened door, Sophie saw an elderly woman in the hallway. Her back was to the door, but Sophie could see she was crying. The woman had long, luxuriant, silver hair that conjured an unexpected wisp of memory. Feeling herself drawn closer, Sophie stepped onto the porch stairs. The woman was clutching a framed photograph of a man and touching her fingertips to his face with loving sadness.

It was a face Sophie knew well.

Grand-père.

The woman had obviously heard the sad news of his death last night.

A board squeaked beneath Sophie's feet, and the woman turned slowly, her sad eyes finding Sophie's. Sophie wanted to run, but she stood transfixed. The woman's fervent gaze never wavered as she set down the photo and approached the screened door. An eternity seemed to pass as the two women stared at one another through the thin mesh. Then, like the slowly gathering swell of an ocean wave, the woman's visage transformed from one of uncertainty . . . to disbelief . . . to hope . . . and finally, to cresting joy.

Throwing open the door, she came out, reaching with soft hands, cradling Sophie's thunderstruck face. "Oh, dear child . . . look at you!"

Although Sophie did not recognize her, she knew who this woman was. She tried to speak but found she could not even breathe.

"Sophie," the woman sobbed, kissing her forehead.

Sophie's words were a choked whisper. "But . . . *Grand-père* said you were . . ."

"I know." The woman placed her tender hands on Sophie's shoulders and gazed at her with familiar eyes. "Your grandfather and I were forced to say so many things. We did what we thought was right. I'm so sorry. It was for your own safety, princess."

Sophie heard her final word, and immediately thought of her grandfather, who had called her princess for so many years. The sound of his voice seemed to echo now in the ancient stones of Rosslyn, settling through the earth and reverberating in the unknown hollows below.

The woman threw her arms around Sophie, the tears flowing faster. "Your grandfather wanted so badly to tell you everything. But things were difficult between you two. He tried so hard. There's so much to explain. So very much to explain." She kissed Sophie's forehead once again, then whispered in her ear. "No more secrets, princess. It's time you learn the truth about our family."

Sophie and her grandmother were seated on the porch stairs in a tearful hug when the young docent dashed across the lawn, his eyes shining with hope and disbelief.

"Sophie?"

Through her tears, Sophie nodded, standing. She did not know the young man's face, but as they embraced, she could feel the power of the blood coursing through his veins . . . the blood she now understood they shared.

W HEN LANGDON walked across the lawn to join them, Sophie could not imagine that only yesterday she had felt so alone in the world. And now, somehow, in this foreign place, in the company of three people she barely knew, she felt at last that she was home.

N IGHT HAD FALLEN over Rosslyn.

Robert Langdon stood alone on the porch of the fieldstone house enjoying the sounds of laughter and reunion drifting through the screened door behind him. The mug of potent Brazilian coffee in his hand had granted him a hazy reprieve from his mounting exhaustion, and yet he sensed the reprieve would be fleeting. The fatigue in his body went to the core.

"You slipped out quietly," a voice behind him said.

He turned. Sophie's grandmother emerged, her silver hair shimmering in the night. Her name, for the last twenty-eight years at least, was Marie Chauvel.

Langdon gave a tired smile. "I thought I'd give your family some time together." Through the window, he could see Sophie talking with her brother.

Marie came over and stood beside him. "Mr. Langdon, when I first heard of Jacques's murder, I was terrified for Sophie's safety. Seeing her standing in my doorway tonight was the greatest relief of my life. I cannot thank you enough."

Langdon had no idea how to respond. Although he had offered to give Sophie and her grandmother time to talk in private, Marie had asked him to stay and listen. *My husband obviously trusted you, Mr. Langdon, so I do as well.*

And so Langdon had remained, standing beside Sophie and listening in mute astonishment while Marie told the story of Sophie's late parents. Incredibly, both had been from Merovingian families—direct descendants of Mary Magdalene and Jesus Christ. Sophie's parents and ancestors, for protection, had changed their family names of Plantard and Saint-Clair. Their children represented the most direct surviving royal bloodline and therefore were carefully guarded by the Priory. When Sophie's parents were killed in a car accident whose cause could not be determined, the Priory feared the identity of the royal line had been discovered.

"Your grandfather and I," Marie had explained in a voice choked with pain, "had to make a grave decision the instant we received the phone call. Your parents' car had just been found in the river." She dabbed at the tears in her eyes. "All six of us—including you two grandchildren—were supposed to be traveling together in that car that very night. Fortunately we changed our plans at the last moment, and your parents were alone. Hearing of the accident, Jacques and I had no way to know what had really happened . . . or if this was truly an *accident.*" Marie looked at Sophie. "We knew we had to protect our grandchildren, and we did what we thought was best. Jacques reported to the police that your brother and I had been in the car . . . our two bodies apparently washed off in the current. Then your brother and I went underground with the Priory. Jacques, being a man of prominence, did not have the luxury of disappearing. It only made sense that Sophie, being the eldest, would stay in Paris to be taught and raised by Jacques, close to the heart and protection of the Priory." Her voice fell to a whisper. "Separating the family was the hardest thing we ever had to do. Jacques and I saw each other only very infrequently, and always in the most secret of settings . . . under the protection of the Priory. There are certain ceremonies to which the brotherhood always stays faithful."

Langdon had sensed the story went far deeper, but he also sensed it was not for him to hear. So he had stepped outside. Now, gazing up at the spires of Rosslyn, Langdon could not escape the hollow gnaw of Rosslyn's unsolved mystery. *Is the Grail really here at Rosslyn? And if so, where are the blade and chalice that Saunière mentioned in his poem?*

"I'll take that," Marie said, motioning to Langdon's hand.

"Oh, thank you." Langdon held out his empty coffee cup.

She stared at him. "I was referring to your *other* hand, Mr. Langdon."

Langdon looked down and realized he was holding Saunière's papyrus. He had taken it from the cryptex once again in hopes of seeing something he had missed earlier. "Of course, I'm sorry."

Marie looked amused as she took the paper. "I know of a man at a bank in Paris who is probably very eager to see the return of this rosewood box. André Vernet was a dear friend of Jacques, and Jacques trusted him explicitly. André would have done anything to honor Jacques's requests for the care of this box."

Including shooting me, Langdon recalled, deciding not to mention that he had probably broken the poor man's nose. Thinking of Paris, Langdon flashed on the three *sénéchaux* who had been killed the night before. "And the Priory? What happens now?"

"The wheels are already in motion, Mr. Langdon. The brotherhood has endured for centuries, and it will endure this. There are always those waiting to move up and rebuild."

All evening Langdon had suspected that Sophie's grandmother was closely tied to the operations of the Priory. After all, the Priory had always had women members. Four Grand Masters had been women. The *sénéchaux* were traditionally men—the guardians—and yet women held far more honored status within the Priory and could ascend to the highest post from virtually any rank.

Langdon thought of Leigh Teabing and Westminster Abbey. It seemed a lifetime ago. "Was the Church pressuring your husband not to release the Sangreal documents at the End of Days?"

"Heavens no. The End of Days is a legend of paranoid minds. There is nothing in the Priory doctrine that identifies a date at which the Grail should be unveiled. In fact the Priory has always maintained that the Grail should *never* be unveiled."

"Never?" Langdon was stunned.

"It is the mystery and wonderment that serve our souls, not the Grail itself. The beauty of the Grail lies in her ethereal nature." Marie Chauvel gazed up at Rosslyn now. "For some, the Grail is a chalice that will bring them everlasting life. For others, it is the quest for lost documents and secret history. And for most, I suspect the Holy Grail is simply a grand idea . . . a glorious unattainable treasure that somehow, even in today's world of chaos, inspires us."

"But if the Sangreal documents remain hidden, the story of Mary Magdalene will be lost forever," Langdon said.

"Will it? Look around you. Her story is being told in art, music, and books. More so every day. The pendulum is swinging. We are starting to sense the dangers of our history . . . and of our destructive paths. We are beginning to sense the need to restore the sacred feminine." She paused. "You mentioned you are writing a manuscript about the symbols of the sacred feminine, are you not?"

"I am."

She smiled. "Finish it, Mr. Langdon. Sing her song. The world needs modern troubadours."

Langdon fell silent, feeling the weight of her message upon him. Across the open spaces, a full moon was rising above the tree line. Turning his eyes toward Rosslyn, Langdon felt a boyish craving to know her secrets. *Don't ask,* he told himself. *This is not the moment.* He glanced at the papyrus in Marie's hand, and then back at Rosslyn.

"Ask the question, Mr. Langdon," Marie said, looking amused. "You have earned the right."

Langdon felt himself flush.

"You want to know if the Grail is here at Rosslyn."

"Can you tell me?"

She sighed in mock exasperation. "Why is it that men simply *cannot* let the Grail rest?" She laughed, obviously enjoying herself. "Why do you think it's here?"

Langdon motioned to the papyrus in her hand. "Your husband's poem speaks specifically of Rosslyn, except it also mentions a blade and chalice watching over the Grail. I didn't see any symbols of the blade and chalice up there."

"The blade and chalice?" Marie asked. "What exactly do they look like?"

Langdon sensed she was toying with him, but he played along, quickly describing the symbols.

A look of vague recollection crossed her face. "Ah, yes, of course. The blade represents all that is masculine. I believe it is drawn like this, no?" Using her index finger, she traced a shape on her palm.

"Yes," Langdon said. Marie had drawn the less common "closed" form of the blade, although Langdon had seen the symbol portrayed both ways.

"And the inverse," she said, drawing again on her palm, "is the chalice, which represents the feminine."

"Correct," Langdon said.

"And you are saying that in all the hundreds of symbols we have here in Rosslyn Chapel, these two shapes appear nowhere?"

"I didn't see them."

"And if I show them to you, will you get some sleep?"

Before Langdon could answer, Marie Chauvel had stepped off the porch and was heading toward the chapel. Langdon hurried after her. Entering the ancient building, Marie turned on the lights and pointed to the center of the sanctuary floor. "There you are, Mr. Langdon. The blade and chalice."

Langdon stared at the scuffed stone floor. It was blank. "There's nothing here. . . ."

Marie sighed and began to walk along the famous path worn into the chapel floor, the same path Langdon had seen the visitors walking earlier this evening. As his eyes adjusted to see the giant symbol, he still felt lost. "But that's the Star of Dav—"

Langdon stopped short, mute with amazement as it dawned on him.

The blade and chalice.

Fused as one.

The Star of David . . . the perfect union of male and female . . . Solomon's Seal . . . marking the Holy of Holies, where the male and female deities—Yahweh and Shekinah—were thought to dwell.

Langdon needed a minute to find his words. "The verse *does* point here to Rosslyn. Completely. Perfectly."

Marie smiled. "Apparently."

The implications chilled him. "So the Holy Grail is in the vault beneath us?"

She laughed. "Only in spirit. One of the Priory's most ancient charges was one day to return the Grail to her homeland of France where she could rest for eternity. For centuries, she was dragged across the countryside to keep her safe. Most undignified. Jacques's charge when he became Grand Master was to restore her honor by returning her to France and building her a resting place fit for a queen."

"And he succeeded?"

Now her face grew serious. "Mr. Langdon, considering what you've done for me tonight, and as curator of the Rosslyn Trust, I can tell you for certain that the Grail is no longer here."

Langdon decided to press. "But the keystone is supposed to point to the place where the Holy Grail is hidden *now*. Why does it point to Rosslyn?"

"Maybe you're misreading its meaning. Remember, the Grail can be deceptive. As could my late husband."

"But how much clearer could he be?" he asked. "We are standing over an underground vault marked by the blade and chalice, underneath a ceiling of stars, surrounded by the art of Master Masons. Everything speaks of Rosslyn."

"Very well, let me see this mysterious verse." She unrolled the papyrus and read the poem aloud in a deliberate tone.

> **The Holy Grail 'neath ancient Roslin waits.**
> **The blade and chalice guarding o'er Her gates.**
> **Adorned in masters' loving art, She lies.**
> **She rests at last beneath the starry skies.**

When she finished, she was still for several seconds, until a knowing smile crossed her lips. "Aah, Jacques."

Langdon watched her expectantly. "You *understand* this?"

"As you have witnessed on the chapel floor, Mr. Langdon, there are many ways to see simple things."

Langdon strained to understand. Everything about Jacques Saunière seemed to have double meanings, and yet Langdon could see no further.

Marie gave a tired yawn. "Mr. Langdon, I will make a confession to you. I have never officially been privy to the present location of the Grail. But, of course, I *was* married to a person of enormous influence . . . and my women's intuition is strong." Langdon started to speak but Marie continued. "I am sorry that after all your hard work, you will be leaving Rosslyn without any real answers. And yet, something tells me you will eventually find what you seek. One day it will dawn on you." She smiled. "And when it does, I trust that you, of all people, can keep a secret."

There was a sound of someone arriving in the doorway. "Both of you disappeared," Sophie said, entering.

"I was just leaving," her grandmother replied, walking over to Sophie at the door. "Good night, princess." She kissed Sophie's forehead. "Don't keep Mr. Langdon out too late."

Langdon and Sophie watched her grandmother walk back toward the fieldstone house. When Sophie turned to him, her eyes were awash in deep emotion. "Not exactly the ending I expected."

That makes two of us, he thought. Langdon could see she was overwhelmed. The news she had received tonight had changed everything in her life. "Are you okay? It's a lot to take in."

She smiled quietly. "I have a family. That's where I'm going to start. Who we are and where we came from will take some time."

Langdon remained silent.

"Beyond tonight, will you stay with us?" Sophie asked. "At least for a few days?"

Langdon sighed, wanting nothing more. "You need some time here with your family, Sophie. I'm going back to Paris in the morning."

She looked disappointed but seemed to know it was the right thing to do. Neither of them spoke for a long time. Finally Sophie reached over and, taking his hand, led him out of the chapel. They walked to a small rise on the bluff. From here, the Scottish countryside spread out before them, suffused in a pale moonlight that sifted through the departing clouds. They stood in silence, holding hands, both of them fighting the descending shroud of exhaustion.

The stars were just now appearing, but to the west, a single point of light glowed brighter than any other. Langdon smiled when he saw it. It was Venus. The ancient Goddess shining down with her steady and patient light.

The night was growing cooler, a crisp breeze rolling up from the lowlands. After a while, Langdon looked over at Sophie. Her eyes were closed, her lips relaxed in a contented smile. Langdon could feel his own eyes growing heavy. Reluctantly, he squeezed her hand. "Sophie?"

Slowly, she opened her eyes and turned to him. Her face was beautiful in the moonlight. She gave him a sleepy smile. "Hi."

Langdon felt an unexpected sadness to realize he would be returning to Paris without her. "I may be gone before you wake up." He paused, a knot growing in his throat. "I'm sorry, I'm not very good at—"

Sophie reached out and placed her soft hand on the side of his face. Then, leaning forward, she kissed him tenderly on the cheek. "When can I see you again?"

Langdon reeled momentarily, lost in her eyes. "When?" He paused, curious if she had any idea how much he had been wondering the same thing. "Well, actually, next month I'm lecturing at a conference in Florence. I'll be there a week without much to do."

"Is that an invitation?"

"We'd be living in luxury. They're giving me a room at the Brunelleschi."

Sophie smiled playfully. "You presume a lot, Mr. Langdon."

He cringed at how it had sounded. "What I meant—"

"I would love nothing more than to meet you in Florence, Robert. But on *one* condition." Her tone turned serious. "No museums, no churches, no tombs, no art, no relics."

"In Florence? For a week? There's nothing else to do."

Sophie leaned forward and kissed him again, now on the lips. Their bodies came together, softly at first, and then completely. When she pulled away, her eyes were full of promise.

"Right," Langdon managed. "It's a date."

ROBERT LANGDON awoke with a start. He had been dreaming. The bathrobe beside his bed bore the monogram *HÔTEL RITZ PARIS*. He saw a dim light filtering through the blinds. *Is it dusk or dawn?* he wondered.

Langdon's body felt warm and deeply contented. He had slept the better part of the last two days. Sitting up slowly in bed, he now realized what had awoken him . . . the strangest thought. For days he had been trying to sort through a barrage of information, but now Langdon found himself fixed on something he'd not considered before.

Could it be?

He remained motionless a long moment.

Getting out of bed, he walked to the marble shower. Stepping inside, he let the powerful jets massage his shoulders. Still, the thought enthralled him.

Impossible.

Twenty minutes later, Langdon stepped out of the Hôtel Ritz into Place Vendôme. Night was falling. The days of sleep had left him disoriented . . . and yet his mind felt oddly lucid. He had promised himself he would stop in the hotel lobby for a café au lait to clear his thoughts, but instead his legs carried him directly out the front door into the gathering Paris night.

Walking east on Rue des Petits-Champs, Langdon felt a growing excitement. He turned south onto Rue Richelieu, where the air grew sweet with the scent of blossoming jasmine from the stately gardens of the Palais Royal.

He continued south until he saw what he was looking for—the famous royal arcade—a glistening expanse of polished black marble. Moving onto it, Langdon scanned the surface beneath his feet. Within seconds, he found what he knew was there—several bronze medallions embedded in the ground in a perfectly straight line. Each disk was five inches in diameter and embossed with the letters N and S.

ARAGO MEDALLIONS

Nord. Sud.

He turned due south, letting his eye trace the extended line formed by the medallions. He began moving again, following the trail, watching the pavement as he walked. As he cut across the corner of the Comédie-Française, another bronze medallion passed beneath his feet. *Yes!*

The streets of Paris, Langdon had learned years ago, were adorned with 135 of these bronze markers, embedded in sidewalks, courtyards, and streets, on a north-south axis across the city. He had once followed the line from Sacré-Coeur, north across the Seine, and finally to the ancient Paris Observatory. There he discovered the significance of the sacred path it traced.

The earth's original prime meridian.

The first zero longitude of the world.

Paris's ancient Rose Line.

Now, as Langdon hurried across Rue de Rivoli, he could feel his destination within reach. Less than a block away.

The Holy Grail 'neath ancient Roslin waits.

The revelations were coming now in waves. Saunière's ancient spelling of Roslin . . . the blade and chalice . . . the tomb adorned with masters' art.

Is that why Saunière needed to talk with me? Had I unknowingly guessed the truth?

He broke into a jog, feeling the Rose Line beneath his feet, guiding him, pulling him toward his destination. As he entered the long tunnel of Passage Richelieu, the hairs on his neck began to bristle with anticipation. He knew that at the end of this tunnel stood the most mysterious of Parisian monuments—conceived and commissioned in the 1980s by the Sphinx himself, François Mitterrand, a man rumored to move in secret circles, a man whose final legacy to Paris was a place Langdon had visited only days before.

Another lifetime.

With a final surge of energy, Langdon burst from the passageway into the familiar courtyard and came to a stop. Breathless, he raised his eyes, slowly, disbelieving, to the glistening structure in front of him.

The Louvre Pyramid.

Gleaming in the darkness.

He admired it only a moment. He was more interested in what lay to his right. Turning, he felt his feet again tracing the invisible path of the ancient Rose Line, carrying him across the courtyard to the Carrousel du Louvre—the enormous circle of grass surrounded by a perimeter of neatly trimmed hedges—once the site of

Paris's primeval nature-worshipping festivals . . . joyous rites to celebrate fertility and the Goddess.

Langdon felt as if he were crossing into another world as he stepped over the bushes to the grassy area within. This hallowed ground was now marked by one of the city's most unusual monuments. There in the center, plunging into the earth like a crystal chasm, gaped the giant inverted pyramid of glass that he had seen a few nights ago when he entered the Louvre's subterranean entresol.

LA PYRAMIDE INVERSÉE FROM ABOVE

La Pyramide Inversée.

Tremulous, Langdon walked to the edge and peered down into the Louvre's sprawling underground complex, aglow with amber light. His eye was trained not just on the massive inverted pyramid, but on what lay directly beneath it. There, on the floor of the chamber below, stood the tiniest of structures . . . a structure Langdon had mentioned in his manuscript.

Langdon felt himself awaken fully now to the thrill of unthinkable possibility.

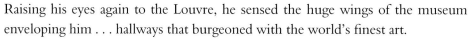

Raising his eyes again to the Louvre, he sensed the huge wings of the museum enveloping him . . . hallways that burgeoned with the world's finest art.

Da Vinci . . . Botticelli . . .

Adorned in masters' loving art, She lies.

Alive with wonder, he stared once again downward through the glass at the tiny structure below.

I must go down there!

Stepping out of the circle, he hurried across the courtyard back toward the towering pyramid entrance of the Louvre. The day's last visitors were trickling out of the museum.

Pushing through the revolving door, Langdon descended the curved staircase into the pyramid. He could feel the air grow cooler. When he reached the bottom, he entered the long tunnel that stretched beneath the Louvre's courtyard, back toward *La Pyramide Inversée.*

At the end of the tunnel, he emerged into a large chamber. Directly before him, hanging down from above, gleamed the inverted pyramid—a breathtaking V-shaped contour of glass.

The Chalice.

Langdon's eyes traced its narrowing form downward to its tip, suspended only six feet above the floor. There, directly beneath it, stood the tiny structure.

A miniature pyramid. Only three feet tall. The only structure in this colossal complex that had been built on a small scale.

Langdon's manuscript, while discussing the Louvre's elaborate collection of goddess art, had made passing note of this modest pyramid. *"The miniature structure itself protrudes up through the floor as though it were the tip of an iceberg—the apex of an enormous, pyramidical vault, submerged below like a hidden chamber."*

Illuminated in the soft lights of the deserted entresol, the two pyramids pointed at one another, their bodies perfectly aligned, their tips almost touching.

The Chalice above. The Blade below.

The blade and chalice guarding o'er Her gates.

Langdon heard Marie Chauvel's words. *One day it will dawn on you.*

He was standing beneath the ancient Rose Line, surrounded by the work of masters. *What better place for Saunière to keep watch?* Now at last, he sensed he under-

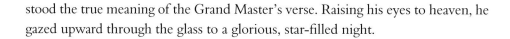

stood the true meaning of the Grand Master's verse. Raising his eyes to heaven, he gazed upward through the glass to a glorious, star-filled night.

She rests at last beneath the starry skies.

Like the murmurs of spirits in the darkness, forgotten words echoed. *The quest for the Holy Grail is the quest to kneel before the bones of Mary Magdalene. A journey to pray at the feet of the outcast one.*

With a sudden upwelling of reverence, Robert Langdon fell to his knees.

For a moment, he thought he heard a woman's voice . . . the wisdom of the ages . . . whispering up from the chasms of the earth.

❧

IMAGE CREDITS

Grateful acknowledgment is made to the following sources for permission to use the images in this book:

Page xii: Dead Sea Scrolls Foundation, Inc./CORBIS

Page 2: Louvre, Paris, France/Bridgeman Art Library

Photos on pages 6, 17, 18, 25, 36, 60, 77, 81, 87, 91, 92, 93, 111, 113, 121, 136, 137, 144, 154, 450T, 450B, 452–453, 455: © 2004 David Henry

Page 7: Vanni Archive/CORBIS

Page 9: Archivo Iconografico, S.A./CORBIS

Photos on pages 12, 14, 15: © 2004 Opus Dei Awareness Network (ODAN)

Page 19: Setboun/CORBIS

Page 20L: Réunion des Musées Nationaux/Art Resource, New York

Page 20R: Louvre, Paris, France/Peter Willi/Bridgeman Art Library

Page 21: Taxi/Getty Images

Page 27L: Roger Wood/CORBIS

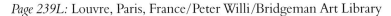

Page 239L: Louvre, Paris, France/Peter Willi/Bridgeman Art Library

Page 239R: Scala/Art Resource, New York

Page 240: Alinari/Art Resource, New York

Page 241: Scala/Art Resource, New York

Page 242: Richard T. Nowitz/CORBIS

Page 247: John Roddam Spencer Stanhope (1829–1908), *Eve Tempted,* © Manchester
    Art Gallery, U.K./ Bridgeman Art Library

Pages 250–251: Scala/Art Resource, New York

Page 253: Scala/Art Resource, New York

Page 255T and B: © David M. Lownie (www.crusader.org.uk)

Page 258TL: The Pierpont Morgan Library/Art Resource, New York

Page 258TR: Giraudon/Art Resource, New York

Page 258B: Private Collection/Bridgeman Art Library

Page 259: Scala/Art Resource, New York

Page 268: Jean-Victor Schnetz (1787–1870), *Procession of Crusaders around Jerusalem the
    Day Before the Taking of the Town, 14th July 1099* (1841), Château de Versailles,

France, Giraudon/Bridgeman Art Library

Page 270: Bildarchiv Preussischer Kulturbesitz/Art Resource, New York

Page 272: © Disney Enterprises, Inc.

Page 278R: The Pierpont Morgan Library/Art Resource, New York

Page 284: © Clipart.com and Jupiter Images, a division of Jupitermedia Corporation

Page 295: Tim Hawkins/Eye Ubiquitous/CORBIS

Page 309: Seth Joel/CORBIS

Page 317: Werner Forman/Art Resource, New York

Page 331: Erich Lessing/Art Resource, New York

Pages 348, 353, 358: Photos by Simon Brighton

Page 351: Judith Stagnitto Abbate/Abbate Design

Page 379: © 2004 Lachlan Cranswick

ACKNOWLEDGMENTS

FIRST AND FOREMOST, to my friend and editor, Jason Kaufman, for working so hard on this project and for truly understanding what this book is all about. And to the incomparable Heide Lange—tireless champion of *The Da Vinci Code*, agent extraordinaire, and trusted friend.

I cannot fully express my gratitude to the exceptional team at Doubleday for their generosity, faith, and superb guidance. Thank you especially to Bill Thomas and Steve Rubin, who believed in this book from the start. My thanks also to the initial core of early in-house supporters, headed by Michael Palgon, Suzanne Herz, Janelle Moburg, Jackie Everly, and Adrienne Sparks, to the talented people of Doubleday's sales force, and to Michael Windsor for the stunning jacket.

For their generous assistance in the research of the book, I would like to acknowledge the Louvre Museum, the French Ministry of Culture, Project Gutenberg, Bibliothèque Nationale, the Gnostic Society Library, the Department of Paintings Study and Documentation Service at the Louvre, Catholic World News, Royal Observatory Greenwich, London Record Society, the Muniment Collection at Westminster Abbey, John Pike and the Federation of American Scientists, and the five members of Opus Dei (three active, two former) who recounted their stories, both positive and negative, regarding their experiences inside Opus Dei.

My gratitude also to Water Street Bookstore for tracking down so many of my research books, my father, Richard Brown—mathematics teacher and author—for his assistance with the Divine Proportion and the Fibonacci Sequence, Stan Planton, Sylvie Baudeloque, Peter McGuigan, Francis McInerney, Margie Wachtel, Andre Vernet, Ken Kelleher at Anchorball Web Media, Cara Sottak, Karyn Popham, Esther Sung, Miriam Abramowitz, William Tunstall-Pedoe, and Griffin Wooden Brown.

And finally, in a novel drawing so heavily on the sacred feminine, I would be remiss if I did not mention the two extraordinary women who have touched my life. First, my mother, Connie Brown—fellow scribe, nurturer, musician, and role model. And my wife, Blythe—art historian, painter, front-line editor, and without a doubt the most astonishingly talented woman I have ever known.

ACKNOWLEDGMENTS

for this Illustrated Edition

To my editor, Jason Kaufman, for his vision, creativity, and monumental effort assembling this edition. To my wife, Blythe, for her superb insights and for sorting through thousands of images. And to Heide Lange, the finest agent in the business.

Sincere thanks also to Rebecca Holland, Jenny Choi, Maria Carella, Luisa Francavilla, Deborah Bull, Deborah Anderson, Ada Yonenaka, David Henry, and Betsy Eble for their invaluable contributions to this edition.